Abuse of Power 2

§

*The Colonials and
the Acadians*

Dedicated to my son Joe and daughter Elaine

Abuse of Power 2

§

The Colonials and the Acadians

By Bill Smallwood

Bill Smallwood (signature)

Borealis Press
Ottawa, Canada
2004

Canada

*The Publishers acknowledge the financial support
of the Government of Canada through the Book Publishing
Industry Development Program (BPIDP)
for our publishing activities.*

National Library of Canada Cataloguing in Publication Data

Smallwood, Bill, 1932 – Abuse of Power 2: The Colonials and the
Acadians / Bill Smallwood

Sequel to: Abuse of Power: The Acadians.
ISBN 0-88887-217-8

1. Maritime Provinces—History—To 1867—Fiction. I. Title. .

PS8587.M354C64 2004   C813'.6   C2004-900193-0

Illustrations by Eugene Kral
Cover design and book typesetting
by Chisholm Communications, Ottawa

Printed and bound in Canada on acid-free paper

Contents

Chapters

1. October 1757, Halifax Harbour 1

2. December 31, 1757, Halifax 21

3. June 1, 1758, Fortress Louisbourg 45

4. June 8, 1758, Gabarus Bay 85

5. June 9, 1758, English Main Camp, Flat Point 107

6. Entrance to Louisbourg Harbour 185

7. July 27, 1758, Grenadier's Redoubt 203

8. July 31, 1758, Fortress Louisbourg. 217

9. September 12, 1758, H.M.S. Sutherland,
   Halifax Harbour Entrance 249

10. December 31, 1758, The Old House, Halifax 255

11. April 17, 1759, Carmichael's Tavern. 269

12. July 18, 1759, Fortress Québec 307

13. August 19, 1759, Québec Lower Town 349

14. October 18, 1759, Hollis Street. 383

Epilogue. 425

Chapter One

October 1757
Halifax Harbour

Pilot Schooner slipped her moorings and, with her lower sails set, allowed the light breeze and the tide to take her down harbour toward the Atlantic Ocean. Not that she ever braved the Atlantic, spending most of her time as she did at the entrance of the harbour, delivering ships' pilots to the ocean-going vessels seeking safe entry to the largest natural harbour in the world.

On this day, *Pilot Schooner* would be more plucky than usual, venturing past Chebucto Head where the pilots waited at the Pilot Station for their client ships, carefully navigating Black Rock and the dangerous Sambro Ledges to find entrance to Sambro Harbour where some of the Halifax Harbour pilots chose to live. The Grays, William and Molly, lived at Sambro. *Pilot Schooner* was taking Molly Gray home.

Molly, the tall woman standing apart from the churning family bustle of the main deck, separated herself even more by strolling to the stern and leaning against the taffrail where she could comfortably look back over the harbour. It wasn't the town that held her interest; her attention was directed toward the warship moored just off Dartmouth Cove. She could identify the figure of her husband as he manoeuvred the small craft away from the side of *H.M.S. Winchelsea.* Molly leaned forward as if to bring the distant scene into better focus. *Yes, William had picked up his passenger ... no, there were two passengers. The small, dark-looking man with the big naval officer's hat, that man would be Captain John Rous. Then who could the other man be?* She watched as the third man seemed to fuss over the captain, getting him settled on the main thwart before sitting further forward where passengers would be subjected to the salt spray from the harbour chop. "The third man is Wimper," she said to herself. She was surprised when someone answered her.

1

"Aren't you worried that Captain John will lure your husband away from us ... away from Sambro?"

Molly turned to see Edith Hiltz, widow lady since four years, who had taken a maternal interest in the young Gray couple.

"Oh, hello, Missus Hiltz." Molly pushed some loose strands of hair back under her bonnet but some of the hair refused to stay put.

Missus Hiltz stood on tippy-toe. "Let me," she said, promptly putting the errant hair in its proper place. "I can't abide those new bonnets. Just because they wear them in Boston, doesn't mean they're proper for Sambro." She lowered her heels and stepped back. "I thought you and William came to Sambro to get away from the likes of Richard Bulkeley and that crook, Joshua Mauger. Your Captain Rous will start it all over again if he's given half a chance." Edith patted the younger woman's hand. "I'm sure you know that, my dear."

The schooner's crew were raising the uppers.

"It looks like our captain wants to make it a quick trip," Molly said, hoping to move Missus Hiltz off the subject of Rous's influence over her husband. She turned away, looking back across the harbour, watching as William set the shallop's single sail. The little craft was falling behind as the schooner moved more quickly down harbour. Soon, George's Island[1] would hide the shallop from her view. She held on to the sight of her man, trying in some way to reach out and protect him from the wiles of Captain John Rous.

"This is the second time you and William have come to Sambro to get away from the navy, the politics, the fighting, and each time," Edith smiled, "that old scallywag comes sniffin' William out." Her smile broadened, "Not that I mind Captain John's visits. He's very personable when he has a mind."

Molly sighed. "Once a shipmate, always a shipmate, my William says. So far, William has served Captain Rous on three ships but he's promised me that, this time, he will stay at Sambro." She watched as the shallop passed behind George's Island, disappearing from her view. *William was heading for the eastern passage. What, in heaven's name, were they going to do out there?*

Published as the Act directs by A. Lockwood 1st May 1818.

J Walker Sculpt.

"You remember the first time you came to Sambro? I remember like it was yesterday. My dear Paul had just passed on and your William was so ...."

Missus Hiltz had started her rant against all things Halifax. Molly had heard it all before. Perhaps it was time to join the other families on the main deck. As she moved away from the taffrail, she took one last look. The shallop was just coming out from behind the island. They were definitely going down the eastern passage.

Eastern Passage

"The Indians are gone!" The bareheaded young man holding the tiller of the shallop pointed with his free hand at the shore. "Some were in there, last month!"

"Good riddance!" The older man was taking a drink from a shiny flask. He continued with his drink rather than make further comment. When he had finished, he handed the flask to the third man who, inserting the cork and replacing the cap, carefully stowed the flask in a sea bag under the thwart.

The third man wiped some spray from his forehead. "Is that your island, Captain?"

The older man, John Rous, captain of His Majesty's sloop of war *Winchelsea*, answered, "No, it's not. That's Cornwallis Island, Wimper.² It divides the harbour entrance into the eastern and western passages." Rous scanned the shore for several moments to see if there were any signs of habitation. "My son-in-law doesn't like the name. He doesn't like to be reminded of the times he was an aide to Governor Cornwallis; when he was just a flunky." The breeze caught his tricorn but he was quick to grab the hat before it left his head. "He plans to change its name," Rous added as he smoothed his hair, arranging his two pigtails so they weren't trapped under the hat while he scrunched the ungainly thing back down on his head. "Used to be that Indians were a problem in here ... "

William Gray,³ the man at the tiller, ruefully commented, "If Richard Bulkeley wants to change the name of that island, there aren't many who will argue with him." William moved the tiller to starboard while releasing the sheet of the single sail to take better advantage of the following wind as they passed to the left of the island. "It will be quicker," William explained for the benefit of Wimper, Captain Rous's manservant, "if we continue down the eastern passage." With the sail set he exclaimed, "God! It's beautiful in here!"

"I think the Rangers got 'em," Rous said, going back to his original subject but not waiting for an answer, "it don't matter, really, as long as the bastards are gone."

"Killed some. The rest left," William answered as he steered down the middle of the narrowing channel. Close as they now were to either shore, there were still no signs of habitation. He shifted his gaze, checking for signs of wear and tear on his former captain; after all, it had been almost a year since William had set eyes on the man. As usual, the Royal Navy captain's uniform made the ex-privateer look smaller than he actually was. *All that gold braid and buttons would be impressive on a larger man*, he thought, *but my old captain appears to be weighed down by it all.*

At that moment the captain turned, looking directly at his young friend.

William revised his mental image of Captain Rous; the high blue collar of the naval jacket provided an effective perch for the hawk nose and the piercing black eyes. Hastily discontinuing his examination, William made a great show of studying the shoreline. It was a glorious day; the beaches full of multicoloured debris from the recent hurricane, dark green trees leading right down to the shoreline, gulls and sunlight, the little craft slicing swiftly through the sparkling waters.

William pointed. "Look ahead. Just beyond the point. That grey smudge, low on the water, is your island, sir."

"Rous's Island." [4] Rous stared hard as they got closer. "It has more trees than I thought. Anyone live there?"

"Nary a soul."

In a grumpy voice, the grey-haired man said, "The fishermen pay their landing fees to my son-in-law."

Neither Wimper nor William Gray made any comment.

"It's my name on the charts! Richard tells me it's my island but what if I wanted to sell it? What if I wanted to give it to you, William? You're like a son to me. What if I wanted to leave it to you? Not likely it would be mine to give."

All three men were silent as the shallop approached the little island known as Rous's Island.[5] William broke the silence. "It looks long and narrow because it's so flat. On the western side of the island, there are several deep gullies. Ships have a devil of a time during storms because the water entering those gullies is thrown great distances, making the island hard to see. When I'm piloting, I keep my ships well clear."

"What good is it, then?" Wimper had taken the captain's glass and surveyed the island as the other two men had discussed it. "I can see nothing but black rocks ..."

"That's slate rock. It comes up everywhere on the island." William held the tiller with his arm while he slipped off his peajacket. He let it fall to the seat and resumed his hold on the tiller.

Wimper continued, "... black rocks, trees and sand. What good is it?"

Rous studied the island as he said, "A sailor knows there's good shelter for small craft in the lee of that island; a good approach and good shelter. The fishermen like to use it"—and there was the petulant voice again—"and my son-in-law gets the landing fees from them. Goddamn! Richard's got no right to take my island!"

William tried to placate the Captain by saying, "That's why I brought you out here today, so's you could have a look at her. I know it's been eatin' at you, Captain. Take a good look! Is that flea-bitten hunk of rock worth fighting with Richard and upsetting Amy?"

When Captain Rous didn't answer, William went on.

"Can you see yourself putting this island to any personal use?"

When the captain still didn't answer, Wimper tried his hand at reasoning with the older man. "Sir, it's all in the family, anyway. Amy would look out for your interests."

Captain Rous made a face. "I wasn't born yesterday, Wimper! Amy, bless her heart, is my daughter, I love her, but she's just a woman in Richard Bulkeley's world!"

"She's his wife ..."

As the two men argued back and forth, William sailed the shallop closer to the island for a better look. He could see where Captain Rous was right; the approach to the lee shore was excellent. He gazed at the shoreline and let the arguments wash over him as he experienced the pleasures of sailing a small craft on a very fine day. His thoughts slowly came to dwell on the current problem with his old captain.[6]

Before becoming a harbour pilot, William Gray had served with Captain Rous during the campaign to push the French off the Isthmus of Chignecto. He had gotten to know and admire the old sea dog but became aware that, while being an audacious sea captain, Rous was suffering from a sickness which, if it became known, would remove him from the active list of the Royal Navy. William had conspired with Wimper, Rous's long-time employee and companion, to hide the Captain's bouts of irritation, anxieties and depression from the crew and from the naval authorities. Now, this 'Rous's Island thing' was weighing upon the captain so much that Wimper had sought William out, asking his help to put the old man back on an even keel.

William realized that it was unlikely that anyone would be able to convince Richard Bulkeley to give the island back. Richard Bulkeley, First Secretary of Nova Scotia, Clerk of the His Majesty's Governing Council, Senior Officer of Militia and husband of Amy Rous, had usurped title to Rous's Island. Whatever caused Bulkeley to use his considerable influence to cheat Captain Rous didn't matter. The deed was done and was chewing up John Rous's innards. William believed it was killing the old man. He turned the boat away from the island and began listening to the arguments, again.

"Sir, this way, the island is in the family. Amy will be able to intervene with her husband if you should ever want to put the island to some personal use, although I can't imagine what you would ever want to do with it."

"It's the principle of the thing," the old man groused. "Richard shouldn't have done that to me! I was in the Gulf of Saint Lawrence with the *Winchelsea* ..."

William jumped in, "And you captured a sixteen-gun

French post ship! I should have stayed with you instead of becoming a harbour pilot! I'd have made more money from that one prize than I made all year as a pilot."

"Aye. I did miss you, William." Rous fixed his eyes upon the young man he would have wished for his son. Beneath the grey, rolled neck jersey were the muscled arms and broad chest of a seaman … *and a damn good one, too.* He began to reminisce about the old days in the Fundy. *It was William who had …*

"Then we don't need the island, do we?" William could see that he had interrupted the old man's thoughts but he persisted. "We don't need that hunk of rock. We have the sea and our shipmates."

The privateer's eyes flashed under the bushy, black eyebrows, "Ye'll come back and serve with me?"

William was flabbergasted! *Was this 'island thing' just two schemers setting me up; getting me alone to talk me into serving again?* He glanced from one to the other. *What a pair! Was that what the old man was up to?* He closed his mouth because it was hanging open. Finally, he answered, "Sir, I left the navy to have a family life. There's no way I'll go back to the Service."

"Christ! Look over there!" Captain Rous pointed to the east. "My God! Whatever happened to her?"

Obviously it was an English ship because she was flying the colours, but not a ship even Captain Rous could identify.

William was the first to speak. "She's big, whatever she is. Look! She's towing another ship."

"They're both badly damaged!" Rous grabbed the glass. "The lead ship is flying Vice Admiral Holbourne's pennant. She must be *Grafton!*"

William found it hard to believe the hulk wallowing along with jury-rigged sails could be the eighty-eight-gun ship of the line, *H.M.S. Grafton.* She was almost unrecognizable because of the extensive damage to her superstructure, as if she had been swept clean by a half-dozen French broadsides.

"I'm making for her! They will need a pilot. It might just as well be me." William short sheeted and set course to intercept the huge ship.

Meanwhile, Captain Rous had identified the ship astern as

H.M.S. Centurion, fifty-two guns. If possible, she was in worse shape than the lead ship: bulwarks and taffrail gone with no standing or running rigging. On the upper decks, it could be easily seen that not a single gun of the ship's armament, in its present condition, could be brought to bear. What it must be like on the lower decks could be imagined because many of the gun port covers were missing or awry.

As the shallop approached the lead warship, she was challenged.

"Ahoy the boat!"

William, cupping his hands to his mouth responded, "*Winchelsea!* Request permission to come aboard!"

"Say again?"

Wimper laughed. "They can't believe that the Captain of *Winchelsea* would be out here in a tiny boat!"

"Better make it plainer to them, William," said Rous.

"Captain John Rous of *H.M.S. Winchelsea* requests permission to come aboard with harbour pilot."

After a few moments, another voice responded, "Carry on, the boat."

As soon as they were able, Wimper and the Captain ascended the ladder while William arranged with *Grafton's* watch officer to hoist the shallop inboard. When he alighted on the deck, he saw Admiral Holbourne shaking hands with Captain Rous.

"I'm not sure I'm glad to see you, Captain, my flagship being somewhat in disarray."

"May I ask what happened, sir? Were you attacked?"

"By a hurricane, Rous. By a hurricane."

"My God! It did this damage?"

"We were several leagues off Îles Royale on the 25th of September. We were struck with such force that every escort ship of the fleet was severely damaged. Look astern!"

From the higher elevation of the man o' war, Rous was able to see other ships slowly moving along, another one in tow, toward Halifax. Knowing what to expect, Rous could identify *Newaark* of eighty guns and *Bedford*, sixty-four guns; the *Bedford* was towing a ship.

"*Bedford* is towing what ship, Admiral?"

"*Defiance*, I would think." The admiral turned to address the Captain of *Grafton*. "What say you, Captain Blenis?"

"Your pardon, Admiral, she's *Nottingham. Defiance* refused a tow. She's in company with *Somerset* and *Sunderland*."[7] Captain Rous nodded his head. He regarded the admiral with some pity, hoping that it wouldn't show in his eyes. All naval officers knew that the Admiralty would not look with favour on any officer who allowed such damage to a fleet he had been entrusted with unless he had left an enemy in a similar or worse condition.

Admiral Holbourne must have sensed the pity. He turned on his heel. "Gentlemen, I have reports to write. Nice to have seen you, Rous, although I can't, for the life of me, understand why you are this distance from your command." He nodded to the captain of *Grafton*, "See to your ship, Captain."

With the admiral gone, Rous was able to ask questions on the subject the admiral had studiously ignored.

"Tell me, Captain Blenis, why was an escort force off Îles Royale this time of year?"

"I understand you had a successful campaign season, eh, Rous? Declared a prize? Where did you take her?"

"In the Gulf. A sixteen gun and, yes, there will be prize money from the Admiralty Court at Halifax." Rous looked at Captain Blenis as if he was going to choke the man. "Captain, what has been going on?"

"As you probably know, our dear Holbourne was to rendezvous with Vice Admiral Hardy. Hardy brought troops from the Mohawk frontier to attack Louisbourg. Too late, dear chap."

"What was too late?"

"The troops. Arrived too late to venture anything at Louisbourg this year." Blenis looked around. "I say, that fellow," he was pointing at the tall, clean-shaven seaman dressed again in his pea-jacket, "first class pilot, wot?" He rubbed his backside with both hands as if he were trying to warm himself in front of a fire. "He was lieutenant when he was in the Service and now he's harbour pilot? Served under you?" He was still rubbing his back, more vigorously, now. "My blood must have gotten thin from my time in Barbados waters. I find it deucedly cold this time of year in the afternoon. Don't you think?"

"I don't understand, Blenis. If the operation was cancelled, what was Holbourne doing sailing off Louisbourg with the escort force?"

"Damned if I really know, old chap. I think he just wanted to take a boo at Louisbourg."

Rous compressed his lips. *Imagine! English fleets in the hands of men like Holbourne and Blenis!* He looked back at the island that was once again a smudge on the surface of the ocean. He shook his head. *There are more important things than arguing about land titles.* The next campaign season he would have to forget the thrill of independent command and gaining rich prizes. He looked down at his feet, realizing his officer's boots were killing him. *Oh well! I've enjoyed the season on Winchelsea, but the next time out I will have to be with the fleet! I must protect our men and the ships from the horse's asses of the Royal Navy. I will have to be there.*

William Gray had been standing off to one side waiting for Captain Blenis to order him to take on his pilot's duties. He hadn't heard any of the conversation but he could see by the set of his mouth that Captain Rous had made up his mind about something. When the captain shifted his feet, William knew the old man had decided to do something that would take him into harm's way. William whispered to Wimper. "The old man has just decided to go into action … his feet are hurting him."

Wimper grinned. "Every time the captain's dogs bark, the Frenchies suffer."

Half aloud William mused, "I wonder where we'll be going."

"You wonder where *we* will be going, young sir? You have decided to serve again with our captain?"

The warship's commander hailed the harbour pilot. "I say, Mister …" Captain Blenis started again. "I say, Pilot. Take us into port, if you will. Mind, now, I have *Centurion* in tow. We won't be performing like a shallop!"

"It's Mister Gray, Captain! Aye, Cap'n! Have your helmsman steer, east nor'east. I mean to give us lots of room. Thrum Cap Shoals come out here a long, long ways."

"Ship's Master! East-northeast! Pilot, you have my ship!"
"Aye, Captain Blenis!"

Government Wharf
Halifax Harbour

As befitting a captain of one of His Majesty's warships, Captain Rous and his man Wimper were taken ashore in the captain's gig from *Grafton*. As the gig left the wharf to begin its return journey to the ship, Rous looked around. "I suppose William will be little while getting his shallop launched from *Grafton*."

Wimper, anticipating his captain's command, volunteered, "I'll wait here, Cap'n, for the lieutenant to come ashore. I suggest you seek some comfort at Carmichael's."

"Well, I don't know if I should go into Carmichael's every time I pass by."

"If Mister Carmichael sees you on the wharf and you don't drop in, he will be sorely disappointed. Have him draw dark ale for me, sir. I'll be right along with the young sir." When the old man still seemed to hesitate, Wimper added, "You could order up some pork crackles for us. It would be much appreciated."

"Yes. Yes, I'll do that. The boy did us good service today. Pork crackles and some biscuit, wouldn't you think?"

"Yes, sir. We'll be right along. I can see some activity on *Grafton*, now."

Captain Rous took the few paces to Carmichael's, hesitating at the front door because the place was packed to the rafters. Every table was full and the ladies of the night were negotiating their encounters with attentive customers in the narrow way-through. Waiters with jugs and mugs made the tobacco smoke swirl as they passed from the tables to the bar. There was no other sound than the din of many voices competing to be heard, all at once.

Carmichael caught sight of the captain and motioned him to his usual corner. The five people who were jammed into the nook caught the barkeep's signal and immediately stood up, joining the throng in the way-through.

Rous had to raise his voice to be heard. "I didn't mean to disturb those people, Mister Carmichael, but I do appreciate it. I'll stand them a round."

"That's not the least bit necessary, Cap'n," but the barkeep was quick to add, "I know they will thank you for it."

"Not at all."

"You'll be joined by your man, as usual?"

"Yes, and a beer for Lieutenant Gray."

"Then it's a dark ale, two beer and crackles."

"And some biscuits, if they're fresh."

"Only this morning, Cap'n."

"That will do fine, thank you." The important business finished, Rous sat back and looked around.

There were so many people! There were the redcoats, of course, a surprising number of militia blues and several ranger greens, but there were more civilians than he had seen before, none of whom he recognized. Since Carmichael always served him personally, Rous planned to ask about the civilians when the barkeep returned.

Wimper and Gray showed up at the door. Gray, towering over the manservant, fairly blocked the light from the open doorway with the breadth of his shoulders. Rous remembered the slip of a boy who had been on the staff of the first Governor in 1749. There were still the same flashing brown eyes and his hair was as black, thick and curly as in earlier days, but the boy had turned into a man and a damn good sailor. He waved them over.

"Have you ever seen so many civilians?"

Mister Carmichael arrived with the drinks and trays of food. The men helped themselves as Carmichael told them what was going on. "Now that the campaign against Louisbourg was cancelled for this year, the troops from the Mohawk frontier had to be garrisoned somewhere. There were too many for New York and Boston. Some of them have been shipped to winter at Halifax."

"Then who are the civilians?"

"The suppliers go where it is most lucrative for them. A lot of them came here. Halifax was caught by surprise by the influx. These men are making a premium on every button, bayonet and bolt of cloth they buy and then sell."

"Gad! Cap'n! This is the year we should have been in molasses!"

Carmichael thought that perhaps he hadn't heard William right over the din of the many voices. "Molasses?" he repeated.

Wimper, usually very quiet, pointed at his two companions. "One year they thought they could anticipate events and bought every drop of molasses they could find. They were going to make a fortune."

William put his mug down. "It was not to be."

Carmichael grinned. "Lose your shirts?"

"No. Mauger took it all off our hands, for a price." William pointed at the captain with his thumb. " That's the last time I'll believe the captain and his crystal ball!"

"Balls!" laughed the captain. "I have balls! But I didn't know they had crystallized!"

The men continued laughing as Carmichael excused himself and went on about his business.

Rous leaned over to touch William's sleeve. "Next season, I'm requesting a more senior command, bigger ship, more say in the war councils. That was a pitiful sight, today. I wonder how many men we lost?"

"While I was working *Grafton*, the men told me *Tilbury* was driven ashore on Îles Royale."[8]

"All were lost?"

"Drowned. On that shore, it's unlikely anyone could survive."

William waited for the captain to respond.

Rous closed his eyes and hunched over his mug. He stayed that way for a time. Finally, the old man pulled himself back from his dark thoughts. "Have you any idea what Blenis told me they were doing off that coast? Why they had all those ships sailing off that miserable coast in hurricane season?" The captain leaned forward to be better heard but the pitch of his voice had risen. "Why he had that fleet on that shore where there is no shelter to run to that isn't French?" Suddenly there was that petulant voice, the tone of a little boy being denied a treat.

"Blenis didn't really know what they were doing up there! He said the Admiral was playing peek-a-boo with the Frenchies!"

"They are inept!" William shared the old man's anger.

"The Admiralty won't stand for the loss of *Tilbury*."

"You're right. Holbourne will be removed. I'm going to request a senior appointment because I want a say in what happens during next season's campaign." Captain Rous put his mug down. He looked across the table at William Gray. "Are you with me, William?"

"How can we do that, sir? I resigned my commission when we came back from the Fundy."

"I put you ashore with no pay. You're still on the books as Lieutenant William Gray, Royal Navy, non-assigned. Are y'with me, boy?"

"Aye sir!"

Wimper clapped William on the back. The three men drank a toast and ordered another round.

"As soon as I get my ship, I'll have you assigned to her."

Wimper, ever the practical man, suggested that the lieutenant should move from Sambro as soon as possible. "We won't have many more nice days like today, this season."

"I'll send a *Winchelsea* shore party back with you. My men will have you moved in a matter of hours."

Wimper could see in the young man's face the sudden realization that there was another consideration, Molly Gray. "We had better send the work party out in a few days, sir. The lieutenant has some campaigning to do at home."

Captain Rous gave his lieutenant a wide smile. "If I know Molly Gray …"

Wimper nudged his captain. "You really don't know her, sir."

"Aye, Wimper." Rous waved at the barkeep for another round. "I must leave it to you, William, to bring that fine lady alongside in our grand enterprise."

Ten days later
Sambro, Nova Scotia

"Grand enterprise! He doesn't really talk that way, does he?"

"When he's in his cups, he does, Molly."

"How much time do we have to decide?"

"The *Winchelsea* work party will be here the day after tomorrow."

There was a silence in the Gray household as Molly tended to her infant son, Charles.

She held the child up for the father to see. "I thought we had decided we didn't like Halifax." She handed the boy to William and said, not unkindly, "We didn't want our sons to grow up amongst the liars and cheats of the town."

William rocked the boy. "Liars and cheats, politicians and businessmen, admirals and pursers, priests and undertakers—Halifax has a lot of them, but it doesn't own all the liars and cheats!"

"At least we know who they are, here at Sambro." She took another approach. "Why does Rous need you, a lieutenant? As a successful captain, he can have his choice, can't he?"

Still holding the boy, William took his wife's hand and led her to the window where they could sit on the little bench and look out over the harbour's sea wall.

"Molly, on a man o' war, we have a sailor we call the Buffer. It's his job to listen to the officer and put the officer's orders into terms the sailors can understand. Not everyone has the knack but, when you have a good Buffer, you have a good ship."

Molly Gray listened as her husband went on to explain.

"In this theatre of war, the army can't march to its battles; it must use the navy. Rous knows that there has to be a very high degree of understanding between the navy and the army if we are ever able to beat the French. The navy has to carry them there, get them ashore, supply them, support them with naval gunfire, and keep the enemy's naval forces off their backs."

"I suppose you're saying that you are the Buffer."

"During the Fundy campaign, I was called a liaison officer. I worked closely with militia officers like Jeremiah Bancroft and naval officers like Captain Cobb. I believe I was a help. Rous knows that our operation at Les Mines moved more smoothly than anywhere else in the Fundy because the navy had better contact with the army, through me, than, say, at Annapolis Royal where there wasn't a liaison officer and they had significant loss of life."

"Where did you learn to be a Buffer?"

William smiled at his wife. He squeezed her hand. "Please, dearest, a Buffer is a sailor. Call me a liaison officer." He took a deep breath. "You know that before I met you, I was on the personal staff of Governor Cornwallis. His aides were army officers." William had a pensive moment as he said, "Perhaps it might have been better if he had chosen naval officers to work with him to build a fortress on the Atlantic seaboard but ..."

"He had you, William."

William acknowledged the loving wife's comment with another squeeze. "Anyhow, I was working with them and, I guess, I learned from them. Later, William taught me a lot."

"William?"

"William Hay." It still hurt William to think of how Hay had died during the siege of Fort Beauséjour so he spoke in a semi-serious tone reminding her which "William" he meant. "Ensign William Hay of the Fortieth Regiment of Foot, generally known as Hopson's Regiment." Dropping his mock serious tone, William said, "We exchanged information about military terms and tactics. He would have been a great help doing liaison work from the army side if he hadn't been killed."

"I remember William and his wife Penelope." Molly touched her husband's cheek in a consoling caress, but she was not to be diverted from her objections to Rous's latest raid on her little family. "So, our dear Captain Rous has such need of my man that he is going to uproot us from our Sambro home and drag us into the sinful town of Halifax."

William could tell from Molly's tone that she wasn't being flippant. He also realized that it was time to come to the heart of the matter. "He needs Wimper and me, Molly."

Relenting somewhat, Molly grasped her husband's hand. "I know, sweetheart. I know he has problems that you keep secret."

"Sometimes the pounding blood in his head makes him see things wrong."

Molly sat there, holding her husband's hand, sensing the surges of strength from his brave heart. If she said yes, this brave heart would soon go into harm's way because that was his nature. Certainly, she had always been proud of her husband's exploits. Prouder even more that he served the Empire as the strong right arm of the famous Captain John Rous. Still, there was the boy, Charles, who deserved his own private Buffer, a father to translate the language of the world for his better understanding.

William saw the hesitation. He waited.

"I know he's worth protecting, your Captain Rous. It's men like him who will keep us safe from the French." She looked wistfully out over the little harbour. Almost in a whisper she said, "I know it has to be." Tears formed in her eyes but didn't spill over. She released William's hand and searched out a linen in case she couldn't keep the tears in check.

Molly Gray gazed out the window, past the sea wall, in the general direction of Cemetery Point where the villagers were building a bigger church. There was a rough scar in the woods where the land had been cleared. Next week the men where going to begin the stone foundation. She sighed, deeply. Everyone believed the roof would be up before the first snow.

Molly reached for her husband's hand. She brought it to her lips, giving a light kiss to the tanned skin. "We'll come back, won't we?"

And then the tears fell.

Endnotes

[1] Originally named George Island, I have found George and George's Island in various references. I settled for George's Island.

[2] McNab's Island was granted to the Cornwallis brothers, Henry, James and William. However, there is an earlier reference to the island as "Cornwallis Island," leading H.W. Hewitt to conclude the island was named after Honourable Edward Cornwallis, the first governor.

[3] Family tradition says that William Gray was a member of the Governor's personal staff. Minutes of the Governor's Council mention that Gray took it upon himself to sign papers in the absence of the Governor due to sickness. (Must have been an enterprising chap.) When Governor Cornwallis returned to England, Gray moved to Sambro and became a harbour pilot. He lived out his life there, having at least five sons.

[4] Documents referred to the island as Rous's instead of Rous.

[5] According to Joan Payzant, "Hewitt's account of Devil's Island says that the island was first named after its original owner, John Rous and called Rous's Island. Later the name was changed to Wood Island because in the beginning it was heavily wooded until a fire destroyed all the timber leaving it altogether barren. Finally, it was owned by a Frenchman by the name of Deval or Devol and a corruption of this left it as 'Devil's Island.'"

[6] During my Gray research, I "found" Captain John Rous, ex-privateer, warship captain and the only colonial officer to be promoted to the rank of Captain in the Royal Navy, who played a role in both sieges of Louisbourg. During the battle for Quebec, it can be argued that the actions of his ship, *H.M.S. Sutherland*, sealed the fate of the French in North America. Coupled with the fact that even though Rous became the father-in-law of Richard Bulkeley, who was confidant of a number of Nova Scotia governors, a general of militia and a thoroughly rich man, Rous was always outside the pale and even a litigant of his powerful son-in-law (concerning Rous's Island). Every Nova Scotian should know about Rous and I just had to put William Gray into a naval uniform and put him on Rous's ships so I could tell the story.

[7] Names of ships and commanders are correct.

[8] *H.M.S. Tilbury* was lost but some of the crew survived. No one at Halifax would have knowledge of any survivors at this point.

Chapter Two

December 31, 1757
Halifax

Lieutenant and Missus Gray hesitated at the front door of the Bulkeley mansion. When William leaned forward to raise the door rapper, Molly stayed his hand. In a low voice she said, "Please don't argue with Colonel Bulkeley. He is far too powerful a man to be on the outs with."

"Yes, my dear," William said as he made a move to lift the rapper.

Molly again stayed his hand. "He might be a trifle overbearing because you were junior to him on the old governor's staff, but I want you to bear with it."

"Yes, dear."

This time Molly allowed the rapper to be lifted. To their surprise they were met at the front door by the lady of the house.

"Come in! Come in, William, Molly, and a Happy New Year's!"

"It's so nice of you to invite us, Missus Bulkeley," William said with a small bow.

"Now, William! I thought we had our little agreement." Amy Bulkeley waited as a manservant took the Grays' winter wraps away to the cloakroom before she went on. "We said that friends must be on a first-name basis."

"Yes, of course," agreed Molly as she gave her husband a little warning with her eyes that he was to comply without any further discussion. "We really appreciate being invited. So many of our friends are gone in the short time we were living at Sambro."

Richard Bulkeley appeared at his wife's side and joined in the greetings. He cast a quick eye over Molly Gray's figure to see if she had recovered from her confinement. Indeed, he thought, *she is a fine-looking filly; firm buttocks and, I wager, she has the lithe limbs of a racer.* By the look on the woman's

21

upturned face, he could tell that she was aware of his examination, so he continued with his welcome. "Yes, as soon as Father Rous told us that you were resuming residence in Halifax, I asked my man to invite you at the very first opportunity." *Beautiful skin, and the widow's peak makes an effective frame for the sparkling eyes and lovely smile. Nice teeth*, he thought. When Amy took Molly by the arm and led her off to the ladies' room to be refreshed after her cab ride in the raw winter air, Bulkeley, with a sigh of regret, ushered William into the drawing room where they both accepted a drink from a serving man. "We might as well wait in here for their return where it is a bit warmer and we can have a quiet drink."

"Thank you, Richard."

"Well, old friend, I see you are assigned to *H.M.S. Sutherland*. Whatever happened to the small cottage by the sea and the life of a harbour pilot?" With a mean-spirited look to his eye he added, "I thought you didn't like us in the big town."

"The Sambro cottage is still there, waiting for us. When we have finished with the French, we shall go home again."

"Every man must do his duty, and all that?"

"Yes, I suppose so."

"Or do you provide particular service to my father-in-law?"

William sipped on his drink.

"I understand the old boy is slipping a little."

"Who would say such a thing about the best captain on the North Atlantic."

"He's had his day. For Amy's sake, I would like to see him cease active service." Richard, when he saw that William was not going to make a response, continued. "I arranged for him to be appointed as a member of His Britannic Majesty's Governing Council. He accepted, attended a few meetings but, when I noticed some irrational behaviour and wanted to discuss it, he stopped coming."

"The ladies should be back by now, Richard." William placed his glass on a nearby table.

"You're not going to tell me, are you." There was no question; it was a statement.

William, turning toward the entrance to the room, said, "I don't have anything to tell."

Holding William by the elbow, Richard persisted, "I want you to know, when he asked for a senior naval appointment, I advised against it."

"You what?" William was shocked. "You spoke against your father-in-law at Council?"

"No! Of course not! I merely dropped my personal opinion in the proper Royal Navy circles."

"Christ, Richard! He's the best sea captain on the Atlantic seaboard!"

"You keep saying that and it might well be, William, but he's not like you or me."

"What do you mean by that?"

"He's not a European. He was born in the wilds of New England. He may be a good enough sea captain but he shouldn't ever have been appointed captain in the King's Navy."

"You prig!"

"Now, now, William. Let's not forget who we are ... and where we are." Richard pulled handkerchief from his pocket and daubed his upper lip. He flicked a wrist in the direction of a manservant, who immediately went to the fireplace and began to bank the fire. "When I first met the man, he showed bad judgement by disagreeing with me in front of the governor ..."

"You mean the day after the Dartmouth massacre?" William didn't wait for any response. "He gave an opinion that differed from yours."

"In front of Governor Cornwallis!"

Remembering what he had promised his Molly, William tried to pull in his horns. "I don't remember it as a disagreement."

Bulkeley made a small motion with his hand. "Whatever. He should have known better than to begin a war with Richard Bulkeley."

William put his glass down. "Captain Rous is a magnificent sailor and does good service for the King."

"You sound like my Amy, bless her little heart. She thinks the sun rises and sets with the man but believe me, it doesn't. He's not good at business and he's slipping as a captain."

"You're jealous of John Rous! He's her father, for pity's sake! It's only natural for her to love him and think the best of him!"

The Honourable Richard Bulkeley stared down at the shorter man. "I hope our little discussion tonight doesn't put a damper on your evening," he turned away and began to leave the drawing room, "and I hope the promise I now make doesn't disturb your relationship with Father Rous." Bulkeley stopped and looked back at William Gray. "I shan't ever have you in this house, again," and he left the room.

March 1758
Halifax

William Gray knocked on the cabin door. When he heard the gruff voice of Captain Rous call out, "Come!" he lifted the latch and entered.

H.M.S. Sutherland, being an older ship of the line, had a smaller captain's cabin than what would be expected for a Royal Navy captain with thirteen years seniority and an impressive record of victories. The moveable bulkheads had been repositioned by the crew to give as much room and privacy as the hull of the ship would permit, but the captain's bunk was still of the "lash and stow" type, the butts of two twenty-four pounders intruded into the living area, and the transom was of the older, smaller type making the cabin dark and, on this day, stuffy.

"Your pardon, sir. This instruction was delivered to the entry port a few minutes ago." William held out an official-looking document with the red seal broken. "It was addressed to me, sir, so I ..."

"So, of course, you opened it. What is it?"

William took two steps forward and handed the document to his captain.

"It was delivered by Bulkeley's man."

"Let's have the proper respect, Lieutenant. Use Mister Bulkeley for the First Secretary, Lieutenant Bulkeley if you want to call him by his Regular Army rank, or Colonel Bulkeley if you are dealing with Bulkeley of the Militia."

"Aye, sir."

"Our system is built upon respect, Lieutenant."

"It was delivered by Colonel Bulkeley's man."

Rous unfolded the document.

3 April

At the request of Brigadier James Wolfe, Lieutenant
William Gray is expected to be present in the east drawing
room of the Bulkeley Residence, 10 am, 4 April 1758.

Thomas Green
(for) Colonel Richard Bulkeley

Rous nodded his head. "And then there is Richard Bulkeley, my
son-in-law, who thinks he can by-pass the chain of command."
Rous instantly regretted making a derogatory comment about
a senior officer in the presence of a junior, even if that junior
was his favourite, William Gray. Rous handed the letter back to
William but didn't seem able to restrain himself: "Richard follows protocol only when it suits him. He should have asked me
to make you available, but Richard is full of himself these
days." Rous frowned as he realized that he was still being criti-
cal of a colonel. He stood up, indicating that the conversation
was ended. "You'll go along, Lieutenant. I'll be there. We will
be talking about the Louisbourg campaign."

"Why me, sir? Why do we meet at Bulkeley's house? I
haven't been invited there since New Year's."

His annoyance with his own lack of self-control still showing, Rous replied, "Wolfe is staying there.[1] He uses one of the
drawing rooms for his planning sessions," Captain Rous
stopped speaking while he listened to a command given by the
watch officer on the deck of *H.M.S. Sutherland* and, apparently satisfied with what he heard as the response, continued, "and
he was the only army commander who expressed an interest in
our liaison efforts in the Fundy."

William opened his mouth as if to speak but the captain
silenced him with a motion of his hand. "He wants the British
naval and military parts of this next operation to work together like two branches of one united service."

"Aye, but …"

"When he asks a question, tell him what you think, directly."

"Very good, sir." William looked down, fiddling with the Bulkeley note.

Obviously there was more, so Rous waited.

William's concerns weren't long in coming out. "Will Colonel Bulkeley be there?"

"Most probably; it's his house, but don't you mind him. He's already tried his best to undercut me but, despite him, I still got *Sutherland*!"

"You should have had the newest and the best, not the old *Sutherland* with her puny fifty guns."

"Don't worry, William. *Sutherland* is my ticket to the meetings," Rous pointed his finger at William, "and she's your ticket, too. Don't pay no never mind to Richard at the meeting … whatever he says."

Captain Rous drew himself up and put a serious look on his face. "Now, Lieutenant, it's time you went about your duties as a ship's officer."

"Aye, sir." William saluted, smartly, and turned to go.

Rous had the last word as the cabin door was closed. "Just give General Wolfe what he wants and pay no mind to Richard."

April 4, 1758
Halifax

William was walking along Argyle Street, enjoying the lovely Nova Scotia spring day but fretting about meeting Richard Bulkeley for the first time since New Year's Eve. They had known each other, Richard and he, for so long and yet William was truly seeing the man for what he was, for the first time. It bothered him that such a petty, malicious person should have so much power over the everyday lives of the people of Nova Scotia.

He hurried along. He mustn't be late.

He wondered if Amy Bulkeley knew about Anne Wenman, Mistress of Orphan House, and of her relationship to Rich

Bulkeley. *Yes, that's what the woman called him, and in public, too! "Dear Rich," she had said on the steps of Saint Paul's for the entire world to hear. Oh, I'd like to be a fly on the wall when those two got together to discuss the "heart-rending concerns of the poor little orphans." And then there was the money!*

It was an open scandal, the amount of money Bulkeley allocated to the Wenman woman for the clothing and maintenance of twenty-five orphans. William's previous ship, *Pilot Schooner*, with a crew of five, was budgeted amongst the Vessels of the Colonial Service at two hundred and two pounds, nine shillings and eleven pence, including such items as "Further supplies," or more blatantly, "Rum charged by Mister Bulkeley." *Not so the Wenman woman. Her orphans received more than five hundred and twenty-five pounds plus thirty pounds here and there for special items like "fuel for the Orphan House." Why, if a few pounds were added to the Orphan House annual budget, there would be enough money to run Lunenburg Settlement!*[2]

Catching sight of the Bulkeley residence, William changed his train of thought. *Richard had purchased two lots on the eastern side of Argyle Street from a departing settler for one hundred pounds in total. Now, he had built a one-storey, framed house with generous proportions, surrounded by a verandah.* As William got closer, he could see the grounds. *Can't wait to see what it's like!* Several men were working on the vegetable gardens. Down by the stables there were other men handling a couple of nice-looking horses.

William remembered how pleased he had been, at the time, that his friend had struck such a fine deal for two prime building lots. He grunted as he hurried up the street. *There were many such "good deals" coming Richard Bulkeley's way now that he had been appointed Judge of the Court of Escheat for the Province of Nova Scotia.*

Money! All it takes is money and a man can afford the luxury of a good library, set a good table and have a well-stocked wine cellar. No wonder men like Brigadier General Wolfe want to visit! He was a little out of breath as he ran along the drive to the front of the house. One rap with the lion's head brass door-knocker and then quickly inside the door where the man took his hat. He was ushered down the hall to the second drawing room, where he hesitated at the door, but the manservant waved him on. He still hesitated, giving a little knock with his knuckles before he pushed the door open. The first person he saw was Colonel Bulkeley, positioned directly opposite the doorway, seated at a long table.

"At last! Lieutenant Gray of *H.M.S. Sutherland*," Richard Bulkeley's voice filled the room.

"Right on time, Lieutenant," said Captain Rous, who was seated off to one side.

A slight, pale-looking Brigadier rose from his chair and pointed to the end of the table. "I'm Wolfe, Lieutenant. Join us at the table. We're going to discuss the taking of Louisbourg."

"Thank you, sir."

Brigadier Wolfe sat down. "We are waiting on Captain Brome, Royal Artillery, but there's no reason why we shouldn't begin discussions. I have had a great deal of army input. Today, I would listen to what you naval types have to say."

What followed was an uncomfortable silence caused by the senior officers who resented sharing space around a planning table with a mere lieutenant, and they were letting it show. Wolfe addressed the matter.

"I have requested Lieutenant Gray be present because he has the most recent experience in combined operations. If any of you have difficulty with that, I request you inform me now …," Richard Bulkeley began to say something but clamped his mouth shut when Wolfe continued, "… so you may be excused from the proceedings."

Wolfe shuffled some papers. "Good!" He looked around the table. "Some of us are too young to remember the last time we captured Louisbourg." At this juncture he smiled at Captain Rous, "But you were there, Captain. What was the key to their downfall last time?"

"Silencing the Island Battery."

"It will probably be the same key this time." Wolfe took some sketches out of his file case and passed them around. "Let's see what we know about Louisbourg. Captain Rous?"

"It's a sheltered harbour about three miles long and short

of a mile wide. You'd think, by taking a quick look at the charts, there'd be easy access through the wide harbour mouth." He looked at the sketch for a moment. "It looks to be a mile wide but it's blocked in its western approach by shoals and islands, leaving a narrow channel a half mile wide."

"What would be the best way to subdue the fortress, Captain?"

"Sail the fleet in and blow it to smithereens!"

The navy men all laughed.

Rous said what they all knew. "But first, someone has to take out the Island Battery. The Island Battery can rake our ships fore and aft before they come to the harbour's mouth …"

"And take them on the side as they pass …," added Captain Spital.

"Then we would be faced with the Grand Battery, jammed right against the mouth of the harbour. We'd be taken fore and aft as we entered," Captain Vaughn said, "while the town's North East Battery, on the high ground, can also rake our ships."

Rous raised his hands. "Still, gentlemen, a quick subjugation of Louisbourg requires the destruction of any French naval force in that harbour."

"Pipe dream!" said Colonel Bulkeley, loud enough for all to hear.

Wolfe attempted to silence further comment with his raised hand.

Rous persisted, "Louisbourg is a walled fortress, a series of bastions and demi-bastions with connecting walls in between. Every bastion of the town wall has embrasures or ports for guns to defend the land side."

At this point, several of the officers began to speak but Colonel Wolfe indicated he wanted to hear what the old captain had to say.

"However, the harbour side to the fortress is both their strong point and their Achilles heel." This time the men around the table waited for Captain Rous to continue.

"Its strength? Any man o'war in that harbour, friendly to the fortress, can lend its firepower to harass an enemy's approach on the land side."

"And the weakness?"

"If the ships in the harbour can be lured out to fight or can be destroyed in the harbour, then the fortress is open to a naval attack from the harbour side!"

"What about the Island Battery?" asked Captain Spital.

"We have to take it out first."

Captain Vaughn gazed down his nose at the older man. "And, my dear Rous, what of the Grand Battery? The North East Battery?" He looked around the room for support. "The French won't have to worry about an attack from the harbour because the channel will be blocked with the hulls of our ships where the French would have sunk us."

"My dear sir, any fighting captain would rely upon the skills of his gunners not to let that happen."

"You are not implying anything, Rous?"

Brigadier Wolfe raised his finger and then pointed theatrically at the table. "I brought you to this table for an exchange of opinions, not for a clash of wills. Oblige me, gentlemen, if you please."

There was a timid knock at the door. An army captain entered and announced, "Captain Brome, Royal Artillery!" He stood at attention.

"Stand easy, Captain; we started a bit early. You haven't missed much."

"Thank you sir."

"To close off our discussion of a land or sea approach to Louisbourg … or a combination, let me tell you that our commanders, Admiral Edward Boscawen and Major General Jeffrey Amherst, are in possession of a plan of attack suggested by Brigadier Samuel Waldo, the New Englander who commanded the land forces during the siege of 1745. It makes interesting reading, let me tell you, but of course, for obvious reasons, we are not going to discuss that plan here today. Added to that is a wealth of information gathered from trading vessels." Here he leaned over so that he could smile at Captain Rous. "Yankee captains never seem to let English laws interfere with making a profit at an enemy port but, in this instance, we are very pleased to have the first-hand intelligence they acquired for us."

If the jibe bothered Rous he didn't let it show. He was here to give his input and he was giving it come hell or high water.

Colonel Bulkeley saw this as an opportunity to grab some of the limelight. "Of such intelligence I would wish to mention we are told by Yankee traders that *H.M.S. Tilbury*, sixty guns, was wrecked on the rocks of Saint Esprit, south of Louisbourg. The captain and half her crew were drowned. Her cannon were recovered and we can expect to meet them again, employed in the defence of the fortress."

"Thank you, Colonel. Now, Brome, tell the gentlemen what preparations we are making during our period of waiting here at Halifax."

Rous tapped the table with a ring he was wearing. "One last word, Brigadier."

"What would that be, Captain Rous?"

"It might not be necessary for us to make an attack through Louisbourg Harbour."

Captain Spital wore a smirk on his face, as he now expected a Rous vacillation; Bulkeley had told him of the old man's periods of irrationality. Perhaps this was going to be a demonstration of one.

"If the Louisbourg governor believed we were in position to make such an attack and," Rous tapped his ring for each word, *"believed we had the guts to do it"*— he opened up his hands and spread them wide— "he would surrender his fortress."

Spital snorted, "Just like that?"

"Yes. Faced with the total destruction of the town, the bloodshed and inevitable defeat ..." Rous stopped speaking as he watched Wolfe search the faces of the officers in the room.

"I don't think your compatriots share your view."

"That's perfectly fine, Brigadier. I hope my view is taken into account, nonetheless."

"Yes. Now, Captain Brome?"

"Yessir!"

"Please tell of your preparations."

"Plenty of good food and exercise has the men fit and raring to go, sir. They're getting lots of drill ..."

"Yes, Brome, but are there any special arrangements for this operation?"

"We are making fascines and gabions ..."

Bulkeley was quick to interrupt Brome. "Would you explain, for the benefit of our seagoing friends, what they are and the uses they would be put to?"

"Yessir. They are cylindrical wicker baskets to be filled with earth and used in field engineering after the siege should commence. There are many ways they can be used: the ground behind the assault area is usually wet and irregular, where they are used to fill in and level the exits from the beach; and around defensive positions they provide quick and easy fortifications. As well, we are making collapsible blockhouses from squared timber to better protect encamped troops ..."

William Gray sat back in his chair. This room held a lot of hostility to his captain, some of it envy for the countless naval successes of an upstart colonial but certainly the major portion of it generated by the jealousies of Richard Bulkeley. And the object of this envy and jealousy? A little man with grey hair tied in pigtails in the style of a much younger privateer, which he once had been. His formal, Royal Navy uniform—silk shirt, white waistcoat, blue jacket, gold buttons and epaulettes—not detracting in the least from the dark eyes (brown or black? who could tell under the craggy forehead and bushy black eyebrows) flashing this way and that. His large, expressive hands were gnarled, as one would expect of a seaman. His face, unscarred by battle, was worn dark by the effects of sun and weather. Only recently had the passage of time added wrinkles to the almost handsome face. With a start, William realized he hadn't been listening, but felt relieved when he heard Captain Brome still listing army activities.

"... sutlers are draining the wine casks, putting rum in them instead of ginger and sugar, which is issued to counter the evil effects of American water."

"And the cannon?" Wolfe asked.

"We begin manhandling guns aboard the ships at the end of the month."

"I'm sorry, Brome, I meant to ask—I saw an engineering design for big-wheeled carts to move the guns from the landing area to where we would need them. Are we actually building any?"

"Yessir. They are a high-box, big-wheeled cart that will easily move the guns to where they are needed. Building hunnerts of 'em, sir." Captain Brome smiled with relief, "And that's it, sir. If there are any questions I will try to oblige."

Wolfe gave it a minute and, when there were no questions, he folded his hands in front of him on the table, saying, "The operation in the Fundy last year was probably the most successful combined operation in the history of the army. Lieutenant Gray was there and I propose we listen to what he has to offer."

Rous indicated that William should stand up, which he did. He cleared his throat and began, somewhat hesitantly, "When Captain Rous ..."

Spital interrupted, "Speak up, man!"

William could see the big grin of satisfaction on Colonel Bulkeley's face as he enjoyed William's discomfort. William threw all caution to the wind and got on with it.

"My first experience with the army was during the landings at Fort Beauséjour ..."

"My God!" Spital interrupted again. "That was barely a year ago. Must we listen to this whelp?"

"Yes, please," said a very patient-sounding Brigadier Wolfe. "Go on, please, Gray."

"The condition of the sea was calm. There was no enemy activity because we were in dense fog. Once we had handled the problem of the fog, conditions were ideal for safe transport of the troops to shore, where they formed up without enemy interference."

"Well!" Captain Spital pushed his chair back, glancing around the room for evidence of support, "What could we possibly have learned from that?"

William, unfazed by this time by anything Spital said or did, continued, "The soldiers had been ordered to get in the boats. They got in the boats. They sat like statues, afraid to move for fear of doing something wrong and upsetting the boat. When they reached shore, they clambered out into the surf before the boat crews were ready for them to disembark. Not every boat had an officer; in fact, the officers went ashore in their own boats."

William had lots of time to take a deep breath before he continued because everyone was listening carefully.

"Think of it, sirs! If there had been a difficult passage, if they had been subject to enemy interference, if conditions had been wrong for the landing, then we would have lost men and, perhaps, the whole operation.

"What are you suggesting?"

"Well, Colonel, during our landing at Les Mines, I was made responsible for getting the men ashore in good order."

"Who would give an order like that to a lieutenant?" Colonel Bulkeley knew the answer but he wanted it out in the open.

"I did," snarled Captain Rous.

"I saw your orders for your operations in the Fundy and you didn't have that kind of authority, Captain," observed Spital.

"Not that it matters, gentlemen. The operation was a huge success," said Wolfe, trying to get the meeting to move along.

Rous was not letting go of it. "Colonel Monckton and I agreed. I signed the order."

William was concerned for his captain because he could see Rous was getting that scrunched-up look in his face that William recognized as the first sign of the Captain's "trouble." He pressed on. "We were early at Les Mines so we did a practice landing at Pisiquid. The sailors and soldiers got to know what was expected, one of the other. They practised getting in and out of the boats. They were thoroughly briefed, navy and army personnel together, on what was expected of them. When the time came, it was like a drill. The soldiers were at ease in the boats and the sailors felt they had an important contribution to make by getting their army comrades to the shore in good order."

"You are suggesting boat drills for our veteran regiments?" asked Captain Vaughn incredulously.

Rous had his head in his hands and, although his voice was

thus muffled, he said it plainly enough for all to hear. "Their only experience has been on European battlefields or on drill squares. They don't know anything about boats! Sure, they'll jump into the surf from a ship's boat and fight any enemy they can see, but," he sighed and rubbed his eyes with the heels of his hands, "you tell them, William."

"I saw the men in the boats at Fort Beauséjour and I saw the same men going ashore at Les Mines. I saw the difference a little practice made."

Bulkeley and some of the others made scoffing noises.

Brigadier Wolfe ignored them. "What do you suggest?"

"The army should have a naval liaison officer. Plain talk gets better results." With a pleading note creeping into his voice he said to the naval officers, "We have a Buffer on the ship! You know how important he is! We need a Buffer between the army and navy on combined operations."

"And you think that arranging boat drills, landing drills, briefings with navy and army together, are the first things this liaison officer should arrange?" asked Captain Vaughn.

The room was quiet, waiting for William's response.

"We could select a beach that has the same characteristics as our objective and practise our manoeuvres!"

Brigadier Wolfe was excited about the prospect. "We have the time, it could be done!"

Captain Spital said. "It makes sense to me, wot, ho! Bulkeley?"

Bulkeley looked as if he had just bitten into a green apple. "It makes sense to rehearse the army in its landing role."

Grasping his head in his hands Captain Rous got up. "Excuse me, I have pressing business," he said as he left the room.

Captain Spital and Bulkeley watched him leave.

Pity, thought Spital, *we didn't get the colonial lout this time but sooner or later, Rous is going to step out of line and show his true lack of breeding.*

May 19, 1758
Eastern Passage

Brigadier General Wolfe watched as the boats, loaded with soldiers, headed for the shore at Scalping Cove just off Cogel's Point. "They're getting better at it, Lieutenant Gray."

"Yes, they are, sir." William checked his pad and read off the times. "Using just the boats of the transports, we put 2,957 ashore. It took them seven minutes to form up on the beach after they landed."[3]

"How many today?"

"Today we're using all the boats of the fleet. There should be over five thousand, seven hundred men out there, right now."

An aide saluted, handed the brigadier a note and stepped back several paces. Wolfe glanced at the paper. He beckoned to the aide, "There will be no answer." He continued holding the paper in his hand. "Interesting name, Scalping Cove. Is there a story behind it?"

"There was an earthen fort manned by ten redcoats ...," William pointed, "... just over there."

Wolfe studied the remains of the fort. "It has no land-side defences, none at all."

"Yes. The Indians saw that, too. That's why it's called Scalping Cove."

Fingering the paper in his hand Wolfe smiled a sad little smile. "Someone seems to have gotten to General Amherst. This is our last drill." He read from the paper: "... not able to continue to risk resources on mock assaults ... must be discontinued immediately upon receipt of this." Wolfe looked up at the boats approaching the shore. "Is there a way to stop them once they are committed to the beach?"

"Only hand signals, sir."

"Good! We can finish this drill." He looked up, sharply, "We have no recall signal?"

"Once committed to the attack, there is no recall. If the landing force suffers a setback, then each boat's coxswain or helmsman would be looking back to the command ship for signals."

"Ship's flags?"

"Aye, sir."

"The control of the assault force must be with me, not with some old fuddy-duddy on a warship. We will have to work something out."

"Aye, sir."

The first of the boats were crunching on the beach. Men were pouring out of the boats, charging to their assembly areas. It looked like mass confusion, but the soldiers sorted themselves out in nine minutes.

"Very good. Since this is the last drill, I must talk to them. Is there somewhere …?"

"Sir, the reverse side of the fort makes a natural amphitheatre. They should be able to hear and see you if we have them gather there."

"Make it so, Lieutenant."

"Aye, sir." William saluted and then turned to face the beach. He raised his arm and gave the jerky hand signals that meant "officers report."

The brigadier smiled. "You learn from us, as well." He walked off in the direction of the fort.

Not ten minutes later, Brigadier General Wolfe was speaking to his men.

"Everybody get their feet wet?" he said in a surprisingly loud voice for such a slight person. "Because, if you didn't … I will speak to Lieutenant Gray … to make sure you get thoroughly wet … the next time we do this."

There were some catcalls and good-natured joshing.

Wolfe raised his arms for quiet and, in a halting manner that permitted his words to be repeated for the benefit of the men at the edges of the assembly, he began his pep talk. "Because, boys … the next time … will be at Louisbourg!" His words, "There will be no more drills," was drowned in the cheering and laughter.

It took some doing for the officers to finally get the men to settle down to hear what else the brigadier had to say.

"I don't know what regiments … will provide the assault troops. I don't even know … which beach we will attack;

General Amherst will decide that ... but I can assure you ... it will be within ... easy walking distance of Louisbourg!"

They laughed. A voice from the mass of men boomed out, "It don't matter, General! We'd follow ye to hell!"

General Wolfe quipped, "And the navy boys will take us there!"

More cheering.

The General raised both arms, "Listen to me! Time is short! I have things to say!"

There was instant silence.

"General Amherst ... will make the selection ... as to which companies hit the beaches first. So, I tell all of you ... what only some of you ... are going to have to know." Wolfe assumed a relaxed pose, a hand on one hip, using the other hand to gesture with.

"First! I will be close to the assault force ... and easily seen by all. Naval boat handlers must watch me for signals. I am a simple man ... so there will only be two signals; my hat on ... and pointing in the direction I want you to advance ..." He paused and seemed to be thinking about something.

The men waited. Finally one of them asked, "Wot's the other, General?"

"I was considering not having any signal for recall!"

"You won't need it, sir!" one of the coxs'n hollered.

"No, I think I should be prudent ... so it will be ... my hat off ... my arm waving you back to the ships."[4] He didn't give anyone time to comment further but proceeded with his briefing.

"All ship's boats ... will be used to take the assault force ashore ... including the boats from the ordnance ships."

One of the General's aides leaned forward and whispered something.

"Except the boats used to take the light, six pounders in. Harrumph!" Wolfe made an embarrassed, throat-clearing sound before continuing to give instructions; this time to his officers. "Officers are to go into the boats in proportion to the number of men without crowding ... particularly if there is surf. Lieutenant Gray tells me he and his boys will be there with

some light boats to save men who might end up in the sea—"
he made a show of giving William a hard look, "—although
why anyone would want to leave a perfectly dry boat and go
swimming is beyond me!"

Wolfe waited for the tittering to die down. Then he raised
his voice and spoke again to all the members of his army.

"The first troops into the Bay ... must carry nothing in the
boats but their arms, ammunition and enough bread and
cheese in their pockets for two days. No fixed bayonets in the
boats .... that's the first thing you do onshore. No shooting
from the boats. If you are taking fire from the shore ... get in
there ... fix bayonets and charge whatever is before you!"

There was renewed cheering.

Speaking again to his officers he concluded, "Commanders
of grenadiers and all field officers are to disembark in light rowing boats so they may land their respective corps and give
orders readily. Right now Major Inch, Intelligence Officer on
the staff of General Amherst, has some information for you.
Good luck to us all." Brigadier Wolfe stepped away from the lip
of the old fort.

A rather portly man with straggly, steel-grey hair (or perhaps a wig) began his briefing.

"We are going to Gabarus Bay. The beaches have a gentle
slope but behind the beach is a cliff that rises sharply some
twenty feet ..."

Screened from the men by the lip of the fort, Wolfe gestured for William to join him.

"The drills went well, Lieutenant. I'm glad we did them."

"I think they did some good, sir."

They stood there, half listening to the major's talk.

"... Gabarus is seven miles west of the fortress ..."

William could sense that the general wanted something
more said. He wondered what it was. "Your briefing went very
well, sir."

"You think so? You don't think it was too flippant?"

"No, sir. I think it was right on the mark."

"... some four thousand people living at close quarters
within the walls. About two hundred houses, mostly of wood,

some with the first storey of stone. The bigger buildings are warehouses but the biggest building of all … a stone building, four stories high, about four hundred feet long with a clock tower … is the Government. The governor lives there. The objective is to get in there and knock on his door."

"Jolly good!" Wolfe said for William to hear.

"What, sir?"

"I said, jolly good that my speech went over well," the general looked into William's eyes. "It did go over well, didn't it?"

"Yes, it did, sir."

"Well, you finish here, Lieutenant. I must be off." He flicked his wrist at his aides and Brigadier Wolfe and his entourage walked down to the shore of Scalping Cove where a navy crew took them back to Halifax.

May 24, 1758
Halifax

William put the last of his gear in the ditty bag, pulling the cord at the top to close it tightly. He looked over to where Molly was packing his trunk. She was heavy with their second child, hopefully a girl this time. He started to say something but changed his mind and walked to the window to look out on Hollis Street. It was early, early in the morning, not yet entirely light, but the lamplighter had been by already, turning out his lamps.

William was feeling odd this morning. He was looking at the things around him as if it were his last time. Of course, he was going into harm's way and he would be a fool if he didn't realize that he could die as a consequence. Spies at Louisbourg had reported there were twelve man o'war in Louisbourg Harbour. The English captains had been briefed and Rous had reported the information to the *Sutherland's* officers.

It certainly didn't look good for an old timer like *Sutherland*, of a mere fifty guns. According to the spy, the enemy ships were: *Prudent* of seventy-four guns; *Entreprenant*, *Capricieux*, *Bienfaisant* and *Célèbre*, all sixty fours; *Apollon*, fifty guns; four frigates, *Arethuse*, *Comète*, *Echo* and *Fidèle*; and two sloops, *Chèvre* and *Biche*.[5]

The English fleet, on the other hand, was much larger, but to be an officer on an old tub like *Sutherland* and consider coming up against something like *Prudent*, broadside to broadside, gave a man pause.

"What are you thinking about, William?"

Never a man to lie to his wife, William told her almost the truth of what he was thinking about. "I'm thinking about the Louisbourg operations." He gave her his most reassuring smile. "We were briefed yesterday. We will have our work cut out for us."

"Can you speak to me about it?"

William sat on the edge of the bed and patted the counterpane for his wife to sit with him. He didn't want to worry her any more than he had to, so he didn't intend to talk about naval operations at all.

"Everyone is pretty well aware that the attack will have to be made in Gabarus Bay, which is close to the fortress." William thought for a moment and then said, "And on Gabarus Bay, the most likely spot to put troops ashore would seem to be La Cormorandière, or Cormorant Cove as we call it."

"What makes the Cove so special?"

"It has a sandy beach coastline bounded by two headlands some six hundred yards apart. The beach has a gentle slope; the cliffs are set back from the shore and are only about twenty feet high. It's almost perfect! There are no rocks to stove in the boats, there's lots of room to get a large number of boats ashore at one time and room for the attacking party to manoeuvre once they overcome resistance on the beach."

"You say, 'everyone' is pretty well aware how perfect the beach is. That includes the French, I suppose."

"The spies told us that Drucourt—he's the French Governor—has his trenches ready and his batteries in place."

"He knows, then."

"Yes, Drucourt ordered them to be manned on April 28th. He's waiting for us."

"Can't our generals do something about it?"

"They're having a strategy meeting today. Rous is going to be there."

"I saw Amy Bulkeley yesterday. She asked how you were, said she hadn't seen you in a long while."

"Um." William was uncomfortable around this beautiful woman, Amy Bulkeley, who spoke so frankly of things a woman shouldn't have knowledge of, such as the goings-on in the dark corners of the 'tween decks and cargo holds out of sight of the officers. He was uncomfortable because she was often coming or going from her father's cabin and she didn't hesitate to touch him to get his attention or brush against him as she passed by in the companionway. Amy spoke of her father's fondness of William and of how the captain thought of him as the son he had never had, and so she attributed her closeness and interest in William's affairs to her natural 'sisterly' concern. He was uncomfortable now speaking with his wife, because he knew the captain's daughter would probably be on the dock to wish him well when he boarded ship this day. In a strange, exciting way, he was looking forward to the encounter and that made him more uncomfortable.

A second "Um" was all he could muster to Molly's comment.

William got up and hefted his trunk. He put it down again. "I think I'll let the cabby take it down for me." He grabbed his ditty bag and went into the next room where baby Charles was sleeping.

"Don't sling the bag over your shoulder, dear. It will get caught up in the gold braid or buttons."

William did as he was told. He gave the sleeping baby a kiss on the cheek and then padded down the narrow staircase to the front door.

"Amy said her Richard has arranged for Rous to get an island."

William looked up in surprise. "Really! That's hard to believe. I never thought that once Richard got his claws into something, he'd ever let it go."

"Well, this time, dear husband, you're wrong."

William peeked out the window. "The cab should be here, any moment now." He faced his wife. "I love you, Molly." He patted her belly. "You look after James."

"What if the baby is a Mary?"

William patted her belly again. "In that case, look after Mary, sweetheart."

Molly pressed in against him.

William folded her in his arms. He said into her hair, "I still can't believe Richard gave him back Rous's Island."

Molly pulled back. "Richard gave him *Sambro* Island— you know, the one we can almost see from the cottage; the one the fishermen said should have a lighthouse on it."

Separating himself from his wife, William said, "Ha! I told you the leopard still has spots! Richard is going to keep Rous's Island!"

"Oh pshaw!" Molly cuddled into William's arms again. "When do you think you will sail?"

"Maybe in a day or two, but we have been ordered back on board so the man o'war can leave ..."

"At a moment's notice. Yes, I know. The navy is all hurry up and wait. Amy Bulkeley said ..." She felt her husband stiffen in her arms. "I won't tell you any more what Amy says."

"Go ahead, tell me."

Molly didn't need to be asked twice. "Amy Bulkeley said the governor has issued a proclamation inviting New Englanders to come to Nova Scotia for free land. There would be a bounty for each family member that comes."

"I'm surprised Richard would let Governor Lawrence invite New Englanders!"

"You know, that's what Amy said! In fact she was more definite about it."

William waited for the revelation.

"Amy said she was surprised that," Molly mimicked Amy, "Richard Bulkeley didn't fill the lands with poor Irish."

"The poor Irish would be Papist. The Bulkeleys, the rich Irish, are very Protestant."

"Amy said Richard wanted the New Englanders to come because it would be cheaper to get them here rather than bring Europeans. Richard wants the New Englanders to farm the countryside and bring their market produce to Halifax. He thinks they will breed lots of sons to support his militia."

"There's the cab, my sweet." He kissed her full on the lips.
"*His* militia? The man's putting on airs!"

"Amy says he plans to be a general."

"There are not many men left who will gainsay the Honourable Richard Bulkeley."

"Amy says ..."

"I must get the cabby to help me with the trunk. Tell me all about what Amy says when I get back."

"I'll remember the tidbits for you, William. You will not allow the French to hurt you?"

"I'll be safe on *Sutherland*. She has fifty guns to protect your loving husband ..." William gave her another hug, savouring the freshness of her hair. "... who is content to leave you only because he knows you will be safe, here, at Halifax, while we go rid the province of the French." He nibbled her ear.

She laughed. "I will pray for your safety, William." Molly pushed her man away. "The cabby awaits, young sir," she said playfully.

He gave her a last smile and then busied himself with the cabby and the luggage.

And then he was, too soon, gone from her sight.

Endnotes

[1] According to the *Dictionary of Canadian Biography*, "Bulkeley had entertained James Wolfe and many other military men during the Seven Years' War and the American Revolution."

[2] According to records at the NS Archives.

[3] Performance figures are from military reports held at the NS Archives.

[4] Signals proposed here were actually used by Wolfe.

[5] Details such as this are from a contemporary handwritten report by an unknown staff officer after the siege. There was a notation made by the NS Archivist that it was the most comprehensive report on the siege that she had seen. When I read the archivist's notation, I allowed the report to be my major guide although the handwriting was often difficult to read.

Chapter Three

June 1, 1758
Fortress Louisbourg

Sieur Poilly, Engineer Assistant to Franquet, Director General of Fortifications, sat in the main room of the tavern on Rue Toulouse inside the walls of the fortress. He had just finished a meal of dark bread, cabbage and meat stew. He had wiped the plate clean with his bread and now licked the two-tined fork, carefully, before he placed it on his pewter plate.

It was late in the day and the room was becoming dark except for the flickering light from the smoky fire in the fireplace. When the maid came to take his plate and fork, he ordered wine and asked her for a candle. He opened an engineer's note pad and turned to the first empty page. From his engineer's case, he removed a quill and ink well. He organized the well, pad and quill, one in relation to the other and to the edge of the table as he waited for the maid to return.

"Hah!" he said when she placed the wine on the table. He held up his hand for her to wait. He took a sip and, nodding his head in satisfaction, indicated that he wanted another. He sat there sipping, as he wrote in his journal.[1]

> June 1, 1758
>
> I walked the circuit of the defences today from the Dauphin Gate, on the harbour side, to the Princess Bastion on the Atlantic side. I do believe that I have built well and the city is impregnable. Impregnable, of course, taking into account the town's outer defences.
>
> Any day now, we expect the English siege forces to arrive. The Governor, Chevalier Augustin de Drucour, commander in chief, does not mean to be caught off guard. He has had our defence forces in place since the end of April. Drucour is brave but inexperienced—but I believe him to be entirely correct in assuming that the English army, tied to supply ships and dependent for cover upon

the guns of the ships of war, cannot stray too far from Gabarus Bay.

The most likely landing place is La Cormorandière. That sick creature with the poisoned mind, Monsieur de Saint Julien,[2] Commandant of l'Artois Regiment, has been chosen to defend La Cormorandière with one thousand men.

To the east, along the Bay, at Pointe Platte, is redoubtable Marin of the Bourgogne Regiment (nine hundred men) while the Commandant of the Volontaires Étrangers, Jacques D'Anthonay, an inexperienced and presumptuous individual, is to defend Pointe Blanche. Beyond Louisbourg, east along the shore from Lighthouse Point, there are several small detachments.

We have done all we can to prepare ourselves for this adventure. Today stormy seas are working in our favour. If the English should appear and can make a landing in such severe conditions, I would be surprised, but the crazy English might try anything and we are ready for them.

Poilly

June 2, 1758
H.M.S. Sutherland
On Gabarus Bay

Captain John Rous watched as the frigate, *H.M.S. Trent,* lost way in the tremendous Atlantic swells. "Mister Gray! Break out the longboat. We must go to the assistance of *Trent!*"

Sutherland, much larger than *Trent,* was heaving and bucking as the winds and waves tore at her, trying to throw her against the shores of Gabarus Bay. Along with the rest of the fleet, she was under storm sails riding out the fearful gale and high seas since there could be no attempt to anchor—just sail back and forth, until the winds blew themselves out.

Trent had been on a parallel course to *Sutherland* a quarter mile to windward when her bow had veered toward the shore. Rous could see the crew working the helm to turn her but to no avail. Unless *Trent* got help, she was going on the rocks just to the west of Flat Point.[3]

"Sailing Master!"

"Aye sir!"

"Prepare to wear ship. I mean to put the longboat in the water upwind of *Trent*. She's beat her rudder off. My God! The French are going to have an early caller if we don't get to 'em in time!"

"Put a boat in the water, sir?"

"In this sea, we can't get *Sutherland* close enough to heave a line but we can get close enough to launch a boat!"

"First Officer! Use *Trent's* number. Make signal, 'prepare to receive tow line.'"

While the *Sutherland's* crew turned their ship around, the men of *Trent* were making a sea anchor so they might slow their ship down and hold her stern-on to the mountainous seas.

With his back to the wind, Rous briefed his lieutenant.

"We haven't much time. We're going to sail back taking *Sutherland* as close inshore as we dare to go. Then we'll come upwind and pass *Trent* to windward. In these seas, we dare not get too close! Sailing Master will position us just upwind of *Trent* for as long as he can—enough time for you to get over there with a line."

William looked over the captain's shoulder as they rapidly approached the frigate. He thought to himself that *Trent* must have a good ship's carpenter because a good ship's carpenter always has the quick makings of a sea anchor in his locker ready to be pulled out in an emergency. He could see that the *Trent's* carpenter had rigged a sea anchor out of spars, canvas and rope. The crew was manhandling the contraption over the taffrail. If it worked, the frame of spars would keep the canvas spread out in the water like a stocking with a hole in the toe. The ship, being driven by the winds, would try to move faster than the water could get out of the sock, thus slowing the ship down— if the sea anchor filled with water properly—if the ropes and canvas held.

William could see the sea anchor was in the water.

"By the time we slow down, your boat should be in the water, in the quiet area downwind of our hull. Row like the furies, m'lad, and take a line to *Trent*."

"Aye sir!"

Sutherland was coming abeam *Trent.*

"You won't have much time before Sailing Master will have to pick up way again."

William crossed the heaving deck. The longboat was positioned for a quick drop, the crew already aboard. William jumped in.

"Boys! We're going to take a line to *Trent.*" That was all he had time for.

Sutherland began to lose momentum. As she was slowing, the longboat was released into the water and the boat's crew rowed as hard and as fast as they could, dragging a line through the water. William cast a last look at *Sutherland* and saw that the men of the duty watch were paying out line as the cutter dashed through the smaller waves in the lee of the man o'war.

Christ! It's still a long way to the frigate and the damn thing is moving away from us!

William took another last look at *Sutherland*; her bow was moving back the way it had been headed before. The ship's crew was paying out line as fast as they could, faster than the longboat was dragging it through the water because *Sutherland*, even under reduced sail, would move away very quickly. The more line in the water, the more time the cutter had to get to the ship and get the line attached. The crew was still paying out line as fast as they could but, now, the ship was moving away faster than the line could be paid out.

Suddenly, the longboat was being thrown about as the protective hull of *Sutherland* moved off. The ten-foot waves were washing over the gunwales and catching at the oars, making it very difficult for the crew to row. In another instant it would be swamped! Fortunately, the little boat was caught at the crest of a wave and planed toward *Trent's* hull where there was some protection that close to the frigate as she swung on the end of her sea anchor. Two *Trent* sailors dropped down into the boat, attaching a hawser to the end of the line that rapidly disappeared toward the bow of the frigate.

Cargo nets were hanging over the side of the ship.

"Drop everything and get off!" William shouted.

The longboat was lifted high in the air and crashed against the side of the ship as *Trent's* bow swung in the other direction. Now the full fury of the wind and sea were pushing against the side of the ship. The second lift and collision destroyed the longboat.

William had one hand tangled in the cargo net as the boat splintered and fell away. Hands from above pulled him to safety as the seas returned to claim anyone clinging to the side of the ship. There was a cut-off scream as a *Sutherland* was captured by a huge swell. He disappeared in the green water to be thrown back on the deck at the next sea's return. Several hands grabbed him before he could be snatched away again.

Looking around, William saw that all his men lay around the deck, clutching at something solid. They were safe, for the moment. Would Rous's daring plan work?

Wiping the salt from his eyes, William searched the wild scene for his ship. He looked over one bulwark and saw nothing but combers and spray. On the other side were huge breakers as the Atlantic swells crashed on the shores of Îles Royale. He grinned. It must be working because *Trent's* bow was pointed away from the shore. He raised himself on his elbows and searched the sea in front of *Trent*. There she was! Carrying full lower sails to give *Sutherland* enough way to pull the other ship, she was a sight! Pride welled up in his throat as he saw how beautiful she was.

William gasped as two of *Sutherland's* lower sails ripped and were carried away in the gale. He held his breath to see what would happen next but both ships were under way and Rous made no effort to replace the shredded canvas as *Trent* was pulled to safety.

Until the storm abated and the fleet was able to safely anchor in Gabarus Bay, William and his men were the honoured guests of Captain Leslie of *H.M.S. Trent*.

Two things happened when the anchor was set; the *Trent* ship's company began the arduous job of making repairs at sea, and Captain Rous sent a boat to bring his sailors back to *Sutherland*.

* * *

"Well done! Well done, boys. You saved *Trent* from Davy Jones Locker, ye did!" Captain Rous greeted each of the returning men individually, and then, pulling Lieutenant Gray off to one side, said quietly, "I need speak with you in my cabin, Lieutenant."

"Aye sir." William followed his captain below.

"You didn't get hurt, none?"

"Got wet, sir, but ..."

"That's good 'cause I need you to do something else today."

William waited. Without thinking, he chaffed his wrist where he had been caught in the cargo net. The captain saw it.

"I thought you told me you weren't hurt?" He reached over and grasped Gray's arm and examined the rope burns on William's wrist and hand. "You should see the ship's doctor about that. Get some balm on it."

"It can wait, sir." He smiled at his Captain. "I gave it a good soaking in salt water; it'll be fine." William withdrew his arm from the Captain's grasp. "Would you tell me what you need me for?"

Rous studied the young man for a minute or two, as if he were trying to make up his mind about something. "You're right! The wrist will be fine." He gestured to the desk. "Come and look at this chart with me."

William could see it was a chart of Gabarus Bay.

"The ships are anchored here," he said pointing, "and here." He ran his finger along the coast. "General Amherst would like to take the same approach the New Englanders took back in '45 by attacking inside the small cove at White Point, here on this beach near Flat Point, and a third assault at Cormorant Cove. "

"Three separate attacks?"

"Yes, but coordinated so they happen all at the same time."

"I'm not an army man, Captain, but wouldn't that spread our forces pretty thin?"

"Amherst has logic on his side. We can better afford to spread ourselves out with a land force of 12,000 men than the French can with 3,500."

"I see what you mean."

"Today, the generals are going to coast along in boats, checking out the landing sites. I want you to be with them."

"What good would I be? I can't make any suggestions as to where the best ..."

"Be patient, young sir!"

"Aye, sir."

"I've checked the charts. They show there is enough water for us to sail in and give close support with our guns."

William waited.

"The charts also showed it was clear sailing where we were waiting out the storm this morning, but *Trent* beat her rudder off on an unmarked rock." He fixed those black eyes of his on the lieutenant. "You get in one of those boats. You take a lead weight and line and make soundings everywhere you think we might have to go with this grand old lady." He patted the bulk-head timber. "She's old and touchy. We mustn't go punching any rocks through her bottom."

"Aye, sir. I understand."

"If you find reason why a man o'war shouldn't pass in there, don't wait to bring the information back to me. Tell Wolfe."

* * *

"Ahoy the boat!"

"Lieutenant Gray from *Sutherland* requests permission to board *H.M.S. Namur*."

William sat in the stern sheets wondering how in the devil he was going to talk himself into joining the generals as they took ship's boats to survey the bay coastline. Perhaps he should have arrived in the captain's cutter rather than the little cock-boat (not much more than a rowboat, really) to present himself at the entry port of the flagship of the fleet, *H.M.S. Namur*, ninety guns. Obviously, *Namur's* watch officer wasn't much impressed.

"What purpose?"

Well, that tore it, he thought. *Should I tell them, 'because my captain says so'? I have to tell the man something.* "I have information for General Wolfe."

"Carry on, the boat."

As he was clambering up the Jacob's ladder he spoke to the two sailors in the boat. "Don't wait for me. Return to *Sutherland*." He grasped the rope rung and began the long climb up the side of the ship. "In for a penny, in for a pound," he said, half aloud. He saluted the quarterdeck and stepped through the entry port.

The duty officer, Lieutenant Sherman, in a smart uniform that had never suffered a briny drop, looked down his nose at the fairly bedraggled-looking *Sutherland* who was in the same uniform he had worn to the storm-tossed *Trent*. William's uniform jacket, made to his Uncle Charles's specifications by a London tailor, was loosely cut to allow the swordsman full play, while what Uncle Charles called the justaucorp (waistcoat) clung, unwrinkled and seemingly unbending, to the young man's torso. William had nicknamed this uniform his 'battle dress' since, like Captain Rous, he had taken to wearing metal-studded gauntlets and a bandana. On this mission, William had forgone the wearing of the gauntlets and bandana.

Slightly out of breath, William paused. He returned the duty officer's look, thinking that the other officer's uniform, untouched by sea, had probably never seen battle either.

"I am Lieutenant Sherman, *Namur* duty officer. If you have dispatches for the general, I will see he gets them."

William cast a quick eye around the deck. "It's ... like a personal word from *Sutherland*."

"I beg your pardon?" The duty officer drew himself up at least three inches. "Like a personal word?"

William was wondering what the brig on a ship the size of the *Namur* might look like when he heard a reedy voice from behind him.

"What say? Lieutenant Gray! You have something for me?" Brigadier General Wolfe looked smaller, somehow, on the deck of a ship, than he did at Scalping Cove when he was briefing the troops. He looked terrible; teary-eyed and wiping at his nose with a handkerchief. With his free hand he waved, dismissively, at the duty officer, "Thank you, Lieutenant Sherman, I will see to Lieutenant Gray." Giving his nose another blow, Wolfe studied the contents of the handkerchief before he tucked it away into his waist pocket. "Bit under the weather," he said by way of explaining his cherry-red nose and watery eyes and then, embarrassed, curtly asked, "So? You have a message for me?"

"I do, sir. Perhaps if I might speak with you ..."

"Alone? My dear fellow, a brigadier has no secrets from his staff," but seeing William's discomfort, he indicated they should walk the deck.

Two more generals came on deck. William supposed the portly one was Amherst and the wiry one was Lawrence.

The generals looked with interest as Wolfe had words with a lieutenant in an untidy uniform. William overheard Lieutenant Sherman tell the wiry one, "He's a *Sutherland*."

The heavier general observed, "What could Wolfe possibly want with him?"

William, very conscious of the generals' interest, was doubly careful not to speak to Wolfe until they were well out of earshot but, during that time, Wolfe became quiet grumpy and impatient.

"Well! What is it! Spit it out, man!" He blew his nose and wiped it, grimacing as he experienced pain from the aggravated nose. "What is the message?"

"Well, sir ..." William still hesitated.

Like a patient school ma'am, Wolfe said, "Start with the name of the person who sent the message."

William blurted out, "Captain Rous wants me to go with you when you do your coasting."

"Captain Rous does, does he?" Wolfe blew his nose again. "Well! Does *Captain* Rous know that *Brigadier General* Wolfe doesn't take kindly to ..." he stopped. The thought flitted through his mind, *why does that wily old man want Gray to come with me?* "Why does Captain Rous want you with me?"

"During any assault on the enemy shore, sir, you will be relying upon the support of a naval bombardment. Captain Rous has ordered me ... er, suggests to you, General, that I accompany you today as you check the terrain." William stopped and examined the general's eyes. *Damn! Why do senior officers always seem to want more when I'm finished what I have to say?* He stumbled on, "I am to make just as careful observations of the inshore waters."

Wolfe wiped his nose. He patted his upper lip which was also reddened from constant wiping. "I have looked at the charts, Lieutenant Gray. There is nothing there to give us concern."

"*H.M.S. Trent* beat her rudder off on a rock that wasn't marked on the charts." William swallowed hard, but he could see that the brigadier was listening. "There may be other uncharted obstacles. I will take soundings …"

"That's a sound idea," Wolfe grimaced; he didn't like being caught making inadvertent puns because it demonstrated a certain lack of foresight that he abhorred. With visible irritation he said, "Wait by the entry port. When it is time, join me."

Sailors were already hoisting out the cutter and the skiff while the sideboys were rigging the boatswain's chair.

Wolfe strolled over to where the other two generals were chatting with *Namur's* captain, Captain Buckle. William felt uncomfortable when Wolfe gestured in his direction and the other officers stared at him as Wolfe said something else.

Leaning on the bulwark in what William hoped was a nonchalant pose, he watched as the boat crews prepared to receive their precious cargo.

The wiry general stepped forward. Allowing a rope and wood sling to be fitted around him, he nodded his head that he was ready. With the twitter of the boatswain's pipe, the sideboys hauled on the rope and the chair gently lifted the general clear of the bulwark and over the side. In a matter of minutes, the two generals were sitting in the larger of the two boats.[4]

As soon as the cutter had pulled away from the side of the *Namur*, the skiff was positioned, ready to receive its passengers.

Throwing any thoughts of naval protocol aside, Wolfe scrambled over the side and then displayed impatience as his aide had difficulty with his hat, sword, the rope ladder and the motion of the boat in the heavy swell. William moved over the side of the ship and into the boat like the accomplished seaman he was.

As they cleared the shelter of the ship, the boats moved heavily through the swell. Three cutters from other ships joined them. William noticed the other cutters maintained a position to seaward of the generals' boat, breaking the swell, thus making their way slightly easier. *The seamen are always doing their best to get the job done. It's not because the sailors love their officers! Dear God, no! It's probably because they are the crew, the ship's company, and they understand that the sea is an unfriendly environment that will take you, and your ship, out of this world in a twinkling.* He shook his head to stop his daydreaming. He opened his pouch and took out the lead weight and line setting the line as best he could between his knees. *How am I going to swing the lead without standing?*

General Wolfe, sitting alone in the stern, motioned for William to join him.

Snugly settled beside the general, William unravelled his lines again. He felt as if he was all elbows and shoulders as he took up position to swing the line ahead of the boat allowing the weight to fall to the bottom. As the boat moved along toward Cormorant Cove, William would pull the line in counting the leather strips marking the depth of the water.

Suddenly, he had all kinds of room as the general joined the aide on the first thwart. William didn't comment. He just went on swinging the lead weight and keeping an eye on the coast so he would know where he was as he measured the depths of the inshore waters.

Major Roberts (that was the aide's name, William found as they went along) was using a sketchbook, pen and inkpot. Occasionally, the cutter and the skiff would come together while the generals discussed the terrain across the interval between the two boats, but most of the time, until they reached Cormorant Cove, the skiff went along quietly, William sounding the waters, the major making his notes and sketches and Wolfe staring at the shore.

William looked up from his work when Wolfe exclaimed, "It's all trees! Where's the beach?"

'That's Cormorant Cove?" William asked the major.

"Yes."

Wolfe was examining the shore with his telescope. Whatever he was thinking, he said nothing.

William had expected to see a gently sloping beach bounded at either end with rocky cliffs. The rocky cliffs were there but, for the rest, the bushes came right to the water. There was no beach, no gun emplacements, no trenches; just trees—right down to the water's edge.[5]

Someone was hailing. "Take your boat in closer. See if you can cause them to reveal themselves!"

Fortunately, at least as far as William was concerned, General Amherst was speaking to one of the other boats.

"Aye, sir," was the cheerful-sounding reply.

The cutter left the little formation and moved, slowly, toward the shore.

William could see by her markings that she was from *H.M.S. Dublin*, Captain Rodney commanding. William's unkind thought was that General Amherst wouldn't have sent the *Dublin's* boat inshore to draw fire if Captain Rodney were on her. "I wouldn't like to be sent in to draw fire!" he blurted.

The major sniffed, as if that was comment enough.

General Wolfe smiled, "No, but I wager you would go."

William acknowledged the truth in that, to himself. *If Rous wanted me to take an open boat inshore to draw fire, to gauge their rate of fire or range, I'd go. Yes, I'd go!*

"You'd win, sir," he finally said.

The three of them watched as the *Dublin's* boat entered musket range of the shore. Just before the line where the combers welled up, the boat turned around and began its return to the flotilla

"I suppose that enough time has passed since 1745 for trees to grow along a beach front," the general said in a thoughtful manner as if speaking to himself. In a louder voice he ordered, "Lieutenant, take this boat in, I want a closer look."

William nodded to the coxswain to move the boat closer to the shore.

The *Dublin's* boat was returning without having raised a single shot.

By the time William's boat (he felt as if he was in charge) came abeam the *Dublin's*, his crew had assumed a nice stroke and, despite the swells, was making good time to the beach.

Pointing at the beach, Wolfe called across to the other boat, "Did you see any activity?"

"None, sir." The coxswain of the other boat cupped his hands as the boats quickly drew apart, "No gun emplacements, nothing!"

Another voice, fainter, called, "General Wolfe, return! We must ..." the rest of the hail was drowned by the noise of the oars and the water.

"I want to see, for myself, what is going on in there!" He turned his head so that he was facing the beach. "You didn't hear the hail, did you, Lieutenant Gray?"

Unfortunately, the coxswain of the *Dublin* boat repeated the hail, "General Amherst wants you to return! General Amherst says to return!"

"Damn!" Wolfe's eyes searched the shoreline. The boat was still moving briskly toward the beach. Another three hundred yards and he would be able to see for himself. He moved to the stern where he could sit and watch the beach without turning his head. Sitting in the stern also meant he could not observe the other boats.

William got up and moved to the spot where the general had been sitting. William could see the other boats by looking past the general's head.

"What are they doing, Lieutenant?"

"Two of the boats have started to come after us."

"Oh, very well!" said an exasperated general, who slumped down in his seat, picking at a piece of gold thread on his sleeve. "Order the boat to return, Lieutenant."

William nodded to the coxswain.

"Lay on starboard! Larboard, hold!" The four sailors on the starboard side of the skiff continued rowing while the other four sailors held their oars, firm, in the water, acting like a brake on the one side. The skiff began its turn.

"Larboard, prepare to backwater!" The coxswain timed his order to the movement of the men who were rowing, "Together! Now! Two! One, two ..."

A fine boat crew, William thought, *performing even better now that the skiff was heading away from the hostile shore.*

The general hadn't noticed the crew's performance.

"Boat crew, hold!"

The sailors held their oars still poised just above the water.

"Ready!"

The men leaned forward, extending their arms so that the oars were behind them as far as they could reach.

"Pull! Together, now."

Without further orders the boat's crew set a steady, even pace as the boat raced along through the rough seas toward the next beach at Flat Point.

At Flat Point it was an entirely different situation; the French had dug trenches anywhere it seemed possible an enemy might attempt a landing. At vulnerable points, cannon had been mounted as well as an abattis of felled trees built with branches pointed at the water. On the crest of the low cliffs overlooking the beach were more trenches, swivel guns and breastworks. Communications trenches connecting the cliff to the beach were visible because of the raw earth that lay exposed.

"Formidable," Wolfe said. "Take us in, Lieutenant. I would like to see if they have ranged their weapons." He was still seated in the stern so Wolfe had a very good view of enemy activity as the skiff moved toward the shore. "They have fired a cannon on the right, Lieutenant. We should see, in a moment, where the shot falls."

In fact, William heard the shot pass overhead and splash in the water fifteen yards in their wake.

"They are ranged, sir, but they forgot to allow for target travel. Must be army gunners."

William nodded at the coxswain. "Take us out of here, coxs'n. We don't want to give them too much practice!"

"Yes, take us back, Lieutenant. It's getting late in the day and we have yet to see White Point. I see Amherst's boat has already moved along."

"Aye, sir. I don't think there will be enough water for a man o'war in here. There's less and less water as we approach White Point." William pulled in the line and read the pieces of leather affixed to the line. "Too shallow, sir. We could send a sloop in here, but nothing any larger. It would seriously cut down the amount of support that you could have available from naval bombardment."

"That's too bad, because Amherst has his heart set on a three-pronged attack." Casting a look at the other boats that were in the lead because of William's activities which had slowed the skiff, Wolfe commented, "I really wanted to take another look at Cormorant Cove, but I suppose you will want to finish your job so we have all the facts." The general slapped his hand on his knee, complaining, "Look at the height of the surf on that beach! What's the usual length of time before this stuff calms down?"

William was reading the lead line. "It's too shallow in here for any serious naval operations, General. To answer your question, this coast can have huge Atlantic swells for a long time after the storm has passed. You see, the storm is still out there making waves that have no place to go but back here to remind us of the storm's passing."

"So, it could be a week, ten days?"

"At least two or three more days, sir."

Brigadier General James Wolfe didn't say any more on the trip back to *Namur*. Leaving the skiff without any comment to crew or officer, he disappeared into the admiral's cabin.

Fortress Louisbourg
June 2, 1758

A courier arrived from Port Dauphin reporting the 2nd Battalion, Cambyse[6] Regiment arrived from France to reinforce the garrison. The presence of English warships off Louisbourg had forced them to divert to Port Dauphin.

The regiment consists of six hundred and eighty-five soldiers and non-commissioned officers divided into 16 companies of musketmen plus one company of Grenadiers.

I pray they will arrive before the English commence their assault.

Weather is still in our favour with very high surf along the Bay.

Poilly

June 3, 1758
H.M.S. Sutherland

Sutherland was hauling anchor. The capstan crew moved around and around the anchor windlass until the ship was pulled up to her anchor. When she was positioned directly over the anchor, the crew would have to bear the full weight of the anchor as they raised it from the bottom of the Bay. By that time, the lower sails would be set and the ship would move off while the anchor was hauled the final distance and secured against the hull.

Ship's officers were standing near the helmsman. Lieutenant Gray was off to one side giving instruction to a junior officer.

"Why is it always us, Lieutenant?" The young midshipman had to raise his voice above the noise of the Royal Marine's drum as the crew was beat to quarters.

"Because, mister," Lieutenant Gray patiently explained to the very young man, "our captain sees things, understands the possible consequences, and acts to correct the situation before anyone else sees it in the first place. Look off to larboard! Several of the transports are in danger of being blown ashore."[7]

"All hands! Set lower sails! Helmsman, starboard the helm until she has way!"

While not as rough as the day before, the sea was still heavy enough to cause a transport to lose her anchor. Before the crew of that transport could get another anchor set, the transport had drifted afoul the cable of a second transport. Now both ships were bearing down on a third.

Rous's voice could be heard above the clatter of rope through pulley, the rumble of anchor chain through hawse pipe, the shouts of the crew and the flapping of yards of canvas still not hardened in the gale winds. "She has way, Sailing Master! Take us upwind of those landlubbers!"

"Aye, sir! Upwind of the ships adrift!"

"Can the Sailing Master correct our captain like that?"

"Not likely, my son! He's just making the captain's orders very plain to the crew," William explained to the young officer. "The Sailing Master is always very precise!"

"Break out the cutter! Lieutenant Gray!"

My God! Here I go again, thought William. "Aye, sir." He unclipped his scabbard and handed it to the midshipman. "Don't think I'll be needing it for a bit." Taking into account the heaving, wet deck, William made good time getting over to where the captain was standing. He arrived as the captain and sailing master were discussing what was going to happen next.

"The *White Dove* might get an anchor out!" Rous pointed. "See! They've cut that mess of cable from the ..."

"There! That's a splash! The *White Dove* is free." Mister Johnson, the sailing master, took the glass from the first officer. He sighted on the second transport.

"Lieutenant Gray, here as ordered, sir."

Rous smiled. "They still might get things under control. The Annabelle is adrift but there's nothin' much stoppin' her from settin' another anchor."

"It's not as rough as yesterday, Cap'n," Sailing Master said. "I can bring *Sutherland* in right some close and put a line to her."

"Make it so, Sailing Master."

"Aye, sir."

They all spoke at once.

"They done it!"

"They've set their anchor!"

Sailing Master, Lieutenant Gray and First Officer looked at their captain to see his reaction.

Captain Rous was studying a ship moving west, parallel to the coast.

"Belay that last order!"

He watched the other ship. "That's *Kennington* and she's got her guns run out. Look's like Cap'n Parry's goin' huntin'." Rous gave his officers a funny little smile. "My feet tell me we're in for some jollies." He stamped his feet on the deck a couple of times. "Since we're already out and about, First Officer, make signal to the flagship, 'am proceeding in company with *H.M.S. Kennington*.'" Rous took one last look at the transports. "Wear ship, Sailing Master. I want to see us catch the *Kennington*, smartly, now!"

The sailing master gave the captain a pained look as he set the crew to follow in the wake of the other English ship.

"I know, Sailing Master! I don't need one of your dark looks to remind me that *Kennington* is newer, bigger and faster but she does have a big disadvantage!" Rous gave one of his perky laughs. "She got sixty guns! Until she finds the enemy, those ten extra cannon are just so much dead weight. If you keep a good weather eye, we'll catch her, Mister Johnson!"

William could hear the chuckles of the crew as they added one more anecdote to the lore of Captain John Rous.

Once settled on a following course, Rous confirmed in a loud voice, "By God, Sailing Master, I think the old girl is doing it! Well done!"

A puff of smoke appeared from *Kennington* and was swiftly carried away by the strong wind.

"They found a target!" Rous leaned forward as if by moving closer to the action two or three inches, he would be better able to see what was on the shore getting the attention of the other warship.

First Officer passed the glass for Rous to take but the old man shook his head.

"Can't stand those newfangled things! The old 'bring 'em nears' were much easier! You look, tell me what you see."

Before First Officer Adams could respond, Rous cackled, "It's got a sting! And they have *Kennington*'s range. Better move it out of there, young Captain Parry!"

The ship was firing guns, in pairs, as they came to bear.

William could see the splashes from the shore guns, two of them, in the water just short of *Kennington*. "They have an excellent rate of fire and they have ranged in very quickly on her." William let his pride in service show. "They must be naval gunners manning that shore battery." He looked anxiously back at the ship. "The next French volley should register!"

Captain Parry must have realized that he would have to silence the battery in his next try or suffer the consequences because there was a pause in the ship's gunfire as the guns crews were especially careful in their sighting.

Stamping his feet as though he were killing ants, Rous hollered at the other English ship, "Goddam, Parry! Get your shot off! You ain't got all day!" He took one last look and then turned his back to the action. "First Officer! Run out the starboard guns! If that shore battery gets in a lucky shot, *Kennington* could be dismasted in there. Duck soup! They'll be duck soup! We'll have to go in and screen Parry and take out that battery ourselves!"

William hadn't taken his eyes off the gun duel. The ship had far more firepower than the shore batteries but the advantage still lay with the French gunners. When they had set up those cannon, they had fired practice shots at different parts of the Bay. The French gunners knew precisely, by azimuth, by weight of shot and by the strength of the powder charge, where a cannonball would land. All they had to do was gauge the movement of the ship and shoot in time for the cannonball and the ship to be at the same point at the same instant. William waited for the next exchange.

Meanwhile, *Sutherland* had piled on more sail and run out her starboard guns as she raced to the aid of a threatened sister.

William, standing off to one side because his duties were with armed boarding parties and away crews, had another vision in mind; *Sutherland* was a second wolf running in to help with the attack on a bear. What if there was a mama bear? So far, they had seen only two batteries. What if *Sutherland* got in there and found another battery or two? What did Rous call it? Duck soup.

The shore batteries fired. William, looking quickly at the ship, waiting for the fall of shot, was in time to see *Kennington* fire a complete broadside. In the next instant there were two hits on the ship, one in the rigging and the other somewhere in the hull.[8] At least one of the French gunners had the right idea! Slow the ship down or stop her and then beat the hell out of her! He turned his head to see if there was any evidence of a hit on the shore. Nothing. He looked around at his own ship. Everything was in readiness to take on the as-yet-unseen shore batteries.

"Guns! Can you see them?" Rous reached for the telescope but, no, he changed his mind. He couldn't bring himself to use it.

"Aye, sir! I got them sighted. They might get off two more rounds each, but then our guns will come to bear and that will be the end of them."

"How many?"

"Two batteries, sir. I swear, only two, Captain."

Kennington and the shore batteries fired at almost the same time.

William watched for the fall of shot on the water. It seemed to take forever. Finally, he could see that a ball smashed into the quarterdeck and the mizzenmast shook as if it had been struck. It was then he did something he hadn't done since he was a kid; he crossed his fingers and prayed. He prayed the mizzenmast hadn't been struck, that it wouldn't come down, that *Sutherland* wouldn't have to put herself in front of a disabled *Kennington* and slug it out with the shore batteries. The mast seemed to be holding and *Kennington* moving serenely as if nothing had happened.

"Ready, guns one and three! On the roll ..."

"Belay, Guns! *Kennington* got 'em! Head her up, Sailing Master. Take us out of here."

"Ahoy the deck! A sail." The lookout in the cross trees pointed astern. "Comin' out of Louisbourg Harbour!"

Since *Sutherland* was already under full sail, the first thought that crossed William's mind was they might commence their turn while the starboard guns were still run out, allowing the sea to rush into the guns ports as the warship heeled in the swells, but he had sailed long enough with Rous to know ...

"Secure starboard guns!"

Almost immediately there was the rumble of two dozen guns being levered back to the stow position and, like clockwork, the ports were closed.

Guns called out, "Starboard guns secured!"

"Sailing Master, put us on an intercept course!" Rous cast a quick glance at the other warship. "Make signal to *Kennington*, 'join in pursuit,' if you please, First Officer." He beckoned to Lieutenant Gray. "Have the armourer open the weapons locker and issue personal weapons to the boarding party."

William watched as the armourer went between decks to open the locker. As he waited, he couldn't help but notice the captain was stamping his feet again. When Wimper appeared with the captain's battle gloves, belt and cutlass, Rous told his manservant, "I thought they were wrong when *Kennington* silenced the guns before we could come into play, Wimper, but they knew! These old feet of mine are never wrong."

Wimper took the captain's hat and helped him put his bandana on, adjusting the set of the cross belt and cutlass as he said, "You are in fine form, Captain. Do you wish your moccasins?"

"No," he said curtly, but smiled at Wimper. "What does she look like to you?"

Wimper took the telescope from the hands of the first officer and, sighting on the ship, said, "She's a frigate, Captain. I can't tell from here what class, but certainly we've got her outgunned."

"Ahoy the deck! The ship is a frigate, flying French colours, taking up a northerly heading, now."

Rous allowed Wimper to tighten one of the ribbons on his pigtails and then ordered, "Marines to muster aft." He got Wimper's nod that everything was in order and he pulled on the black battle gloves with the metal studs over the back of the hands and wrists. "Mister Gray! Have the purser serve up a tot all 'round!"

The ship's company, to a man, cheered loud enough to be heard all the way to the enemy ship.

Lieutenant Gray, as leader of the boarding party, was almost the first to be served his tot. Enjoying the feel of the black rum warming the 'cockles of his heart,' as his Uncle Charles used to say, he realized, for the first time, that he also liked the feel of the sand on the deck which had been spread so the crew would have sure footing no matter how much fluid of whatever kind was spilled underfoot. The guns, flints attached, while not run out, were loaded: larboard side with grape, and starboard side with ball (that had been meant for the shore batteries). The acrid smell of the fuses hanging over the water barrel, in case of a flint misfire, was a special smell that William would remember to his dying day, *although, please Lord, I would like to sail home again to see Molly and our next baby before that event.*

"Intercept course set, Captain, nor', nor' east. I estimate three miles."

"Where away *Kennington*?" Rous twisted his head from

side to side as he tried to locate her. "What course has Captain Parry set?"

"He follows on, sir, a mile astern, setting his tops'ls," was the sailing master's reply.

"Set course, east, nor' east, Mister Johnson. If she wants to fight, I mean to pin her against the shore. First Officer, keep an eye on *Kennington*. I want her to take the most direct course to challenge the Frenchie."

"That'd be north, north east, Captain?"

"It would indeed, First Officer. Captain Parry will see what I mean, have no fear." He gave his first officer a devilish grin. "But I want you to keep an eye on him, nonetheless."

Captain Rous looked around the deck, at the guns, at the boarding party standing near the mainmast and the set of the sails. "You have the deck, First Officer," he said as he proceeded below to his cabin.

"Aye, sir."

William walked far enough over to where he could speak in a normal voice to Lieutenant Adams. "He's gone below to have Wimper put his moccasins on." William was wearing a huge grin. "Some things never change."

"Do you think he does it for luck? I've seen him do it every time we've gone into battle."

"I don't know, but it works. The crew is always looking to see if the old man has his moccasins on and, when he has, they feel better about whatever comes next."

Ten minutes later, Captain Rous reappeared on the deck. "What is the situation, First Officer?"

Everyone on the deck—the officers, the boarding party, the gun crews, the working watch—all tried to catch a glimpse of the captain's feet.

"Sir, the enemy ship carries on north, north east. *Kennington* continues on a following course, a mile and a half astern. We are a mile east, south east of our target."

"Sail a parallel course, now, Mister Johnson." Pointing at the French ship, Rous said, "I wish to be no more than a mile away when we begin our interception. When *Kennington* is a half-mile from the target, she will begin using her bowchaser.

We have until that time to position ourselves to pin that bastard against the coast." Rous ran his eyes over the set of the sails. "Keep a weather eye, Mister Johnson."

"Aye sir. I'll get the best out of 'er, you can count on me for that."

"I do, Mister Johnson." Captain Rous walked forward on the quarterdeck so the rest of the crew could see that he was wearing moccasins. There was a great deal of nudging and smiles.

The captain disappeared into the companionway leading to his cabin.

Various activities went on as the English ships positioned themselves to attack the French frigate. Each man of the boarding party passed the time in his own way as he waited for the battle to begin. Some repaired worn belts and leggings while others sharpened whatever blade they were going to carry into the battle. A few, not the least bit self-conscious, said their prayers, and two of the men sat with some of their mates and made apology for slights or wrongs they had done. The officers on the quarterdeck chatted as they sighted on the enemy ship, measuring the change of azimuth as *Sutherland* overtook her. William, on the main deck with the boarding party, kept pretty much to himself, leaning against the bulkhead, gazing out over the water at the two ships.

Kennington was almost within range where she would begin to use her bowchaser and it was expected that the French ship would use its stern gun in reply. *Sutherland* had passed the enemy ship, a mile to larboard, and was in excellent position to turn and run down on her. It was typical of Rous to leave nothing to chance, pinning the enemy against the shore, swooping down on her from the northeast while *Kennington* struck from the south.

Kennington fired her bowchaser, the shot falling short a small distance.

William had been so intent on the action between the other two ships he hadn't noticed the captain's return to the quarterdeck until he heard the warning, "Captain on deck!"

Rous must have given commands because the ship heeled

as *Sutherland* changed course to go on the attack. The guns were run out and the men of the boarding party gathered, nervously, around their lieutenant.

Rous appeared at the edge of the quarterdeck where the boarding party could see him.

"I mean to close with Frenchie as quickly as I can. We will deliver a broadside, turn and give her a dose of grape. Follow the orders of Lieutenant Gray but you know I expect each of you to get over there and take that ship and come back to *Sutherland* all in one piece. Don't you boys let me down!"

"We'll give it to 'em, sir!"

The captain's head and shoulders had already disappeared as he went about his duties so William gave the men a hearty smile, "It's been a while since we had some prize money, boys! Don't do too much damage as we take her! We want a good price at Admiralty Court!"

The men laughed and cheered.

One of the men, pointing, said, "She's changed course! The blighter is comin' at us!"

"The Frenchie is doing the only thing he can, trying to take us one at a time," William shouted. "Boarding party take cover!" William would have sent them to cover anyway and he was sorry he hadn't done it before now. Now it sounded like he was having his men hide from the approaching enemy. He stepped into the companionway where he had some shelter but could still see the action, unhappy with himself that he hadn't thought ahead, just a little bit.

She was a pretty ship (the French made lovely frigates), her guns run out, battle flags flying, the glint of steel on her decks as her men prepared to repel boarders.

William shouted to his men, "She looks like she wants a good fight! There's a party of men on her deck with personal arms waiting to entertain us. We'll not let them down, will we?"

There was a rousing cheer.

Soon, *Sutherland* would turn to larboard and fire a broadside. William tried to guess when the best time would be; close enough for an effective delivery of the shot, leaving enough room to reverse course and fire the grape across her decks and then close. He watched with fascination as the French ship turned away and presented her starboard side, all guns run out, to deliver a broadside! "But she's out of range," William spluttered, "what the hell!"

A full broadside was discharged into the ocean three hundred yards in front of *Sutherland,* one spent ball bouncing along the waves and thumping against her hull. In the same instant, the French colours came down, a white flag was raised and the ship turned into the wind, coming almost to a standstill while reducing sail and then reversing course.

Waving his boarding party out to where they could see, William yelled, "Goddamit, boys! She surrendered!"

"I heard her fire a broadside, sir. Why did she do that if she was goin' to give it up?"

William couldn't think of a reason right off but, as he stood there, he remembered something his Uncle Charles had told him when he was a boy in Scotland: *pour l'honneur du roi.* He repeated it out loud for the men to hear. "Pour l'honneur du roi. The French have a thing about surrender ..."

"Aye, sir! They does it all the time!"

William looked at the man who always seemed to have something to say. *I should learn that man's name because, in a way, he's good for morale.*

The man must have felt what William was thinking because he volunteered, "Fink, sir. We was with you on *Success,* in the hold we was, doin' the trim for the old man."

"You mean for the captain, Fink."

"Aye, sir, I do mean that, sir. Meanin' no disrespect, sir, we woulda gone with you and done you proud 'cept for the Frenchies takin' a shot at us and then quittin'."

"They didn't mean to hit us ..."

Jake Fink was going to say something else but the quiet voice of the Buffer could be heard. "That'll be quite enough, Fink."

"They didn't mean to hit us. They fired, in our general direction, for the honour of their King. Honour being satisfied, they could lower their flag."

"Stand down boarding party, Lieutenant Gray," came from

Captain Rous. "Reduce sail, Mister Johnson! Guns, stay in readiness, just in case."

William was surprised at the order for the boarding party but he repeated it without question. "Boarding party report to the gun locker to stow weapons."

Of course, Jake Fink couldn't stop himself, "Wot's the trouble? Ain't we goin' over there to take the ship?"

"Fink!"

"Aye, Buffer. I'll carry on."

As for Lieutenant Gray, he was every bit as curious. He reported to the quarterdeck where he was surprised to see *Kennington* positioned near the French frigate, lowering boats to send a boarding party to take possession of the ship.

"I suppose you're disappointed, William." Rous was handing his cutlass and belt to Wimper, who quickly slipped the bandana off the Captain's head and handed him his hat.

"The men are wondering why they aren't going over to the …"

"*L'Écho*, William, *Echo*, she's called, thirty-two guns, bound for Quebec with news of our arrival here at Louisbourg, I wager." Rous made a face and waggled his finger. "Captain Parry will have to deal with all that … and lose some men to crew the ship to Halifax as prize." Rous was as gleeful as if he had won another victory. "We get the same prize money and a lot less trouble by havin' Captain Parry take her."

"With your permission, Captain, I'd like to tell the boarding party why we didn't board her."

"Don't bother, Lieutenant. In five minutes, the ship's crew will believe they know more about it than the officers."

"Aye, sir."

Captain Rous turned his back on *Echo* and gave over to the First Officer the task of taking *Sutherland* back to her mooring while he went below to do whatever it is captains do in the solitude of their cabin after a well executed operation.

Fortress Louisbourg
June 3, 1758

With the departure of the frigate *L'Écho* to Québec, there are now eleven warships in the harbour; *Prudent* and *Entreprenant* (each of 74 guns), *Capricieux, Célèbre* and *Bienfaisant* (64's), the *Apollon* of fifty guns, the frigates *Arethuse, Comète* and *Fidèle* and the two sloops *Chèvre* and *Biche*. I have drawn up a berthing plan that would make the best use of the space along the Rue d'Orléans waterfront, giving the ships the protection of the cannon of the Bastions while allowing them to add their firepower to that of the fortress. Governor Drucour has approved the berthing plan and will recommend it to the ships' captains for implementation.

L'Écho has taken the news to Québec of the presence of a large English fleet at Louisbourg; fishermen have reported counting forty warships in Gabarus Bay. With so many English ships here, a show of force at Halifax by our second squadron of warships at Québec would probably cause the English to withdraw to protect their home port. Our prayers go with *L'Écho*.

Poilly

June 5, 1758
H.M.S. Sutherland

"There they go again."

First Officer Adams and Lieutenant Gray were leaning on the bulwark watching the boat leave *H.M.S. Princess Amelia*, eighty guns, flagship of the Third Division.

"You're sure they're not going to another conference on *Namur?*" Adams asked as he lifted the eyeglass and studied the Second Division's flagship, *H.M.S. Royal William*, an eighty-four, for similar activity.

At the same time, Gray was watching *Namur*, which was closer to *Sutherland*, to see if they had sideboys out to help the senior officers board ship. "No, there's nothing going on at

Namur." He raised his eyes and studied the signal pennants. "There's just the usual signal, 'maintain position.' I don't see the 'Division Commanders attend the flagship' or 'ships' captains report to flag.' There's nothing new at all."

"Then it's Commodore Durell out to have another look at the inshore," said Adams with a hearty laugh and a slap on his thigh, "and you sure put the fox in with the chickens when you told General Wolfe there wasn't enough water at White Point."

"Captain on deck!"

"Good morning, gentlemen." Captain Rous came right over to them and joined them at the bulwark. "Who has the watch?"

"Almost eight bells, sir," answered Lieutenant Adams. "I have the mid-watch, and Lieutenant Gray will be the morning watch."

"You were discussing White Point?"

"Aye sir. Commodore Durell was out there yesterday, checking the inshore, and he's out there again this morning." Adams refrained from offering the eyeglass to the captain. "You can see it's the commodore by his fore and aft."

"Yes, thank you, I can see he's wearing his commodore's hat. He'll lose the thing in this weather."

The three of them regarded the heavy swells sweeping by the ships and crashing on the shores.

"The French appear to have King Neptune on their side," said Adams with a smile. "Our assault will be delayed at least another day."

Gray gave a snort. "He just took his hat off, sir."

"Sensible thing to do," was all Rous had to say, and the junior officers knew that the subject of the commodore's hat was closed.

"They broach!" Adams said as a wave, larger than the others, caught the ship's boat on the stern and turned her enough so that most of the wave crashed over the gunwales and into the boat. "They'd better …"

Almost immediately, the boat turned enough to meet the next wave, not as large as the previous one, with the boat's bow. "Now, there's a good coxs'n!" said William.

"I wager, not in the commodore's books," Captain Rous

commented, "because he's drenched and he still has a couple hours of work to do."

"Your pardon, sir, but why is the commodore rechecking something we have done before—and he has done before?" Adams pushed his officer's hat back and scratched at a spot just behind his ear. He readjusted his hat the moment he realized what he was doing, maintaining an open-eyed expression of inquiry on his face as he waited for the captain's reply.

"General Amherst finds it difficult to give up his plan of three assaults at the same time." Rous leaned out a bit over the edge of the bulwark as he pointed to various points on the shore. "There's a little bay at White Point, or as the Frenchies call it, Pointe Blanche, that the general took a fancy to."

"That'd be the assault beach where we wouldn't be able to give him full naval support."

"Right-o! The other little bay at Flat Point, or Pointe Platte as the Frenchies like to say, is all right." Rous sucked some food from between his teeth; "I'm not partial to the beach at Cormorant Cove because the trees come right down to the water. Can't see if there's anything there. If there's troops and guns there, we can't see them." Rous shook his head, "No, I don't like the Cove as a landing beach."

"I don't think General Wolfe liked it, either, sir. The other day, in the boat, he wanted to go in close and take a real good look but we weren't able to. One of the other boats went to the edge of the surf and saw nothing, but that didn't satisfy the general."

"And there's your answer why Commodore Durell is out in the bay in rough seas, measuring the depth of water. It's because General Amherst wasn't satisfied."⁹ Looking at *Namur*, Captain Rous asked, "Are there any signals from the flag?" He squinted his eyes and stared, blinking, trying to make the signal halyards on *Namur* come into focus for him.

"There has been no change, sir." Adams looked at Gray as eight bells sounded, "You have the watch, Lieutenant Gray," and handed William the eyeglass. He touched his hat. "With your permission, sir, I will go below."

"Carry on, First Officer."

"Thank you, sir."

Captain Rous pointed at *Namur*, "Keep an eye on the flagship for signals, William, because I know in my bones, General Amherst will call a conference as soon as he sees Durell head back to his ship. I wager Durell won't get a chance to dry off before he's telling Amherst the bad new about his three-pronged attack." Rous stood in silence watching the combers on the beach. "This is the only place in the world where there's strong winds in thick fog. Did you ever see the like of it this morning? Pea soup fog and a strong blow with seas that make a man wonder why he ever pushed away from his mother's teats in the first place."

"Aye, sir, but the fog burned off quickly."

"The fog'll be back as soon as the sun goes down. Louisbourg is lucky; there'll be no assault tomorrow no matter what Amherst decides today."

"French pea soup fog, sir?"

Chuckling, Captain Rous began his exercise walk around *Sutherland's* decks leaving Gray to his thoughts about home and his Molly.

Fortress Louisbourg
June 5, 1758

Thick morning fog and very high surf.

We believe that the weather has delayed the English assault and hope it will continue long enough for the Cambyse Regiment to arrive to reinforce the garrison. Even if the Cambyse arrive in time, the fortress is seriously undermanned. If the outer defences should be breached, the Governor's plan is to recall his forces within the fortress itself.

We are well supplied. For once I have as much Virginia tobacco as I can use, thanks to the Yankee traders.

P

June 6, 1758
H.M.S. Sutherland

"Lookit that!" Adams didn't have to use the eyeglass to see that two ships of their Division were going into action. "The *Squirrel* and the *Hawke* are headin' out!"[10]

Gray and Mister Johnson had been taking their morning walk. They joined Adams at the bulwark, gaping at what they saw.

The frigates were beautiful in the brisk winds and pale sunlight, battle flags streaming, with several companies of soldiers massed on the decks, passing almost within cannon range of the Island Battery at the mouth of Louisbourg Harbour.

"Christ! That's tempting fate!" Mister Johnson, usually a very quiet person whose spoken words were most often an echo of the captain's orders, was quite agitated. "There must be thirty or thirty-five cannon on that island!"

The First Officer ordered the Marine guard to ask the captain to come on deck.

"If they're going to make an assault," William complained, "they shouldn't have the soldiers in plain sight." He unconsciously made fists and half-raised them as if he wanted to beat some sense into a head or two. "The French will send troops along the coast road. By the time our boys get ready and get into the boats ..." He stopped, took a breath, and started again. "Can you imagine doing something like this in broad daylight? The French will be waiting for them anywhere they go to land!"

"Captain on deck."

The officers saluted and waited for their captain to speak first.

"You have something to report, First Officer?"

"Aye, sir. The *Squirrel* and *Hawke* are transporting troops down the shore. They sailed so close to the harbour guns, we were surprised they didn't get their asses shot off! Beggin' your pardon, Cap'n, but it does seem most unprofessional."

Rous walked to the side of the ship and checked the scene. "They do seem to be a couple of inept captains. After witnessing this kind of performance, today, it would be hard to believe that we could do anything better, say, tomorrow, when we plan to put an attack force together in the dark, out here in these rough seas, and pounce on them at first light." He smiled as his officers. "No, I would think, after today's little exercise by the *Hawke* and *Squirrel,* the French would be able to believe that we can be pretty stupid."

"It's a feint!" William exclaimed.

"Right-o!" Gesturing at the receding ships, Rous assumed a mock serious tone, "Those boys will make every effort to land at Lorembec but the presence of dusty and tired first line troops, from some other Louisbourg defence position, will frighten our boys away."

There was laughter at the captain's performance. Even the marine guard, duty helmsman and signaller were hard put not to laugh.

Rous seemed to catch himself, turning abruptly on his men so that the levity disappeared like a passing shadow. "There will be briefings on *Namur,* later this afternoon. Lieutenant Gray will attend." With that, he turned and left the deck so quickly the marine guard couldn't perform a butt salute on his musket in time.

The officers stood in silence, wondering why their captain was so moody lately.

After a little while, Mister Johnson and Lieutenant Gray returned to their walking exercise.

Fortress Louisbourg
June 6, 1758

What a magnificent sight! Row after row of the splendid musketmen and Grenadiers of the Cambyse Regiment paraded down the road from Mire into the fortress. Their uniforms were spectacular: white waistcoats with red collars and cuffs, red vests and white knee breeches. Upon the cuffs and pockets of the waistcoat were shiny buttons, alternating silver and then gold. The black hats, which had silver and gold lace trimming, made each soldier appear to be over six feet tall. It was a moment of tremendous pride for every Frenchman.

The first contingent was immediately assigned to Pointe Blanche and Pointe Platte, where it is expected the English might attempt to make a landing.

The second contingent will spend the night at Mire except for two companies of musketmen. Our coastal watchers had reported enemy ships moving troops toward Lorraine. The two detached companies were sent to patrol the coastal road.

Thick morning fog, high winds, and rough surf continue in our favour, limiting the English capacity to mount and launch an assault during the hours of darkness. For them to mount such an attack during daylight would be suicidal but, it must always be remembered, the English are a cunning foe.

Poilly

June 7, 1758
Gabarus Bay

There were sounds of other boats but Lieutenant Gray couldn't see them; the fog was too thick, or was it a heavy mist, he couldn't tell the difference in the pitch black of the very early morning. In circumstances other than the loading and marshalling of the attack force, he would have given a signal on his whistle and the boats of his command would have responded, but not this morning. This morning the boats were to be as silent as possible and gather behind the warships and transports. There was to be no sight or sound of the hundreds of boats, most of them loaded with troops, until the last moments before dawn, when the signal would be given and the three attack groups would pull for the shore.

William allowed his boat to move away from *Sutherland's* hull to give room for the grenadiers to disembark from her. He was searching for some way to position his boat in the attack force; one of the five 'follow-on craft' meant to rescue any man of the attack force who was lost overboard. Each of his boats had been assigned a position and William was supposed to be directly astern of General Wolfe's group.

The rendezvous system was simple.[11] Using three lights hanging near the water on the off side of *Violet* as the far right, two lights hanging from *Saint George* as the far left, and the red flag flying from a boat as the centre, boat captains were to position themselves and wait for the signal to come out from behind the warships and transports and surprise the French at first light.

General Whitcomb's attack group would make a feint at White Point, meant to hold the French troops there until it was too late to reinforce the real point of attack. General Lawrence was to make a similar feint at Flat Point where, at the last possible minute, General Wolfe, with over 3,000 Grenadiers, was to break away and make the actual assault at Cormorant Cove. Designated warships would bombard all three locations so there would be no hint of whether one or all the beaches would receive an attack.

Great plan, William thought, but where the hell is everybody? The fog, the dark, the heavy swell and the number of boats made a circus of the rendezvous system. Boats were going every which way, and then it started to rain, washing the powder out of the muskets' firing pans.

The signal to abort, three short blasts from a reed horn, wasn't the end of the operation because it was going to take several hours to get all the men and boats out of the water. The 'follow-on boats,' of course, would be last.

Shivering, sitting in the stern of his boat, William was entirely miserable. His boat, lighter than most of the other boats because there was just himself, four sailors and the coxs'n, rode higher in the water and was tossed by the swells and the wind. It was hard, strenuous work keeping the bow into the wind, but without this effort the bow would be blown one way or the other allowing the swells to catch her broadside. The most recent broach brought another three or four inches of water from a rogue wave that had threatened to capsize them. With the boat righted and steady again into the wind, William reached for the old-fashioned bailer and began the back-breaking job of putting some water back over the side where it belonged. The activity was good for him; it brought some warmth to his upper body, but not to his feet, which were awash in the freezing seawater.

He set a rhythm as he said a child's play-verse to himself, "One for the money and two for the show, three to get ready, and four to go ..." After a while, he became silent and thought about other things, about home, about Sambro, about Richard Bulkeley.

Bulkeley had always been patronizing to William, probably because William's family could only arrange a junior position on the staff of the new Governor of Nova Scotia, whereas Bulkeley was a lieutenant of Irish Dragoons and Aide de Camp. At first, William thought it was because he was so much younger than anyone on the governor's officer staff that Richard was so condescending but, after a while, he realized that Richard Bulkeley was a prig; if a man didn't have wealth or title, Bulkeley believed he could be used without concern as to the rights and wrongs of it. And not just men, he thought, as Amy Bulkeley came to mind.

Bulkeley had the choice of any maid in Ireland, and perhaps a few in England, although in England, a son of an Irish Lord was not a desirable prospective son-in-law if there were any sons of English titles available. So, Richard had chosen the loveliest, most vivacious, educated woman in Nova Scotia as his bride—Amy Rous, daughter of the only colonial to reach the exalted rank of captain of the Royal Navy, a rank of distinction. Despite Bulkeley being only a lieutenant and, more recently, a self-made colonel of militia, and far outranked by a Royal Navy captain, he managed to look down on Rous and undercut him any way he could from his political position as Provincial First Secretary. Of course, Amy Rous idolized her father and that made Bulkeley more determined to do the father harm. And then there were the abuses of power.

Richard Bulkeley was involved with that man, Joshua Mauger, slave trader, smuggler ... perhaps piracy was the only thing the man didn't indulge in. They were hand in glove; Mauger had been granted title to a handy dandy little beach inside Halifax Harbour (Bulkeley having the keys to every box of goodies in the province) where almost anything, from anywhere in the world, was delivered for a price or for a perk.

William rubbed his legs where the cold was creeping up his body from his soaking feet. *No, he thought, it wasn't just the stipend from an indulgent father that was supporting the Bulkeley lifestyle! He was, most likely, in the night trades up to his hocks.*

"Up to his hocks!"

"Did you say sumthin', Lieutenant?"

"No, Coxs'n. Just talking to myself."

"It'll be our turn soon, sir. I think you should stop bailing, sir. There are other boats within sight, now that the rain has let up."

William sat back on the thwart and wrapped his arms around his chest. *It was cold, so cold. I wouldn't be cold for long at Sambro. We have such a grand fireplace at Sambro. On a cold, wet day like today, I would come home; Molly would take my wet clothes and rub me down with a big blanket and then sit me down in front of the fire. Usually there would be an iron pot on the side of the hearth with soup or stew and I would have a mouthful or two before Molly would bring me a toddy. Perhaps I would cuddle little Charles and talk about my day, the name of the ship, the tides and times, because Molly was always interested, being the daughter of a New England fisherman, and it was never too early for Charles to learn—because the Grays were going to be a family of Halifax Harbour pilots. It was the better of two worlds, being a harbour pilot: ships and the sea as the vocation, and the honest and sane life of the little village of Sambro. Yessir! Sambro, not Halifax, for the Gray family, away from the dirty politics and double dealing of the likes of the Honourable Richard Bulkeley or the supposedly respectable merchant, Joshua Mauger.*

Why, then, was he sitting in an open boat, freezing his ass off? Certainly not for the King! No, the Grays were Scots and not much in favour of English Kings in Scotland—nor New Scotland, for that matter. It was for survival. Surviving was something Scots were good at.

With his father dead and mother remarrying, there was no place for a Gray in the new Munro household. Uncle Charles had purchased a position for him with the new governor for Nova Scotia, Colonel Edward Cornwallis, notorious in Scotland as an oppressor, but no matter to young William Gray—

for there was little choice. He accepted the position and, when the time came, chose a life at Sambro. Quickly realizing that he needed more money to establish himself at Sambro, William attached himself to the most successful captain on the Atlantic seaboard, Captain John Rous. Strictly for the prize money, he had told himself and Molly as he had joined the ship's company of *H.M.S. Albany*, and, in the beginning, it had been strictly for the prize money. Lately, he had to admit, as he served his captain, the adventure and excitement was like a hot meal to a starving man; he couldn't seem to get enough of it, quickly enough. He had followed Captain Rous to *H.M.S. Success* and the campaign to rid Nova Scotia of the Acadian threat and now, here he was, with the crew of *Sutherland*, freezing his ass off at Louisbourg.

William had a bad attack of the shivers. He made no attempt to control it or hide it from the crew, as his body was doing its best to keep him warm. *No shame in that*, he thought. But he did find it a bit difficult to return to his thoughts.

No, it wasn't the prize money any more, or the adventure. A bond had developed between Rous and young Lieutenant Gray, probably because Rous didn't have a son and Gray didn't have a father, or perhaps Rous realized that Gray performed all of his duties in a good, seaman-like manner, the highest praise Rous could give to another human being. And the captain was coming to rely upon Gray as Rous became frailer; there was something wrong with the old man and he knew it.

Rous knew he had something wrong 'in his head,' as he told Wimper, who passed the information along to William Gray, the only person he would trust and who might be of additional service to the captain if he were aware of it. Wimper knew that some incidents, like the Rous's Island thing, would wear at the old man until Rous would lose sight of immediate problems and dwell upon the incident instead. With Bulkeley's determination to belittle the old captain in the eyes of his daughter, there were many such incidents generated by the powerful son-in-law.

Lately, the captain had been suffering from mood swings during which he expressed himself inappropriately to his crew and, at the last Council of War on *Namur*, to the admiral and generals. In his own words, repeating the details of the meeting to Wimper and William, he had told General Amherst, "Attacking the three beaches is like trying to kill the Christmas goose by sticking your nose up the goose's arsehole. All you get for your trouble is a dose of shit! We should be goin' after the goose's head, the ships in the harbour, even if we have to suffer from the bites. At least, when we're done with them, we have goose for dinner." He said he had slammed his fist on the meeting table and advised them, "Take out the French ships, or threaten to take out the ships, and the French will surrender! If you attack the beaches, you have to roll up the outer defences and, eventually, you still have to take out the ships before that goddamn fortress will surrender!" In the silence that had followed, Captain John Rous had excused himself and returned to *Sutherland*.

Shivering again, William realized he was suffering from exposure to the cold and wet but, with nothing else to do, continued with his thoughts. *I'm here out of loyalty to the old man. The captain's moments of stress might reinforce the European officers' view of the crusty old colonial who shouldn't ever have been made a Royal Navy captain, but, on Rous's worst days, he was better than all those upper crust officers on their best.*

"It'll be our turn, Lieutenant Gray."

"Fine, coxs'n." William stood, holding the gunwales of the boat to steady himself since he couldn't feel his feet.

"Mind the ladder, sir. Wouldn't want to have you as our first customer."

"Thank you, coxs'n." He looked around, for the first time in what seemed like hours. It would soon be dawn and, with the lifting of his boat out of the water, there would be no sign that there had been any sort of activity on Gabarus Bay, the early morning of the seventh day of June.

Fortress Louisbourg
June 7, 1758

Siege of Louisbourg: 2nd day

I mark today, for the purposes of my journal, as the second day of the siege.

Up until yesterday, there had been no overt action by the enemy to hinder the port/fortress of Louisbourg from going about its normal business; the frigate *L'Écho* sailed for Québec, a schooner bound for Guadeloupe took on a cargo of cod, local fishermen brought their fresh catch to the market where the previous days' catches are drying on the flakes and, this afternoon, now that the weather has improved slightly, hospital patients are again taking the air in the gardens.

This evening Madame Courserac de Drucour will host the officers of the garrison at the Château St. Louis for dinner. My priority of seating should improve immensely since Saint Julian, D'Anthonay and Marin must remain with their troops and my immediate superior, the Director General of Fortifications, has been laid low with la grippe. If the opportunity should arise, I will ask Governor Drucour why my berthing plan for the warships has not been implemented. Everything takes time to accomplish and the warships should be berthed properly for their best protection, and to the fortress's best advantage, before the English become more aggressive.

But, as I began this entry—yesterday, the soldiers of the second contingent, Cambyse Regiment, prevented the English from landing at two separate locations on the coast road. Since this is the first enemy action against the Fortress, I note the Cambyse Regiment's success by marking the 6th of June as the first day of the siege.

Poilly

Endnotes

[1] In real life, Poilly kept a journal. Cyril Robinson of *Weekend Magazine* had translated entries for significant dates for an article. I read them and then made up some entries for the person who was Poilly in the novel.

[2] The real-life Poilly recorded his views of his fellow officers. The adjectives are taken from his journal.

[3] *H.M.S. Trent* lost her rudder on this date.

[4] Actual detail from notes in Archives. "On June 2, Amherst and Lawrence and Wolfe recce'd the shore coasting along in small boats for several miles and approaching as close as the French guns would permit. Sent boats in to draw fire. Amherst had rejected landing further east of Louisbourg. Too hard to cross rough and unknown land from Mire to Louisbourg. Amherst still thought of three assaults. Inside the small Bay at Blanche, right, Whitmore left Lawrence in two little bays about a mile and 1/2 west. Wolfe at the beach. Man of war cannot come close enough to Blanche to provide support."

[5] Actual detail from *James Wolfe: Man and Soldier* by WT Waugh. "… wherever the beach was smooth and level the French had tried to render it impassable by an abattis of trees, placed with their branches towards the sea. This abbatis was particularly formidable at Cormorandière Cove; so dense was it, indeed, that the British took it for a natural thicket of scrubby bush …"

[6] I found two spellings: Cambise and Cambyse.

[7] According to the unknown staff officer's report, the transports did get into trouble that day. If any ship's captain were to help them, it would have been Captain John Rous.

[8] *H.M.S. Kennington* suffered some damage in her action against the French batteries but there was no detail in the army officer's report.

[9] Commodore Durell was sent out to recheck the soundings.

[10] The two ships did make a feint on this date that was successful in drawing off some of the Cambyse Regiment down the shore.

[11] Details such as this were taken from the staff officer's operational assessment report held at the Archives.

Chapter Four

June 8, 1758
Gabarus Bay

The Bay was not as rough this morning. Certainly, the waves still threatened to swamp any boat that allowed itself to broadside the swell but, so far, the five 'follow-on-boats' of William's command had not been called upon to rescue any of the men from the assault force.

William was stationed just astern the boats holding General Wolfe's four grenadier companies who would be the first to storm the beach at Cormorant Cove. Although William could only see the nearest boat in the morning darkness, he remembered how handsome the grenadiers were, most of them sporting heavy moustaches so that, at a glance, they looked like a band of brothers. Here and there, a clean-shaven face made the resemblance of the rest even more striking. In the nearest boat, a sergeant reached across to straighten a cross strap on one of the clean-shaven men but, otherwise, there was no movement among the redcoats. They sat there, muskets between their knees, heads and shoulders swaying with the boat's motion, eyes gazing impassively seaward as their crew kept the bow of their boat pointed into the ocean swell.

The men in the boats could hear the slap of bare feet running across the decks of the nearest ship, *Sutherland*, probably getting ready to man the anchor windlass. Soon, the warships of the fleet would move away to begin their bombardment revealing to the enemy the assault forces that had been gathering out of sight behind the ships.

"When the warships move, we'll get our first piece of business, coxs'n."

"Aye, sir. A boat or two might swamp as they turn t'ward the beach."

"Make for the nearest boat ..." William started to say, but his words were drowned by the sharp, heavy sounds of the beginning of the naval bombardment. The bomb ketch, *Hali-fax*, and the frigate, *Kennington*, had been scheduled to enter the Cove at 4 a.m. and, in the words of Captain Rous, 'dust 'em up a bit,' while larger ships of the fleet would begin the bombardment of the other possible landing sites ten minutes later. With only two small ships shelling the Cove, the English activity off Flat and White Points would appear to be more intense, so perhaps the French would take troops away from the Cove. It was all part of the English plan to disguise the actual attack point until the last possible moment.

Using hand signals, William ordered the coxs'n to move their boat closer to the grenadiers in an effort to reduce the ocean swell for at least one of the assault boats. He cast a quick look around to see if he could give a similar order to any of the other 'follow-ons' but it was still too dark.

The great, black shape that was *H.M.S. Sutherland* began to move.

"There she goes!" William said, although no one would be able to hear him over the sound of the guns. As *Sutherland* moved out of the way, the men in the boats could see that several fires had started in the trees that grew right to the water's edge in the Cove.

The ketch and the frigate had surely done a good job of 'dusting up' the shore, William thought. *Funny those trees should catch fire like that. Of course, we could expect that those two ships would inflict severe damage on whatever was there since they had started their bombardment much earlier than any of the other ships. Still, the trees seemed to be burning as if they were bone dry!* William was distracted from that line of thought as *Sutherland* opened fire on the beaches near Flat Point. *God! She was such a beautiful sight! Rous was taking her right in, daring the French to reveal the location of the batteries by shooting at him. There! Several French cannon took the bait.* William smiled as Rous reversed course, bringing the port broadside to bear, cannon by cannon, on the unfortunate French gunners. The unmasked shore batteries were quickly silenced.

William thought that it must now be obvious to the French defenders that there were two large groups of boats preparing to attack somewhere along their shores. They could guess that the one group, the one on the English right (commanded by General Whitmore), was aimed at White Point. The second group (Generals Lawrence and Wolfe) seemed to be poised to attack the beaches near Flat Point where *Sutherland* and the larger ships were conducting a furious bombardment. If the French were ever going to rearrange their forces, it would be in the next few minutes. William could see the French were stoutly defending themselves against the English ships at Flat Point and at White Point, while in Cormorant Cove, *Halifax* and *Kennington* continued their shelling, setting substantial blazes in the trees, and suffering no return fire from the featureless shore.

It was fascinating to witness unbridled naval power tearing and rending any enemy forces with the temerity to resist its approach. There! *Sutherland* had found another French battery! William glanced back at the Cove where *Halifax* and *Kennington* were withdrawing, supposedly, to lend their firepower to the Flat Point bombardment, but actually to get out of the way of the assault force that would soon be headed into the Cove.

"They're movin,' Lieutenant Gray." The coxs'n pointed at the first line of boats. "Didn't see no signal, but they's goin', that's fer sure."

The sailors in the assault boats were bending to their oars. William could see that the grenadiers were leaning forward on their thwarts in anticipation of being targeted by muskets hidden in the trees. They were still far out of musket range but the grenadiers, not unfamiliar with battle, never took a chance with a stray shot if they could help it.

The line of boats turned, taking a heavy swell broadside before they were settled on their course to the beaches of Flat Point. Several of them had shipped a quantity of water and sat lower in the water than normal, but the soldiers were using the bailers as they had been trained to do at Scalping Cove, the first two soldiers in the middle holding the muskets of the next two soldiers, who were bent over bailing.

"Let's move out, coxs'n." William's boat executed a smart turn toward the beach. "Be prepared to change course when the grenadiers make their dash into the Cove."

"Aye, sir."

It was hard rowing in the heavy swells, the waves slowing down the cadence. William looked astern in time to see the second line of assault boats, the one carrying the light infantry and the rangers, complete its turn and begin the trip toward the shore. An assault boat was in trouble, not yet capsized, but had taken on enough water to be threatened. The follow-on boat had thrown them a towline while the sailors in the troubled boat bailed as quickly as they could. With the tow from the follow-on, they were still headed to shore.

"So far so good!"

The boats holding Fraser's Highlanders were the next to make the turn and, as far as William could see, did so without difficulty. He faced the beaches. He wouldn't have the time to watch the final portion of the assault force, eight grenadier companies, make their turn for the run-in to the Cove. By the time they began their turn, all pretence of this being an attack at Flat Point would be over and Wolfe's soldiers would be firmly committed to the beaches of Cormorant Cove.

General Lawrence's force was now taking cannon fire from the enemy located above the beaches at Flat Point. William marvelled there were any French batteries left after such an intensive naval bombardment, but even as he watched, one of Lawrence's assault boats disappeared in a spray of wood splinters and red foam.

The enemy gunners didn't seem to be the least bit rattled by the naval shelling, William observed. They were right on the mark. Of course, these French gunners had waited until the English naval forces had withdrawn (to provide room for the attack forces in front of the beach) before they had revealed themselves. If Lawrence were to continue with a real attack, he would be in serious trouble. Even now, his men were being badly hurt and it would get worse as they continued into the artillery's killing zone, waiting for the signal from General Wolfe that the real attack was proceeding.

A quick movement off to the left took William's eye; it was General Wolfe's signal for the grenadier companies to begin their dash for Cormorant Cove. William indicated to the coxs'n that his sailors would have to row harder to keep up.

It was tough going for all the boats because the seas were
heavy, still catching on the sailors' oars; the morning was bit-
terly cold although bright and sunny, while the spray and the
onrushing swells drenched the soldiers and sailors alike, turning them blue with the cold.

"Man overboard, sir!"

"Where away?"

"Dead ahead, sir!"

Carefully, William raised himself on flexing knees to maintain his balance as he scanned the waters. He noted that the
boat directly in front of them had a blank space and one of the
soldiers was pointing back to a spot in the water. Nothing.

"He went right down, sir, didn't come up again, he didn't."

"Continue on, coxs'n." William could see the shore more
clearly now. There was no enemy movement. Looking back at
Lawrence's force, he could see that they had withdrawn out of
cannon range and were moving laterally along the coast to be
available to provide support to Wolfe once his men had gained
the shore.

"Sir! Those trees ain't right!"

William scanned the shore but it was pretty much what the
intelligence officer had described during the briefing at Halifax.
There was a sandy beach with a gentle slope. Behind the beach,
a cliff rose about twenty feet and was thickly covered with trees.
*What was wrong with the trees? The coxs'n was right; there was
something wrong with the trees! My God! The branches all faced
the water! Those trees had been cut down and placed there like an
… what had Uncle Charles called it? Like an abattis!* William
quickly looked left and right. *More trees to the left! No shelter
there. To the right was a rocky point and beyond that nothing but
rocks where boats would be dashed to pieces in the surf! Shit! The
presence of the abattis meant that the French were there, waiting
for them.* He squinted, trying to keep the salt spray out of his
eyes, as he searched for signs of the enemy. He could see the
lead boat was entering the surf; the sailors bracing their oars to
hold the boat steady as they rode into the beach. The grenadiers
were getting ready to move but the coxs'n held his hand up
steadying the soldiers to keep in their places. William felt a

moment of pride as he saw the soldiers respond by settling back as they were told. All that training at Halifax is paying off! The boat was riding the surf when the coxs'n threw his hands in the air and fell over backward. Then, two sailors slumped over their oars. The boat broached and tipped some of the crew and the soldiers into the water where, weighted down by their equipment, they quickly disappeared. The remaining sailors worked to regain control of the boat. They were thrown about and finally torn apart by the dozens of musket balls fired at them from the trees and the cliff. The coup de grâce was a cannonball tearing what was left of the boat into pieces small enough to vanish into the foam.

A volley of musket fire met the next boat, killing all the boat's crew in an instant. The boat, almost as if it sensed that its handlers were gone, immediately dumped the soldiers into shoulder-deep water. The grenadiers struggled to keep their footing and get onto the beach and it looked to William as though they might make it since the French musketmen were busy killing the sailors in the next boat to come through the breakers.

William ordered his crew to rest on their oars as he searched for the best way to help the attack. He could see that ten or eleven boats were in trouble, mostly because the enemy sharpshooters were ignoring the soldiers and killing the boat handlers. Cannon or musket fire was coming from behind every tree. The entire cliff was shrouded in heavy smoke as the French increased their rate of fire. The boat William had been following came under fire and was loosing the crew. Their coxs'n had been the first to go; the sergeant, taking charge of the boat, died a moment later; then the last of the sailors. As if by magic, the buzzing of musket balls around that boat stopped and went off to concentrate on another target.

The grenadiers from the first boat had reached the beach. They must have realized that their muskets were too wet to shoot because they formed up and were fixing bayonets when a volley of musket fire cut them down to one man.[1] That soldier took a couple of steps toward the cliffs and seemed to change his mind. Trotting down the beach, stripping off his equipment, he dove into the incoming waves and began to swim to the closest boat.

It was then that William saw what the lone soldier must have seen: General Wolfe standing in the command boat with his hat off, waving the boats away from the shore. Recall!

Motioning to the coxs'n to move the boat closer to the beach, William shouted, "We'll put a line to that boat and tow her out of there," he shouted. The boat moved into the surf, the coxs'n looping a rope for easy throwing. William expected the French sharpshooters to begin their execution of himself and his crew, but they were able to get a line to the other boat and begin to tow her out of the surf without the loss of a man. *It's the smoke from the French guns! Their own gun smoke was shrouding them so they couldn't see us!. That was good luck!*

Something kept nagging at William. *Yes! That lone soldier—had he made it? No, he was still in the surf.* The soldier made a feeble wave when he saw William looking his way, but the surf was so high he was being tumbled this way and that. As William watched, the soldier rolled over on his back for a rest but a wave swamped him. He surfaced a few feet away, spluttering and thrashing his arms. He wasn't going to last much longer.

"We can go back in, sir. We could get him …"

"Aye, coxs'n." William tossed his end of the towline to the soldiers in the other boat. "Take up the oars, boys. Learn what it's like to be a sailor. We'll be back!" With that, William's boat headed back into the surf.

They didn't have far to go. The soldier was doing surprisingly well; only ten or fifteen feet and they would have him but the smoke had cleared enough for the sharpshooters to resume their deadly work. The coxs'n and one of the sailors were down almost at the same moment. Another sailor yelped with pain but he kept on rowing. William grabbed an oar before it was lost over the side. Stripping off his gauntlets and dropping them to the bottom of the boat, he sat on the rowing thwart and began to row furiously.

"Beggin' your pardon, sir, but stop your rowin' until I gets him in!" The sailor next to William reached over the side and pulled the soldier in by his collar. They had him! "We'll have to get the hell outta here, sir!"

"Right-o! You lead, I'll follow!"

"That's good, sir. The boys always said you wuz one of the smarter ones and knowed when to stop bein' officer."

With the salt spray in his eyes, William blinked several times to see who was doing the talking, but his sight was blurry. He grinned. "Fink! You must be Fink."

"Aye, sir, and it's almost a pleasure servin' with you agin." After several minutes of serious rowing, Fink said, "Yer pardon, sir, but you can stop all that rowin' while we gets a towline to t'other boat. Them sojers are tryin' but the ways they's goin', it's no better'n bein' adrift."

Gratefully, William stopped and wiped his eyes with his cuff. He raised his head and looked around. The beach and cliff where they had made the assault were completely covered with smoke again. Realizing that the smoke had probably saved their lives, William shivered. His shoulders slumped as he felt the extent of the English defeat: *all those grenadiers, slaughtered— and the sailors of the boat crews*—he scanned the Cove, looking for survivors. Three boats were still inshore being driven onto the rocks beyond the point. *Poor souls!* He noted with grim satisfaction that the boat crews were still handling the boats well, guiding them through the surf properly, bracing for the impact on that terrible shore.

There was General Wolfe with his hat off, still waving! Damned little man! Couldn't he see those of us who were able had already retreated? Recall meant defeat and defeat was especially bitter when so many men had died for absolutely nothing. William leaned over to check the coxs'n and found that he was still breathing. *Must get him back to the ship …*

The rescued soldier raised himself on his elbows. "Attack the beach!"

"No, no, soldier. We won't be attacking." William pushed the man back down for fear he would rock the boat. "Take it easy."

"But, sir! Three of our boats have made it ashore beyond Rocky Point!"

William couldn't believe his eyes. British soldiers were forming up on the rocky beach out of sight of the French defenders of the Cove!

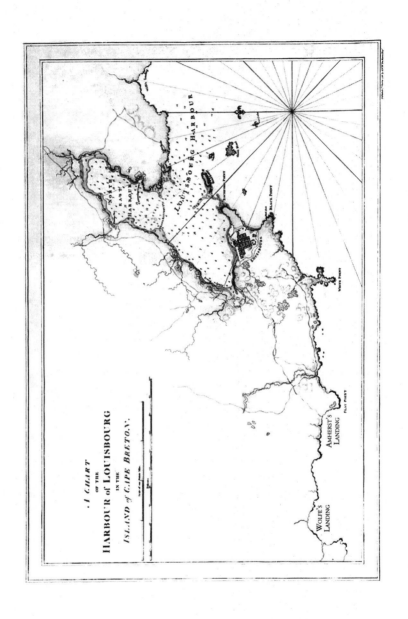

A CHART
OF THE
HARBOUR of LOUISBOURG
IN THE
ISLAND of CAPE BRETON.

The soldier sat bolt upright in the bottom of the boat and, pointing to the shore, shouted, "General Wolfe wants us to attack!"

It was true! General Wolfe was bareheaded[3] but he was waving his cane in the air and his boat was moving as fast as possible to the other side of the rocky point closely followed by the boats of the light infantry and the American Rangers. The English on the rocky beach were now fighting against a mixed force of French and Indians. It was obvious that Wolfe meant to reinforce them.

"Come on, boys!" William pointed at the oars. "We have to get these grenadiers to the party."

Fink straightened out the towline to the second boat and indicated by a nod of his head that they were ready to move off. He called the stroke, mainly for the benefit of the officer who, by now, was having trouble handling the oars because of his blistering hands. With the boat in tow, they were moving slower than the boats with the light infantry and were soon passed by some of the boats of Fraser's Highlanders as well. Just off Rocky Point, William ordered his crew to rest on their oars. He turned in his seat so he could see what was going on.

Some grenadiers were mixed in with the light infantry formation and they were shooting at an enemy further up the slope. That was the only organization that William could see. The rest was chaos!

As expected, this beach was very rocky but there was a small sandy piece, about one boat length wide, where a boat crew could land their human cargo without being stove in or hung up on the rocks in the deadly surf. Each coxs'n, of course, headed for that tiny stretch of sand and, with the arrival of each boat, there were more and more collisions and upsets.

As William watched, two boats approached the safe area at the same time. The wave lifted the one and thrust it onto the oars of the other, snapping the oars and flipping the oarsmen into the water. The lifted boat continued, crushing the sailors in the water and forcing both boats onto the rocks where they turned turtle, trapping the occupants underneath. The next wave moved both wrecks further onto the rocks, ensuring the death of the trapped men. For the moment, then, the sandy space was free and two more boats tried to approach.

The sailors braced their oars, keeping the boat straight on to the beach. The wave carried both boats up the slope where the light infantry disembarked without incident. Since the boats were considerably lighter, the next wave pushed the boats further up the beach.

Another boat raced into the beach, slamming into the small space between the first two boats. Before these new arrivals could get out of the way, another boat crashed ashore, destroying itself on the rocks. Some of the soldiers of both boats were knocked down and crushed or drowned by the next boat to arrive. The surviving soldiers scampered up the beach and were forming up by the time the sailors on the beach began to get a handle on things.

Standing in the wreckage of the two boats, sailors used ropes and brute strength to stop the next boat before it destroyed itself on the rocks. Lashing it to the wrecked boats on the beach, they used it as a sort of pier to capture the next boat before the combers could rush it to its destruction. Now they had space to work from.

By the time William led his boat in, the grenadiers were unloaded and, with a helping hand from the sailors, made it to shore without further harm. The empty boat was pushed back out where William's crew caught it and moved it out of the way.

A soldier waved at William from the jury-rigged pier to get his attention. He shouted, "Lieutenant Hopkins compliments, sir. Please direct the grenadiers to the Cove." He pointed toward Cormorant Cove on the other side of the rocky point.

William gave the soldier a casual salute to show he understood. Fink was already moving the boat away from the beach.

"What about me?" the grenadier asked. "I got to fight!"

The wounded sailor groaned and fell over, too weak from his wounds to row any more.

"What's your name, grenadier?"

"Jenkins, sir."

"Do you know how to handle an oar, Jenkins?" William asked as he lifted the unconscious sailor from the rowing thwart and pushed him onto the sternsheet.

Jenkins grabbed the oar before it slipped away and, giving a broad smile to the naval officer, said, "I guess I can learn. If the navy can do it, I guess it can't be too tough."

William snorted. "What do you think of that, Fink?"

"Tell 'im to row, sir."

William looked at the oar he had been using; it was smeared with blood from his hands. He sighed as he sat on the rowing thwart. "Right-o, Fink. Call it out!"

"Ready! Pull, two. One, two …"

It seemed much easier now that they weren't towing a boat-load of soldiers. As they cleared the rocky point, William turned his boat so they were headed into the Cormorant Cove beach. William shipped his oar and gave hand signals to the boats carrying the final group of Wolfe's troops. They understood and followed him to the beach.

Grenadier Jenkins looked with very solemn eyes at the bodies of his comrades on the beach. "That's a hostile shore, Lieutenant. Let the other boats go in first. We don't have a musket 'tween us."

William thought that was a good idea. "Try to hold her here, Fink."

"Aye, sir," but of course, the heavy swells kept pushing the boat toward the beach. They reached the shore at the same time as the first of the grenadiers.

William watched them disembark, form up and then move off. Other English soldiers appeared at the top of the cliff, rolling up the French flanks. In the Cove, *Sutherland*, under full sail, had returned from the feint action off Flat Point and was delivering broadsides into that part of the cliff still occupied by French troops.

"Beautiful, beautiful birds of the morning are flying my way, flying my way!" William sang the old Scottish ballad and, if he hadn't been so tired, he would have done a jig. Walking along the beach, intent on borrowing a sailor from one of the other boats to take the wounded back to the ship, he failed to see the line of musketmen, with black hats, red collars and cuffs, white waistcoats and knee britches, emerge from the abattis and raise their weapons, aiming at the unarmed sailors. He did notice Jenkins diving for cover and looked around to see why. William turned, just in time to stare down the muzzles of four or five muskets aimed right at him. He drew his cutlass, raising it above his head.

"Molly Gray!" he challenged as he charged the enemy.

They fired.

Fortress Louisbourg
June 8, 1758

The English launched assaults against Anse de la Cormorandière, Pointe Blanche and Pointe Platte this morning at first light. Our troops discouraged the landings at Pointe Blanche and Pointe Platte by concentrated and well-directed cannon fire.[4]

When the sound of musketry at la Cormorandière reached the fortress, confirming that the English were attempting a landing there, preparations were made to send reinforcements. Before the relief column could get out the gate, they were met by a wave of white uniforms in full rout, the valiant de Saint Julien in the fore.[5]

Unfortunately, the commandant at la Cormorandière, Monsieur de Saint Julien, had devised a plan in his pea-sized brain that meant to surprise the English on the beach and destroy them before they had a chance to form up. His plan might have worked but for the smoke from his own guns that hid the landings of English troops beyond a rocky promontory. A lookout tower had been built on this headland to provide warning of just such an enemy manoeuvre, but de Saint Julien, in his great wisdom, had failed to man it.

L'Artois Regiment and the veteran Cambyse Regiment found their trenches enfiladed by American Rangers. Still, I am informed that all might have been saved if our brave de Saint Jullien had acted resolutely against the Rangers who were approaching his flank with wet muskets, but his nerve failed him. When larger numbers of English Light Infantry and Highlanders launched a strong attack, de Saint Julien deserted his defences, abandoned his artillery and stores and fled to the fortress.

My friend Marin, Commandant of the forces at Pointe Platte, in danger of being overrun by the Light Infantry, retired to the fortress.

The inexperienced Jacques D'Anthonay,[6] when it came time for him to retreat from Pointe Blanche, neglected to spike his cannon, which fell, intact, into enemy hands. D'Anthonay fought a rear guard action, being pursued by the English to the very fortress gates. Driven back by the fortress cannon, the English retired, setting up camp north of Pointe Platte.

By midday of this, the third day of the siege, the only Frenchmen outside my fortifications are either prisoners or dead. A sad day for French Arms.

Poilly

The little man stared at what he had written while he sipped his wine. At this time of day, not quite 1400 hours, he was the Inn's only patron. With a sigh, he closed his notebook and stuffed it in his case along with the inkpot and pen. His chair scraped on the pine floor planks as he rose to leave, causing the cook's helper to peek out into the dining room to see if there was something more he might want, although he had already ordered one more than his usual two drinks. When she saw the dark looks on the engineer's face, she ducked back into the pantry, hoping she hadn't been seen.

Poilly scowled in the direction of the anxious face but then relaxed his features. *It wasn't the girl's fault that Fortress Louisbourg was well on its way to a catastrophe. It wasn't the girl who had arranged the contracts for the fortress walls, selected the materials and personally supervised the construction of the pads that were the support for the heavy cannon. No, it wasn't! It was the Director General of Fortifications, the man of such impeccable credentials that he was always well placed at Madame Drucour's dinners, fawning over her hand, dripping compliments so that he could continue to draw his engineer's fees from the Crown for every stone and board that had gone into the construction of the defences—and probably receive an even larger fee from the suppliers for the stones and boards that hadn't gone into the construction.*

He pulled the door closed behind him and stepped out into the sunny afternoon. The street was bustling with the usual activity for that time of day, despite the siege. Looking down to make sure he had closed his case, he patted his pockets for his purse and keys. He had so many things to keep track of now there was an enemy at the gates of his beloved Louisbourg.

A tall man, dressed as a baker with white apron and hat, hurried out from the side door of the inn. "Sieur Poilly! If you would allow me a minute!"

"Of course, but be brief, my man. I am busy these days," he said as he opened his engineer's pad.

"I know the guns of the fortress drove the English away because I looked out through the open gate and saw them run," he waved his hands expressively, as if he were kneading dough, "so, why are we still shooting? Nobody is shooting back at us. Who is out there?"

Running his finger down an impressive-looking list on the opened page, Sieur Poilly made several disapproving, sucking noises through his teeth before he replied, "All morning the English have been landing troops and supplies. Our gunners, both in the fortress and on board our ships in the harbour, are able to fire on them." Apparently having found the piece of information he had been searching for, he snapped the pad closed and tucked it under his arm.

"Why don't the English shoot back?"

Poilly gave the baker a patronizing look as he explained that the English guns were mired in a bog. "Why, my dear man, it will be many, many days before they have any guns heavy enough to reach the harbour and, even then, they will have to dig ditches to drain away the water and fill in the bog so that it is firm enough to support the weight of the guns and accept their recoil when the shot is thrown." Yes, he knew the English would have a problem placing their guns, but the fortress was going to have problems with its cannon, too! In his mind's eye, he remembered the tiny fractures in the masonry pads in the fortress gun emplacements. The fort's guns had been shooting for less than a day and there was already evidence of structural failure. He prayed it was merely superficial, but—Assistant Engineer Poilly grimaced—the Director General of Fortifications, Monsieur Franquet, had been too friendly with the contractors and suppliers and now the chickens were coming home to roost. The tiny fractures were most likely early signs of the serious structural problems to come. It was something he would have to look into but, for now, he smiled warmly at the baker. "Don't you worry, my fine fellow. We have the very best of circumstances; we can shoot at the English and they cannot shoot back at us."

"I thank you, Sieur Poilly. I told my wife I should ask you because you are an educated man and would know such things." The baker bowed to the little man who turned to walk on. The baker had a second thought. "But sir," he held his hand out to stop the engineer, "the Lighthouse Point Battery and the Royal Battery are silent. They are much closer to the English. Why aren't they shooting?"

That was a question not so easily answered. Fortress Louisbourg was so seriously undermanned it had been the governor's plan to withdraw all his forces within the walls of the fortress if the English were able to establish a foothold on the shore. He had done so, this very afternoon. The governor believed it would probably be a week, maybe more, before anyone (the English included) realized that the Royal Battery and Lighthouse Point had been abandoned. That the baker had raised the question was not a good sign. With a feeling of irritation Poilly said to himself, *the matter should be of no concern to this pie-making dolt, particularly when he works at the Inn where everyone gossips.* Poilly's smile was not so broad this time. "I am not a military man but I can assure you, the governor and his council have a grand plan that will drive these English from our land." As he walked away, Poilly called back over his shoulder, "Now, you must excuse me, I see Madame Drucour coming this way and I must pay my usual respects." With that, Sieur Poilly briskly walked toward the governor's wife and her escort.

Strange, he thought. *She is usually in the company of ladies, whereas today she's chatting with several officers.* As he slowed so their paths would intersect, Poilly could hear what they were talking about.

"… every day at this time. I want to be seen walking down this street. I want our people to know that the governor's wife is willing to carry the fight right into the teeth of these English. You gentlemen …" She noticed the little figure standing almost in her way, waiting as if to speak. *Oh, yes. It's that assistant engineer. Insufferable little pip-squeak! The last time I was forced to speak to him was when I hadn't been able to avoid him. He did what he is doing now—putting himself directly in my way so I have to acknowledge him just to get by.*

"Good day, Monsieur." She hoped that would be the extent of it. She sighed when she saw he was going to make one of those meaningless little speeches about her appearance or the weather.

"It is a beautiful day for taking the air, Madame." He stared at the woman's bosom, memorizing the delicate line from the narrowing of her waist to the roundness of her breasts. In the middle of that roundness there was a suggestion of hardened nipples, as if the woman were aroused, perhaps as a consequence of their encounter?

Letting her exasperation show a little she replied, "I am not, as you say, just taking the air, Monsieur. I mean to shoot some iron into the hides of Englishmen." She pulled her skirts together as if to pass but it looked to her as if the engineer was overwhelmed with a moment of anxiety. *He was concerned for her safety on the walls of the fortress?*

Poilly was definitely suffering a moment of panic. *If the governor's wife were on the parapet and saw the cracks in the pads—well, they weren't really cracks—not really. They were tiny little fractures, perhaps only in the masonry. Perhaps they weren't anything at all but he would rather the governor's wife wasn't going to be where she might possibly see them, at least not until Poilly was able to verify that there wasn't anything to worry about or arrange for the blame to be placed on Franquet, where it rightly belonged.* "It's noisy and dirty, Madame. Certainly not the place for the governor's wife!"

"Thank you for your concern, Sieur Poilly, but these gentlemen tell me that Ensign deBaralon is the best gunner in all New France. He is going to find me an apt pupil. Good day, sir." With that, she brushed by the engineer and walked toward Dauphin Gate.

Poilly breathed in deeply the better to catch the scent of her as she passed him by. Delicious! He watched her go. *No need for that woman to wear a wig or augment her figure with any sort of padding*, he thought. *She sports gorgeous buttocks, the delight of any lusty man, and the glimpse of her ankle is enough to make me lick my lips.* He realized that any number of people would be able to see him staring after the governor's wife but he continued to stare. He watched as the sunlight caressed her raven locks which were neatly held off her collar by a fine, golden net. Poilly imagined there were other, equally black, crinkled hairs that neither he nor the sun would ever be permitted to do homage to. He sighed again. "She is a woman fit for a king," he said, softly. *Certainly, she's dressed as if she were to be presented to the King! She carries herself so proudly, shoulders back, holding her skirts with the one hand and a parasol with the other as she takes firm, purposeful strides, smiling at the people she encounters, gathering a crowd by the time she reaches the gate. She must have said something because the citizens and soldiers are cheering.* She disappeared onto the parapet.

Sieur Poilly turned away, forcing himself to think of engineering problems. *He had to inspect the other pads. Surely Franquet hadn't been so stupid as to allow the contractors to ... but then, if I had been in the position to acquire an extra coin or two, would I have not done so? Just look away at the proper time and the contractors and suppliers would make me a millionaire!* He sighed. *That's not my problem. My job is to keep the fortress in the best state of repair I can. If there were a problem with the quality of the materials that went into those walls, it isn't up to me to report it, no, not at all. Whether damage is caused by shot thrown by English cannon or by the recoil of French cannon, I will do the best I can for as long as I can.* But he feared the worst for his beloved fortress.

He had a moment's thought of a defeated Louisbourg where a hairy Highlander, his kilt tucked up and out of the way, was ravishing Madame Drucour. "Things like that happen at the end of a siege, even in Europe," he uttered.

At the house, the slave housekeeper noticed that her owner was breathing heavily when she opened the door for him. Poor man, she thought. "You don't get enough exercise, Sieur Poilly," she commented, but wasn't surprised when he marched straight to his room without acknowledging her presence.

June 9, 1758
H.M.S. Sutherland
Gabarus Bay

It was the first time in the captain's cabin for Able Seaman Fink. Since he was fairly certain he hadn't done anything wrong recently, he was still his usual cocky self when he entered.

"You were with him when he died." Captain Rous was seated at his desk and hadn't looked up when the first officer brought Fink into the cabin. "What happened?"

"We was on the beach ..."

"At Cormorant Cove?"

"Yes, and the lieutenant, he was ..."

The petty officer who had charge of the able seaman nudged him with his elbow.

Fink bobbed his head and restarted. "Beg your pardon, sir." He bobbed his head, again, "Aye, sir. The lieutenant was walkin' away from me boat. He wanted some help to take the coxs'n and the other boys that was hurt back to the ship. *Sutherland* was in the Bay, sir, an' the lieutenant was keen to get back on board. You unnerstand, Captain, we didn't have enough crew left for our boat ..."

Rous swivelled in his chair and fixed his deep-set eyes on the sailor. Somewhat patiently, Rous said, "I don't want a history of the operations, sailor. I want to know how Lieutenant Gray died when the rest of you lived."

"He was wearin' a cutlass, sir. When he saw the Frenchies come out of the trees an' aim their muskets at us, he drew his blade an' charged the bastards! Beggin' your pardon, sir. He waved his sword around his head an' ran at 'em, howlin' like a highlander when they's goin' to put 'em to the sword."

The first officer huffed and turned his head. "How would you know, Fink, what Highlanders do?"

"It's all right, Lieutenant Adams. Let him tell it his way." Rous waved his hand at Fink. "Then what happened?"

"A sojer officer told us to get the boats off the beach and take the wounded with us."

"No, Fink!" Rous was losing his patience. "No! What happened to the lieutenant? What did the French soldiers do?"

Fink leaned forward as if he were sharing a drink and a story with a friend at the pub. "Cap'n. He scared the bejesus outa them Frenchies. Two of 'em threw down their guns and run off. One of them pulled his trigger while his gun was pointed at the sand. Honest to God, the ball hit not three feet from where I was standin'! The others, maybe three, maybe four, shot him down."

"You saw him fall?"

"Aye, sir. He took a step and fell on his face. I thought he was goin' to get up, but he rolled over and was real quiet like. The French sojers ran back into the trees so I went to him, right away. He had blood comin' from his head and he had two holes in his chest."

"You left him there?"

"The sojer officer was givin' the orders and he said to take the livin' only. I wanted to bring the lieutenant back, sir. I really wanted to."

The first officer could see that Rous wasn't paying any attention. "That's all, Fink. You're dismissed."

The petty officer led Fink out of the captain's cabin and closed the door.

"It sounds like William died fightin' mad, Captain." When the captain didn't answer, the first officer quietly left the cabin.

Fortress Louisbourg
June 9, 1758

Choppy seas and high surf have returned, making it difficult for the English to land artillery and stores. God must be French!

The English main camp is plain to see, just north of Pointe Platte. It is being carefully entrenched. I smile when I think of the effort that will be spent digging those trenches because the ground at that site is excessively rocky.[7] Nonetheless, several blockhouses are being erected as well. The English general, Amherst, is reputed to be very methodical and is probably seeking to protect his camp from attack by Indians and Irregulars. We are expecting just such a force under the command of Boishebert to arrive from Acadia but we have no word, as yet, of his whereabouts.

Madame La Gouvernoress has made good her promise, gathering a large crowd to witness her defiance as she fired three carefully sighted cannon at the English. Morale is very high, I believe, as a consequence of her actions. The citizens are calling her Madame La Bombardière.

Poilly

Endnotes

[1] Grenadier Jenkins is my creation.

[2] Smoke from the French muskets also hid the British soldiers who were able to land in the next cove.

[3] The historical accounts gave no reason why he didn't have his hat on as planned. Probably lost his hat.

[4] I found no record that the French were misled but I thought it would be all right for Poilly to think so.

[5] Poilly didn't like de Julien, the commandant of the l'Artois Regiment. He said Julien was "the most dangerous mind I know, full of jealousy."

[6] Poilly viewed D'Anthonay as "inexperienced and presumptuous."

[7] According to the operational report, the ground was very rocky.

Chapter Five

"Sergeant Major!" General Wolfe's voice was hoarse from his cough and runny nose. He wasn't sure the sergeant major had heard him so he called again, just as the senior non-commissioned officer, bent over, entered the tent, straightened up and made a parade ground salute.

"Sergeant Major!"

"Yessir!"

Wolfe wasn't startled by the sudden and unexpected appearance of the major (or at least he didn't show it) whereas many another man would have been. He continued without pause, "I need a personal runner. He must be in excellent shape," Wolfe looked up at the non-commissioned officer, "but you'll know what I want. I need a man who keeps his wits about him."

"I have just the man in mind, sir."

"At ease, Sergeant Major. Who is he?"

The sergeant major snapped his left foot a half-pace to the side and clasped his hands in front but, otherwise, he continued as before, staring at some point three feet over the general's head. "Grenadier Jenkins, sir. He's the sole survivor of the grenadier company from the Cove beach, sir. He saw what was goin' on and swum back to us." The sergeant major leaned forward and, for the first time, made eye contact with his general. "He's a good lad, sir."

"Right. Send him to me." Wolfe went back to his maps. "Thank you, Sergeant Major." When the major was gone, he adjusted the position of the candles on his campaign desk and then pulled several sheets of paper from a file case and began writing. He finished writing and sanded the sheets to make the ink set more quickly and firmly. After two folds, he laid the

107

papers down and searched for a stick of red wax in a haversack lying by his foot. Holding the stick to the candle, he dropped a blob of wax on one of the sheets.

A voice called out from the other side of the tent flap, "Grenadier Jenkins, reporting as ordered, sir."

"Enter, Jenkins." Wolfe licked his ring and pressed it into the wax. He held it firmly for a second and then released it, holding the paper up to the light so he could examine the resulting seal. Nodding his head in approval, he put it on the table while he looked the grenadier over.

Standing in front of him was a dark-haired and, in the somewhat obscure light of the tent, seemingly sun-weathered soldier, with moustache, slightly protruding ears and sparkling eyes. *Probably a good lad*, the general thought.

The grenadier seemed flustered about something. He made up his mind about whatever was bothering him and saluted the general saying, "Beg your pardon, sir, but I lost my headgear on the beach and there's none to spare in the camp." He held his salute until the general nodded acknowledgement of the salute.

"Stand easy, Jenkins."

The young soldier snapped his left foot to the side and clasped his hands in front but, unlike the sergeant major, the grenadier kept his eyes fixed on the general's face.

The general, unused to the direct stare of one of his men, stood. He faced the grenadier. "I need a personal runner and the sergeant major says you are the man." Wolfe didn't wait for any answer or comment. He reached to the side and picked up the paper with the red seal. "This is a laissez-passer. Do you know what it is?"

"It means that the bearer is on the general's business and must be let pass." Jenkins had seen one while he was training in England, where he had gotten into trouble by calling out the guard. He didn't regret that experience, now.

Wolfe handed it to the man. "There are two things I need done before morning." He held up one finger. "I want prisoners and I want them brought to me as soon as they are captured—day or night, early or late, I want them brought to me.

You will tell all the companies manning the perimeter as quickly as you can that it is a personal order from me. Use the laissez-passer if needs be."

Jenkins nodded that he understood and waited for the other order.

"We lost our naval liaison officer this morning." Jenkins, surprisingly, interrupted his general. "I was there, sir. Lieutenant Gray saved my life and the lives of several others."

Wolfe looked at his man for a moment or two.

"Beggin' your pardon, sir. If I spoke out of ..."

Wolfe handed Jenkins the second folded paper. "This note asks the navy for a replacement for Gray.[1] Find someone in the navy and tell them I need another liaison officer." Wolfe continued to look at Jenkins, or perhaps beyond Jenkins. "Yes. Gray was a good man. I'm not surprised he did the right thing on the beach." Wolfe sat down. "You have your orders, Grenadier Jenkins." He appeared to be studying the maps spread out on the little table.

Grenadier Jenkins jumped to attention, paused, did an about face and, in the flickering candlelight caused by his rapid movements, departed.

June 10, 1758
H.M.S. Sutherland
Gabarus Bay

"Captain on deck!"

The officers on the quarterdeck saluted. Lieutenant Adams had been in the process of opening a dispatch bag so it took him a little longer to pay the usual compliments to his captain.

Rous didn't seem to notice or care about navy protocol this morning. His interest was in the dispatch bag.

"What is it, First?"

Wimper, following closely behind his captain, was carrying a steaming cup of tea. He touched the captain's sleeve to get his attention and handed him the cup.

Rous shook his head, "No." He looked as if he had spent a sleepless night. Of course, everyone knew he was deeply disturbed about the loss of William Gray. In recent years, each death in the ship's company seemed to affect the captain more and more. In this case, he had given orders that a search be made for the young man's body. The ship's company had come to the conclusion that their captain wasn't going to accept this particular death until someone produced a corpse.

The Captain's Man, Wimper, hovered nearby, which was unusual by itself, but for him to speak up on the quarterdeck was unheard of. "Any news about the lieutenant, Mister Adams?"

"Not yet, Wimper."

"I asked you a question, Mister Adams. Do me the courtesy of a reply." The captain turned to glare at Wimper. "And you, Wimper, can stop trying to be a mother hen. Go about your duties," he softened his voice slightly as he added, "if you please."

Wimper went below.

His face the colour of the marine guard's tunic, Adams said, hastily, "Dispatch pouch, captain. I was just going to open it … with your permission?"

"Carry on, First Officer." Rous walked to the rail and placed both hands on it, leaning forward a bit, looking out at the Louisbourg Harbour entrance. "If we had the balls, we'd sail in there and destroy their ships. The game would be over in a day or two and we could go on and take Quebec, this year. Montreal would surrender when they got hungry enough. It would be all over by next spring. Instead, we're going to fart around here until it's too late to take Quebec …

"There's a packet from Halifax for you, Captain."

"Send it down to Wimper, Mister Adams."

The marine guard took the packet and went below.

Adams shuffled the next packet for a second or two, "The transport ship, *Neptune*, reports they have Lieutenant Gray, sir." The First Officer's voice rose with excitement. "It says, since we have a ship's doctor, they'll send him over to us in the next hour."

"Eh? What good's a ship's doctor for poor William," Captain Rous looked up and turned swiftly to face the other officers, "unless he's alive?"

"Yes, sir. He's alive."

General Wolfe's Tent
English Main Camp
Flat Point

Grenadier Jenkins had altered his uniform to allow him to perform his new duties more effectively. He still wore the redcoat of the grenadiers but he had removed the crossed belts and other grenadier accoutrements. In their place, he wore a single strap across one shoulder with a message pouch at breast level. His waist belt held a bayonet sheath and water bottle. He had been offered a pistol as a personal weapon, but he felt more comfortable with the musket he carried at the trail when he was moving. Jenkins thought it necessary to wear some sort of headdress since it wouldn't do for him to be uncovered in the presence of officers. A fisherman's cap with a grenadier collar badge affixed to the brim had seemed appropriate (when he was in the company of other grenadiers, he did feel a bit foolish) but a grenadier's shako wasn't meant to be worn by a runner. The cap would have to do.

At the moment he was seated on a camp stool outside the general's tent being kept company by several light infantrymen who had brought three French prisoners, as ordered, directly to the general. Jenkins wasn't paying any attention to the infantrymen's small talk as they waited. He was listening, very carefully, to every word from inside the tent, where an English officer asked questions in French and repeated the answers in English so that the other English officers would understand. (Whether or not the general understood French, Jenkins couldn't tell, because the general didn't speak a word during the interrogation.) After the prisoners were led away, General Wolfe discussed the interrogation with his staff. Jenkins continued to listen.

General Wolfe summed it up. "We have three deserters who say the Lighthouse Battery is deserted and they were ordered to throw the cannon over the cliff onto the rocks."

Another voice, probably the fat major, said, "The Royal Battery has been abandoned, too, if you want to believe them."

A third voice, "Remember, the information about the Royal Battery is hearsay. They only heard it from other soldiers of the regiment ..."

"... Who said they were ordered to destroy the Royal Battery emplacements," interrupted the fat major. "They wouldn't make up that kind of thing."

Silence.

"It could be a set-up, false information, to lure us onto the beaches again," said the third voice.

Jenkins could hear a long sigh followed by, "I believe their story." General Wolfe had made up his mind. "I believe that, for whatever stupid reason, the French have made us a gift of the two batteries."

"We launch an attack?" asked the major.

Next came the sound of General Wolfe's bitter laughter. "No, Major, 'launch' isn't the word I would use. Because I don't like the shoreline at Lighthouse Point, I won't risk our men in those little boats again. No, I'll lead my men in a wide arc around the fortress and approach Lighthouse Point from the land side. Look at the map."

For the next ten minutes, the officers discussed possibilities and alternatives. Jenkins slipped on his cap, stood up and straightened his tunic when he heard the words, "I'll ask for a meeting with General Amherst. He is being exceedingly slow in the envelopment of the French positions but I think I will gain his approval to risk an attack on an unoccupied position."

The other officers made no further comment following this obvious criticism of the commanding general.

"Jenkins!"

"Yessir!"

Captain's Cabin
H.M.S. Sutherland

"My God, William! You were reported dead," the captain smiled, "but, for the first time in my years of service, I'm glad I received poor intelligence."

The officers who had gathered in the captain's cabin to see the modern day Lazarus politely laughed at their captain's humour.

Captain Rous had put Lieutenant Gray in the chair in

front of the captain's desk, the most comfortable seat on the ship. He backed away to get a better look at him.

William's tunic had been slipped over his shoulders with no attempt to pull his bandaged hands through the sleeves. The tunic was not fastened so Rous and the other officers could see that his chest was bound with white linen and there was a stain of blood. His hands were bandaged while, where he had worn a bandana into battle, he now sported a bandage over one side of his head like a girl's tam.

His voice noticeably hoarse, Rous ordered the officers out of the cabin. "Come, now, boys! You can talk to him later. Right now, I want to speak to him alone." He motioned to his man, Wimper. "Get the lieutenant some barley soup."

"Of course, sir." Wimper, as he passed by William whispered, "We were both devastated when you were reported ..."

"Wimper!"

"Aye. I'm on my way, sir." He smiled again at William as he followed the officers up the companionway. "I will ask Cook to make biscuit for the lieutenant, sir."

The cabin door closed, quietly.

Captain Rous pulled the campaign stool over so he sat directly opposite William. "Tell me what happened. Fink said you were dead."

"I guess I should have been, sir."

"Tell me."

"French musketmen came out of the smoke and took aim at my men. I had the only weapon, so I drew it and charged them."

"That must have jarred them a trifle—a Scot brandishing his shillelagh ..."

"You know it was a cutlass, sir."

"Yes, but when the story was repeated by the crew, the whole fleet knows it was a shillelagh." Rous looked closely at his lieutenant. "You in much pain?"

"No, sir. I'm fit to resume duties."

"Like hell you are! My God, man! You took a ball in the chest and one in the head from musketmen shooting at close range." He considered what he had just said. "How did you survive?"

"I saw they were aiming at the sailors. I guess they were still operating under their orders to kill the boat handlers. I took them by surprise." William smiled as he thought of it. "A couple of them threw down their arms and fled. The rest switched their target in a hurry to me. I took a musket ball fair in the chest …"

"Fink said you were bleeding from the head and had a hole in the middle of your chest."

"I lost the top of my ear. Lot of blood but not much damage … except to my good looks. Fink must have seen the blood coming out from under my bandana."

"And the hole in the middle of your chest?"

"I was wearing a uniform my Uncle Charles had made for me in London. The coat is large enough to allow me to wear a waistcoat …"

"We all wear waistcoats."

"This waistcoat is a chain mail justaucorps covered with material so it looks just like everyone else's waistcoat except it will thwart the thrust of a dagger or the slash of a sword."

"But not a musket ball."

"It's a family foible. Uncle Charlie's grandfather, my great-grandfather, was wearing chain mail when he was killed by a peasant's arrow. Bowmen were trained to aim for the centre of the body and musketmen are trained the same way." William paused, taking a slow, deep breath. He continued. "Uncle Charles reasoned that if a musketman ever got close enough to you, he might just hit his mark. So, my father and Uncle Charles had a breast plate, three inches square, in the centre of their chain mail vest. They wore the vest all the time they were in the field." William sighed. "Yesterday, I almost didn't wear the damn thing …"

"It's two days ago, now, William."

"Well, I almost didn't wear it because I was going to be in a small boat on a rough sea …"

"Good thing the musketman kept his head and aimed true." Rous laughed.

"I can't laugh, sir. It hurts!"

Rous continued laughing. "What if you had fallen overboard?"

"My waistcoat would have rusted by the time I walked ashore." William crossed his arms to hold his chest as he started to laugh. "I—mustn't—laugh."

The handle of the cabin door rattled and Wimper entered, pushing the door with his foot. "Barley soup and biscuit, sir." He set the bowl and plate on the desk. "The biscuit is this morning's so it will be good. Eat hearty!" Wimper looked from William to the captain, "Why can't he laugh?"

William already had a mouthful of biscuit so Rous answered, "He's got a musket ball in the chest."

"Beggin' your pardon, sir," William pushed the biscuit to the side of his mouth, " but the ball flattened against the plate. The plate was pushed into my chest until it bent." Lieutenant Gray tried to make a joke of it. "I've got the damnedest looking hole in the middle of my chest you ever saw. There's still little pieces of chain mail sticking out. The doc says he'll fix that in a couple of days."

"In a couple of days you'll be in Halifax. I'm goin' to send you back on the first transport."

"Please, sir. I want to remain here. I want to continue as naval liaison to General Wolfe ..."

"You've been replaced." In a firmer tone Captain Rous said, "The siege of Louisbourg is over for you, laddie."

Lieutenant William Gray pushed the bowl away with his bandaged hands and stood up. "I can walk and talk ..." but he put his hand on the back of the chair as his knees bent. Wimper helped him back into the chair. "I'll be fine tomorrow," he said in a noticeably weaker voice. "I don't want to be sent back, Captain."

"You eat your soup, Lieutenant. Wimper, get a couple of ship's company down here to help the lieutenant to his quarters."

Wimper left the cabin while William slurped more soup.

"While we are waiting, I can tell you about Halifax." He pulled a folded and refolded letter from his pocket. "Molly is fine, Amy says. Your baby is fine. They see each other every week now that Amy ..." The captain put the letter back in his pocket. "Everything is fine. Molly is having a good pregnancy." Rous rolled his eyes in mock terror. "I find it hard to believe that my Amy would talk about such things in a letter to her father, but she does."

There was a knock on the door and two sailors, one of them Fink, entered.

"For Christ's sake, Lieutenant Gray! I wouldn't have left yer, sir! I saw yer dead!"

From the entranceway, the Buffer called out, "Are you talking again, Fink?"

Ducking his head done between his shoulders as if to avoid a blow, Fink answered, "Aye, Buffer." The two sailors worked their hands under the lieutenant's shoulders and buttocks and formed a cradle with their arms.

Allowing himself to be lifted, William caught the Buffer's eyes with his. "He means well, Buffer. We were on the beach together ..." but it was all too much for William. He closed his eyes as the sailors carried him from the cabin.

When the door closed, leaving Wimper and the captain alone, Wimper shook his head. "You didn't tell him about Halifax, did you."

"No, I didn't and it's not your place nor duty to give me advice on such matters."

"Aye, sir."

Wimper cleaned up the bits of biscuit and drops of soup from the desktop. He took the bowl in his hands and walked to the door. He grasped the latch. "Anything else, sir?"

"No, Wimper. Goodnight."

"You should tell the young man, sir. He might be of help."

"I said good night, Wimper."

"Good night, sir."

John Rous, Captain of the Royal Navy fourth-rate ship of the line, *Sutherland*, absent-mindedly picked at a small crumb that had been overlooked by his man. He sat down and pushed the crumb first one way and then the other. Lining up his thumb and forefinger, he flicked the crumb out of sight. "If only it were that easy to rid my life of the Honourable Richard Bulkeley."

Fortress Louisbourg
June 10, 1758

Marquis Charry Des Gouttes today requested that the Governor release the ships of his fleet so they might escape the harbour and return to France. The Governor refused. Des Gouttes then suggested that at least the five first-line ships be permitted to escape to France. Again refused. Jean Vauquelin, captain of the thirty-six gun frigate, *L'Arethuse*, after seeking permission of the Marquis, suggested that the presence of the Louisbourg fleet on the Atlantic seaboard would pose such a threat to Halifax that the English might be forced to lift the siege rather than divide their forces. He recommended the fleet make the escape and at least be seen to sail south toward Halifax. Neither the Governor nor the Marquis supported the Vauquelin suggestion.

The fleet will remain in the harbour.

I had asked my superior, Franquet, to suggest the ships be repositioned in the harbour according to my berthing plan. He informed me there was no opportunity to bring the subject up.

Today I inspected all of the gun emplacements. I found no further deterioration of the stonework.

The daily parade to the guns of Madame La Bombardière and her entourage is inspiring. There is little risk to the Madame and perhaps some damage to the English but it certainly proved good for morale.

Poilly

Lieutenant William Gray had not admitted to the full truth of his condition. The musket ball that had cut the top of his ear also grazed his head. The ball that hit him in the chest was reported correctly but another ball had passed between his left arm and chest, near enough to the armpit to wound arm, chest and armpit in its passage. It was eleven days before he ventured on deck again.

Fortress Louisbourg
June 13, 1758

Yesterday, under cover of thick fog, enemy grenadiers took possession of our abandoned positions at Lighthouse Point. The move took us so much by surprise that it wasn't until today the Governor was able to organize a countermove, when, early this morning, 700 garrison troops attacked the English pickets defending Lighthouse Point. (Enemy light infantry had occupied the small rise, Green Hill, about 900 yards from our walls.) Our forces were repulsed. The English continued to reinforce their grenadiers by sea from the small cove adjacent to the lighthouse.

Following the withdrawal of our troops, Captain Jean Vauquelin positioned his frigate at Barachois Lagoon, where he is able to add his thirty-four cannon to the fortress bombardment of the Green Hill position.

Now that the cannon of the west batteries are in action, I will be able to better determine if our walls have been constructed well enough to withstand the continuous recoil of our guns.

Madame Drucour continues her daily parade to the guns. The last time I spoke to her, I sensed some animosity in her responses to my polite inquires. Given her influence, it will not be Sieur Poilly who is the bearer of bad tidings about any faulty construction at this fortress.

Poilly

June 21, 1758
H.M.S. Sutherland

Lieutenant Gray grasped the side of the doorway with his right hand as he pulled himself from the companionway to the main deck. Once there, he straightened, although, if anyone were watching, they would have seen in his face the reflection of the pain the effort cost him. *Right foot! Left foot!* He walked the short distance to the starboard bulwark and rested. He heard cannon in the distance. *Naval cannon! Perhaps the fleet was acting on Rous's idea of sinking the French squadron in the harbour. Wouldn't that be great!* He felt a moment of loss. He believed, as the captain did, if the French ships were neutralized, the fortress would soon surrender. *It's just my luck to miss the action. The guns of the fortress have a deeper, heavier sound. By the sounds of it, the ships are getting off as many rounds as the fortress! Maybe I could see something from larboard.* He turned. *One foot! Two ... one ...*

"Ahoy! Sleeping beauty!" It was the first officer. "Join us on the quarterdeck."

Gray thought that Adams probably meant well. *Or maybe he didn't.* William quite often gained favour from the captain over the first officer. It would be natural for Adams to resent the captain's obvious favourite and be glad to see the back of him if he were sent to Halifax medically unfit. The smile on Adams' face seemed innocent enough but that didn't change the fact that he had invited Gray to climb the ladder to the higher deck. Somehow, Gray was going to have to do it! He gritted his teeth.

"You look fine, William," Adams lied. Actually, Gray had the colour of his name and walked stiff as a ramrod. He wore a fresh bandage over his ear while his head, which remained unbandaged, showed where his hair had been cut away to allow the doctor to apply ointments to the wound. He wasn't wearing a vest, his chest being bound with linen. His blue coat was slung over his heavily bandaged left arm, which Gray held out at an angle of about fifteen degrees from his side. All and all, he didn't look very good.

"Take your time, old man. I've still three hours to stand watch."

William thought, *a quick jibe or a thoughtful suggestion?* However, William didn't have time to ponder the motives of the other officer; he was at the bottom of the ladder and had to climb, somehow. He raised his foot for the first rung. He had only the one arm to boost himself with. He would have to lean into the ladder and, once he got moving, keep moving until he hit the top. He started.

"Just listen, William."

William thought he had gone up the ladder quickly but during the time it took him to reach the top, Adams had moved to the taffrail and was pointing astern.

"There's a little French pisscutter in the harbour annoying the hell out of our troops. Hear it?"

Out of breath and a little dizzy, William paused as if he were taking a good look around.

Adams hadn't witnessed Gray's breathlessness. He continued talking as if William had joined him at the rail. Pointing at the shore he groused, "The light infantry have pretty well entrenched themselves on the top of that hill but getting supplies to them has been a bit of a bother."

William's first step was almost a stagger but he caught himself. He strolled across the deck. "The naval guns I heard aren't our guns?"

Pointing, Adams indicated a gun emplacement on the road to Green Hill. "Wolfe's cannon are there," he swept his arm to the Point, "and there, bombarding the Island Battery."

"And the naval gunfire?"

"One of the French ships is pounding the hell out of our boys who are trying to get supplies up that little road to Green Hill." Pointing to the shore he added, "She's over there in the lagoon at the end of the harbour."

"Oh." William took in the scene for a bit and then asked, "Only one French ship in action? Where are the rest?"

"Our spies tell us they are moored, higgledy-piggledy, all over the harbour. Haven't moved or twitched since we got here …except for one," Adams nodded his head, "*Arethuse*. Let's hope it's *Sutherland's* good fortune to meet up with her if we sack the harbour."

"You don't doubt we'll attack the harbour?"

"It's the only plan that makes sense," Adams leaned forward so he could whisper and be heard only by William, "but Captain Rous seems to have lost his smarts." He whispered even more quietly, "You didn't hear this from me but, at the last meeting on *Namur*, our captain was told to withdraw and, before the door closed, and so's our captain could hear, the admiral announced to the assembled officers that not all ship's captains are meant to be *Royal Navy* captains."

William thought of the recent signs of change in Captain Rous: blatantly showing favouritism to William, discussing tactics with Wimper and not with the first officer, arguing with the admiral (or anyone else who held a contrary opinion), leaving his assigned post (the *Trent* rescue, the *Echo* capture) with hardly a thought to the consequence; and nursing a grudge against his son-in-law. He steadied himself at the rail, "But Captain Rous is right."

Adams nodded is head in agreement. "There are captains who believe he's right but can't side with a colonial against the man who is Admiral of the Blue, Commander in Chief of his Majesty's Ships employed or going to be employed in North America."

"They should be thinking of what's best for the fleet!"

Adams was going to nudge William with his elbow but thought better of it; he might knock the poor blighter over. Instead, he made a friendly smile and whispered, "Davy Jones Locker is full of naval officers who relied on would'ves, could'ves and should'ves." When William didn't reply, he added, "The way things are right now, the admiral won't ever allow an English warship to enter that harbour before the fortress surrenders."

"Because it was Rous who suggested such an attack?"

"You can bet your life on it."

Fortress Louisbourg
June 25, 1758

Early this morning, the last of our serviceable cannons on the Island Battery were destroyed by enemy fire. Our surviving gunners were ferried by boat to the fortress. The enemy can now take possession of the Island. Once their guns have been placed, they might be able to reach the ships in the harbour with their shot. As a consequence, the various captains have drawn their ships in closer to the city but they have not implemented my berthing plan. My superior officer tells me that there has not been the proper moment to suggest it at the Council of War. Apparently, it is a very sensitive matter to tell a naval officer that an engineer knows better how to berth his ship.

The Governor directs our guns at the English trench lines and battery positions. He hopes to deter, as long as possible, the expected assault upon the fortress.

For my part, I have been busy checking the gun emplacements. Ominous cracks are forming in the gun pads. Additionally, there are stress lines in the fortress walls adjacent to any of the cannon that are in continuous use. Somehow, I must arrange for my esteemed Director General to conduct his own inspection.

P

July 3, 1758
British Grenadier's Redoubt

Grenadier Jenkins could see the man he was looking for. He called out to him. "Lord Dundonald!"

The officer working with the soldiers strengthening the outer walls of the redoubt recognized General Wolfe's messenger. He handed the trenching tool he had been using to the nearest grenadier with a smile. "I'm sure you weren't needin' me to show you how to dig a hole, son!" He stepped back from the wall, raising his hand to acknowledge he had heard the call. "Over here, Jenkins!"

Another grenadier, who had been sitting on the top of the wall looking out over Louisbourg Harbour, suddenly shouted, "Take cover! She's ready!" and dove into the bottom of the trench where he crouched down, putting his hands over his head.

Dundonald jumped back into the hole and pushed his head and shoulders as close to the earthen wall as he could, squinting his eyes shut as he waited.

Jenkins was standing at the lip of the trench looking down at the members of the working party who were making themselves as small as possible. "I have a message ..."

Lord Dundonald opened his eyes. "You soon won't have

anything, Jenkins!" The officer reached up and pulled the startled Jenkins down beside him.

It was as if everything that was solid in the world had turned to jelly as a dozen or so cannonballs smashed into the redoubt. Logs and tree trunks that had been embedded in the earth were torn loose and thrown about as if they were straw, but it was over in an instant. Each man checked himself to see if he were still all in one piece and then looked to see how his fellows had fared.

Three grenadiers who had been working on the reverse side of the wall were buried, their shoeless feet sticking out of the mud.

"Come on!" Dundonald was the first up, followed quickly by a corporal. They began to dig the men out. It was a small space. Only two men could dig at a time. Jenkins watched with a feeling of helplessness as the minutes passed. There would be no hope for the buried men, but the grenadiers didn't give up. They kept digging and changing places and digging until they had recovered the bodies of their comrades.

Lord Dundonald nodded at Jenkins. "I'll be a few minutes. I want to see to my men." The officer went with the litter party to the reverse side of the hill where the wounded and the dead were gathered out of reach of the French guns.

Jenkins stood up with his hands on his hips. "What the hell!" he said to no one in particular.

"You mean 'im?" The corporal jerked his thumb at the departing officer. "'e looks out for us, 'e does."

"Shit, no! I know Major Lord Dundonald is a right smart officer." Jenkins peeked over the wall at the harbour. "No, what I meant was, where the hell did all the cannonballs come from?"

"H'it's that little ship at the edge of the harbour. A frig-it, they calls it." He stuck his hand out to Jenkins. "I'm Turnbull and you're the General's Runner." Turnbull looked Jenkins up and down as they shook hands. "Bein' the General's Runner is better'n a promotion, I bet. You gets lots to eat, real regular like, and hears all the gossip." Turnbull leaned forward and spoke in lowered tones. "They gonna send our ships into the harbour and sink that frig-it?" He shook his head from side to side. "It needs some sinkin' real bad! It's been pesterin' us ever since we took this knoll five days ago."

Jenkins continued peeking over the edge of the wall, watching the frigate. He didn't take his eyes off her, as he said, "No. I guess not. I heard the general ask the naval liaison officer to arrange an attack but the admiral won't risk his ships under the guns of the fort."

"We 'ave to do it all by 'rselves?" There was disbelief and then anger in Corporal Turnbull's voice.

"Well, General Wolfe wasn't none too happy, either. He sent the naval officer packin'! Told him not to come back if he couldn't be more help than that." Jenkins took his eyes off the French ship and looked around for Dundonald. "I've got this message to deliver ..."

"The major will be back, soon as he looks after the boys."

The frigate fired a single cannon.

"What's the frigate doing?"

"The sergeant says the Frenchie don't want to wear out his guns, no he don't. Every four hours, that Frenchie captain, 'e turns his ship around. Ya see, 'e lets one side cool off by switchin' sides. When 'e gets all lined up after a switch, 'e shoots 'em all at once."

"They fire a broadside."

"Yep, and we watch and take cover when it's about to happen."

"But now he's shooting one at a time."

"That's right! For the most part, 'e shoots 'em one at a time. The sergeant says it's 'cause 'e ain't got 'nuff iron left to shoot ..."

"Broadsides."

"... broadsides all the time. We don't pay no never mind to 'im 'til 'e does 'nother switch. Them ... er ... broadsides are murder! We watches fer 'em real careful like."

Both men straightened up at the approach of Lord Dundonald.

"What do you have for me, Jenkins? Good news, I hope?" Dundonald jumped down into the trench.

Grenadier Jenkins opened his leather case and removed a sheaf with a red seal on it. He handed it to the major. The officer broke the seal. He signalled for his section commanders to join him; several non-commissioned officers and a lieutenant quickly surrounded him.

He glanced at Jenkins's face as he smoothed out the paper. "You always have a verbal message from the old man, Jenkins." "Yes, sir. Not good, I'm afraid ..."

Lord Dundonald held his hand up to stop the messenger. "Then let me read the message." He scanned the three lines and slowly lifted his head to study the terrain in front of the redoubt. "Well, boys, we've been ordered to build a redan in front of the redoubt ... nearer the harbour."

The lieutenant pressed his lips together and several of the non-coms cast swift glances one to the other but, otherwise, no comment was made from the section commanders.

Dundonald continued. "The general says a redan could be built much quicker than another redoubt. He thinks fused mortar shells will drive the French ships out of the harbour into the arms of our fleet and that's why we're going to build a redan—for the mortars."

The lieutenant asked, "We only have eight-inch mortars. We'd have to build the redan pretty close in to them."

A sergeant said, "We could pull a thirteen incher up from the beach but that frig-it would see us. Our men would be in the open ..."

"Do it at night." The way Dundonald spoke, there was to be no more discussion as to how difficult it would be to get a thirteen-inch mortar up the hill and down into a redan that wasn't even built yet.

But the lieutenant persisted, "Sir, we're going to be working closer to the West Gate under continuous bombardment from that infernal frigate and the fort ..."

An older, grizzled sergeant picked up on his thoughts, "... and probably from the other shipping in the harbour."

Jenkins shifted from foot to foot, obviously uncomfortable but intent on delivering the general's message. "Beggin' your pardon, sir."

When Jenkins saw that he had the major's permission to speak, he carried on. "The general knows that. He says to tell you the Royal Navy won't send a single man o' war into that harbour. It's up to us to do something about the French fleet."

There was no comment made so Jenkins continued. "The general says your batteries have damaged their West Gate but, unless something is done about those ships, our losses are going to be unacceptable. The general will set up a battery on your right as support against attacks from Irregulars or from the fort. The guns from the other battery will play on the fort while you build the redan."

Major Lord Dundonald quickly folded the message into a small square to fit in his breast pocket. "Tell the general we'll need five mortars ..."

"Perhaps we can make room for a howitzer?" the older sergeant asked.

Dundonald checked around the circle of men and nodded. "Jenkins, please present my compliments to the general and tell him that the new redan for the Grenadier's Redoubt will require five mortars and two howitzers. Please inform him of our appreciation for the covering batteries on our right."

"Yes, sir!" With sharp salute, Jenkins jumped up out of the trench and began the fluid, graceful lope that would return him quickly to the beach where the cannon and supplies were being landed. As he departed, the last words he heard from the section commanders were, "What if we're attacked? A redan isn't much of a defence ... at least not as much as a redoubt." He didn't hear Lord Dundonald's answer.

July 5, 1758
English Grenadier's Redoubt

Major Dundonald was pleased with himself and his men. It was amazing what four companies of grenadiers could accomplish even under the worst of circumstances. Mind you, he thought, his childhood governess, or one of his many governesses (which one he couldn't quite remember), had told him "Pride goeth before the fall!" She had reminded him that the Dundonald men were particularly prideful and, because of their exalted position in society, their fall often led to the destruction of their supporters. She then would tell him stories of prideful men and their fall from grace, supposedly all Dundonalds ...

"Sir!" It was Turnbull. "The four twelve pounders on our right will begin to play at the top of the hour. They want to know if our mortars will be ready at the same time."

"Yes, Turnbull. Tell them we will begin bombardment on the hour." He waved the corporal on his way.

The sense of pride of accomplishment returned as Dundonald reviewed the situation. *Our redan is finished, giving shelter to five mortars. We have seventeen cannon and the two new howitzers located in the redoubt.*

He lifted his hand and signalled for one of the lieutenants to approach and continued with his thoughts as the officer made his way up the traverse to where the major was standing.

That little French ship, the Arethuse, still maintains her position like a thorn in our side. Her rate of fire has been reduced— probably running short of ammunition. He smiled. In the next hour, we will deliver as many cannonballs as that French captain can possibly handle. With luck, maybe my men will shove one right up his bum.

The lieutenant stood in front of him. He saluted.

Major Dundonald stared at the young man while running his fingers along his moustache and, with his other hand, lightly holding his sword scabbard, making no attempt to acknowledge or return the salute.

Dropping his salute, the lieutenant apologized. "I'm sorry, sir. It's hard to break the habit."

"Right-o! We don't want enemy sharpshooters picking us off just because our boys run around drawing attention to us with a lot of infernal saluting, do we?" He reached over and gave the lieutenant a friendly tap on the shoulder. "Set the example for the boys, Lieutenant."

"Yes, sir."

"Pass the word. I will give the order from here. I want all guns to begin to play at ten o'clock. I will take my hat off and wave it twice. Give the order to fire from my signal. Targets of opportunity, of course, but I want as many guns as can reach her, to be brought to bear on the French frigate."

He watched the lieutenant scramble along the trenches, giving the orders to each battery commander. Dundonald raised his eyeglass to examine the work being done on the last mortar to be installed, breathing a sigh of satisfaction when activity ceased, indicating that all was in readiness for his signal.

Eleven minutes to go.

He had often tried to remember her name, the governess who had told him splendid tales of the Dundonalds. There was the Dundonald who had planted his shield upright in the middle of a battlefield daring any of the enemy to come to him and engage in personal combat. He had stood there, taunting the enemy, while his men had formed line around him. She had said he was a big man, like all the Dundonalds, with his nostrils flaring in anger and disdain for the foe who would not accept his challenge. He had stepped around his shield, beating his chest, shouting …

It was time. He raised his hat and waved, once, twice.

The crash of the English guns felt good. The western gate of the fort, some of the ships in the harbour were struck but it gave him great satisfaction to see that damned frigate engulfed in the blasts from his mortar bombs. He waited for the smoke to clear. He waited. She was still there! Yes, there was visible damage, but she was still there! Her crews were cutting away fallen rigging and spars but she was still there. She returned fire, a broadside! The redan took the hits. One of his mortars fell silent, the men serving the mortar all dead, the gun probably damaged if not destroyed.

Arethuse cut her anchors. Several sheets of canvas billowed into the breeze and the little ship began to move. When the next mortar bombs were delivered, *Arethuse* wasn't there to receive them.

"Probably had that all planned out," the Major said to himself. "A damned good man!" He put his hat back on and walked toward the cook's tent. He might as well get a meal. By the looks of it, it would be a long afternoon what with his guns and the enemy's guns trading shots on an equal footing for the very first time in this campaign. As he passed the lieutenant he called out, "Have the men go eat. Every third man to the cook's tent until all fed." He sauntered to the reverse side of the hill where tending the wounded, feeding the well and attending to the dead could be done out of reach of French guns.

It was a long afternoon. The shot came hot and heavy from the ships and the town. By early evening, the backside of the hill was littered with the English wounded and the dead and still the damned *Arethuse* flitted about the harbour like an angel of death delivering broadsides on the unfortunate grenadiers in the exposed redan.

"Five guineas to the gunner who puts the next hole in her!" the Major hollered. "Pass the word along!"

The General's Runner, Jenkins, arrived at about this time. He watched *Arethuse* approach as the major seemed to take his own sweet time opening the message. Jenkins remembered the last *Arethuse* broadside he had experienced and he was most anxious to be on his way, but his discipline and training wouldn't let him show his uneasiness.

"It says here," and the major pointed at the paper, " I can use my discretion as to how many grenadiers I hold in the trenches to defend the mortars." He scratched the back of his neck where some mosquitoes had gotten under his hair and drawn blood. "What does the general mean, Jenkins? I didn't ask for any relief from company procedures. I have the usual four companies up and two in reserve."

"The general saw the casualties from the bombardment. He means to give you as much flexibility as you may need, sir."

Major Dundonald rubbed his neck vigorously. He nodded his head. "Please tell the general I appreciate his confidence in us."

"Yes, sir." Jenkins could see where *Arethuse* was making her turn to present her broadside to the shore. All of the English mortars barked at the same moment, sending their bombs high into the air in a trajectory calculated to catch *Arethuse* as she made her firing run, but the ship swerved back to her original course, resuming her head-on approach to the shore. The bombs were going to miss.

Turning to go, Jenkins asked, "Anything else, sir?"

The bombs exploded harmlessly a hundred yards from *Arethuse.* Now she was making her final turn to present her broadside. There she was, sailing a predictable course with the length of her exposed to mouths of the English guns but the mortars were not going to be able to reload in time to catch her. She would deliver her blow and then turn on her heels and scamper out of range.

"No, grenadier. That will be fine."

Grenadier Jenkins began what he hoped was his usual gait up the hill and out of range of the guns of *Arethuse.* As he crested the hill, he could feel the earth shudder with the impact of the broadside.

July 6, 1758
Grenadier's Redoubt

Two grenadier companies up and four held back in reserve. Even with that reduction of troops held in the firing line, casualties were bad. Major Dundonald watched as *Arethuse* began another approach to the English shore. What trick would the French captain pull this time?

He heard a voice behind him. It was Turnbull, again.

"Beggin' your pardon, sir, but Sergeant Mitchell says 'e heard drums at the fort. 'e thinks the Frenchies might be puttin' together a sally force.[2] 'e asks, sir, if you are wantin' to call up the reserves in case they attack?" Turnbull could see that the major was studying the approach of the enemy ship. He waited.

Dundonald was thoroughly tired of that little ship strafing his grenadiers, time after time, and getting away unscathed. Always, the ship pranced to the shore, fired a broadside, and retreated to the further reaches of the harbour while the English mortars riled the water with impotent fury. He remembered his astonishment, early this morning, when the *Arethuse* delivered her broadside and then reversed course and delivered another as if there were no threat to her existence within a dozen country miles. "What audacity!" he said, as the thought about it.

That wasn't one of the answers that Corporal Turnbull was expecting, so he held his tongue and continued to wait.

Call up the reserves so that Arethuse could peck away at them? "No, corporal. Tell the sergeant that we can hold the line with two companies." He continued to watch the French ship. It raised some signal flags and turned early.

The twelve pounders couldn't withhold their fire and their volley churned the waters where the ship might have been. The mortars, being of shorter range, had time to order the ceasefire.

Arethuse, pulled up into the breeze and almost stationary, seemed to be waiting for something—maybe a signal from the fort. Dundonald used his glass and examined the open ground between the redan and the western gate. White uniforms; sunlight glinting off gold and silver buttons. It was the Cambyse Regiment, the regulars from Breton, who were coming to test the defences of his redan! His mouth went dry. Maybe he should have called the reserves forward. He sent a runner to the rear doing just that but, at the same time, he knew that the fate of his mortars would rest upon the two companies currently at the fore. He forced himself to walk sedately as he signalled for the assembly of his commanders.

Sergeant Mitchell was the first to arrive, followed almost immediately by the lieutenants and the other sergeants.

"Looks like a hundred, maybe a hundred and fifty of them Regulars, sir." Mitchell growled.

Lieutenant Brown raised his arm and pointed, "*Arethuse* has resumed her approach."

"All right, boys," the major said in a hearty voice. "Here's our chance to dirty up some fancy French uniforms." He inclined his head toward the beach. "Sergeant, put a man at the top of the redoubt. When *Arethuse* takes her final turn, have him give three blasts on his company whistle. Commanders should be able to order the men to take cover because there's no sense sitting up to watch the frigate spit in our eye. The mortars will chase the frigate away and we can then deal with the intruders using normal company tactics. If any of the fancy pants reach the redan wall, have our men climb out the reverse side and allow the enemy to enter the trenches, where we'll greet them with our volley fire from above." Major Dundonald swept his eyes around the small group. "Clear?"

Sergeant Mitchell asked, "Who has command of the reserves?"

"There are no reserves, sergeant. Every man jack of us will be at this party from the very first." Dundonald didn't give time for any further comment. "Let's have a go, boys!"

As the commanders assumed their positions with their men, they could see *Arethuse* coming on in her usual fashion, a white bone in her teeth due to the brisk breeze.

Dundonald smiled a grim little smile as he remembered the surprise he had planned for *Arethuse*. He had ordered every gun in the redoubt, the redan and the battery to the right of the redan to shoot at the frigate on her next approach. This was her next approach. Perhaps it might have been wiser to divert some of the guns to the support of the redan during an assault by French Regulars, but Dundonald's pride would have none of it. The gunners were ready for *Arethuse*; his grenadiers, albeit only two companies of grenadiers, were ready to receive the Cambyse. So be it.

The English watched as the Cambyse officers gave the signal to advance. It was impressive: a hundred huge-looking men, formed up in two walls of white, marching with a steady rhythm, advancing on the low walls of the redan. Dundonald watched them. Even on the rough ground, the lines didn't waver. Behind those firm lines of men was *Arethuse*, her sails full, signal flags flying and those deadly little guns run out on both sides. She was coming closer to the shore than she had ever come before. Major Dundonald thought, *what magnificent naval support! That captain is intent on giving as much …*

With a start, Dundonald realized that the closer the ship came to the shore to get off her best shots, the less choices she had to avoid the English guns! He held his breath. *Now, if the gunners would only …*

The twelve pounders to the right were the first to fire. Shooting high, they took out some of her standing rigging. The mortar bombs straddled her, killing numbers of the crew and putting rents in her sails. The twelve pounders shot again, this time aiming for her hull: at least two hits! *Arethuse* was being forced to turn, her broadside not yet delivered. The *Arethuse* gunnery officer tried to shoot during the turn away, but the shots were wild, some of them landing closer to the Cambyse than the redan.

The white line faltered, several men going down from shrapnel or flying debris from the *Arethuse* shots but, with excellent direction from the commanders, the Cambyse resumed its advance.

Another twelve pounder hit the *Arethuse* as she picked up her skirts and ran. It was obvious that the frigate was out of the battle for now.

The grenadiers were cheering the hasty departure of their worst enemy, some standing on the redan walls and raising their muskets over their heads in the glorious feeling of victory.

Feeling better now about the coming fight, Major Dundonald watched as his men settled down to the business of killing as many Frenchmen as they could before the white wall engulfed the redan.

The first English musket volley sounded firm, sure, but not as heavy as Dundonald would have liked. He was reassured when a single mortar ranged in on the French was followed almost immediately by bombs from the entire battery. Frenchmen fell.

With precision, the Cambyse Regiment halted. Non-commissioned officers could be seen dressing the line. The second rank, taking a half step to the right, lifted their muskets in time with the front rank, aiming at the redan. Smoke from their muskets shrouded the French line. When the smoke cleared, the Cambyse were marching away. They formed column from line as they approached the western gates, which were open. They marched into the fortress, the gates closing firmly with a thud that could be heard by the grenadiers.

For a moment it was so quiet that the grenadiers could hear the screeching of the seagulls and, from somewhere in the distance, the mooing of a cow. The grenadiers in the redan cheered and clapped each other on the backs. They were joined by the reserve companies who had just arrived, some of them doing a dance or a jig on the walls of the redoubt, hopefully under watchful eyes in the fort.

Major Dundonald let the celebrations continue until he noticed that the gunners were attempting to service their guns and the grenadiers were in the way. He quickly restored order so there would be no interruption of the bombardment of the fort and the shipping in the harbour. He raised his eyeglass, searching for that old thorn in the side, *Arethuse*. She was somewhere in the harbour, but among the taller, bigger warships, he couldn't pick her out.

"Lieutenant Brown! Get me a runner!"

"Grenadier Jenkins is here, sir," was the reply.

"Good! Have him report to me."

Major Dundonald took the dispatch case from his clerk and wrote a quick note to the general in his own hand.

> An attack by one hundred Regulars was repulsed. *Arethuse* acted in support of the attack. Concentrated cannon fire drove her from her station. Extent of *Arethuse* damage unknown. Our casualty figures are light and I will make them available to you as soon as possible.
>
> Your faithful servant,
> Dundonald

"Oh, there you are Jenkins!" Dundonald stood up and handed the paper to the messenger. "Please take this to the general. If he asks, tell him I am reducing the grenadiers in the redan to one company. The boys did a smart bit of work today and I want to give them a good rest and some hot food."

Jenkins took the message and placed it in his case. He nodded to the officer and trotted off over the hill.

"Lieutenant! Have the two active companies relieved. Send them over the hill for a rest. Order up one of the reserve companies to take duty."

"One company, sir?"

"Yes. Tell them they'll be relieved, first thing in the morning."

July 7, 1758
Grenadier's Redoubt

"Your pardon, sir." Grenadier Jenkins had approached his general, who had been studying the lay of the land in front of the West Gate for the placement of another six-gun battery.

Without turning around, the general asked, "What is it Jenkins?"

Jenkins could hear the annoyance in the general's voice; the general didn't like to be disturbed while he was working out a tactical problem. He hesitated.

Now turning, the general demanded, "What is it?" in that tone of voice that his staff officers called 'nasty' and always attempted to avoid the general when they heard it.

The grenadier pointed across the redoubt to the back gate where two naval personnel were entering: one of them an officer, the other a seaman. "I think it's a ghost come walking, sir!" There was a tremor in Jenkins's voice. "It's that lieutenant who saved me life!"

"Really!" General Wolfe took a step or two in that direction to get a better look. "By Jove! He's a bit the worse for wear, but it is our Lieutenant Gray!" There was a broad smile on the general's face. "Present my compliments and ask him to join me."

"Yes sir." As was now his habit, Jenkins placed his musket at the trail and trotted even the short distance to the rear gate. When Jenkins was several paces from the naval officer, he slowed to a walk. He shouldered his weapon and came to a halt. He slapped the butt of his musket with his right hand, holding it there in a butt salute. "Lieutenant Gray, sir. The general presents his compliments and asks that you join him."

"Thank you, Grenadier …"

"Jenkins, sir. You saved my life …"

"I remember you, Jenkins." Somewhat uncomfortable with the obvious display of respect and appreciation, Gray returned the salute. "Where is the general right now?"

"I'll take you to him, sir." Jenkins glanced at the seaman. "You were there, too."

Gray wished that the subject of the conversation could be changed. "Yes, Fink was in the boat that picked you out of water, Jenkins, and is every bit as responsible for your current condition." Gray looked around the enclosure. "Could we hurry on to the general? I don't want to keep him waiting."

The three of them walked to where the general was standing, Lieutenant Gray moving with a show of stiffness or, perhaps, pain. In the interval, Major Dundonald had joined the general. They were discussing the battlefield, both of them pointing and making comments. As Gray approached, General Wolfe raised his hand to halt the conversation. He took several steps to meet the lieutenant and extended his hand in greeting. "Reports of your death were exaggerations, I see. I will have to chastise my intelligence sources."

Taking the proffered hand, Gray replied, "They weren't much exaggerated, sir. Even Able Seaman Fink thought I was a goner."

"Indeed he was, sir, with blood pouring out of ..."

General Wolfe nodded to Grenadier Jenkins. "You can take the seaman off for a bit. Get him something ..."

"Yes, sir." Jenkins took Fink's sleeve in his left hand and firmly led him away before he could say anything else.

"Mustn't get too fond of any of them, Lieutenant," General Wolfe had turned so that he could look right into the younger man's eyes, "because, the next time, it may be your duty to expend his life and the lives of a dozen more just like him."

"Aye, sir. I mean, yes, sir."

"Major, do you remember Lieutenant Gray?"

"Yes, of course. The boat training at Halifax." He offered his hand. "I'm Dundonald."

They shook hands, Gray wincing a trifle at the major's enthusiastic shake.

Gray looked beyond the two men at the view of the harbour. "It was your guns, Major, that got rid of *Arethuse*."

"It was. The general and I were just discussing how much better it would be for the siege if we could get more guns closer to the harbour."

General Wolfe sucked his teeth. "It is a long, long job to creep ever closer to those walls." He turned his head to one side and blew some small fragment of food from his mouth. "You are right, Lord Dundonald. We will have to place another battery on that tiny rise. Perhaps six guns. Draw the noose ever tighter."

"I'll take an engineer with me and scout that area tonight."

"American Rangers as escort?"

"I would prefer my grenadiers, sir."

"As you will, Major. I leave that sort of thing to your good judgement."

His business completed, Major Dundonald nodded to the two officers and left.

Wolfe then turned his watery eyes on the naval officer. "You are aware I sacked the naval liaison officer the admiral assigned to me."

"Yes, sir. I ask permission to resume my duties."

"Under whose authority?"

"Captain Rous says that you can ask for my services. It is unlikely the admiral would refuse such a request."

"I'll expect results, Gray."

"I'll do my best to get you what you need."

Wolfe pointed at the ships in the harbour. "I need an attack on those ships and as many of them destroyed or neutralized as possible."

Gray didn't respond.

The general continued. "Every time we make a move to tighten the ring around that fort, those ships help the cannon of the fort pound my men. Of course, we persevere and accomplish what must be accomplished, but," he paused. It was if he was searching for some words. "But it's like fighting a big dog with a knife. If you can rip his belly open, all the fight drains out of him. Getting rid of those ships would take all the fight out of the French."

"That's what Captain Rous thinks, too."

"I will speak plainly, young man. Your Captain Rous is his own worst enemy. Those Royal Navy types aren't going to listen to his theories. In fact, I think they go out of their way to act contrary to anything Rous suggests."

William Gray felt anger at the haughtiness of upper-class Englishmen who were born to positions of Imperial power. As a Scot, Gray could only be accepted if he performed extremely well for the Empire. Captain Rous, a lowborn colonial, would never be accepted. Gray hoped he masked what he was thinking. "Please have me reinstated, sir, as your naval liaison officer. Having me around can't be worse than having no liaison officer, and, consequently, no direct contact with the navy."

General Wolfe didn't hesitate. "Done! By the time you get back to *Sutherland,* I will have made arrangements to have you transferred ashore."

"Permission to carry on, sir?"

"Aye, Gray."

Both men smiled at the general's lapse into the naval response.

July 8, 1758
250 yards north of the redan

The moon had come up in the late evening and now, at one o'clock in the morning, was hanging over Louisbourg. It gave the small party of Englishmen a lighted view of anyone approaching their position from the fort. At the same time, Frenchmen coming from the fort would be staring into the shadows caused by the moon at their back; they would be at a distinct disadvantage.

The English party, eight grenadiers and the two officers, Major Dundonald and Lieutenant Brown, were fanned out in a semi-circle around a man on his knees at the top of the knoll. That man, an engineer named Schmidt, who spoke English with a German accent, had his head down in a little hole he had dug, carefully examining the texture of the soil.

"I hafe vat I need, Herr Major. Dis is a goot platz for our guns. Ve kan leaf now."

Schmidt had spoken in a normal voice. Perhaps the constant barrage of the English guns might drown the sound of his voice but Major Dundonald wanted to take no chances. He motioned to Sergeant Mitchell, who placed his hand over the engineer's mouth and whispered in the man's ear to be quiet.

Surprised by the sergeant's action, Schmidt pulled the hand away and said, angrily, "Vhat are you doink?"

A French voice spoke out of the darkness. There was movement off to the left.

Sergeant Mitchell put his arm around Schmidt's neck and clamped his hand down, tightly, on the engineer's mouth.

Major Dundonald, facing the threat in the further darkness, could hear the scuffling behind him as Schmidt struggled against the pressures on his face and head. Motioning to one of the grenadiers, Dundonald continued to stare into the darkness.

The grenadier crept over to the struggling pair and brought the butt of his musket down, sharply, against the skull of the engineer, who slumped in the sergeant's arms, but not without making a loud groan.

"Let him be!" the major whispered. "Form up! We've got company!"

The English party could see patches of grey in the moonlight. Moving patches of grey! The Cambyse in their white uniforms! How many could there be? Dundonald strained his eyes to get a better look.

Perhaps it was a raiding party ... but that would be bad enough since there's only a single company manning the redan. Dundonald felt sick at heart because he had believed that his boys needed the rest and it was unlikely the Cambyse would be quick to come back to face their guns. *But here they were! The Cambyse were forming up. Shit! There must be a couple of hundred! In a moment, they would begin their advance. With two hundred men, they would overwhelm the redan! His boys put to the bayonet! Well, I'm not going to have it!*

"Grenadiers! Present! Fire!" The left end of the grey line crumpled from the onslaught of English musket balls. "Reload!" Dundonald could see some confusion in the French line. They didn't know where their attackers were.

"Present! Fire!" A rocket from the redan arched into the sky, giving a flickering light to the scene. "Reload!"

A French officer waved his sword in the direction of the

knoll. With precision, half of the Cambyse line of white giants wheeled to the left to defend their flank.

"Present! Fire!" More Frenchmen crumpled to the ground. Another rocket spluttered into the air. There were no holes in the white line; the French Regulars accepted their losses and closed up. They advanced toward the knoll. "Reload!"

At the far end, in front of the redan, there was concentrated musket fire. Dundonald's company was meeting the assault with professionalism. He felt a surge of fierce pride. Yesterday his boys had beaten off a hundred of the French best. Now they would beat off two hundred!

The Cambyse halted.

"Grenadiers! Present!" The French also raised their muskets, sighting on the small band of grenadiers. Dundonald gave the last order of his life. "Fire!" English and French volleys were delivered at the same time.

Numb with pain, Dundonald staggered upright. All of his men were down. Schmidt, waking from his slumber, looked dazedly up at the solitary figure standing in the moonlight. "Was fehlt ihnen?" he asked.[3]

Another rocket faltered into the sky. The French officer gave a command to a section of men who began an advance on the English officer.

Dundonald picked up a musket from one of the fallen. It had been discharged. He dug in the man's pouch and began to load.

Six Cambyse were now close enough to see what he was doing. They stopped. One of them gave him an order.

Dundonald stood with the musket held in both hands across the front of his body. He cast a quick glance in the direction of the redan. His boys were doing well by the sounds of it. Turning back to face the enemy, he smiled. *I remember her name! It was Mary Lodge.* He felt the small hairs at the back of his neck bristle just the way they did when Mary Lodge had told him the stories of Dundonald courage and defiance. He raised his musket. "A Dundonald!" he shouted.[4]

Fortress Louisbourg
July 9, 1758

Madame La Bombardière made her daily procession to the West Gate today. This time her cannon were sighted on the new English battery being constructed. This battery is so much closer to the walls that the Madame could actually see the destruction inflicted by her ball. The crowd cheered.

Prisoners were taken by the Cambyse Regiment. I was allowed to be present during the interrogation. I was surprised to find a fellow engineer packed in with the soldiers. I had him paroled to me. He is a continental gentleman, schooled in Heidelberg, speaking German, French and Italian. Herr Schmidt was leading an engineering work party when guerrillas beset them. He fought his attackers and was the sole officer survivor. As colleagues we have been discussing the soil and drainage problems in this area for providing a good base for the cannon pads.

Regarding my concerns about structural failure in the fortress cannon pads, his suggestion is that perhaps our walls were not given sufficient base to support heavy calibre cannon. Since the walls were commenced before my Director General or I arrived, perhaps there was no chicanery during the construction of the pads.

P

July 11, 1758
Grenadier's Redoubt

"Come over here, Lieutenant Gray!"

General Wolfe was standing at the wall of the Grenadier's Redoubt that gave the best view of the western approaches to the fortress. Impatiently, he motioned the lieutenant to hurry.

"Dammit, Gray! Come see this!"

William hurried to the general's side. As he got closer, he could see the general was in a rage and so he made a great show of staring over the edge of the wall and not looking into the general's mottled face. The first thing he noted was, only the English guns were firing. There was no return fire from the fort.

"It's that she-devil again! See her? The bitch comes to the parapet and exposes herself. It's like a goddamn ritual. The French guns fall silent and ..."

As William watched, a single gun was discharged, the ball traveling the short distance to the new six-gun battery where several English gunners were hurled into the air and the gun they were serving knocked off its carriage. Even over the noise of the continuing English barrage, the French cheers could be heard.

The French resumed their counter barrage. Several more Englishmen died in the new battery.

"We are sitting ducks! They can rain havoc on us from those walls while we peck away at them. We have to bring enough of that wall down to send troops in and take that Bastion." Wolfe handed Gray his eyeglass. "We have some success, as you can see, but it will take us another ten days or two weeks to breach that wall sufficiently."

William could see where part of the Dauphin's Bastion had fallen away into the moat. Through the glass, he could see a man was standing at the edge of the damage and, despite the cannon fire, seemed to be taking measurements! William was about to comment on the man's strange behaviour when the general grabbed him by the arm and turned him round to face him.

"I need an attack on those ships, Gray!" Wolfe continued in a surprisingly mild-mannered voice, "You said you would get it for me. When will it happen?"

William gazed at his feet. He was finding it hard to tell the man that Admiral Boscawen wasn't going to allow an English warship into the harbour for as long as there were hostile French guns on that shore.

In an even quieter tone the general said, "I need something to counter the effect of Madame Bomber. My men are becoming disheartened by her daily performance. We are now close enough to see her. It's always the same. She arrives, talking light-heartedly with the French officers, and walks to the parapet where she stares down at us. She turns and lays aside her little parasol. She sights her guns and delivers death to her audience. When the smoke clears, she is gone, only to return the next day for another performance." General Wolfe cleared his throat. His voice firmer he said, "Speak up man! I need to know what the navy will do!"

"Well, sir, Admiral Boscawen hasn't changed his mind."

General Wolfe moved his lips as if to say something but, changing his mind, clamped his mouth firmly tight

"Captain Rous had meetings with a number of captains seeking their support for a harbour incursion."

General Wolfe waited, unmoving.

"He did receive some support before the Admiral heard about it and ordered Rous on board *Namur* to receive new orders."

"Which were?"

"Any further activity to undermine the admiral's authority and Rous would be transported to England in chains." William smiled. "Cap'n Rous said the admiral was having a fair fit by the time he left him!"

"Your Captain Rous is an undisciplined man."

William could hear the unspoken part. 'And I wouldn't have him in my command for a moment.'

For William's part, the unspoken words were, 'Rous knows better what should be done than inbred, self-opinionated asses who inherit their rank.' Aloud, he asked, "If you want those ships destroyed, my captain has a plan."

"Despite the admiral's wishes?"

William persisted. "The captain believes the same way you do—doing the right thing at the right time overcomes the odds. If you agree ..."

"I couldn't agree." General Wolfe put his hands behind his back and stomped off to the other end of the parapet. He twirled his officer's cane, once, twice, and then walked back to rejoin Gray. "I couldn't agree," he repeated, "but what would be his plan if he decided to carry on with it?"

"Rous has two captains who would follow him into Hades."

"Two? Only two?"

William continued. "Right now, the winds are better for coming out of that harbour than going in. As soon as he has the proper wind, and two hours before the flood tide, he would lead *Squirrel* and *Hawke* ..."

"Only three ships of the line would go?"

Again, William looked down at his boots. He lifted his chin and stared the general in the eyes. "*Sutherland* is a ship of the line, fifty guns, but the other two ships are frigates ..."

"Two frigates and a fourth rate! Gad!" General Wolfe chewed on his lip. He tapped his cane against a stone jutting out of the wall. "It would be suicide!"

William gestured at the gunners in the new gun pit, without saying a word.

"Um. Yes." Wolfe sighed. "How soon might we expect a favourable wind?"

"That's hard to say, but at the moment it's a soldier's wind for anyone coming out of that harbour and we'll have to wait for it to change."

Wolfe smiled. "A soldier's wind? Meaning?"

Gray caught himself smirking so he quickly composed his face. "I didn't mean to be disrespectful, sir, but we call it a soldier's wind when the wind pushes the ship where it is meant to go no matter that a soldier is steering."

"Hah!" Wolfe nodded his head at the lieutenant and turned to walk away. He thought about something and came back several paces. "I want you to make another official request for a harbour attack. I can't be seen to be associated with Rous's scheme."

"Aye, sir. I understand. I will make another formal request."

Shaking his head, the general turned again to leave. "The audacity of it," he said.

"Audacity is worth a couple of broadsides, sir."

If the departing figure heard, it gave no sign.

Fortress Louisbourg
July 13, 1758

There is serious damage to the walls at the Dauphin's Gate. It would be impossible to attempt any repair on the exterior of the walls with the enemy muskets so close. I have devised a buttress that would strengthen the wall from the inside and, in the event the original wall should be breached, the enemy gunners would be faced with another wall, recessed in the fortifications, constructed of timbers. There is no supply of timber in the fort and, now that the fortress is encircled, it is unlikely that we will be able to procure any from outside. My suggestion that certain houses be razed and their timber used for the walls was not well received by the Governor, I am told.

I spent some time composing letters and reports to be taken to France. *L'Arethuse* will depart as soon as possible, the winds being very favourable for such an enterprise. The ship's Purser, Guy Leblanc, will take charge of my letters and ensure their delivery to my mother and sister.

My paroled colleague, Herr Schmidt, returned from his evening constitutional and informed me there is a great deal of activity at the waterfront. He reflects the very best of his engineering background so I was not surprised that he produced a list of the ships to discuss with me upon his return.

(The notations after each name are mine.)

L'Apollon (54 guns)
La Chèvre (22 guns)
La Fidèle (26 guns)
La Biche (24 guns) and
La Ville de Saint Malo (transport)[5]

I must walk Rue d'Orléans to see what those ships' captains are doing. Perhaps they are finally implementing my berthing plan.

Poilly

July 15, 1758
H.M.S. Sutherland

"What a rascal!"

Captain Rous had just received word that a French ship had passed through the entire English fleet during the night. "Remember, last night was foggy and the Bay full of hostile ships and still the little bugger cleared the harbour as if it were a fishing trip in peacetime." He chortled. "And there won't be much said about the escape in his lordship's report to the Admiralty. No, sirree, there won't!" Rous stamped his feet as he stood at the transom, staring out at the morning mists. Continuing to gaze at the water, Rous ordered his first officer and William Gray to take the two seats in the captain's cabin.

William glanced at First Officer Adams to see which of them would have the temerity to sit in the captain's chair.

Rous looked back over his shoulder. "Sit down, sit down. We have some plannin' to do." He continued with his original thoughts. "No, there won't be much said in the official reports."

Obviously, the captain wanted the question asked so William asked, "Why is that, sir?"

Just as obviously, Rous was enjoying himself. "The Frenchman passed within two leagues of Admiral Sir Charles Hardy's flagship ..."

"The *Royal William* ..."

"Yes, and even closer to the old man himself on *Namur*. If our dear Admiral of the Blue, Commander in Chief of his Majesty's Ships in North America, had rolled over in his sumptuous bed, he could have waved bye-bye to the Frenchie as he set sail for home."

"Ships were sent after him?" Adams had decided to avoid the captain's chair.

William shrugged and sat down in the captain's chair.

"Yes." Rous rubbed his hands together as if to take the morning chill off his hands. "*Northumberland* and *Vanguard;* but they'll never catch him. They'll be back in a few days. Captain Colville will give it up first. He's the better seaman and probably knew it was futile when he got the admiral's order, but dear old Captain Mantle always allows his stubbornness to overcome any sense of seamanship he might posses. Yes, we'll see *Vanguard* limp back here in about a week with tales of rough seas, pirates and sea monsters." Captain Rous picked up the campaign stool and drew it up close to the other two officers. "Like I said, we got some plannin' to do."

July 15,1758
The Forest near
North East Harbour

Reine Cameron held her breath. It was difficult to listen for movement in the night forest what with all the noise coming from the Acadian and Indian campsite. The fact that her heart was pounding and her breath unsteady in anticipation of being with her husband further hampered her. Nothing was going to stop her from stealing a few moments with her Robert but, still, she had to be careful.

Satisfied that she was alone, she continued through the forest toward the picket area assigned to Robert Cameron. *Typical,* she thought. *Boishebert, the leader of the French Irregulars, and his cronies were drinking the remains of the bière d'épinette the inhabitants of the village of Mire had given them, not too willingly, while Robert Cameron, known as Carrot Top, the English Turncoat, was on guard duty, serving as a tripwire in the unlikely case the English should send a probe in this direction.*

Reine Cameron halted again. *Was there someone behind her, in the pines?* She dropped to one knee and closed her eyes. Concentrating, thinking she had heard a small sound down the path she had just travelled, she opened her eyes as wide as possible. She stared into the darkness, not directly at the place she thought she had heard something but slightly to the right and then off to the left, letting her peripheral vision work its night magic. Nothing.

She decided to wait, motionless, to find out what had made the sound. Ears and eyes acutely fixed on the pines, she settled back on her haunches. She thought, *there shouldn't be anyone in the camp interested in the small man with the stinky leather jerkin and leggings even if he chose to go into the woods when there was bière to be had.* As far as everyone in the camp was concerned, she was the smelly Acadian, Stinky Claude, who had joined Boishebert's raiding party the third day of his recruiting tour on Île Saint Jean. Recruiting? Hah! Her Robert, as a British deserter, had had no choice but to join the war party or be handed over to the Mi'kmaq who made up over half of the two hundred-man force.

As soon as Boishebert and his war party had moved on to the next Acadian hamlet, Reine had begged leggings and jerkin from one of the wives whose husband had also been 'volunteered.' Using the last of her silver coin from her bread-making at Grand Pré, she bought an old musket and knife. Donning the leathers, cutting her hair and binding her breasts had turned her into a young man. Adding cow dung to the ensemble had ensured that she was always assigned the furthermost sentry post and that she ate and slept alone. In the two and one half months she had travelled with the war party, her disguise had not been questioned. In that same period, she had not been alone with her husband.

Tomorrow, they would do battle with the English at Louisbourg.

Tonight, she would be with her man.

Was there movement in the pines? Reine knew that, by this time, even the most cautious animal would have shown itself. Only when the hunted was a man would the quarry wait endlessly until the hunter had moved. Just a few minutes more and, if there wasn't an animal, she must assume the thing on her trail was a man. *Ah! Movement!* She saw the flash of silver feathers, *probably an owl.* She smiled a smile of relief. Reine crossed herself. After a brief prayer, she rose and resumed her silent passage through the forest.

Getting away from the camp without drawing attention to herself had not been easy, but searching out her husband's position in the dark forest she knew would be a daunting task. She stopped to catch a breath. Standing there, she had the sense that she was not alone, that someone was watching her in the darkness. Robert must be waiting to see who she was.

"Row-bear!" she whispered. "C'est moi, cheri!" There was no answer.

Moving along about thirty paces, she tried again, only this time she spoke in a normal voice. She waited for an answer. The feeling that she was not alone grew more intense. Perhaps she had lived in villages too long and had lost her forest skills. For the very first time she doubted herself and her ability to find Robert.

* * *

Beau Soleil, the Acadian who had been brought up Mi'kmaq, watched the stinky little Acadian's growing frustration. He continued to follow, carefully, as Puant Claude moved closer to where Beau Soleil as second-in-command of the French Irregulars knew a sentry post should be.

Five minutes and three hundred metres later, the sentry stepped out of the trees with his musket at the ready. He challenged the little man.

Beau Soleil could not hear the exchange of words. He was surprised when the two figures embraced. Reattaching his hawk's feathers that he had used to simulate the flight of an owl to his belt, Beau Soleil settled down to watch developments.

* * *

"You can't build a fire, sweetheart."

"You will be too cold, Reine. I'll build a small fire in this copse. I don't expect any English visitors. Boisehebert sent me out here just to get rid of me for the night."

Reine helped her man gather some wood. "More bière for him." She brought an armful of dry twigs to the spot Robert had chosen for his fire. "We will need water."

"I have water, Reine." He kissed her passionately, his hands moving over her body.

"If I get cleaned for you, Row-bear, where will I find more cow dung for my disguise?" She was being coy, now.

Robert slid the jerkin and undershirt over her head. In the

flickering light of the very small fire, he unwound the wraps that confined her breasts. He fondled one of them as he worked at the tie at the top of the leggings.

"No, Row-bear. I must be clean for you. Get me the water. I would wash before ..."

He had found the end of the tie and the leggings fell to her ankles. "Oh God! You are so beautiful!"

* * *

Beau Soleil could now see, for the first time, that the smelly little Acadian was a white woman and the sentry was the English Turncoat!

He did not often allow himself to be surprised; to that end, he had followed the little Acadian out of the camp when he saw him leave. "I smelled cow dung," he said to himself. He didn't allow a smile to appear on his face, even in the dark of the forest where there was no one to see. "But I smelled woman, too." He was pleased with himself.

The Englishman was washing the woman's face and shoulders, kissing her as he cleaned each erotic spot; mouth, eyes, nape of the neck, throat ...

* * *

Beau Soleil half rose from his vantage place and then thought better of it. The immediate satisfaction of killing the Turncoat, smearing Englishman's blood over the white woman's belly and mounting her, would leave him open to possible surprise if there were other conspirators involved in this deception. He observed that the woman was lying on her back, never taking her eyes off the man as he stripped off his clothes. Beau Soleil noted that the man's penis was erect and of reasonable size for an Englishman.

Quietly, he withdrew. It would be better if he observed them for a few days to discover what they were after .... British spies? He would place the woman next to him during the coming battle.

He glanced back as he withdrew to the camp. The fire was low and the man and woman were still entwined. The woman was encouraging the man to greater haste with her hands pushing hard on the small of his back. This time Beau Soleil allowed himself to smile. He would look forward to mounting her and then killing her.

July 16, 1758
Before Dawn
North East Harbour

As far as Robert Cameron was concerned, the sun seemed to be a long time coming this morning. He fidgeted. *I haven't been trained for this type of warfare, no, indeed, and I don't have the patience for it.* His training had been as a foot soldier on a formal parade square in England. His battle experience? Former Private Robert Cameron grimaced. Hiding behind the walls of the fort at Dartmouth as the settlers were massacred. He was flogged for his efforts that night. He did manage to save that naval officer's life. *What was his name? His name was …*

He lifted his head a little to make sure he was still well positioned. He was.

Gray. William Gray was his name. Was he a lieutenant? No matter, there was no reward for saving an officer's life; just a flogging for trying to lead a sally from the blockhouse to rescue the settlers. Officers do the leading. Soldiers do as they are told, without question.

It was the flogging that decided it for him. As soon as he could, he had deserted.

Oh, yes! He had some other battle experience. There was that time he helped the French garrison of Beauséjour defend the bridge. Not much of an action. The English took the bridge with little trouble.

The birdcall. Get ready!

He waited, his musket ready, his legs bunched under him ready to spring forward.

Today, he was in the fore of an attack on a small English post at the head of North East Harbour.[6] Now that he had thought about it, he supposed he could include the time he rescued those three farmers near Annapolis Royal as battle experience. He shook his head. It hadn't been necessary for the New England sergeant to be shot. He really didn't understand why he had meddled in the Indian business of taking scalps. One of the poor colonial buggers had already been done by the time he involved himself. He hadn't gained anything by it. He had certainly earned Beau Soleil's enmity. He supposed that was why he was in the fore of this, their first attack.

He was fidgeting again. *What was the hold-up?* Cameron lifted his head but could see no movement. He ducked down and soon resumed his train of thought.

Beau Soleil. Now there was a piece of merchandise! He was more Indian than the natural-born ones. More mean than the most callous warriors. Beau Soleil would never let it be that I had questioned his leadership at Annapolis Royal.

It's getting light. What's the delay? If we don't move off soon, we will be approaching the earthwork defences in full daylight.

An English sentry called the alarm. A musket fired. Robert Cameron rose up and advanced on the English position.

July 16, 1758
Grenadier's Redoubt

"Come in, Jenkins." General Wolfe was seated on a campaign stool while a steward finished shaving him. "What do you have for me so early in the morning?" The general dismissed the steward. Wiping his face and neck with a small towel he said, "It's all right, my man. I will dress myself if my gear is laid out."

The man nodded his head and went out through the flap in the tent.

Wolfe slipped on his shirt.

Jenkins marvelled that the officer was so slight. His chest wasn't the least manly and, if anything, he was rather stoop-shouldered. "It is a verbal message, sir." Jenkins put his head back as if he were retrieving the message from the back of his eyeballs. "About an hour before dawn, a small post of ours at the head of the North East Harbour was assaulted by about one hundred French and Indians without affecting anything, the post being fortified and the men alert."

"No casualties?"

"The enemy had casualties but we had none, sir."

"Jolly good!" He fussed with the buttons of his tunic before he said any more.

Jenkins waited.

The general pushed through the flap of the tent. "You know, Jenkins, when an operation doesn't go the way you plan, it sets up a frame of mind." He grinned at the grenadier who had followed him outside. "I like it when the other fellow has his mind set for him by circumstances." He walked briskly along the catwalk into the redoubt itself, Jenkins still following. He jumped up on the parapet, looking over the wall at the landscape below. He examined it for several minutes and then pointed. "There's a little bridge down there with a French name I can't pronounce; Bonnie-chew-lice." He laughed.[7] "They have a small post there, just like ours, the one they attacked this morning at North East Harbour." He picked at something between his teeth. Finding a piece of food on his fingernail, he examined it and then put it back in his mouth. "Now, you run along to the adjutant of the light infantry and tell them I will want a small party to go with me down to that bridge. Also, tell the grenadiers I need twenty brawny chaps to follow us over to the other side."

Jenkins was about to leave when the general motioned him to wait.

"In for a penny, in for a pound, eh, Jenkins?" Wolfe turned and began to walk back to his tent. "Don't bother with the light infantry or the grenadiers. Instead, call my staff officers, Jenkins. Round then up and have them report to me by three."

"Yes sir."

* * *

In the evening, General Wolfe ordered a small party of light infantry against the bridge in front of Grenadier's Redoubt. There might have been some resistance from the French post, but a second light infantry force, which crossed the small stream several hundred yards further down, flanked them.

The French knew they were outflanked and retired, quickly, into the fortress.

Even before the gates had closed, General Wolfe and his personal escort of twenty grenadiers crossed the bridge.

Using a prearranged signal, Wolfe ordered a company of grenadiers across the bridge to take up defensive positions along with the light infantry.

"Jenkins! Where are you, man?"

"I'm here, sir!" he answered but he was unable to pass through the grenadiers' defensive ring around the general.

Wolfe stepped through the grenadiers and bent his head close to Jenkins's so that the runner was sure to hear. "There are two more companies of grenadiers in readiness. Have them join me here. I will need a third company. Go to the redoubt and have them form up and come as quickly as possible. By that time, I should be on that little crest over there, about 250 yards from the gate. Hurry on, now. It will get hot here."

Jenkins had to wait at the bridge as the grenadiers crossed. It was almost dark but he could see the twenty grenadiers moving toward the hill some 250 yards from the walls of the fort. Grape shot started to fly. He could hear the whiz of musket balls. "The general was right," Jenkins said to himself as he trotted up the incline to the redoubt. "It's going to get hot around here."

When Jenkins returned in the fore of a company of grenadiers from the redoubt, he saw that most of the soldiers with Wolfe were digging trenches. He went, immediately, to the general's side.

"Good man, Jenkins. You brought my grenadiers. Wait here but a moment. I have more for you to do."

The officer in charge of the newly arrived grenadiers reported to the general, who knew him by name, but Jenkins couldn't hear because of the number of musket balls passing by his head at that moment.

"… dig a trench from the bush to where you see those light infantry standing. By morning light, we must have cover here." He returned to Jenkins.

"I want to order up as many Highland companies as are available. Struthers. Find Struthers and tell him to bring up two ... no! Tell Struthers to bring up three companies. He put his hand on Jenkins's shoulder. "If you ever ran before, fly now, Jenkins! If we can hold here, it is the end of Louisbourg!"

In the darkness, Jenkins could see the shiny eyes, the high flush on the general's face. *Wolfe is enjoying himself!*

Another storm of grape shot. The officer of the newly arrived grenadiers fell in a crumpled heap as if he had lost all the bones in his body. Jenkins stepped over him. As he ran, he sent little messages out all over his body to see if he were still all right—he seemed to be in one piece. When he reached the Highlanders, he wasn't breathing hard from his uphill run and had no difficulty passing the orders to the colonel. He stood out of the way and watched as the colonel rapidly put his companies on the move. While drinking some water at the commissary tent, Jenkins wondered at his own calmness. Finished with the water, he went behind the tent and relieved himself. Jenkins studied his hands. They were steady as ever. He realized that he was looking forward to returning to the general, to be standing by his side, to be part of this great endeavour.

A cannonball made its passage overhead. Jenkins buttoned up his pants and pushed his way to the front of the redoubt but there wasn't room for him to pass down the side of Redoubt Hill; three companies of formed-up Highlanders, maintaining contact section by section, were efficiently moving to where the general needed them. Jenkins waited. What was it the general had said? 'If we can hold here, it is the end of Louisbourg.' He was strangely excited and couldn't wait for the Highlanders to get out of the way so he could get to where it was hot—where he was needed.

Fortress Louisbourg
July 16, 1748

It is not widely known in the town or garrison, but the harbour mouth is effectively sealed off. The ships mentioned in my last entry were emptied, their masts removed and the ships towed to the narrows. As soon as the *L'Arethuse* had passed on her way to the open sea, they were sunk. It is unlikely the English will find the hulks until, or if, they attempt to attack the harbour with their ships. I suppose it is good tactics but I am sorry to think of *La Biche* rotting on the bottom of the harbour. She was beautifully constructed.

There is the other side to that same coin; the English are prevented from entering the harbour, that is true, but it also means that what is left of our squadron is bottled up in Louisbourg Harbour. Huddled as they are as close to the town wall as possible, the ships have been shielded with cordage and bales of tobacco. (There is plenty of tobacco available because of the earlier successes of French privateers.) As of this morning, however, larger calibre guns have been inflicting extensive damage to their rigging. The hulls have received a prodigious number of shots. The ships' crews have been ordered ashore and the ships' armaments will be removed during the night when the populace will not be witness. Since the ships of the squadron are the most visible symbol of French power and prestige, it would not do for the citizens to be aware that they will soon be disarmed.

Poilly

July 18, 1758
Grenadier's Redoubt

"I took some of the chill off the water, sir." Wolfe's manservant laid out a fresh uniform as the general doused his head and shoulders with the water from a small basin. "Bad night, sir?"

Busy scrubbing his chest and arms with a dry towel, Wolfe didn't respond.

The man knew better than to speak again until the officer had made his reply. If he didn't reply, then there would be no more conversation.

Wolfe tossed the towel at the man who deftly caught it and, folding it very carefully, put it on the top of a pile of dirty clothes he was collecting. "We lost ten men and one officer. Thirty men wounded, most of them Highlanders." He allowed the man to help him get dressed. "Do you know what that little hill is called?"

"I'm afraid I do not, sir."

"The French call it 'Gallows Hill.'" Wolfe patted his sparse hair into place with his hands while looking into a steel mirror the man was holding. "Well, in a day or two, Gallows Hill will be bristling with English mortar and cannon and they will make the end of Louisbourg. We will hang Louisbourg from Gallows Hill. Heh, heh." Wolfe liked his own jokes but didn't appreciate them from others.

"What are the French doing about it? Have they attacked, sir?"

"No. I don't think they wanted to face our ladies from hell."

"What, sir? I mean, I beg your pardon, sir."

"They didn't want to fight the Highlanders. They are called the ladies from hell because of their kilts."

"Yes, sir." The man gathered up the soiled clothing. "Is that all, sir?"

"Send Jenkins in."

Grenadier Jenkins was at the flap of the tent before the manservant passed through it.

"You wanted me, sir?"

"You're never far away, are you, Jenkins? Tell the adjutant to arrange for the relief of those Highlanders."

"Yes, sir."

"Oh, and have you seen the naval liaison officer around this morning?

"He's been waiting outside, sir."

Wolfe pushed through the flap and stepped out into the early morning sun. He beckoned Lieutenant Gray to accompany him as he walked to the parapet overlooking the battlefield. "You see what my Highlanders have done." He pointed. "Two trenches, a traverse and the solid beginnings of a redoubt over there, at the far side."

"That's amazing, sir." William had something to say and he tried to start. "I must tell you …"

"That little hill. Do you know what it is called?"

"No, sir, I don't. But I would like ..."

"It's called Gallows Hill. The day after tomorrow, when we install the mortars, we are going to hang Louisbourg from ..."

"Your pardon, sir, but the French have blocked the entrance to the harbour."

"Yes. We found out from a French deserter. I meant to tell you first thing, but I was otherwise occupied. The ships in the harbour haven't been much of a bother this last while, so I haven't been too concerned about them." Wolfe frowned. "Actually, that's not true. If we could get at those ships and destroy them, burn them, it would rip the fight out of the French. They would lose heart."

"That's what Captain Rous thinks, too. When he found out he sent ..."

"But they haven't been what's been annoying me. It's that damn woman. She comes every day. She sights and fires three cannon now. It's always the same time, always the same cannon. We are so close to the walls now, she can't miss!"

William was thoughtful.

"What's the matter, lieutenant? What are you thinking?"

"If it's the same place every day and at the same time, you could range in some cannon and destroy her."

"My gunners have thought of that." Wolfe smiled at the naval officer. "I had to give orders, very discreetly, that no attempt was to be made on her life. When she appears, our men who are in her sights are told to seek cover. They wait for the three shots and then resume their duties."

As it dawned on him, William said, "If we killed her, she would become the martyr ..."

"Like a Joan of Arc. It would cost a thousand lives as the garrison—and probably the entire town—fought us to the death in her memory."

"Shit!" William cast a quick look at the general to see if he reacted to such an inappropriate remark from a junior officer in the presence of the commander. He was relieved when he saw that the general was continuing with the conversation as if he hadn't heard it, or hadn't minded it.

"That's why I would still like to see those ships destroyed. The Madame gives them heart. Sinking the ships might destroy the garrison's morale, once and for all."

"Captain Rous sent me out in the cutter to see if the entrance was completely sealed. It isn't. I did a careful survey and reported back to him that there was enough room for even *H.M.S. Namur* to enter the harbour."

General Wolfe looked around from side to side to make sure no one was close enough to overhear him. "Is he still going to proceed with his three-ship attack?"

"No, sir. With the obstacles in the harbour entrance, there is no way he could make a swift approach. There can be no attack."

Wolfe said nothing.

"I'm sorry, sir."

They stood there in silence, watching a company of Highlanders file by.

"Well done, my lads!" The general called out to several of the men by name as they passed. "Because of your efforts, we will hang Louisbourg from Gallows Hill."

The men cheered.

When they were alone again, General Wolfe commented, "If the French ships have been a thorn in our side, that French woman has been a sword thrust to our heart."

William was surprised. The man who would be known as the Conqueror of Louisbourg, the Hero of Cormorant Cove, was disheartened. He didn't know what to say.

Disheartened, perhaps, but not for long. "Come let me show you my babies." Wolfe walked briskly to the reverse side of the hill. There, lined up in neat rows, were guns. He put his hand on the first. "This is my favourite. She's an eighteen inch mortar; we have two of them." He grinned like a schoolboy in an apple orchard when the farmer has gone to church. "I have one thirteen inch," he walked by it indicating another row, "these are all eight inch mortars, handy little devils, but this one and this one," he touched first one and then the other, "are thirty-two pound cannon!"

"Gad, sir! Those are magnificent! We should be able to hit Quebec from here with those two."

"We'll be able to hit anything, anywhere in Fortress Louisbourg."

To William, the thought of the amount of destruction that could be delivered by the huge, black cannon was frightening. He was just going to say so when the general asked, "Have you had breakfast?"

"No, sir, I haven't."

"Then we had better go get some while it's still hot."

William smiled a discreet smile because there would always be hot food ready for the general and he knew how—Jenkins would run ahead to give warning to the cooks.

July 21, 1758
H.M.S. Sutherland
Entrance to Louisbourg Harbour

It was early afternoon and *Sutherland* was positioned near the mouth of the harbour at the orders of Commodore Durell. Small boats from *Sutherland* had been deployed most of the morning taking soundings so that the charts of the vessels of the English fleet could be amended to show the location of the French wrecks.

Gray, Adams and the ship's doctor, Proctor, were watching as the last of the boats returned to *Sutherland*.

"Hazardous work," the doctor commented. "I looked at the battle plan when I learned we were coming in here. I saw it was estimated that there were over thirty forty-two-pound cannon at that battery." He pointed at the stone bastion that was planted hard against the mouth of the harbour. "What's it called, again?"

"The Grand Battery," Adams answered.

Proctor shook his head from side to side. "It gives me the shivers, sitting here, knowing that all of that iron is in there. It probably wouldn't take much to motivate a few Frenchmen to put a hole in this old tub."

"From where we are, it's not a good shot; we're probably out of range. Besides, they know what we are doing and we're not much of a threat." Adams took the eyeglass and studied the tower of the battery. "They are extremely short of powder and ball." He swung his glass to study the far, west end of the harbour. "Now, that's where the threat is. Any ammunition the French have will be used against Wolfe's gunners in front of Dauphin Gate."

"Then why doesn't *Sutherland* deliver a broadside or two at the Grand Battery? If they don't have ..."

"We are supposed to gather information about the wrecks." Adams swung his glass back toward the town. "If we started a duel with that battery, we'd lose. But you're right. I'll breathe easier when we get the hell out of here." He handed the eyeglass to Gray. Walking to the far side of the ship where the boats were being hoisted in he called out, "Buffer! How much longer?"

"Ten minutes, sir."

William continued studying Louisbourg. "Look at the small fires in the town. There isn't a part of the fortress that can't be reached by the new guns at Gallows Hill." William gave the glass back to Adams. "Do you know what General Wolfe calls his thirty-two pound cannons?"

Proctor grinned as he said, "Big?"

"You're really funny, Doctor Proctor. He calls them his babies."

William glanced at Lieutenant Adams, who had drawn a sharp breath.

"Marine! Go below and ask the captain if I may see our copy of the battle plan. Tell him one of the ships is burning in the harbour."

"Which one do you think it is?"

"I don't know. It's a sixty-four, I think."

William was dying for a look, but Adams wasn't letting go of the glass.

"That would make it *Bienfaisant*. The rest of the ships are seventy-fours."

"It's burning on her poop. Gad! There goes her mizzen-mast, up in flames."

"Captain on deck!"

Rous acknowledged the three officers and almost ran to the bulwark. Passing William, he handed him the battle plan. Even without the glass, he identified the burning ship. "She's a 64, my hearties. She would be the *Celèbre*." Pointing at Gray he said, "Check the plan. Second outboard of the sea wall, last to the east."[8]

"*Celèbre*, sir, a 64."

"The army gunners are pouring it into her!"

"They cut her lines." Rous was putting himself in the *Celèbre* captain's shoes. "Now, with the crew working her, they should be able to move to deeper water and flood her. That way they'll save the hull."

Adams, still holding the glass, said quietly, "There's no one working the sheets. She's drifting against the next ship …"

William consulted the battle plan. "*Entreprenant*."

Most of *Sutherland's* crew were now watching the spectacle, some of them from the rigging.

Both ships were now burning, giving off a tall, black pillar of smoke.

"Oakum and pitch," someone said. "They must have a lot of ship repair supplies on their decks."

Small boats were leaving the pier, the men rowing as fast as they could to the burning ships or to the other seventy-fours.

"The crews," Rous said, shaking his head from side to side in disbelief. "They were ashore."

The *Sutherland* ship's company gave a collective gasp as the first of the boats was blown out of the water by the English gunners; then another and another.

"Just like shooting sitting ducks."

The English gunners switched targets and concentrated on the warship at anchor.

"Now they want *Capricieux*."

"They don't have to bother." Rous pointed. "See! The hot draft from the burning ships is carrying cinders and sparks into her rigging." There was some emotion in the captain's voice. It was hard for seamen to watch beautiful ships die this way,— even enemy ships.

Several moments later, there was a huge explosion.

The *Sutherland* crew ducked down, concerned that they might be hit with something even at this distance. When they felt it was safe to look back again, *Capricieux* was aflame. What was left of *Celèbre* was low in the water, giving off a dense, black smoke.

"She must have had some powder on board ..."

Entreprenant exploded, spewing flaming debris into the town. *Celèbre* and what was left of any of the boats in the harbour disappeared below the wave that also broke against the sea wall and the other two ships, *Prudent* and *Bienfaisant*. Their crews had managed to swing their ships clear, out of the danger zone.

"They will live to fight another day." Captain Rous was scanning the shore. "Beat to quarters, Mister Adams!" He studied the Grand Battery, closely. "Prepare to raise the anchor! Move lively now!" Rous walked the few paces so he could have an unobstructed view of the North East Battery, whose 24 pounders also commanded the harbour entrance. "Raise the anchor! Set the uppers!"

The noise of scurrying feet and the pock, pock of the capstan couldn't hide the sounds of wedges being set on the heavy guns of the Grand Battery.

Adams said, in a quiet voice, "They must be some pissed at losing their ships like that! They're going to try for us, even at this range."

Sutherland was hauled toward her anchor, bringing her slightly closer to the Grand Battery where two guns were now run out.

"Straight up and down!" the sailor in charge of the anchor windlass called out, meaning that all the available anchor cable had been pulled in and the ship was now directly over the anchor.

The Buffer repeated it to the quarterdeck. "Taking the strain on the anchor, sir."

"Anchor clear and rising!"

"We are clear, sir."

Rous snapped his head toward the sailing master. "Move us out of here, Mister!"

"Aye, sir."

The outgoing tide and the off-shore breeze pushed against *Sutherland's* bow, turning her toward the passage to the sea; turning, turning ...

"Set the lowers, Mister!"

A puff of smoke appeared on the face of the Grand Battery. The men of *Sutherland* held their breath. They waited. The ball was a long time coming.

Lieutenant Adams laughed. "They charged their cannon but didn't want to waste a ball at this distance. Just wanted to scare us!"

Whumfph! A huge spout of water raised in the narrows some ten yards astern, where forty-two pounds of iron completed its long journey.

Boom! The hollow sound of the cannon echoed and re-echoed in the confined space.

Most of the ship's company had been looking at the Grand Battery so they saw the second and third puffs of smoke.

"Starboard the helm! Sailing Master, get more men on the sheets! We will have to be quick." There wasn't much room, but the captain was moving *Sutherland* out of the channel toward the opposite shore.

"Steady!" In a conversational tone the captain said, "Ya see, Lieutenant Adams,"—Captain Rous didn't seem the least bit perturbed with the gunfire and the closeness of the shallow water—"they don't think our charts are accurate enough for us to leave the channel so they will have placed their next shots just four boat lengths ahead of their last one, one on the starboard side of the channel and one on the larboard."

"Beggin' your pardon sir, but it's true! Our charts aren't very good!"

Rous continued as if he hadn't heard his first officer, "Meanwhile, we'll dogleg to the left."

The first ball plunged into the water on the right side of the channel about twenty yards ahead. The *Sutherland* could feel the force of the projectile as it impacted.

"... And if the Frenchmen are good gunners, both shots should rile the water where we might have been. One for the hull ..."

The second ball thundered into the water not ten feet from the bow. *Sutherland* bucked and shifted as if she had been hit.

"… and one for the riggin'. Larboard the helm! Send a man below to check our hull! Move lively on the sheets!" Rous took a long look at the Battery. "The second gunner wasn't as precise as the first. He was off his mark and so we might have some underwater damage from his shot." Rous continued to watch the Battery.

"Sir! We are mid-channel. Should we resume passage down the channel?"

Rous kept his eyes on the Battery.

"Aren't we out of range, sir? Even of forty-two pounders?" Adams cast an anxious glance at the approaching shallow waters.

Rous gave a snort, like a laugh, when there was a puff of smoke and a cherry-red explosion at the Grand Battery.

"Helmsman, steady. First Officer, take her down the middle of the channel."

"Aye, sir."

A second and third explosion could be seen by anyone who was looking, the sounds of the first explosion just reaching *Sutherland.*

Captain Rous gave his officers a smile. "General Wolfe sinkin' them ships must have got that Grand Battery feller right some mad. He'd been double charging his guns, and then he tried a triple charge. Really wanted to reach us and take a piece out of this old girl, but his gun failed him."

A voice from the ship's hold reported, "All secure below! No sign of damage."

"Right!" Rous looked at the sky and forward to the Bay. He nodded to his officers. "I'll be in my cabin, if you need me, gentlemen."[9]

Lieutenant Gray took a step or two and said, "Your pardon, sir, but might I have a word …"

"Yes, William. What is it?" Captain Rous, for the first time in months, held his hand out for the eyeglass. While William spoke to him, he studied the Grand Battery, where smoke was still pouring out of a gun port.

"Sir, General Wolfe can now reach anywhere in Louisbourg with his guns. There are only two ships left in the harbour.

Rather than have the general destroy them, I have a plan where we might take them in prize."

Rous put the glass down. "Take them in prize, you say! How's that? Admiral Boscawen won't let an English ship enter that harbour until the cannon are silenced. You know that."

William could tell by Rous's voice that he was interested. "We saw today that the French ships are not manned with a full crew. It probably wouldn't take much. A little surprise …"

"A lot of luck." Rous rubbed his chin. "But this is different; those Froggie ships are vulnerable. They would be …"

"Sitting ducks," they both said at the same time.

The captain thought for a moment. He shook his head, "We'd never get Admiral Boscawen's approval."

"Your pardon sir! Commodore Durell is always interested in prize money and he is our Division Commander. He could approve an attack on the harbour."

"We couldn't call it an attack on the harbour because of the admiral. We'd have to say …"

"A night operation, sir."

"That's the ticket! A night operation against the two remaining unmanned ships! It wouldn't be an attack on the harbour."

"Not at all, sir."

"Make it so. You draft a warning order, William." Rous grinned. "Check the fleet roster to find two junior captains … we would need at least two of them to lead this … expedition." He smiled at the word, "Yes, expedition. We'll use the word, expedition, William."

Captain Rous paused before descending to his cabin. He chuckled as he lifted the latch on the companionway door. "Those two junior captains … they must not be seen as friends of mine."

After the door closed, William said, "That shouldn't be at all difficult."

Fortress Louisbourg
July 22, 1758

Much has gone amiss since my last entry.

In the early afternoon of the 21st, a lucky British shot struck the poop of the *Celèbre* causing it to catch fire. As we watched, horrified, the fire spread and a great column of black smoke rose high above the harbour. Then the burning craft swung toward *L'Entreprenant*, which also caught fire.

Flames spread to the *Capricieux*. As boats put out from the shore, the British poured their heaviest fire on the three ships and the boats trying to reach them. The horror of this day was increased when the loaded guns of the ships began exploding from the intense heat. These explosions had a telling effect on the ships, on the boats, and on the town itself.

We have had a lot of people killed because our ships were not lined up according to my plan. I don't understand why this was not done.

Our bad luck continued today (July 22nd).

The town is undergoing fire from twelve encircling batteries and there is not a spot within the walls safe from the storm. A bomb fell on the barracks and a blaze demolished a great portion. There was so much confusion we had no success in containing the fires. During the fire, the English continued a heavy bombardment, giving us as many dead as wounded. I pray that the fire may serve as a valid excuse for our great inefficiency in the repairing of our parapets.[10]

The Queen's Bastion has a breach in it but not serious enough, as yet, for the English to attempt an assault.

Poilly

July 24, 1758
Grenadier's Redoubt

Lieutenant William Gray, naval liaison officer for General Wolfe, had been explaining the plan for capturing the remaining French warships.

Wolfe interrupted him. "The plan sounds simple enough, Lieutenant. What do you want from me?"

William swallowed, visibly. He cleared his throat. "Don't sink the ships before we get a chance to capture them." He vigorously rubbed his chin and nose. "What I mean, sir, you said you wanted to sink those ships to destroy the French morale but ..."

Wolfe, keeping his head bowed so it didn't touch the slanted ceiling of the tent, moved over to where a small table was standing close to the tent wall.

"... but we would like a chance at capturing them. We'll do it right away. Tomorrow night, sir, if you would give us the chance."

"Come over here, Lieutenant." General Wolfe put a small, well-cared-for finger on the position that William knew to be the Redoubt. He moved his finger toward the Western Gate of the fortress. "Last night, two hundred and fifty volunteers built a new battery right here. The gunners will move up four guns tonight." He shifted his finger. "Tonight, those same two hundred and fifty men will build a five gun battery, here, to the left. With the addition of those nine cannon, Louisbourg will fall. We should be able to storm, either here," he pointed to the Dauphin's Gate, "or here," and this time he indicated the Cavalier.

The lieutenant said nothing, his plans for capturing the French warships fading with each point made by the general.

It was silent in the tent for the next several moments. Both men could hear the continuous roar of the English guns near at hand with the occasional response from the fortress.

Wolfe smiled. "They don't have many working guns, perhaps nine or ten. Three of them are the ones that damned woman uses each day."

"We still leave her alone, sir?"

He shook his head, ruefully, from side to side. "It would be foolhardy to interfere with her theatrics." He sighed. "Anyway, she will soon have nothing to shoot at us. They are so low on ammunition that they are digging out our cannonballs and throwing them back at us." He snorted a sort of laugh. He indicated the campstool for Gray to sit. Wolfe sat on the edge of the table. "Like some tea?"

"Why, yes, sir. That would be nice."

"Jenkins!"

From the other side of the tent flap Jenkins replied, "Yes, sir. Two tea."

"I'm glad you saved that man's life." He hurried on with his thoughts. "With all the new guns positioned, I could sink those ships at any time, except for one thing; the French are using them as prison ships. Thirty-five or forty of my boys are locked up in them."

"How did you find out?"

"They paraded the boys to the ships in the middle of the day. Our spies reported it yesterday."

"Very clever. They know we won't shoot on our men and they have gun ships in the harbour."

"No, they moved all the cannon off them or, at least, they are not shooting the ships' cannons if they're still there. *Prudent* and *Bienfaisant* aren't part of the French cannonade; they are just prison ships."

Jenkins cleared his throat as he pushed his way into the tent carrying a tray with a silver teapot and a brown honey jar.

General Wolfe moved so the grenadier could place the tray on the table.

"Sorry, sir. I know you like cream but the goat died."

"That's fine, Grenadier. We'll look after it. Thank you."

General Wolfe poured the tea and offered the naval officer some honey.

Lieutenant Gray declined. He sipped his tea, waiting for whatever the general had to say.

"If you captured the ships, I would have the best of both worlds. I believe French morale will nosedive when they see their pretty little ships in English hands. They might even sur-render the fortress and save us a bloody assault." He sipped his tea. "And my boys would be released from the prison ships before any harm that might befall them during such an assault." General Wolfe stood up. "I agree to give you one night. We will not use rockets or heated shot so as not cause new fires that might cast a light upon your attack." He walked to the tent flap. "Please, finish your tea; however, I must ensure those four guns are ready to be moved up tonight."

"Jenkins!"

"Yes, sir."

"I want the commanders to meet with me at the mess tent, three o'clock."

William put his cup down and watched General Wolfe leave. He stood up and adjusted his tunic. Peeking out the tent flap he ensured that no one could see him. He stepped back into the tent and, holding his sword close to his side, did several seconds of a vigorous jig. "Oh, my, Molly! A prize or two is jolly!"

He adjusted his tunic again and exited the tent. As he walked down the reverse side of the Grenadier Redoubt hill, he cautioned himself against counting his chickens before they hatched.

Fortress Louisbourg
July 24, 1758

Ah! My poor Louisbourg. The English have ringed her with steel and are tearing at the heart of her. Many of the buildings are destroyed. The hospital is gone as well as much of the citadel. There is no refuge from the English guns. Large pieces of the walls fall into the moat. Where the English are not knocking down the walls, they are being shaken down by the constant firing of our cannon. There is a shortage of ammunition. A party of sailors and citizenry has been organized to seek out fallen English cannonballs so they may be returned. In some instances our batteries have been firing back scrap iron.

Madame de Drucour is an inspiration to the town. Now, at great personal risk, she continues her parade to the guns and fires three cannon daily. She walks along the parapets (where they are still intact) and exhorts the soldiers to maintain their courage in the face of the formidable English. Louisbourg has only five cannon to reply to the British barrage—two on the wall between the Dauphin Bastion and the citadel, and three on its northern flank. Her efforts are worth a half-dozen more.

Before sunset, our troops claimed to have seen a considerable movement in the enemy's trenches. They said that scaling ladders had been brought up in readiness for the final assault. Just an hour later, the English increased the tempo of their barrage. Anticipating an attack, the Governor called assembly. All the off-duty troops had been allowed to scatter throughout the town in an attempt to reduce the number of casualties from the effects of the cannon fire. They were a long time assembling. It was said that all of the enemy were attacking at once but the thick fog prevented us from finding out the exact cause of our terror.

Panic is ugly.

It is now past midnight. The officers have finally achieved order. Fortunately, the English failed to appear at our walls.

Poilly

It must be well past midnight, Reine thought as she moved quickly along the street. There was no real darkness in Fortress Louisbourg any more; everywhere she looked, there were fires in the standing buildings caused by the British guns. In the smoking ruins, there were huddles of citizens or off-duty troops seeking any kind of shelter from the rain of British shot. She ducked, instinctively, when there was another explosion off to the left but didn't slacken her pace. She had responded to the assembly call (still posing as Puant Claude) to repel the British assault. *Fortunately*, she thought, *no attack materialized because the garrison would not have been ready.* She had been amazed at the extent of the garrison's demoralization. *Even the Cambyse had seemed disorganized.*

"It won't be long, now," she said. She meant to say something else to herself about getting Robert out of the fortress before the inevitable surrender but coughed instead, quickly covering her mouth and nose with her free hand. Thick, black smoke was wafting along, drawn by the fires into the centre of the settlement. It smelled like coal. Of course! The coal yard had been set ablaze this morning and now the other fires had created a strong draft, like a bellows, forcing air through the mounds of coal. "Hades must be like this."

She reached the corner of Rue d'Orléans and Rue Toulouse.

Robert had been given shelter in a little shop where the windows had been blown out but, otherwise, the eleven-foot-high building had been intact. Reine gasped. All that was left was the stone foundation. The rest was a smouldering ruin.

"Oh! Mary Mother of God!" She stood at the doorway, staring into the debris, as if she might get some sort of message as to what had happened to her wounded husband.

A heavy-set woman picked her way down the street, heading to the waterfront.

"Please, Madame. This morning, there were some wounded in this building …"

"There's wounded everywhere," she said, brusquely, as she hurried on.

"I hate townspeople," Reine shouted after the thick-bodied back as it disappeared into the coal smoke.

Another figure, clutching an engineer's pad and a notebook, came out of the darkness.

"Please, monsieur, tell me what have they done with the wounded who were being sheltered in these houses." She reached out and grasped his arm, delaying his passage. "Please!"

"Don't touch me, you filthy cretin! I have no time for the likes of you!" He pulled his arm out of her grasp and made as if to pass her by.

Reine blocked his way.

"Vat haf ve here, Herr Poilly?" A larger man, slightly out of breath from hurrying down the lane, took up position by the little man. "Ve need der security patrol?"

Obviously reassured by the presence of the bigger man, Monsieur Poilly assumed a haughtier air. "What do you want, my man?"

Allowing her voice to lose its tone of urgency, Reine asked, politely, "Do you know where they would have taken the patients after these buildings were struck?"

Monsieur Poilly sensed something about the dirty man. What was it? As he opened his notebook to consult his planning charts, he studied the face of the younger man. *Under all the dirt, the boy, because he was young enough to be a boy, was clean-shaven. There was a nice, nice line from the throat to where the first rise of the breasts could be seen. Breasts?*

The boy must have seen something in his eyes because he moved back. "Thank you, sir. I didn't mean to bother an important man like you. I will go ..."

Poilly was quick to respond. "No, no, not at all. It is no trouble." He opened his pad and held it, slanted toward the nearest fire so that the page was lighted. "You see, the hospital, right here," he said, pointing at the chart, "is destroyed and we are using the gardens for the hospital wounded, but any patients from these buildings would have been taken to the pier." He gave the boy a wide smile as he indicated another position on the chart while he said, in German, "When I give the word, Schmidt, grab him and hold him tight." He nodded his head to reassure the boy as he continued speaking in French, "The British are not bombarding the piers. I would look there first, if I were you."

"Grab him!"

Schmidt dropped his arms over the boy and held him in a bear hug.

The boy struggled but was fully restrained.

Poilly, putting his pad down on the ground, loosened the ties at the boy's waist and slid his hand down his belly, inside the clothing, and was not the least bit surprised when he found female genitalia. He looked into her eyes as he inserted his fingers into her. She struggled; he curled his fingers and held her tightly. "Now, my dear girl, who are you and what are you doing in my fortress?" He applied pressure to her private parts for emphasis as he said, "Hmm? Tell me!" this time with a vicious squeeze.

A heavy, male voice said, "Filthy pig!"

Poilly half-turned to confront the source of the outcry. He had time to realize that he was facing a hairy brute with a broad, toothy grin before he was smashed in the side of the head by a musket butt.

Schmidt suffered the same fate but he required two blows before he went down.

"What in hell were they doin' in your drawers, Puant Claude?" the big horse of a man asked. He gave the unconscious

Poilly a kick. "The Louisbourg women must be pretty hard tickets for him to take a go at you!"

The Irregulars all laughed, all except Beau Soleil who stood off to one side, his face a mask. If anyone of the war party took notice of his lack of participation in the joking about the Frenchman's interest in Stinky Claude's crotch, they would have presumed that he was being careful not to move his facial muscles; Beau Soleil had been wounded just above the eye by the near miss of a musket ball and there would be considerable pain with such a wound. Of course, they all knew that Beau Soleil, an Acadian who had been brought up Mi'kmaq, was more Mi'kmaq than the Miramichi—and he didn't like the smelly little Acadian, anyway. So, on second thought, if he didn't participate in the camaraderie, it probably didn't have anything to do with the musket ball wound; it was probably just Beau Soleil being Mi'kmaq.

Horse had noticed Beau Soleil's lack of comment and withdrawal from the group's leadership. He gave it a moment's thought and then shrugged his shoulders. After one last, hard kick at the inert Poilly, Horse asked Stinky Claude, "Did you find out where our boys are?"

"Probably down by the waterfront," Claude replied.

"Let's go get 'em. Boishebert says it's time to leave. The fortress will soon fall."

July 25, 1758
Fortress Louisbourg

When the Irregulars found him on the pier, Robert Cameron wasn't in good shape. He had received a nasty shoulder wound and, while he had been waiting for his turn on the surgeon's table, someone had stolen his boots. Following the surgery, his shoulder had stiffened to such an extent that his right arm was virtually useless. Even though he was suffering from fever, had only one usable arm, and would have to walk in bare feet, he still refused to allow himself to be carried on a litter by the Irregulars. Since he certainly couldn't march away with the war party, Robert was going to have to stay in Louisbourg.

Only one voice was raised in objection when Claude volunteered to remain behind with him. Beau Soleil gave no reason for his opposition so the Irregulars agreed to leave their two comrades behind.

The Irregulars departed before dawn, planning to make their way, slowly, to Bras d'Or Lake, where their boats were hidden. They would rest for a day or two at Bras d'Or and then depart for River St. John and safety. Perhaps Robert and Claude could catch up to them, they said as they bade farewell.

With the Irregulars gone, Reine realized that, if she were to remain by her husband's side, she must pretend she was one of the wounded. She wrapped soiled bandages around her head, covering one eye. A small amount of pus showed from under the bandage and dribbled down her cheek where she neglected to wipe it away. It was an effective disguise.

Reine was trying to make her husband comfortable when she noticed the heavy-set woman passing by, heading back to the coal yard. The woman was carrying a bundle of clothes in both arms. Reine got her to stop, this time, by holding out a piece of silver where the woman could see it.

The woman demanded, "Well, what do you want?"

Still annoyed by the woman's manner, Reine said, "What makes you think I want something?"

"People who have money always want something."

She's right on that point, Reine said to herself. "Boots. Boots for that man over there."

The woman shifted her bundle to free up a hand. She held it out, palm up, for the money.

Reine closed her fist on the silver piece. "How do I know you will come back?"

"I am the fishmonger's wife. Go to our stall. Wait for me there. I will be back in a couple of hours." She made a demanding motion with her outstretched hand. "Give me the money."

Reine tossed the coin to the woman. "If you don't bring me my boots, I will search you out. If you aren't in hell when I find you, I will send you there."

"I'm sure you would," the woman said as she departed.

Reine watched the woman out of sight while walking back

to where Robert lay. "Come, chéri. We must move away from here." She grasped his good arm, half supporting him to his feet. "I know of a better place for us to rest. We might be able to get some fresh fish there."

Robert made protesting noises.

"Shhh, my darling. When we get there, I will be able to get you some boots."

It was several blocks to the market. Robert moved along like a drunken sailor, but he walked surprisingly well, even in his bare feet. They found the stall. Robert immediately settled into a corner by the wall and fell into a deep sleep. Reine went around to the front of the building to see if anyone was there. To her surprise, the fishmonger was setting out a few fish for sale.

"Bonjour, Monsieur," he said cheerfully. "There are not many fish, but they are fresh! I caught them, not ten minutes ago, from the end of the pier."

"I spoke to your wife. She promised ..."

Without looking up the man interrupted, "I regret, Monsieur, I do not have a wife. She departed three years ago. Back to France, I believe. One of the street girls having a joke, no?"

"No! I spoke to her and she promised me ..." Reine's voice trailed off and she became silent.

The fishmonger stopped working with his fish. "These are not good times." He gave Reine an apologetic smile and a shrug of his shoulders as he repeated, "I do not have a wife."

July 25, 1758
H.M.S. Sutherland
Gabarus Bay

"How did you get permission?" If Lieutenant Adams hadn't been jealous of Gray before, he was certainly having a serious case of it now. Adams was chagrined that he was going to stand deck watch on *Sutherland* while William Gray would be leading an assault against the two remaining French warships. *The upstart Scot had all the fun!*

As if he could sense what was in his fellow officer's mind, William said, "I won't be leading an assault group. I haven't recovered enough from my wounds." He put a hand on his fellow officer's shoulder and gave it a friendly squeeze. "But I volunteered, anyway."

"So did I," Adams said, morosely. "I think I was the first officer to volunteer."

Gray answered the unspoken question. "Well, the operation was my idea. I guess that's why I was assigned as a supernumerary officer under Captain LeForey."

Adams couldn't stop himself, "LeForey shouldn't have accepted you. You're still on the sick list, officially."

"Captain Rous assigned sixty *Sutherlands* to the expedition. He made it very clear to Captain LeForey that I was to be the senior officer of the *Sutherlands.*"

"Your pardon, sirs." It was a seaman on the main deck asking permission to approach the two officers, saying that the Buffer had sent him.

Lieutenant Gray nodded at Adams.

Adams ordered, "Approach and state your business."

Both officers recognized Able Seaman Fink as he assumed his best position of attention at the foot of the ladder to the quarterdeck. "Seaman Fink, sir. The Buffer wants Lieutenant Gray t'pick his boat, sir."

"The longboat, Fink," Gray replied.

"Buffer says he'll have two pistols under the thwart for yer use, sir." The sailor smiled directly at Gray. "You'll be bringin' your shillelagh, sir, this time, too?"

Gray looked down from the quarterdeck at the upturned face of this irrepressible sailor. "You know better than that, Fink." William looked along the main deck to see who else was a party to this conversation; at least a dozen sailors waited for the officer's reply. "You know that I didn't carry a shillelagh."

"Aye, sir. I know that, but there's no telling the crew of this ship or any other ship in the fleet that you ain't the man who charged the Cambyse with a shillelagh and …"

"That will be enough, Fink."

"Aye, sir." Fink touched his knuckles to his forehead as a salute and backed away. "The longboat it is, sir. Pistols under the thwart, sir. Thank you, sir."

Adams turned toward the taffrail so none of the crew could see his smile. "And you saved that man?"

"Yes, I'm afraid I did." William was glad to have the conversation changed from who was going on the expedition and why. "But he's a good man."

"The crew thinks he's your man." Adams turned and looked Gray in the eyes to gauge his reply.

William sucked on his teeth. He probed a tooth with a fingernail as he had seen General Wolfe do. He studied a supposed piece of material and put it back into his mouth. He then returned his companion's stare. "I suppose he is. He's always there, on my off side, watching out."

"I suppose it can't hurt to have a big man like that on your left."

"Particularly tonight."

"Yes, I suppose so."

"Time for me to check on the boats. Permission to leave the quarterdeck?"

"Granted."

Fortress Louisbourg

"They ... they p-p-p-picked up their wo-wo-wounded last night, they d-d-di-did." The sentry was overwhelmed that a senior officer of the Cambyse Regiment should be speaking to him. He tried very hard to supply all the information he possibly could. "They br-brought litters and-and t-took them ..."

"Took all of them?"

"Yes, sir."

"There are no Irregulars or Indians left?"[11]

More comfortable now that the sentry knew what the officer wanted he added, "They were laughing and singing, ha-happy to be going ho-home, they said."

The major directed his next remark to the little man who had been standing in the shade of the wall of a ruined building. It was still morning but the sun already had a certain warmth that must have been too harsh for the tormented and torn skin of the man's battered face, forcing him to seek the shelter of the wall during the sentry's interrogation. "I'm very sorry, Sieur Poilly, the men who assaulted you appear to have gone, taking their wounded with them."

"One of them is a spy, Major. It is unlikely she, I mean, it is unlikely he would have departed without fulfilling his mission and we have no reports of any spy activity."

The major fiddled with his sword handle, trying to come to a decision. He finally concluded that he would be well advised to satisfy the whims of this official because, nearly every day, the major had seen Sieur Poilly speaking with the governor's wife as she made her way to the cannon. Yes, he obviously was a man of considerable influence and one to be toadied to.

"You understand, dear sir, that I cannot spare many men from their duties at this stage of the siege." The little man made a face as if to protest so the major hurried on. "However, I will lend you six of my men for an hour to help you in whatever type of search you deem appropriate."

Before the engineer could make a response, or perhaps an objection, the major excused himself and marched off. He stopped to give directions to the sergeant at the end of the pier and, without a backward glance, continued up the street to the administration building.

In a moment, six soldiers and a corporal were standing in the bright sunlight waiting for orders.

Sieur Poilly couldn't believe his good fortune. *This is better than sitting in the second tier of tables at Madame Drucour's soirée. Even if I don't find the renegade, how many of the citizens would see me with my elite guard! Oh, they are so handsome in their uniforms! And they are right here: tall, strong-looking, Cambyse musketmen waiting for their orders from Sieur Poilly, Assistant Engineer for Fortress Louisbourg. Yes, it is becoming a fine, fine day.*

"Follow me!" He set out to walk by his lodgings where his neighbours would be able to see him. Then he would go to the market where he would finally get to impress that haughty bitch that managed the women's dry goods store. It was going to be a wonderful day.

* * *

Reine stood up as the heavy-set woman approached. She shook her fist at the woman. "You told me you were the fishmonger's wife!"

"I also told you I was going to get you a pair of shoes." She pulled a pair of square-toed shoes out of her apron.

Reine snatched the shoes out of her hands. "Why did you lie to me?"

"You could have been one of the governor's spies. He has men everywhere checking to see the taxes are paid." The woman was startled by something that she could see over Reine's shoulder. She smoothed her apron and abruptly turned away.

Reine was taken by surprise and watched as the woman walked casually to the corner, where she gathered up her skirts and ran up the alley as fast as she could.

Holding the shoes close to her side and not looking toward the other end of the street, Reine returned to the corner where Robert was sleeping. She woke him.

"Here are your shoes, Robert. Please put them on, quickly," and she helped him pull them on. They weren't a bad fit, although perhaps a bit wide. She still didn't raise her eyes to look down the street to see what had frightened the heavy-set woman but she could hear the clatter of infantry accoutrements and the crunch of boots on the gravel. Soldiers were coming.

"Lie down Robert. Pretend you are asleep."

Reine settled down beside him and, supporting her head with the side of her arm, turned the pus side of her face to the street. She opened her mouth and allowed herself to drool. Through the bandages of her covered eye, she could see a half-dozen soldiers being led by a civilian marching up the street as if led by fife and drum. She recognized the civilian. *It's that shit of a man who hurt me last night!* She closed both eyes and relaxed as if in sleep but her mind was racing, thinking desperate thoughts as to what she could do if they were discovered. She put her mind at ease. *Robert couldn't run. We will have to make the best of whatever happens.*

A voice called, "Corporal! There's two Irregulars over here!"

There were the sounds of rapid movement and Reine was hauled upright.

She feigned surprise and concern. "What do you want of me, comrades?"

The soldiers said nothing but held her tightly, waiting for the corporal and the civilian to come back to the corner. Two soldiers dragged Robert to her side.

"That's the one! That's the one who is the spy!" The little man was smiling so broadly that one of the wounds on his face broke open and began to bleed. He took no notice of it. "That's the one, for sure!"

"They are wounded French Auxiliaries, Sieur Poilly. What makes you so sure they are spies?"

"That one has something to hide. I can prove ..." He stopped and thought a moment. "I can prove they are hiding something. Take off her ... I mean take off the bandage. There is no wound." As the corporal gingerly removed the filthy bandage, Sieur Poilly moved closer to her. When they could all see there was no wound, Poilly moved even closer. He said, in a very low, husky voice, "And now the game will be played by my rules." He leered at her, "You might even enjoy it."

Poilly stepped back. "Lock them up! I will call for them tomorrow ... for interrogation purposes."

"You do not have that authority, Sieur Poilly. I must get ..."

The corporal's opposition to his wishes angered Poilly. "I haven't the authority!" He took two steps toward the corporal. "What did you need to lock up the British soldiers?" He didn't wait for the reply. "Commonsense is all you need. The enemy isn't left to walk around in our fortress! They are locked up!" Sieur Poilly drew himself up to his maximum height. "Well, take these spies and just lock them up!" He clasped his hands behind his back and rocked on his heels. "And when I call for that one," he pointed at Reine, "you had better deliver her to me."

The corporal stared at the civilian.

Poilly stared back, his face becoming crimson. "You have your orders, corporal. Take charge of your prisoners!"

"Yes, sir."

Endnotes

[1] Actual detail from the *Canadian Historical Review*. "On June 9 Boscawen sent an officer to shore to attend the General to continue the close liaison with the military."

[2] Actual detail from the Archives report that is the basis for this incident in the novel. "(July) 6th about daybreak 100 of the enemy came pretty near the redoubt but soon return, the frigate whose fire had interrupted the approaches on the side of green hill being raked by one of our batteries was obliged to quit her station, there was a continual fire this day from our batteries and from the ships and town."

[3] That the engineer spoke German is fiction.

[4] "(July) 8th between one and two in the morning the enemy made a sortie from the town on our workers to the right (?) killed Lord Dundonald and 7 or 8 Grenadiers of Forbe's regiment and took an engineer and about 30 prisoners but they were soon obliged to retire by Whitmore's Grenadiers leaving behind them 17 killed about as many wounded and prisoners."

[5] In the Archives report the officer had made up an order of battle for the French ships that I drew upon.

[6] Actual detail of the incident. "(July) 16th about an hour before dawn, a small post of ours at the head of the Northeast Harbour was assaulted by about 100 French and Indians who retired without effecting anything, the Post being fortified and the party alert."

[7] Detail of the incident. "In the evening (July 16th), General Wolfe ordered a small party of light infantry followed by light infantry and 20 Grenadiers against the Barachouolice bridge in the front of the Grenadiers redoubt and drove a French piquet from their post on the other side, a party from green hill advancing at the same time to flank the enemy, the parties who attacked them in front met with little opposition and the picket retired into the town with precipitation, a company of Grenadiers of general wolf's corps were detached to sustain those who had passed over ..." "A picket of Struthers's regiment and three companies of Highlanders who belonged to his detachment were encamped near the Grenadiers redoubt, being in possession of a spot called Gallows Hill within 250 yds of the west gate. He immediately began to break ground of their (?) and opened the trenches under a most terrible fire all of round and grape shot this work was continued all night the troops were tolerably covered."

[8] Detail from the staff officer's report. "(July 21st) working at a parallel; about 2:00 in the afternoon a shot from one of Wolfe's batteries by some means set the French men of war on fire which blew up immediately the fire communicated to two others that lay near and before 10:00 all three were burned to the waters edge."

[9] I created the incident of the *Sutherland* at the mouth of the harbour so that I would have a method of telling the story of the sinking of the French ships.

[10] Poilly actually wrote on July 22: "Our bad luck increases daily ... A bomb fell on the barracks and demolished them with such rapidity that we did not have time to stop the progress of the fire despite all the aid we received. The general confusion was to such a degree that it was the principal reason for the lack of success in extinguishing the fire. During the fire, the enemy did a lot of damage and there were as many dead as wounded. I hope that the fire may serve as a valid excuse for the great inefficiency in the repairing of our parapets. We were all very surprised that the fire did not kill more people than it did."

[11] The Irregulars withdrew when it seemed the fortress was lost. The Irregulars/Poilly incident is fiction.

Chapter Six

Entrance to Louisbourg Harbour

It was a recipe for disaster: six hundred English seamen packed cheek by jowl into small boats wallowing through choppy waters in the fog and midnight darkness toward a hostile shore. If they were discovered, there would be no supporting fire from the English warships because they were stationed in the Bay. Neither would General Wolfe's guns be able to provide any cover since they were too far away. No, if the boats were discovered, they would be under the muzzles of Louisbourg's largest cannon, the largest of the large being the Grand Battery.

Although it was difficult to tell in the darkness, Lieutenant Gray believed they were approaching the portion of the channel where it swung in close to the Grand Battery. He stared and stared to the left where he knew the gun towers should be but could see nothing. That was just fine as far as he was concerned; perhaps the Frogs would not be able to see him. He prayed that was the case. He took comfort in the fact that, sitting in the stern of *Sutherland's* longboat, he could see no further than the first row of men. He rubbed his hands together to shake off some of the damp, night chill but immediately thought better of it and stopped; you could never tell what sounds might carry across the water and warn the enemy of their presence.

A squeak was developing on the oarlock of the second larboard oar. He passed some spruce gum forward and the sailor sitting next to the oarsman applied it to the oarlock. The noise disappeared.

A French voice sounded in the darkness! It was almost as if the speaker were sitting on the sternsheet next to him but, of course, after a moment's consideration, William realized it was coming from somewhere off in the night.

If there was any other sound from the English seamen, it was the intake of six hundred breaths. The crew of each boat ceased rowing; they had been briefed, since it would be too dark for hand signals, to rest their oars and lift the blades out of the water at the first indication of an enemy presence. In that way, the boats would continue moving forward by their own momentum. As they listened for any alarm that might be raised from the shore, the boats glided, silently, in the dark mists of the night.

A second voice replied. There was some laughter from the first voice and then the sounds were moving astern. The sailors resumed rowing.

William strained his eyes looking forward. *Where the hell were those two ships?* Despite the fires in the town, he wasn't able to identify anything along the shore. *Fog and darkness were fine for when we were trying to sneak into the place,* he thought ruefully, *but not so good now when we're trying to find our targets.*

* * *

About twenty minutes later, they were close enough to the town to be able to make out the individual fires but still no sight of the enemy ships.

William was getting worried; *if I could see the shore, could the Frogs see our boats?* He scanned the harbour but saw nothing other than the huge mass of English small boats. *Good God! How could the French miss seeing us!* He noticed that the boats nearest the fortress were bunching up as if they were coming to a stop. In fact, it looked as if they were milling around in confusion.

Someone in the commander's boat was waving to him. It was obvious that Captain LeForey wanted him alongside. It took several minutes for William's boat to pass through the throng and, during that time, the rear of the expedition caught up with the fore. The boats were now in a jumble, the two assault groups all mixed up.

As William's boat approached, Captain LeForey broke the silence protocol. "I say, Lieutenant Gray, you are familiar with these waters? Which way do we go from here?"

"I did some mapping of the wrecks at the mouth of …"

"Yes, yes, my good man. So now, tell me, where are we and, more importantly, my fine fellow, which way to the beastly *Prudent?*"

William knew he was going to have to give a response, which would probably be acted upon as if he were an oracle. He cast his mind back to the day he was standing with General Wolfe at the Grenadier's Redoubt where he had had a view of the harbour. He took a deep breath. "Captain, we seem to be directly opposite the town."

"Good man! I knew you wouldn't let me down!" He swivelled in his seat and spoke to someone in the next boat. He raised his arm, "The *Bienfaisant* party go that way. The remainder, follow me!"

There was cursing as boats collided and oars threatened to impale the unwary or the unfortunate. *Sutherland* boats followed the example of their lieutenant's boat, shipping their oars and waiting for the confusion to subside. When it had, they began a steady stroke following in the wake of their assault group leader, Captain LeForey.

They rowed on, roughly parallel to the harbour-front of the fortress, able to see plenty of action on the shore, explosions and muzzle flashes, but no sign of the two ships. A little voice, way deep inside him, was telling William that he had been wrong. Perhaps they had been closer to the North East Battery. "I've never been inside this harbour," he muttered to himself, "I only did a little mapping out near the Grand Battery." He squirmed in his seat, "Dammit! The bloody captain should have used his own judgement and not put me in such a bind."

Another oar began squeaking. William passed more spruce gum forward and the noise stopped. He began counting the strokes. One, two, three, but then couldn't stand it. "I ruined this whole expedition! I should have told LeForey I didn't know where we were!"

Fink, on the first starboard oar, said in a hoarse whisper, "You said something, sir?"

William waved, negatively, with his hand.

At the front of the fleet of boats came a shouted order. Even with William's limited French, he knew what it was; a

French sentry was demanding to know who was approaching in the boats.

The coxs'n signalled 'rest' but William ordered him to resume the original, strong cadence. On flexed knees, he raised himself and stared ahead. There was *Prudent*, or rather, because he couldn't make positive identification in the darkness, there was the long, black shadow of a warship.

The sentry, in what seemed like a casual voice to William, repeated his challenge, "Qui êtes-vous?"

William, his boat moving more swiftly through the water than the others, was rapidly approaching the fore of the assault group. He couldn't yet see the sentry but he could see the boat that must have attracted the sentry's attention. All of the other English boats were holding back, most probably still out of sight of the Frenchman.

"We are from the town," an Englishman responded in very good French, "and coming aboard."[1]

"Come on, then," was the nonchalant reply in French. William was now close enough to see the sentry's head disappear from the bulwark.

There were the sounds of many oars biting into the water as all the boats that had held back in the darkness began the dash for the side of the ship. William's boat passed through the pack and would be first to arrive.

"No grapples! Use boat hooks!" William whispered to his men.

"Ship starboard oars!" The coxs'n ordered in his normal voice. "Larboard, hold, now!" The boat swung to the left, banging hard against the side of the ship. Boat hooks, bow and stern, held the boat steady.

"Boarders away," William ordered and he grabbed the side of the ship, hoping to boost himself up to the first gun port where he might get a toehold. His wounded arm wouldn't support him.

Two *Sutherlands* leaped halfway up the ship's hull and reached down for him. From behind, he was firmly lifted upward. William could hear Fink as he grunted beneath him, "Can't have our lieutenant missing any of the fun, now can we boys!"

As William's feet were lifted over the bulwark, there was a scream from the *Prudent's* quarterdeck. To William, it sounded as though the sentry had met his end.

"Careful men, watch for English prisoners."

Captain LeForey joined William. "Have your men check the hold for English prisoners. I will take the cabins."

"Aye, sir."

It was then William realized that he had left the pistols under the thwart of the boat. "Damn!" he said. A sword wouldn't be much help to him in a confined space but he drew it anyway. "*Sutherlands* open the hatches!" A French sailor came out of nowhere and attacked him with what looked like an old-fashioned pike; probably would have run him through except Fink was there with a pistol. He shot the French sailor in the face. William deflected the pike with his cutlass.

"Thank you, Fink."

"Beggin' your pardon, sir, me usin' your pistol like that." Fink tossed the empty pistol to the deck. He pulled the second pistol from his belt and handed it to William. "She's well primed, she is, sir." He drew his cutlass. "Come on, boys! Open the hatches like the lieutenant says."

From the quarterdeck came the call, "The ship is ours!"

The smiles of the English attackers could be seen even in the darkness but there was no cheering. The plan was to cut the ship loose and take her to the far end of the harbour. Cheering might attract the attention of French shore batteries.

"Lieutenant Gray, the forward hold is empty, sir!"

"Herd the French crew into the forward hold and batten it down." That sounded like Captain LeForey. "Red crew, check the rudder and cables. Green, get aloft and break out the tops'ls." Yes, it was the captain. All was going as planned.

William looked around the deck appreciating the fact that this beautiful ship would soon be an English warship. *She would keep her name, of course. It's bad luck to change her name. Perhaps, next year, Prudent, would be part of the fleet attacking Fortress Quebec.* He shook his head. *That's next year!* He shouted, "*Sutherland!* What about any English prisoners!"

"We're still checking the main hold, sir!"

"Red crew sir! Anchor cables cut."

"Tops'ls set and drawing, sir."

"No English prisoners found, sir!"

"Set the lowers!"

More English seamen scrambled into the rigging, responding to Captain LeForey's order for additional sail.

"We have no steerage, sir!"

What the hell! There was enough sail now for the ship to respond even in this sheltered part of the harbour. Something was amiss.

"Light a torch!"

It took a few minutes for a torch to appear and, in the meantime, the *Sutherlands* reported there was five feet of water in the main hold. Holding the torch over the side of the ship, Captain LeForey could see the *Prudent* was in shallow water. The ship had been run aground to prevent her from sinking.

Captain LeForey grabbed the torch from the sailor. "I am going to fire the ship! Abandon this ship!"

William found it easier going down the side of the ship to the boat but he was aware of Fink at his side all the way. "All accounted for, coxs'n?"

"All present, sir."

"Push away!"

"Good Christ!" someone said, as brilliant light burst over their heads. Looking up they could see Captain LeForey scramble over the bulwark closely followed by a billow of fire. He still held the torch in his hand as he started down but dropped it, needing both hands to slow his descent. The torch fell into William's boat where the *Sutherlands* easily doused it.

"Whouf!" LeForey said, as he fell the last three feet onto the backs of some of the boat's crew.

Of course, Fink had something to say. "Glad to be of service, sir." He shouldered the captain, none too gently, to one side.

"What did you say, sailor?" The captain was dishevelled, red-faced and breathing hard with his exertions but there was no mistaking the tone; he was every inch a Royal Navy captain, who would brook no familiarity from a common sailor.

William wondered what he could say to deflect the officer's anger and embarrassment at being handled by sailors and then addressed with no 'by your leave.' He couldn't think of anything. Fink was a breath away from a flogging.

Fink handed the officer his hat. "I said, I was glad to be of service in findin' and savin' your hat, sir."

The hat was dripping wet and Fink held it out, reverently, as if it were the silver collection plate at chapel. "It was in the drink, sir, and would soon have been lost to sight."

LeForey took the hat, somewhat imperiously. He cast an irate look at the lieutenant. "The deportment of the crew bespeaks the quality of the officer." The captain pushed his way onto the stern sheet. "You're Irish, lieutenant?"

William swallowed the anger welling in his throat. "Push away, coxs'n."

"Aye, sir, but what of them Frenchies in the forward hold?" The coxs'n gave William a searching look in the flickering light. "We locked 'em down."

Fink leaned forward to speak to his lieutenant. "Beggin' your pardon, sir, but I could free 'em up in a mo.'"

Nodding his head to give Fink the permission he needed, William responded to the English officer. "Actually, Captain, the Grays are Scots." He leaned back, watching Fink as he almost flew up the side of the ship, his long legs and arms reminding William of an ape he had once seen in Edinburgh. "Able Seaman Fink would like to save something more than a hat, it seems."

"Must I remind you I am senior officer here? If you had not been of such good service on this mission, I would report you to your captain for ..."

William gazed into the eyes of the Englishman. Both of them knew that the captain could not, or should not, criticize the more junior officer in front of the men. "May I wait upon the return of our crewman?"

Burning shards of canvas fell, sizzling, into the water. Part of a spar crashed onto the bow of the boat and across the shoulders of one of the men, who hollered more in surprise than hurt. Above the boat, the night sky was gone, filled instead with roiling flames being fed by the ship repair stores that had been stacked on the *Prudent's* deck.

"Lieutenant, I want us moved out of here."

"Aye, sir."

The coxs'n gave the orders and the boat started to move away from the doomed vessel.

Fink came vaulting over the side of the ship. He didn't look down because he expected the boat to be there.

Without a word, the *Sutherland* crew backwatered and had the boat positioned where Fink could jump onto the stern. Fink landed in the arms of the already dangerously rankled senior officer.

"Beggin' your pardon, sir, but you know what a hard trip down that is ..."

Captain LeForey sputtered something about 'speaking of this at a later time' but finally, in a clear, controlled voice said, "I won't have any more of it, Lieutenant. Take me to my own boat, now!" And he pointed to where the rest of the *Prudent* attack force had withdrawn, some hundred yards into the comparative darkness, to watch the spectacle of the burning ship.

William sighted the captain's boat and had him transferred without any further exchange of words. Relieved of the Englishman's presence, William checked his crew for wounds and injuries. Absentmindedly, he listened to Fink tell of how the French ensign had kissed his hand for coming back to release the Frenchmen from the forward hold.

William didn't take his eyes off *Prudent* as he asked, "Did they all get away, Fink?" and was immediately sorry when Fink went into the details of how each sailor jumped over the side to swim to the shore. At the seventh or eighth escape out of the hold, the dash across the burning deck with a brave and steadfast Fink helping each Frenchman over the side with a kick in the ass, William ordered, "That will be enough, Fink."

By now, *Prudent* was a torch, every part of her burning right to the water line, but she was going to take a long time to meet her spluttering end. Her gun port covers and hatches blew off as her guns exploded in the intense heat, debris being thrown dangerously close to the English boats. It was then the order was given for the boats to retire.

As LeForey's assault group approached the north-east end of the harbour, they could see that Captain Balfour's attack group had been successful in capturing *Bienfaisant* and towing her to the head of the harbour where both the French and English land forces could see her flying English colours. By the early light of the dawn, William and his crews watched as the English prisoners debarked. There was cheering and loud huzzahs as each boatload of prisoners reached the shore.

The *Sutherlands* rowed with renewed vigour to join the celebration.

Fortress Louisbourg
Morning, July 26, 1758

The British, under cover of the fog, attacked both the *Prudent* and the *Bienfaisant*.

I sit here making this entry as the last of our mighty naval squadron burns at the water's edge. It brings tears to my eyes as I watch one brave soul near the bow of the *Prudent* risk his life helping his comrades over the side to safety.

Prudent had been damaged below the water line by the British bombardment and her captain had beached her where she could be worked on without the danger of sinking. The fact she was beached probably prevented her from being taken in tow as *Bienfaisant* was. Right now, *Bienfaisant* is sitting at the north end of the harbour, out of reach of French forces and, regrettably, flying English colours.

My God! The sails of *Prudent* have burst their lashing and are burning so fiercely that the entire sky is one great sheet of flame.

(I was forced to seek shelter near the embrasures of the King's Bastion as the cannon of the *Prudent* exploded, one after the other, raining further destruction on this poor town. I lost my candle in my haste to get here and write the rest of this entry by the light of the rising sun.)

With the loss of *Bienfaisant* and *Prudent*, the fortress is open to attack from the harbour side. As for our defences from the landside, our walls are in such a bad state that the firing of our own cannon is shaking them down. Further, it is my opinion the walls will be sufficiently breached during the next day of bombardment for the British to attempt an assault.

I pray the Governor will seek terms for the surrender of the fortress.

P

North East Louisbourg Harbour

Rubbing his hand across the stubble on his chin, William Gray breathed a deep, deep sigh while thinking to himself it had been a long night. He stepped back a few paces to the water line and scooped up a handful of water and dashed it into his face. He licked his lips, enjoying the salty taste. If he were any judge, Captain LeForey would probably make it an even longer day by raising observations with the senior officers about Gray's personal behaviour and the deportment of his boat crews. William shook the water off his face. He couldn't expect any support from that little circle of upper class Englishmen. Wiping the remains of the water from his eyes, he recognized a familiar figure trotting across the beach in his direction.

"Grenadier Jenkins! You're not looking for me, are you?" Thinking about the report he would have to write in answer to LeForey's allegations, William was suddenly very tired. He would like nothing better than a few hours' sleep in the comparative quiet of his tent on the other side of Grenadier's Redoubt. Hopefully, Jenkins would pass on by. No such luck!

"General Wolfe's compliments, Lieutenant Gray. He asks that you make arrangements to have his boys taken off this beach as soon as the naval surgeons have checked them over."

"His boys? Oh, yes, you mean the soldiers rescued from *Bienfaisant.*"

"Yes sir. He is confident that you will permit the Navy to cause no delay gettin' 'em to the rest area behind the Redoubt."

William was going to say something but the grenadier carried on, "I took the liberty of arranging a dozen litters on my way here, Lieutenant, in case they were needed."

"Thank you, Jenkins."

"And, beggin' your pardon, sir, I'm to run ahead the minute you're ready to leave so the general can be present when the hot meal is served."

"Thank y ..."

"And there will be a double ration of rum for every man jack of them, the general says."

William waited to see if there was anything else the grenadier might add but he seemed to be finished.

"Thank you, Jenkins."

"Beggin' the lieutenant's pardon, but there are two prisoners who aren't the general's boys. I would suggest ..."

"Where away, grenadier?"

"Pardon, sir?" but as he understood the intent of the naval term, Grenadier Jenkins pointed to the end of the beach. "Still sittin' in the boat next to where the senior officers are standing."

Let's see, near to where Captains LeForey and Balfour are standing. Yes, two figures, one smaller than the other ... William knew who the second one was, instantly. *Carrot Top! That bugger should have been captured at Grand Pré, flogged as a deserter and sent to Halifax to swing from the end of a rope. How the hell did he get away?* William could see Captain LeForey was deep in conversation with Captain Balfour, probably comparing notes about the assault and, no doubt, talking about what they would do with an upstart Northerner named Gray! In a moment, one of them would turn and see the two prisoners who obviously weren't British soldiers. Acting without thought of the possible consequences, William beckoned Jenkins to stand closer.

"Move the one with the red hair off the beach, immediately, with as little notice as possible. Stay with him," William looked around for some place to put him, "over there near those scrub bushes until I come for you."

Jenkins turned to obey.

William stopped the grenadier with his hand. "Treat him well but give him no opportunity to escape, Jenkins."

With a "Yes, sir," Grenadier Jenkins was gone.

Litter carriers came through the scrub trees to the beach. *There must be a dozen litters,* William thought as he ordered his coxs'n to organize an escort party to take the rescued soldiers to the Grenadier's Redoubt. In ten minutes, the first of the litters began moving off the beach, the able-bodied walking alongside. *There! That's started! It was time to do something about Carrot Top.*

Carrot Top didn't get up as Lieutenant Gray approached.

Pointing at the smaller prisoner and, with a questioning look at Jenkins, William exclaimed, "I thought I told you to bring one prisoner over here!"

"Sorry sir! The blighter wouldn't come unless the other one came too. You said to do it without any fuss."

Oh, well! He turned his attention to the redhead. "You're wounded. What's your right name?"

"Nothing serious, Lieutenant, and it's Cameron, Robert Cameron."

"You deserted your regiment at Halifax and joined the French."

"I joined the Acadians."

"It's the same death sentence."

Both men were silent: William, remembering that it was he who had recognized Cameron as a deserter at Grand Pré and had arranged for him to be caught and hanged, and Robert, thinking about his single musket shot at Dartmouth that had saved this lieutenant's life.

Finally, William spoke. "Who's your friend, a deserter, too?"

"Hello, Lieutenant," Reine said, softly. "Where is Jerrie?"

It was difficult for William to think of this smelly little bandit as the lovely Reine LeBlanc whom his New England friend, Jeremiah Bancroft, had taken a fancy to, but yes, he could see her under the dirt and the disguise. She wanted to know about Jeremiah. Poor Jerry! Even as William told Reine that Jerry had died of smallpox in New England, he recalled the glorious moment when Jerry had led his company of Massachusetts colonials in a charge against the French infantry and cannon on the shores of the Misaquash River. By their bold, perhaps rash attack, they had saved the sloop of war, *H.M.S. Yorke*, from capture or destruction. They had also saved William Gray, whose eyes misted as he recounted the closing of his friend's mortal toil.

The Cameron woman, for that was how William now thought of her, was thoughtful for a moment, seemingly studying the fortress that was still being bombarded by the British guns while actually thinking back to their time at Grand Pré. She then raised her eyes, searching for the lie that would possibly come from the lips of this Englishman: "And my cousin, Sylvie?"

"Sylvie and Aunt Matilde went on the ships. They left on the last day." William suffered a moment of guilt.

He could recall Jerry telling him how sweet little Sylvie had refused to escape the deportations with the Camerons. She had chosen to return to English captivity to be with her aunt. Aunt Matilde would need her, she had said. She and her aunt would always be together, she had believed.

"They are together, Lieutenant?"

William hoped the lie would not show on his face. "They boarded at the same time, Reine." He remembered the scene. Little Sylvie was delayed by the guard as she sought to keep the family strong box with them, the box that held all that was dear to her aunt. Arguing to keep their treasures meant she missed the boat carrying Matilde to one of the ships. Sylvie took the last boat to the only other ship in the Bay, believing both ships were going to the same place. Probably believing until the very end of the voyage that she would see her aunt again. "Yes, at the same time," he repeated.

Damn! He could see the way Reine turned her face away that she had heard and understood the evasion; Sylvie was not with her aunt. Reine Cameron would ask no more questions about Grand Pré.

"What happens now, Lieutenant?"

William could hear the Scots burr in Robert's words. *By God, we're both a long, long way from home and our enemies abound.*

"You are a deserter. You know what happens."

Reine sucked in her breath. She put her hand in Robert's and looked the lieutenant in the face. "You English are ... tout le même!"

Without even thinking, William replied, "I am not English," *but it would be English officers who would judge this man. They would have him flogged and, if the dirty little Northerner survived that, he would be shipped to Halifax for hanging. Someone like LeForey would put a notation on the file, 'private soldier, deserted, executed' and Cameron would rot in the paupers' field on the north side of Halifax Common.* William suffered a pang in his gut as he realized he was about to do something that might change all that ... and put him and his little family at risk. He cast a quick look at the grenadier. *Could he trust the soldier?* His gut growled and churned. He had made up his mind.

"Grenadier, I want you to escort these people to my tent, put them inside and then go about your duties." His tent was the only place he could think of where he could hide them. No one ever disturbed him there. Usually, if anyone wanted him, they sent Jenkins. Yes, his tent was the safest place he could think of while he considered what he would do next.

"Yes, Lieutenant." Jenkins beckoned to the two Irregulars, "Move along now. I'll have to get to see my general and I don't have much time for the likes of you."

William helped Cameron to his feet. "When you get to the tent, stay inside and be quiet." He watched as they joined the procession going up the hill, the grenadier helping the wounded Cameron, probably so they could move along more quickly.

William ordered the *Sutherlands* back to their boats. As the sailors took up their first strokes, William looked back over his shoulder at the beach. Balfour and LeForey were still in much the same position, talking, although now they were gazing after William as they continued their very serious-looking conversation.

Lieutenant William Gray sat, unseeing, in the stern, pondering the possible consequences of his run-in with Captain LeForey. *How much of the incident was my fault and how much was the result of the English captain's prejudice against anyone who wasn't a member of the upper class?* "It must be bloody wonder-ful to be rich and English!"

"Your pardon, sir. Did you speak?" Fink didn't miss a beat on the oar but his big, homely face looked up, expectantly, at his officer, wondering what the muttering was about.

"Oh, for Christ's sake, Fink! That'll be enough out of you."

Fink's expression didn't change as he replied, "Aye, sir," and continued rowing.

At *Sutherland* the entire ship's crew was under a pall. William noticed it the moment he set foot on deck. He glanced questioningly at the duty officer but didn't have time to ask what was wrong before he was summoned to the captain's cabin. Even the marine guard at the door of the captain's cabin seemed to be in a funk. William knocked on the door but there was no answer. He asked the marine if the captain were in the cabin and the guard nodded that he was. So William waited.

The companionway where William and the guard were standing was stifling; not a breath of air. William became aware of an odour and realized that he was the source of it. Of course he was sooty from the *Prudent* fires, sweaty and dirty from his exertions, smelly from the acrid gunpowder and fouled with the splattered blood of the Frenchman Fink had shot in the face. Wouldn't it be just fine if the captain's man, Wimper, would show up with water and a cloth? *Now's the time, Wimper,* William thought. *You've done it before when I didn't appreciate it, but I would relish some hot water and a cloth right now.*

The cabin door was suddenly opened. Wimper stepped out. William half expected to be handed a cloth, but there wasn't one.

"The captain wants to see you, right now. He's got anoth-er letter from Halifax," Wimper said in a very low voice. "He's very upset."

"I don't need you blabbing to all the world, Wimper."

"No, sir. It's the lieutenant. He's coming right in, sir."

William stepped over the threshold and stood to attention. When his eyes became accustomed to the darkened cabin, he wasn't prepared for the wild-eyed, dishevelled-looking man who better resembled a barfly at Carmichael's Tavern than a senior captain of the Royal Navy.

In a false-hearty voice, Captain Rous greeted his favourite young officer. "You had an exciting time, me young bucko!"

"Yes, sir, I …"

"Too bad about *Prudent*. She would have made a grand prize."

"Yes, sir. We thought …"

"Admiral Boscawen is sending a squadron into the harbour to take Louisbourg from the sea. Now that the French have no ships, only two or three cannon and virtually no ammunition, Admiral Boscawen will risk a squadron to capture the fortress."

"That's wonderful, sir!"

"No, it isn't!" Captain Rous waved his arms around, "You haven't seen our ship's company?"

"Well, yes, sir. I noticed as I came aboard that …"

"We're not going. Six ships are going, but not *Sutherland*. *Sutherland*, that charted the obstacles at the harbour entrance. The *Sutherland* …" Here, the Captain paused and then laughed but, actually, the laugh was more like a cackle. "Those six crews will be just as pissed as our ship's company when they find out that they won't be going either." Captain Rous sat down. "They won't get to see action, nosirree." Rous gazed at the sea through the narrow, old-fashioned transom. He seemed to be lost in thought.

William waited.

As if speaking to himself, Rous said, "I told those upper crust dandies that we could take this fortress if the French believed we were capable of attacking them from the sea"—he paused again—"and if they were convinced we had the guts to do it."

"Yes, I remember you saying that, sir."

Abruptly, Rous's eyes cleared. He ran his hands over his head, calming his hair somewhat. "The six ships have been given their orders to attack this afternoon." He smiled the rogue's grin that made him look so much like a pirate. "Our dear Admiral made sure the French were informed, as early this morning as he could arrange, that there would be a naval attack."[2]

"They'll surrender?"

"Aye, William. That they will." Captain John Rous toyed with a letter that he had picked up from the desk. William thought he was going to speak of it, but instead Rous ordered, "Go tell the crew the fortress will surrender this afternoon. That'll make them more chipper."

"But, sir! We don't know the fortress will surrender."

"Every man gets an extra tot."

When William still hesitated, Rous growled, "Go tell the crew, Lieutenant. Do as you're told," and in a strangely disconnected tone he added, "now that's a good laddie."

Lieutenant Gray saluted and left, closing the cabin door softly.

Rous unfolded the letter. He read, silently, his lips moving for each word. Not looking up when the ship's company began cheering, Rous read aloud the portion of the letter that troubled him most.

> "I admit that I am not the most pleasant company and have come to accept that we do not eat at the same table nor do I share my husband's bed. A few days ago, I was moved to the master bedroom of the old house. Now I do not see Richard at all. Father, I do not deserve this. What can I do?"

In that same, disconnected voice, Rous said, "Shoot the bastard. We'll shoot the bastard, my dear."

Endnotes

[1] Detail from the report held by the Archives. "(July 26th) about 1:00 in the morning the *Prudent* and *Bienfaisant* were boarded by 500 English sailors in (boats). The *Prudent* (being) aground was set on fire, the other was towed off into the Northeast Harbour. 11 officers and 50 sailors were made prisoners on board the *Bienfaisant* and 28 English prisoners retaken."

[2] Details of the surrender are from *Rise and Fall of Louisbourg* by J.C. Webster and a Canadian Historical Society paper. "Boscawen now decided to send six ships into the harbour to attack the town at short range. Drucour hearing of this, decided that it was time to capitulate and he sent a messenger offering to yield on the same terms which were granted the English at Port Mahon in Minorca. This was refused and Drucour was forced to accept the British terms, surrendering on July 26th ..."

Chapter Seven

July 27, 1758
Grenadier's Redoubt

If anyone had been watching, they might have wondered why Lieutenant Gray was knocking at the flap of his own tent but there was no one there to see; everyone was gathered at the front of the Grenadier's Redoubt watching the three grenadier companies preparing to march through the Dauphin Gate of Fortress Louisbourg. Captain Rous had been right; the mere threat of a sea attack on the fortress had forced the French to capitulate.

The English had offered no terms.[1] Yesterday the French were given an hour to surrender or be blown to hell by the guns of the Royal Navy and Wolfe's batteries. Then the city would have been put to the bayonet with little or no quarter given. The French had had no choice but to capitulate. Today, in the next hour, the British Army would take possession of Fortress Louisbourg.

William tapped on the metal knocker again. There was no answer. He slipped the loops on the flap and entered. Reine and her husband were standing in the middle of the tent, Robert with his arm around his wife's waist. They relaxed visibly when they saw it was William.

"The guns have stopped?" Robert said with a question in his voice.

"The fortress hung a white flag over the Cavalier, yesterday, at ten in the morning. They argued over terms but none were granted. The garrison will be treated as prisoners of war."

Robert Cameron understood these things because of his service in an English regiment. "The regiments?"

"They were granted no terms. They will be ordered to ground their arms and fold their colours."

"The Cambyse won't do that."

"We shall see. Three of our companies are going to march into the fortress in the next hour." William put a grim little smile on his face. "I am told they go with fixed bayonets."

"And the Irregulars?"

"Hunted down and killed, I suppose."

Reine hadn't grasped all that was said, but 'hunted down and killed' she understood well enough. "Robert, what shall we do?" she asked in French.

"We are in God's hands, chéri."

"No," she answered, "we are in this Englishman's hands. What is he going to do with us?"

William could see the distress in her face. He didn't have to guess what was upsetting her. "I have a plan ... no, it really isn't a plan ... we have one chance to get you out of here and we had better go right now." He lifted the flap of the tent. "Follow me." Without looking back, William marched out of the tent and up the path to the Redoubt. At the top of the hill he was met by Jenkins, who led them through the communications trench, past the redan, and into the open where they crossed over the stream and into another communications trench. That trench led to a fortified position in front of the main gate. Here, Jenkins and William paused as they listened to the strains of the fifes as the British Grenadiers marched through the gate. When the three companies had disappeared into the fortress, Jenkins took a deep breath and climbed over the parapet into the open. He waited for the other three to join him and then he unslung his musket. Motioning for the Camerons to go ahead, he followed closely behind, apparently herding them through the gate.

Inside was a sight. There was destruction everywhere. Some of the debris was still smoking. Several hundred people were gathered in little bunches to witness the official surrender of the French regiments. What struck William was the absolute quiet of the populace as they watched their garrison give up their weapons and colours to the victorious British.

The Volontaires Étrangers must have just been ordered to ground their arms because they were bent at the knees, their muskets on the ground by their feet, each weapon lined up perfectly with the next man's weapon. Then the order was given to "recover" and the French soldiers stood erect, disarmed, their arms hanging uselessly at their sides. "Three paces forward, march," and the regiment moved away from their weapons.

When the soldiers completed their movements there was a moment of silence. Then a sergeant carried the Volontaires Étrangers' colours through the regiment to the front of the nearest British company. He stopped. He stood there, ignoring the English officers at the front of the centre company, the emblem of his regiment bravely flying in the breeze. There was no other movement.

It was then William noted the other piles of muskets and swords. He glanced around and could see the small groups of disbanded men of other regiments who had already been subjected to the disgrace of giving up their arms and banner to the enemy.[2]

In the hush of the general crowd, several Bourgogne soldiers could be heard arguing. They discontinued their argument to watch the spectacle of what the damned English officers would do about the determined Étrangers sergeant who wanted to surrender his colours to the actual men who had won it, the men of the British Grenadiers.

Jenkins took the opportunity to move his party further into the fort and away from the gate, all the while appearing to be interested in the ceremony.[3]

The French sergeant wasn't moving to the centre of the English parade where the standards of the Artois, Bourgogne and Marine regiments had already been folded and were now in the hands of the English officers. The officers, for their part, seemed to be enjoying the light breeze of the afternoon and, if they were aware of the sergeant, they did not show it. One of them made a comment, which must have been amusing because the others laughed, softly.

The French sergeant, unmoving, must have heard the laughter; his face reddened. His eyes fell from a fixed position over the heads of the English soldiers and, instead, searched the faces of the front row of the grenadiers.

The grenadiers' right marker stepped forward, executing a smart 'one, two' movement. He turned to the right and marched with a left wheel along the front of the grenadier company. Coming to a halt in front of the sergeant, he executed a 'one, two' halt, paused, and then right-turned to face the sergeant.

Both men, filled with pride for their regiments, took the moment to study the other's face as if to remember it for all time. The Frenchman, without breaking his gaze, folded his colours and extended his arm, holding the flagstaff away from his body. The Englishman grasped the staff and held it steady until the Frenchman released his hold. Both soldiers executed a turn and went in opposite directions, the grenadier managing, somehow, to hold onto the colours while carrying his musket at the shoulder.

The Regiment Volontaires Étrangers was ordered to disband, the soldiers moving off the parade ground in small groups. Now it was the turn of the proud Cambyse.

Jenkins had guided his party to the furthest edge of the parade. He stopped and whispered to the lieutenant, "I think we should wait here until the ceremonies are over. We don't want to draw attention to our actions."

"Right-o." William indicated to the Camerons that they should pretend to be interested in the next regiment to surrender.

They were impressive, the Cambyse. Their parade formation was perfect, the men in absolutely straight lines. An officer did an about-turn to face his men, perhaps to give an order, William thought. Glistening on his cheeks were tears of embarrassment and rage against the British who would give such insult to a fine, regular army regiment. He opened his mouth but said nothing, at least nothing that William could hear from the distance that separated them. The officer's mouth moved again. William and everyone in the area could hear the one word the officer shouted: "Cambyse!" He grasped the blade of his sword and, raising his knee, brought the flat of the blade down to shatter on his leg. In disgust, he threw the pieces of the sword to the ground and marched off the parade.

The Cambyse broke ranks. Muskets were slammed against walls and steps, breaking the stocks and bending the barrels. With their weapons destroyed, the colours were held high while an ordinary soldier set fire to them with a torch. When it was burned, the flagstaff was hurled to the ground. The Cambyse had disbanded as much on their own terms as they could manage.[4]

There was movement on the edges of the crowd. More grenadiers came through the gate and fanned out in patrol formation to take up positions throughout the fortress. It was time for Jenkins to get his party out of there.

Someone was shouting, almost screaming. William understood enough French to realize that the little Frenchman making all the noise was telling the newly arrived grenadiers to stop the Camerons.

It looked as if Reine and Robert were going to try to make a run for it, but Jenkins raised his musket enough to stop them in mid-stride. When he was sure that the Camerons and the naval lieutenant weren't going anywhere, he turned to face the Frenchman who was still yelling his head off. Raising his musket to the level of the Frenchman's belly button, Jenkins said, "Ferme ta bouche!"

The grenadier patrol had taken skirmish formation and was approaching with caution.

"The Frenchman knows us!" Robert Cameron said to Jenkins. "He knows one of us is a woman disguised as a man."

"Shut up, then!" Jenkins said without looking at Cameron.

The corporal in charge of the patrol approached Jenkins. "You're out of uniform, son! Your sergeant is going to have a purple fit when he sees you!"

"I lost most of my uniform on Cormorant Beach. I had to strip to swim back."

"Oh, my laddie! I've heard about you. You were the only grenadier to come back from that place. You are the General's Runner!"

Engineer Poilly, because that's who it was, was dancing from one foot to the other as the soldiers spoke to each other. When he couldn't stand it any more he began his shouting again: "He's a she! That man's a woman!"

The corporal glanced at the Frenchman. "Any idea what his problem is?"

"No. I was passing with my party when he started yelling."

"He's a she. Take a look!" Poilly poked at Reine's crotch with his fingers. She tried to jump back but he had grabbed a handful of her clothing and held on.

Jenkins casually knocked Poilly on the side of the head with the butt of his musket. "I don't know what he's trying to prove but he's in my way."

"You have orders?"

"Yes, I do." Jenkins reached into his message pouch and pulled out a document with a red seal on it. "This is from the general. That's his seal. It tells me that ..."

"Cor' blimy, I don't want to know the general's business. You just get on with it."

Jenkins pointed at the crumpled form on the street. "What about him?"

The corporal pulled on Poilly's collar and lifted him enough to see his face. "He seems all right." The corporal let him fall to the street. "We'll just leave him there. He'll come around and have a nice lump to remind him not to get in the way of British Grenadiers."

"Thanks, corp."

With his musket, Jenkins motioned his party to continue. They marched without comment or interruption through the streets and, when they reached the gate that led to the Mire Road, Jenkins halted his group.

"The gate is open and unguarded," he said to the Camerons. "You should move away from here as quickly as your wounds allow." With nothing more to say to the two Irregulars, Jenkins stepped back several paces, away from the gate.

William Gray had been silent for most of the trip. He really didn't have anything to say to these people and he was wondering why he had done as much as he had. Probably for Jerry, he thought. *Yes, I did this in memory of Jeremiah Bancroft.*

"Thank you, lieutenant." Robert Cameron extended his hand.

When William heard the man's Scots accent he knew why he had helped them. He took Cameron's hand and shook it strongly. It was to spite Englishmen like Boscawen, Balfour and LeForey who seemed to rule the world with a system based firmly on prejudice.

Without another word, the Camerons went through the

gate and down the hill into the marshes surrounding this part of the fortress.

William continued the same train of thought as he watched them walk quickly along the trail. *And not only the English! Men like Rous's son-in-law, the Honourable Richard Bulkeley, had their own twisted sense of values that raised them above anyone with supposed lesser breeding, position or wealth.*

Grenadier Jenkins cleared his throat to get the lieutenant's attention. "Hm-hmm. I hope they hurry, sir. I would hate to think of what might happen if they were caught up in the sweep."

"Sweep? What sweep?"

"I carried orders to the Highlanders, sir. As soon as the fort is secured, they are to sortie. They will be searching for Irregulars." Jenkins pointed at the distant Camerons. "If those two are caught in the sweep, I hope they are killed. Otherwise, they might tell how they escaped from Louisbourg."

William Gray had a cold, tight feeling in his nose and throat. He attempted to ignore it by changing the subject. "What was that document you waved around in front of the corporal?"

"A laissez-passer, signed and sealed by the general. I haven't had to use it up until now and didn't want to use it for them," he gestured in the direction the Cameron's had gone, " but it looked like the only way we were going to get away with it."

"It was good you had it."

Both men turned to go back into the fortress. They walked without speaking for a while. William broke the silence. "You didn't ask me why."

"I didn't have to know, sir. It was enough that you wanted it done."

"Thank you, grenadier."

July 30, 1758
Bras d'Or Lakes

It was a rough shoreline, the beach very rocky. When Boishebert's band of Irregulars had come by here on their way to

Fortress Louisbourg, they had hidden their boats at intervals wherever there was suitable cover. Now that they were in retreat, the recovery of each boat was a small miracle that raised the spirits of the band immensely.

"There are three more beyond the next point," Boishebert said. "I'm sure of it." He waved his arm, expressively. "In the cove by the fallen trees."

Beau Soleil grunted. "I will send my brothers to look." Grunting again, he added, "but they will find nothing in the cove. It is a waste of time. We must move away from this shore before dark. It is better we load the boats now, and leave."

Boishebert allowed his disdain for the Acadian-turned-Mi'kmaq to show on his face. "Why move away from this shore in darkness? That is folly."

"The British come."

"Looking for us, I suppose? You become an old woman, Beau Soleil."

Beau Soleil betrayed no sign of his irritation and anger as he pointed at the skyline of the low hill to the east. "The British come."

Boishebert flinched as if he had been doused in the face with cold water when he looked where Beau Soleil was pointing. Cresting the hill were dozens of Highlanders[5] carrying muskets at the high port, bayonets glistening, their uniforms crimson in the setting sun. As he watched, even more appeared on the hill. "It must be a full company!" Boishebert was again every inch the soldier. "How long before they get here, Beau Soleil?"

"After dusk, my friend." If there was irony in his voice, Boishebert was not aware of it. Beau Soleil continued, "We load now. Then we leave."

"Forget everything else! Load up! As soon as you are ready, push off. Assemble offshore out of musket range."

It wasn't long before the boats were pushed away from the rocky beach, Beau Soleil being in the very last boat.

English voices could be heard in the woods. A musket was fired followed by more shouting. Two figures, hand in hand, burst through the trees onto the beach.

Beau Soleil gave the order for the men to row away from the beach.

One of his crew objected. "It's Puant Claude and Robert!"

"I know. Keep rowing."

"We should go get them! The English will kill them."

Beau Soleil was tempted to go back; the woman was lovely. He remembered her in the woods, *washing her private parts getting ready for ...* "No. We must get out of musket range. Keep rowing." *Getting ready for the Englishman to spew his seed into her.* "Keep rowing." *She must be flawed.* Beau Soleil had watched as the Englishman had done his part and yet she still had the body of a boy. *Yes, she is probably flawed and not worthy of my concern or interest.*

"Please come back for us!" It was a voice from the beach. In the approaching darkness, it was difficult to see which one was shouting. Beau Soleil hoped it was the woman. He did not answer.

"Help us, brothers!"

That was definitely the man, Beau Soleil thought. He realized that his crew had stopped rowing. In a moment they might force him to take the boat back to the beach. Cupping his hands, Beau Soleil shouted to the shore, "There are boats around the point!" He waved his arms and gestured in the direction of the point. "In the cove by the fallen trees." He didn't know he was grinning as he watched the two of them run toward the point but by the looks on the faces of his crew he knew he was doing something wrong. He became very serious. He lifted his hand as a salute, "Bonne chance! We will see you at River Saint John!" He turned his back on the shore, sitting down in the stern. "Row, my brothers. We are not out of musket range yet." *Perhaps the woman would die from many thrusts before the final one from a bayonet.*

There was a volley of musket fire on the beach.

Well, perhaps not, he thought.

* * *

"They are not shooting at us. Keep running." Robert said that to encourage his wife because he really didn't know where musket balls were going in the dusk. And, in the deepening dark, the Camerons were tripping and sliding on the wet rocks as they raced past the point to the cove beyond. Maybe the Highlanders didn't see which direction they went. It was their only hope—and the hope that Beau Soleil wasn't lying to them. *There has to be a boat in the fallen trees. Please dear God! Let there be a boat in the brush!*

"God damn him!" Robert had charged into the nearest likely thicket and come out empty-handed. He was panting with the effort, frantic with the creeping terror that there would be no boat in this cove.

Reine had no doubt to whom Robert's curses were directed. She had thought of Beau Soleil as a constant threat. It was almost as if he knew about them, knew that they were husband and wife, not comrades-in-arms.

The next likely place to hide a boat was also empty. Robert ran on.

Reine sank to her knees, bruising herself on the beach stones. She clasped her hands in front of her. "Holy Mary, Mother of God, blessed be the fruit of thy womb …"

"Reine! I found one!" Robert had shouted when he found the boat and instantly regretted it. First one, and then a dozen English voices sprang up at different places along the beach. They had heard him. Throwing all caution aside, Robert called again, "There are several boats here. Come! Help me!"

There were three boats, one of them smaller than the other two. Robert was dragging the smallest one to the waterline. With Reine's help, it was quickly in the water. Robert ran back to the other boats. He stove them in with rocks and carried their oars to the small boat.

"Push off!" He fitted a set of oars into the oarlocks and began to pull as hard as he could. Reine fiddled with another set of oars and soon had her oars working the water as well.

The Highlanders were lighting torches so they might be able to search better. Robert rested on his oars to catch his breath. "Take it easy, Reine," he whispered. "As long as we don't make any noise, they won't be able to see us, now. The torches will blind them to us out here on the water."

After a few minutes of rest, they rowed away into the darkness, using the light from the English torches to guide them away from that dangerous shore.

When the lights could no longer be seen, Robert had them stop rowing, saying they could rest on the lake until morning light, when they would be able to pick a direction.

Robert giggled with relief. Reine joined in, the two of them giggling like children. Robert gave a huge sigh. "When Beau Soleil told us to go to the right down the beach to find the boats, I almost went in the opposite direction. I didn't believe him ... that he would help us."

"After all, he could have come back to save us, but he didn't." Reine shrugged, "I didn't like that man."

"He said they were going to River Saint John." Robert slipped his tunic off and put it over his wife's shoulders. "It will get cold out here in the early morning."

Reine took her husband's tunic and handed it back to him. "You will need it as much as I do. You put it on, chéri."

There were no stars, no lights to be seen on the shore. They were in a world of their own but they both knew it would be short-lived. Robert voiced his concerns.

"If we go to River Saint John, Boishebert will have us fighting for the French until ..."

"Until we get killed," Reine finished for him. "We must not go to River Saint John."

"There is nothing for us in Acadia. The English are there ..."

"And now they are in Îles Royale."

"Perhaps they will not come to Île Saint Jean. We have a house there ..."

"And we have our land."

"Yes. We have our land." With great conviction Robert said, "This time, no one will take it from us."

Endnotes

[1] Poilly wrote in his diary, "As a preliminary to surrender, the British say Governor de Drucour must give up his garrison as prisoners of war. He has only one hour to think it over. All members of the Council of War were scandalized by such a humiliating proposition ... the officers of the garrison felt rebellious and nearly caused a riot.

[2] Poilly wrote, "July 27—8A.M. we went out and by 9 o'clock the enemy had taken over. The garrison, who had served bravely and patiently, felt greatly the effects of this hardship. The humiliation of it all brought tears to my eyes."

[3] The Cameron escape is fiction as well as the Poilly/Gray interface.

[4] From the archives: "When the news leaked out soldiers of the Cambis regiment broke their muskets and burned their colours."

[5] From the archives I found, "The partisan leaders, Boishebert and Villejouin, had escaped. They evaded the Scottish Highlanders sent to pursue them, and carrying their sick in litters, had reached their boats on the Bras d'Or Lakes. From there they returned to the St. John River in French Acadia only to find that Monckton occupied the old French Fort and raised the British colours."

Chapter Eight

July 31, 1758
Fortress Louisbourg

"What a magnificent sight!" Standing as he was on the front steps of the Government Building, his view unobstructed by any of the structural ruins, Lieutenant William Gray was enjoying the historic moment as the English Fleet, under the command of Admiral Boscawen, entered Louisbourg Harbour. The ships were dressed for the occasion, with every sort of pennant and flag streaming in the light breeze as all hands stood to their stations waving their caps. As each ship passed the Grand Battery, it announced the arrival with a broadside of colourful smoke discharges, some blue but mostly red and white.

It was now the turn of *H.M.S. Namur*, Admiral Boscawen's flagship, to pass the Grand Battery: a huge ship, dwarfing all that had gone before.[1] William couldn't help but pray there wasn't enough room for the old bastard and his ship to pass through the channel, but Captain Buckle, *Namur's* captain, was too good a seaman to have anything like that happen. *Namur* passed without incident into the harbour, where she received ceremonial salutes from the English cannon that had been hauled into the fortress just for that purpose.

Major Inch, Wolfe's Senior Intelligence Officer, dressed in his best uniform and ceremonial sword for the occasion, joined William, who was less formally attired, on the step. "Which is your ship, Lieutenant?" Inch had found some unsupervised wine in the governor's apartment and, since there were no pressing duties for an intelligence officer once the enemy had capitulated, he thought to sample several of the bottles. He was already unsteady on his feet but still coherent. He waved his hand in a wide theatrical movement that almost pushed William off the step. The major continued, unconcerned, "To which of those little cockle shells do you regularly entrust your precious family jewels?"

"*Sutherland* is my ship but she won't be here today. She's on patrol in case the French Squadron from Quebec should sally forth and try to catch us in the harbour."[2]

The intelligence officer gave it a moment's thought and then blurted out, "That's not the least bit likely!" He studied William's face to make sure the lieutenant wasn't joking. "If they tried to enter, we could blow them out of the water, one by one, as they come past the Grand Battery!" He shook his head. "No, that's not the least bit likely!"

William made no comment and made a great show of watching the activity on the water.

"It's a known fact!"

"What is that, Major Inch?"

"We could blow them out of the water, one at a time. Admiral Boscawen said it over and over again when we were in War Council: any English ship assaulting this harbour would be blown to smithereens." Smirking, he added, "Now that we have the fort, we can do the same to them. Not a problem. Don't need patrol ships out there in the Bay."

Pleased with himself, Inch turned to re-enter the Government Building where the governor's apartment was. He paused in mid-step. "Of course! I know why *Sunderland* is doing patrol duty!"

"It's *Sutherland*, Major."

"The *Sutherland*, then. It's because your captain is the Redoubtable Rous: the Colonial Cavalier, Hero of a Thousand Prize Takings, Ruination of the Righteous Royal Navy, a Rude, Crude and Tattooed Privateer, a True Son of …"

"For God's sake, Major! Let it go! It's enough that my mates are out there doing useless duty while the rest of the fleet is celebrating!" William gulped, aghast at his own complete lack of discretion in the presence of this well-connected, senior English officer.

Major Inch, apparently too drunk to notice, made a deep, formal bow, causing him to loose his hat. Red-faced, following its recovery, Inch continued in good humour, "Yes, celebrating! We need to vent ourselves over a doxy or two but there aren't enough of 'em to go 'round." He grinned, "I'd even share, if we had to." Major Inch pointed at some civilians approaching from the direction of the guardhouse. "Here's one being delivered right to the door!"

Two Frenchmen, by their dress and deportment obviously citizens of distinction, were leading a young, dark woman by a tether attached to her bound wrists. The girl was weeping and, with every audible sob, the shorter of the two men yanked on the tether, causing her to skip forward a step or two to take the pressure off her wrists.

"You're wrong, Major. They seem to be parading her around."

Paying no heed to the two officers, the threesome walked along in front of the Government Building and then turned down Rue Toulouse, heading toward the harbour front.

William was full of curiosity since he recognized the little man as the Frenchman who had interfered when he was helping the Camerons leave the fortress. "I'm going along to see what this is all about," he said over his shoulder as he stepped down. "With your permission, sir."

"Not at all, my fine fellow."

Major Inch was sorely tempted to return to the apartment for more wine but his loins were all a-tingle. There were no women in the building but there might be some more tethered women where this one was being taken. Besides, not everyone had easy access to the apartment, as did an intelligence officer—the wine would still be there—and, if he were successful in finding a partner, there would be more than enough for two. "I will join you, Lieutenant." His descent from the step was more of a dismount. He staggered, off balance, for several paces before he was able to assume a semblance of a walking cadence. He tried to match step with William but then gave it up. By the time they reached the gate called Porte Frederic, Major Inch was out of breath and regretting that he hadn't followed his first inclination to get more wine.

"For Christ's sake, how much further?" he complained.

"Catch your breath, Major, they have stopped in front of that red post and platform. There's going to be some sort of ceremony." William Gray looked around at the small gathering of citizens and disbanded soldiers. "Does anyone speak English?"

Most of the small crowd just stared at him but two men, one of them a priest, looked away as soon as William asked his question.

"You, there! Yes, you in the cassock!" He beckoned for the man to approach. "What is going on here?"

The priest walked, slowly, with hands folded in front of him, to within a few paces of William and the major. "She has been found guilty by one of our judges and will be locked in the stocks as punishment for her transgressions."

"What is she guilty of?"

"The charges and sentence will be read by the judge, Monsieur. I will translate, if you wish."

The taller of the two officials unrolled a document. He cleared his throat and began reading. Meanwhile, the other man, the little man and troublemaker as William thought of him, began untying the girl's wrists. He pushed at her, hard, in the chest, attempting to hush the girl or perhaps to intimidate her, but the sobs became howls of mortification and fear. He slapped her and she quickly became silent.

Whatever the judge was reading was short and to the point. He rolled up the document and tucked it under his arm. Taking one of the girl's arms, he forced her to climb the two steps of the red platform. The little man followed closely behind, roughly pushing her against the pole in the middle of the platform. Chains and manacles were draped over the pole's crosspiece.

The priest whispered, "She is the slave housekeeper of Sieur Poilly, the engineer."

William interrupted. "Let me guess. The little man is the owner."

Nodding his head the priest went on, "She is a thief and is to be punished by four hours in the stocks. We discussed the matter yesterday—the judge, Sieur Poilly and the Sergeant of the Guard. Despite the capitulation, matters of such importance as a slave stealing from a master must continue to be judged, a punishment determined and delivered."

William watched as the heavy iron collar was fitted around the girl's neck. Her habit had been pulled down somewhat to bare her throat, allowing the collar to be fitted snugly. Her smooth, tawny skin made William think of his wife because Molly's skin took on a similar hue after a few days at sea, fishing with her father. Perhaps that's what prompted him to do what he did next, or perhaps it was the fact that he didn't like the little man, the Sir Polly fellow, from the way he had been poking at Reine Cameron the other day. Either way, William knew he was 'for it.'

"What did she steal?"

"Bread," was the reply.

"Her master didn't give her bread?"

"Oh, she had enough bread, Monsieur. She had dark bread but that wasn't good enough for her. She had to take her master's white bread for her own use."

"How do you know she took some white bread?"

"Sieur Poilly caught her and made her spit it out. He had the evidence with him when he witnessed against her."

"Thank, you, priest." William indicated that the priest could move off, which he did.

Beckoning to an English soldier on patrol, William requested him to fetch his corporal. As he waited, he made some corrections to the appearance of the now silent major. He straightened the army tunic, pulling it taut under the gold sword belt and fastening the metal clasp at the throat so the tunic was closed at the top. Major Inch suffered through the adjustments without a word of complaint although, from the look in his eyes, William thought he might have wanted to ask a question but wasn't able to manipulate his tongue at this stage of his intoxication.

"That's a good officer," William whispered to him. "You're on parade. Stand tall."

Heavy footsteps behind him announced the arrival of a corporal and four grenadiers. Six paces in front of the major the corporal gave the command for the patrol to halt. He stepped forward, smartly, two paces, and gave a butt salute on his weapon. Addressing the major he asked, "You require assistance, sir?"

William returned the salute. "Major Inch, of the general's personal staff, wants that woman released from the stocks. If there is any difficulty, particularly from that little man over there, take him into custody for making a public disturbance."

The corporal glanced over to where the woman was standing with her chin raised by the width of the iron collar and her arms lifted to their fullest extent by the short chain on the wrist manacles; she looked as if she were pleading with an unkind god.

"Beggin' your pardon, sir," said the corporal, for the first time recognizing the presence of the naval officer, "we only have room for the governor and his staff in custody, Lieutenant."

"I see. Well, the major expects the little man will make a fuss …"

"I will take care of anyone makin' a fuss, sir!" He saluted and moved his patrol off.

William decided he had better lead the glassy-eyed major back to the Government Building where they had first met. "Christ! You're pissed, mate," William hissed as he slung the other man's arm across his shoulders and half dragged, half carried him along. Halfway, William found the going a lot easier as he gained support from someone on the other side of the drooping body. Peeking around the big stomach, he saw that the slave girl had a firm grasp of the other arm. Together, they guided Major Inch to the vestibule and seated him on a wooden bench. The girl unfastened the army officer's collar and belt. She smiled at William, saying something in French. It sounded comforting or reassuring, so William left them there while he took the opportunity to look around the edifice.

He was impressed. It was a wonderful building, made of the finest materials, by the best craftsmen. Truly a work of art, he thought. He wandered from room to room until he came to what must have been the apartment of the governor. The doors being ajar, he knocked timidly on the double doors and then pushed them open. He was startled to find a civilian, with a measuring stick, telling off the measurements of a stupendous stone mantel and fireplace to a sapper of an army engineering company. The civilian turned to face the intruder. William was dumbfounded!

"Mister Mauger!" He was so surprised to find Joshua Mauger in Louisbourg, let alone in the governor's apartment, that he couldn't stop the next question. "What in hell are you doing here?"

"Mindin' my own business, Lieutenant Gray, which I suggest you do immediately." With that he resumed his task of measuring the fireplace. He spoke to the sapper as if William wasn't there. "What do you think, Amos? Cut it into sections?"

"Christ!" William said when he realized that the man in the sapper's uniform was Amos Skinner! Amos Skinner who had attacked him one night on the Halifax waterfront when William had been trying to apprehend a gang of rum smugglers. With these two rogues together, there must be skulduggery afoot! William had no doubt in his mind that Skinner was a liar and thief and possibly a murderer, and here he was disguised as a soldier in league with Joshua Mauger, reputed to be a successful Halifax businessman and friend of the English Court, who was, as far as William was concerned, the most unsavoury peddler, smuggler and all-around thug on the eastern seaboard. Mauger and Skinner—here was a pair up to no good!

"Amos Skinner is not a soldier! He's a convicted smuggler!"

Unperturbed by William's comment or presence, Mauger didn't even bother to look up. "He's a soldier right now, Gray, and please be so kind as to mind yer own business. Ye've caused me deep troubles before with your pettifoggin' interference in my legitimate dealings and …

"Legitimate dealings! Governor Cornwallis ordered me to stop you in your nefarious schemes and it's too bad we only caught people of the likes of Skinner! This time, I've got *you!*"

"Well, laddie, Cornwallis is no longer governor," Mauger said as he gestured for Skinner to continue, "and we'll soon be on our way."

Without another word, William turned on his heel and stormed out of the apartment. He descended as quickly as he could to the street level, looking for an army patrol. No luck! There was no one within hailing distance. Re-entering the building, he considered going back to try to detain them but only for a moment; Skinner was a huge man and William had already lost one encounter to the bastard. "I don't need to do that again!"

"Pardon, M'sieu?" The girl had loosened the major's tunic and the top of his trousers. He was now stretched out, full length, wearing a stupid smile as she washed his face and neck with a damp cloth. She looked up at William with large, brown eyes, waiting for his instructions.

"Damn!"

"Oui, M'sieu."

"I'm going to borrow the major's sword, Madam."

"Oui, M'sieu."

Hefting the light, ceremonial sword to better get the feel of it, William tiptoed down the corridor until he came to the apartment's double doors. Someone had closed them. He turned the handle but the doors remained closed; they were locked. Without hesitation he used the sword to pry them open.

From the street William could hear Amos Skinner as he shouted, "Hurry, sergeant! There are looters in the governor's apartment!"

William had time to determine that there appeared to be nothing missing and that the only damage was the splintered wood of the double doors where he had, himself, forced entry before he heard a voice behind him say, "If you move, sir, you will be shot."

With his arms spread wide and the ceremonial sword dangling from one finger, he turned to face the security patrol. Lieutenant William Gray was disarmed and taken into custody.

Of course, there was no sign of Amos Skinner.

July 31, 1758
Porte Frederic

Two Royal Navy lieutenants watched as the French civilians and disbanded soldiers lined up to be registered for deportation.

"They line up to get food, to get blankets, to get medicines and now we have them line up to get out of here." Lieutenant Sherman of *H.M.S. Namur* glanced at his companion. "I guess you didn't think that was clever, eh, Gray?" Sherman nudged the other officer, "What say you, Gray?"

William didn't know Sherman very well. In fact, this was only the second time he had encountered the man. The first time (and it seemed so long ago, now) was when William boarded *H.M.S. Namur* to brief General Wolfe about determining the depth of the water off White Point before any English warships were committed to the assault. Sherman had been the *Namur* duty officer who challenged William at the ship's entry port. William had considered him a bit of a dandy then, what with his beautifully tailored uniform that had never encountered seawater and his haughty flagship airs. Bit of a prig, William had reckoned. Now, William's whole career, perhaps his life, would rest in Sherman's hands, but William still considered the other fellow a prig. William turned his back on Sherman, pretending to study the long line of Frenchmen.

Sherman sounded annoyed when he spoke again. "It's not my fault that your ship is on patrol right now."

With a start, William recognized someone in the line-up. Intrigued, William took a few steps in the direction of the line-up.

Following Gray's movement, Sherman persisted in making his point. "You are entitled to an officer of your ship to advise you and speak up for you. We both know that isn't possible while your ship is at sea." Sherman moved around so he could see the expression on Gray's face. "What in hell are you smiling at? In your position I wouldn't be smiling."

William was deep in his own thoughts; *I guess the little bastard did make a fuss.* William took another pace or two toward the line because the Frenchman had moved behind someone, out of William's sight. *Yes, there were two more lumps on the man's face. He must have been struck two or three times by the looks of it.* William felt a glow of satisfaction. *The bastard goes around poking at defenceless women he deserves a few pokes back—with a musket butt!*

The Frenchman noticed the English naval officer staring at him. He said something with a pleading tone in his voice.

Without taking his eyes of the small man, William asked Sherman, "Do you understand what he is saying?"

"Yes, of course."

The Frenchman spoke again.

William waited for Sherman to translate while the Frenchman continued speaking. Sherman was plucking at some lint on his tunic, not making any effort to comply with William's request.

Irritated by Sherman's lack of response, William abruptly turned. "Will you get on with it and tell me what he is saying?"

Surprised that Gray would be interested in the complaints of a French prisoner, Sherman huffily replied, "Prisoners are always bitching, but if you insist, he says he is Engineer Poilly and he is being treated as a common citizen. He says he should have been quartered with the governor's staff and not left to fend for himself. Worse, he has been beaten by English soldiers and ..." here Sherman hesitated and then recommenced his translation, "... one of our officers interfered with the proper punishment of his slave and then took her for his own uses." Sherman stared at Poilly for a moment and then, turning his attention to Gray, exclaimed, "This bugger confirms one of the charges laid against you, Gray!" He slapped his hand against his thigh. "The devil! He's a witness against you!"

William didn't say anything although there was a look of surprise on his face.

"It's bad enough that I was ordered to represent you, Gray, but to discover that you are actually guilty ... I can't imagine anything worse for my career." He pulled his sword close to his side as if it might brush against Gray and be contaminated. He stepped several paces toward the gate, away from William. For a long while he stood there, staring out through Porte Frederic Gate at the water. "Oh, jolly good! Here comes the communications craft."

Neither officer spoke while they waited for the bumboat. When it arrived, Sherman allowed Gray to board first and then conspicuously seated himself as far from William as space would allow. "Take us to *Royal William*, boatman," was all he had to say.

H.M.S. Royal William was the flagship of Sir Charles Hardy, Rear Admiral of the White, and Commander of one of the three Divisions of the English Fleet. It fell to Admiral Hardy to convene the Board to investigate the charges laid against an officer of one of the other Divisions, namely William Gray, Lieutenant of *H.M.S. Sutherland*, a fourth rate warship of Commodore Durell's Division.

At the entry port of the ship, William surrendered his sword. He and his official representative, Lieutenant Sherman, were told to wait off to one side, while the board members arrived from their respective ships.

The first to arrive was Captain Swanton of *H.M.S. Vanguard*, a third rate warship of seventy guns belonging to Hardy's Division. He nodded at the two men as he passed by on his way to the captain's cabin where the hearing was to be held. Captain Parry of the *Kennington*, a sixty-gun fourth rate of Hardy's Division, did not acknowledge their presence. When the *Namur's* Captain Buckle arrived, he spent a few minutes with the two lieutenants enquiring after Sherman's uncle and his naval successes in the Mediterranean. Captain Buckle excused himself and proceeded aft.

Lieutenant Sherman sighed. Then he spoke to Gray for the first time since their arrival on the *Royal William*. "Splendid fellow! Old friend of the family."

"Will it do us any good during the hearing?" William asked.

Sherman fidgeted with his sword handle. Finally he said, "I will go see how long we will have to wait." Before William could comment, Sherman pushed past whispering, "I won't be very long, old chum."

Standing there, William felt truly alone in the world. *Well, at least Molly, my Molly, wouldn't know anything about this until it was all over. In a way, that was good because she wouldn't have to go through the worry of my guilt or innocence, dismissal of the charges or death. No, this way was better for Molly. She wouldn't know until it was all over and, besides, Captain LeForey had laid the stiffest charge he could: in that, Lieutenant William Gray, whilst an officer of His Majesty's Navy and in the face of the enemy, did disregard the orders of competent authority.* William sucked his teeth and then swallowed. *Of course, if Sutherland had been in port, Captain Rous would have ... but my captain, my ship, my mates, my friends were somewhere to the northeast prowling for French warships. All the help I will have is what I would get from that prig, Sherman. Where was the prig, anyway? Taking long enough, he was.* William stared at his boots as he continued his thoughts. *If I'm found guilty of any charge with an 'in the face of the enemy' clause attached to it, there would be a death sentence.* "An automatic death sentence," he said to himself. "The Royal Navy doesn't like to leave anything to chance. Found guilty? Hang him!"

William glanced over at the marine guards to see if they were listening but they weren't.

Then there's the second charge: in that, Lieutenant William Gray, whilst an officer of His Majesty's Navy, did interfere with the actions of competent civilian authority. Captain LeForey had *probably found out about freeing the girl from the stockade.* Wistfully, he wished he hadn't gotten involved in that one. *It seemed like the right thing to do at the time—the little Frenchman getting poked back. No, I don't regret helping the slave girl, but the last charge, the one that should have been laid against Mauger and Skinner, I don't deserve, and yet I have no defence! In my heart of hearts I know I'll be condemned to death as a looter! If Uncle Charles were still alive, what would he think of a Gray being executed for looting? What would my sainted mother think?* He said a little prayer that he would have their understanding in the afterlife. When he had finished, he looked up to watch his defending officer approach.

"Sorry to take so long, old man, but they are ready for us now." Lieutenant Sherman seemed to be calm and in control. He took William by the elbow and propelled him toward the companionway leading to the captain's cabin. "Knock twice on the cabin door," he said in William's ear as they moved along. "You are to enter, hat off and under your arm, and sit on the empty chair to the right. You will not speak unless spoken to." Sherman stopped William in front of a mahogany door. "Knock twice," he hissed.

William knocked and entered.

William didn't remember anything of the first half hour in the cabin. He was sitting in front of three senior Royal Navy officers who were giving various instructions to the clerks, the friend of the accused, and the prosecuting officer, but William might just as well have been at Carmichael's in Halifax for all the attention he was giving to it. His mind wandering, he could see, in the half-light of the tavern, Wimper smiling as Rous said something interesting …

Sherman was pulling at his sleeve and whispering in his ear.

"What did you say, Sherman?"

"I have been named as the friend of the accused. You have no trouble with that?"

"No. I agree." William retreated into his thoughts. *When we get back to Halifax, I'll have to find out what is troubling Rous—something really serious by the sounds of it.*

"The prosecutor is Lieutenant James Campbell. You can't object, but do you have any observation about their using another Northerner to prosecute you?"

The Campbells and the Grays were allied clans at home. It was a typically English touch to have one Scot seek the death penalty for another. "No. I agree."

"They will proceed with the 'disregarding competent authority' charge first. Do you have any problem with that?"

"No, I agree."

Sherman stood up. "The accused is ready to proceed." He sat down.

Captain Buckle smiled as he said, "Lieutenant Sherman, the friend of the accused is not expected to call him 'the accused.'"

Lieutenant Sherman stood. "Then what should I call him, sir?" He sat down.

Adjusting some papers on the wide plotting table that was being used as a bench by the three officers, Captain Buckle seemed to be taking his time making a response. He glanced at the clerks. One of the two clerks was seated, off to one side, at the captain's desk; the other clerk was near the large transom where the light was better but having to use his knees to support his tablet. Making up his mind, Buckle rapped his heavy gold ring on the table to get everyone's attention.

"There is to be no record of this next exchange." He waited until the clerks had put their pens down before he continued. Leaning forward on his elbows, Captain Buckle fixed his steely eyes on Sherman, who had risen to his feet as a consequence. "Robert, Lieutenant Gray's life is threatened by these proceedings, so stop worrying about *your* career and commence working to represent your fellow officer." Captain Buckle placed a pair of spectacles on the end of his nose and peered over them at the red-faced lieutenant. "Have I made myself clear, Robert?"

Lieutenant Sherman stood. "Yes sir, you have, sir." He sat down.

"Then call Lieutenant Gray what you will as long as it isn't 'the accused.'" Captain Buckle coughed and dabbed at his mouth and nose with a linen from his wrist. "And you may address this hearing while seated, Lieutenant."

Sherman bobbed up and down twice before deciding to remain seated as he responded, "Yes, sir."

Shuffling the papers again Captain Buckle intoned, "The clerks may resume." He chose one sheet and passed it to the nearest clerk, the one sitting at the transom, for him to read, but he immediately dropped it on the deck.

While the clerk fumbled with his pen, tablet and inkpot, Captain Buckle recovered the charge sheet. "No matter, clerk, you may make notes as I read." He read from the sheet.

"The Charge
In that, Lieutenant William Gray, whilst an officer of His Majesty's Navy and in the face of the enemy, did disregard the orders of competent authority."

He ran his finger down the page.

"The Particulars
    One: the night of July 25, 1758, on Louisbourg Harbour, while leading an independent command against the French warship, *Prudent*, Captain LeForey gave the signal for the attacking force to hold its position while a response

was made to interrogations from enemy lookouts. Disregarding the orders of Captain LeForey, Lieutenant Gray led *Sutherland* boats through the middle of the attacking force thus endangering the entire operation.

Two: the early morning of July 26, 1758, on Louisbourg Harbour, following a successful assault on the French warship, *Prudent*, Captain LeForey ordered the withdrawal of the English forces. One of the *Sutherland* boats, under the command of Lieutenant Gray, disregarded the order thus endangering the lives of the boat's personnel."

Captain Buckle paused in the reading. He locked his eyes on the handsome officer in the salt-stained uniform as he said, "The recommendation is imposition of the maximum penalty, death." Again, the captain paused, "We will hear from the prosecuting officer."

The prosecuting officer was an older man with thinning hair, a weather-beaten face and a lithe, young-looking body sheathed in a well-worn uniform. Without hesitation he began, "I have provided the presiding officers with copies of the general statement by Captain LeForey which bear out in detail the nature of the charge. Before the beginning of the hearing I gave the friend of the accused a copy of the good captain's statement and therefore recommend that we forgo the reading into the record of the statement.

Captain Buckle raised a questioning eyebrow at Lieutenant Sherman. Before Sherman could reply William tugged at his sleeve.

"I didn't know you were given anything. What does it say?"

Seemingly flustered, Sherman shielded his mouth from the eyes of the presiding officers as he whispered to William, "It is virtually a copy of Captain LeForey's report to the admiral on the details of the assault. I could see no harm ..."

"I want to know what it says," William reached and pulled Sherman down by the collar of his tunic, "before we go any further with this!"

From the bench, Captain Parry commented to the other

captains, "I can see no harm in passing the report into the record; the admiral has already approved it."

"So be it." Buckle pointed at one of the clerks. "Attach a copy to the record with the proper notations and I will sign it." The clerk nodded as Captain Parry handed over his copy.

"Do you plan to call witnesses, Lieutenant Campbell?"

"No, sir. The record is plain; Lieutenant Gray is guilty of crass disobedience on both counts."

"Let us not be too vivid with our language, Lieutenant. And your recommendation?"

"Maximum penalty, sir."

"Hmm." Buckle nodded at the prosecuting officer as if complimenting him on an efficient, effective presentation. He gestured to Sherman. "The friend of the accused will call witnesses?"

"No, sir. There are no witnesses."

"Rebuttal?"

William raised his hand like a schoolboy. "I wish to make a rebuttal, sir."

"You may not speak unless addressed by one of the officers on the bench, Lieutenant. That is why you have an officer to assist you."

Captain Parry, nodding his head in agreement, added, "The admiral's staff drew up these regulations before we left Halifax. In an operation this grand, there must be simple, efficient administrative procedures to handle the many disciplinary problems that were bound to arise or we would never have found time to trounce the Frogs."

Silent up to now, Captain Swanton, his face more florid than usual, harrumphed and then said, "We would spend all our time in hearings, yes, we would. This is our second hearing today and we have one more to go before we can toast the King's health. Many things to do, so let's get on with it!"

A look of panic passed over William's face. Somehow he was going to have to speak through this dolt of a Lieutenant Sherman and convince the captains that he had not seen the signal to 'hold' and had not disobeyed when he recovered his sailor from the burning *Prudent*. He stared into Sherman's eyes and saw there that he was doomed. Sherman was only concerned with his own performance in front of the captains. The captains, in their turn, were concerned with looking efficient in the eyes of the admiral. The fate of a Scotsman named Gray was incidental.

There was a timid knock on the mahogany door.

The captains were not certain where the noise had come from so they didn't address it until a second, stronger knock was made. All three responded at the same time, "Enter!"

A very frightened naval officer stood in the doorway with his hat on and standing stiffly at attention. "Lieutenant Adams, sirs, with a message from *Sutherland*." Probably everyone in the cabin counted his steps as Adams marched to the front of the bench and handed a sealed letter to Captain Buckle. Once relieved of his burden, he saluted and took two paces back. He waited.

Captain Buckle expelled his breath, almost as a sigh, as he said, "Our Captain Rous is back!" He slit the seal with a sailor's knife that he produced from somewhere and read the contents. He looked up at the petrified officer. "How many do you say?"

"Fifteen, sir."

Buckle stroked his chin as he pondered the contents of the letter. Then he began to read the text out loud, "Charges have been laid against a *Sutherland* officer concerning his actions during the assault of the French ship, *Prudent*. I have such confidence in my officer that I have made available for your examination all of the ship's company who were with Lieutenant Gray during that action. They are encouraged to reveal whatever information they possess so the Board can be sure of the absolute truth of the matter before a decision is rendered." Captain Buckle put the letter to one side. "It is signed, 'Rous.'"

"Well!" It was Captain Swanton shaking his head. "I never …"

"The *Sutherland* has always sailed his own course," was all Captain Parry would say.

Pointing a finger at Lieutenant Sherman, Buckle demanded, "I thought you said there were no witnesses?"

"There weren't, sir." Seeing the disapproval in the three captains, he hurried on. "At least, not until *Sutherland* returned."

"You could have sought a postponement, Lieutenant."

Sherman sputtered and stuttered, "I- I- I s-saw the B-Board's s-schedule, sir and … I- I thought …"

Buckle waved the officer to silence. "Lieutenant …?"

"Adams, sir."

"Lieutenant Adams, we will hear from one, and only one, of the witnesses. Please pick the most articulate and accompany him in here."

"Aye, sir."

William Gray was not the least bit surprised when Adams led a self-important Able Seaman Fink into the cabin.

"Lieutenant Adams reports, sirs, that this seaman has been ordered to answer all questions, fully and truthfully, without fear or favour. His name is Fink, sirs. Able Seaman Fink."

"Very well, Fink, were you with Lieutenant Gray during the *Prudent* assault?"

"I was, sir, I certainly was. Sittin' on the thwart right in front of the young officer, sir, rowin' me very heart out as were all me mates."

"Why did you keep on rowing when the assault commander gave the order to hold?"

"Weren't no order given like that as I could see, sir. We rowed right through the whole mess of 'em, the coxs'n steering us through the jumble of boats as neat as you please. Ya see, it was the second time we was all in a jumble that night but we hit the side of the ship; 'no grapples' our lieutenant says. Used boat hooks, we did, so our boats could be moved away, allowin' the slower boats to get in. Up on the deck like thieves in the night and we was clearin' the deck of all Frenchmen 'fore the other crews got there. Had it all nice and tidy for 'em and Captain LeForey we did."

Lieutenant Campbell indicated that he wanted to pose questions. Receiving Buckle's permission he asked, "You were rowing?"

Fink nodded, 'yes.'

"So you must have been facing Lieutenant Gray?"

"Aye, sir."

"Then you would be facing the wrong way to be able to see the commander's signals. You don't know if the signal was given or not."

"Well, he did sumpthin' 'cause all the boats was in a jumble again."

"Ha!" Captain Swanton clapped his hands together. "That's the point! The order must have been given because all the other boats were stopped!"

Captain Parry said, slowly, "and your boat didn't stop because …"

"Because we couldn't see far enough in the dark and mist … couldn't see two boat lengths."

Campbell looked annoyed. "You don't know what was going on, Seaman Bink."

"Fink, sir. Seaman Fink, and the French lookout couldn't see none too good either, since he couldn't see we wusn't French! We destroyed that ship because Lieutenant Gray got us there 'fore the French lookout got a good look at us."

"I think we have enough information on that score," Captain Buckle interceded. "Tell me, sailor, where were you when the order to withdraw was given?"

Fink swelled with pride, "I was the last *Sutherland* on the *Prudent's* deck, helpin' the Frenchies what was trapped over the side with a friendly boot. If anyone gave an order to leave me there, I don't know about it. Me mates was there waitin' for me when I came back down." Fink grinned, "I came down so hard I near come to flatten Captain LeForey. He was a gentleman about it all, his bein' an officer and all that."

William could see the surprise in Buckle's face. "You mean to tell me that Captain LeForey was in the boat that went back to *Prudent* after the withdraw order was given?"

"I know nuthin' about them comin' back, sir. I know they was there when I jumped down from that burnin' deck and Captain LeForey broke me fall, he did."

Captain Buckle glanced at his companions and then pushed back his chair. "I ask that all persons vacate the cabin while we have a discussion." Seeing the protest forming in the prosecuting officer's face, Buckle added, "We will recall you as soon as possible." With that he waved them out of the cabin.

As soon as they were alone, the presiding officers all tried to speak at once.

"LeForey was with him during the withdrawal ..."

"If it was so dark the Frenchman couldn't see who it was, how could Gray ..."

"LeForey was going to abandon that sailor, Bink?"

"Fink," the other two officers said in unison.

They all smiled at each other. It was Swanton who spoke next, "Could we have LeForey called to testify?"

"I'm afraid not. As a reward for his service, LeForey was given command of *Echo*. He's working up his new crew." Buckle breathed a long sigh, adding, "*Echo* is at sea."

"The whole *Prudent* operation was Gray's idea, I'm told." It was Parry's turn to sigh. "The man who actually captured *Prudent* is charged with disobedience ..."

"While LeForey gets a new ship."

There was silence in the cabin. Finally, Swanton spoke. "We haven't all day, you know. Got another one of these to go through before the end of the day and there are two more charges to hear on this one."

"Right!" Buckle leaned back in his chair to enable him to see both officers. "What say you on this first charge?"

"Deferred until we speak with LeForey."

"Dismissed," said Swanton. "These things can go on and on if we are not decisive."

Buckle nodded his head, "I suggest 'not guilty' since we have two more charges, one of them with the death penalty."

"And he seems to be a good man." Parry had another thought. "He was involved in the *Trent* rescue, you know; led the boarding party."

"I agree to not guilty. We should be decisive," answered Swanton.

"Not guilty it is then."

Captain Buckle cleared his throat as a sign that he had a pronouncement to make. "I must tell you that Lieutenant

Sherman informed me of a Frenchman who is, apparently, an excellent witness to the next charge. The Frenchman would be a witness for the prosecuting officer."

"No!" Parry allowed his disbelief to show in his voice. "That's not playing fair!" He banged his fist on the table, "The friend of the accused is, well, the *friend* of the accused. He shouldn't be finding witnesses for the prosecuting officer."

"If the Frenchman is credible, we will get to the truth much quicker ..."

"And be more decisive."

"I ordered him here and I arranged for an interpreter." Buckle glanced swiftly from one officer to the other to gauge the reaction. Seeing no further dissent he clapped his hands together. "Right. Parry, you're the junior, get the unwashed multitude back in here."

By the time William re-entered the cabin, everyone was nicely settled in his place. Captain Buckle motioned for William to remain standing. "Lieutenant Gray, by virtue of the Admiral's new administrative procedures, we are not obliged to give our decision in writing. On the charge ..." here Captain Buckle riffled through some papers but not finding what he was looking for, continued, "disobeying some orders from Captain LeForey, you are found to be not guilty. There are two other charges and we will proceed with them immediately." He waved his hand at William saying, "You should sit. Lieutenant Campbell has a witness who will be brought in now."

William watched with open-mouthed astonishment as Sieur Poilly was led into the cabin. William turned to say something to the scarlet-faced Sherman but thought better of it. *I'll kill the bastard*, he promised himself as the second charge was read.

It was tedious process as far as William was concerned. The question in English, repeated in French, a long-winded response in French, back into English, and then the observations and opinions of Campbell and, occasionally, Sherman. It was so tedious that William wanted to stand up and scream that he was guilty. *Matter of fact, I am guilty. No doubt of it. I had given the order to release the slave woman ...*

"Major Hinch? Who cares about Major Hinch?" Captain Buckle shook his finger vigorously at the interpreter, "Find out what he is talking about! I don't want to hear about Major anybody! I want information about Lieutenant somebody! So far he hasn't mentioned Lieutenant Gray!"

Quickly the interpreter verified with Sieur Poilly that he did not know of a Lieutenant Gray. It was Major Hinch who had given the order to stop the punishment. It was Major Hinch who had taken Poilly's slave to Government House where the major had been drinking the governor's wine; there were many empty bottles. Yes, right in the Government Building the slave girl had loosened the major's clothing and might have taken off her own clothing if the patrol had not come upon them.

"Ask him how he knows all this."

"He says the patrol corporal told him where Major Hinch had gone. Sieur Polly followed to recover his property."

"The slave girl?"

"Yes. The slave girl."

"Do we know who this major is?"

Lieutenant Campbell opened his file. "Yes sir, we do."

"Well?"

"I didn't get it from the main file because it had been sequestered and marked 'no further action.'" Lieutenant Campbell hesitated. "I only have his name because it was inscribed on the army sword Lieutenant Gray had in his possession when he was apprehended."

"Lieutenant Campbell! Please identify, for the record, who this major is."

"He's an army intelligence officer. Major ..."

"That's enough, Lieutenant!" Captain Buckle's face had gone stark white.

Captain Parry looked very much as if he was going to be sick.

"Well, man!" Captain Swanton was leaning forward, intent upon learning the identity of the army major who was probably guiltier of looting than Lieutenant Gray; at least Gray hadn't been caught drinking the governor's wine. "Spit it out! We want to know who he is so we can have the army disciplinary board have a go at him! Can't have looters, no we can't."

Captain Buckle grasped Captain Swanton by the wrist. "If you please, Captain Swanton, arrange to have the cabin cleared, again."

Swanton managed to gain control of his arm as he objected, "I am not the junior on this board!"

"That, sir, is correct, but, if you please ..."

"Aye, Captain Buckle." Swanton rose. " Clear out, the pack of you! We'll let you know when we want you back."

Swanton waited until the door close before turning and facing Captain Buckle. "Now, see here, Charles."

"Who is the staff intelligence officer?"

"We all know that. It's Major Geoffrey Inch."

"And why was he given his majority and made senior intelligence officer on his first field assignment?"

"Because he's the bastard son of Prince ..."

"Yes."

Swanton sat down. "Christ!"

"You want his name read into the record?"

"Christ!"

"And you want him to be charged as a looter?"

"Oh, Christ!"

The three officers sat, contemplating the end of their careers.

Finally, Parry said in a soft voice, "Louisbourg was not granted terms. Therefore, it could be reasoned that, since all the inhabitants are prisoners of war ..."

"Yes, of course. There is no harm in drinking a bottle of the enemy's wine."

"Or going into a building to see if there are any enemy soldiers skulking there."

"For heaven's sake. We must dismiss the charges against Gray."

"If we expunge them, there is no report to the admiral."

"Expunge the record, then."

"Who will explain the facts of life to Captain LeForey?" Parry had been adjusting his sword. When he looked up he found both officers staring at him. "Well?" He repeated, "Who will tell the good captain ..." He stopped his fiddling and shrugged his shoulders, "Oh." He was the junior captain.

* * *

Afterwards, Lieutenant William Gray, his sword returned to him, was standing in the lee of the water casks at the mainmast of the *Royal William* as he waited for the senior officers to depart.

Lieutenant Campbell, also obliged to wait his turn, joined him. "When I get the chance, I must congratulate your friend Sherman on an admirable defence strategy."

"I wasn't aware of it."

"Well, let me tell you."

"Don't bother, Campbell."

The subject of their conversation passed by in company of Captain Buckle. Buckle was commending the lieutenant on his handling of the case. "I must admit you had us bamboozled, Sherman. Supplying the prosecutor with the one witness who could prove the innocence of your friend and," here he lowered his voice so much that if he hadn't been standing on the other side of the water barrel Gray and Campbell would not have been able to hear him, "if there were to be repercussions about the involvement of the prince's son, it would have been that Northerner, Campbell, who would have borne the royal displeasure." He let his voice resume its normal level. "Jolly clever work, my boy!" The captain clapped the younger man on the back. "I will be sure to tell your father."

"And my uncle, sir?"

"Certainly. I will tell him next time I see him at the Admiralty."

It was Captain Buckle's turn to leave the ship. He motioned for Sherman to join him and they departed.

The two lieutenants studied the other ships in the harbour.

When the deck officer motioned to William that his boat had arrived in its turn, William nodded to Campbell as he gathered his sword scabbard to his side.

"We have no friends here." Campbell was still studying the ships and not looking at the other Scotsman.

William held out his hand. "I think I have just made a friend, Campbell."

"Aye, you have, Gray." Campbell took the proffered hand and shook it warmly.

Stepping along to the entry port, William was conscious that the other Scot was closely following as if loath to see him depart. *It's true,* he thought; *we are a solitary pair of Scotsmen surrounded by English sailors and marines on an English ship where some English officers had attempted to arrange for my death— arrange for me to 'take the low road,' as a Scot would say.* William was the first to speak. "Keep taking the high road, Campbell."

"Aye, Gray." Campbell stepped back to give William room to salute the quarterdeck and the pennant. "I'll watch for ye along the way."

August 22, 1758
General Wolfe's Tent
Fortress Louisbourg

"Jenkins! Is that you skulking around outside my tent?"

Corporal Jenkins had been hunched down near the wall of the tent seeking some shelter against the glare of the morning sun. He stood as he responded to his general's voice. "Yes, General. I am right here."

General Wolfe was lying on his bunk with a hot towel draped over his eyes, enduring his continuing problem of a runny nose, puffy eyes and a severe headache. "I thought I told you to report back to your company!"

"You did, sir."

"Well! What are you doing here next to my tent? I told you to go, Corporal."

"There was no one left in my old company to report to, General, and I thought you might have need of me until you take ship back to Halifax."

Jenkins heard the bunk squeak. The tent flap flipped up and out came the general's batman, a slopping basin of water and a towel in his hands as he got out of the way of an irritated General Wolfe.

"Dammit! No one seems to be able to do what they are told lately."

"No, sir," was all Jenkins had time to say before Wolfe exclaimed, "By the gods, I think they are trying to kill my boys." He pointed at the harbour front by Porte Frederic. "The navy loaded them last night! Why are they taking them off this morning?" Wolfe didn't expect a reply because he didn't pause or take a breath. "Do I still have a naval liaison officer?" This time he did want a reply because he asked, "Well, do I?"

"I saw him on the pier this morning. There was a problem …"

"I'll give him a problem if the navy keeps pushing my wounded boys around. They're supposed to be taken to Halifax without delay. Instead, they're being moved on and off the ship as if they were straw dummies for bayonet practice!" Stamping his foot in exasperation Wolfe spoke in his 'I will brook no nonsense' voice, "Bring him here, Corporal!"

Jenkins saluted and took off.

Wolfe stood with his hands on his hips as Jenkins loped down the street in search of Lieutenant Gray. When the corporal had disappeared around the corner, Wolfe beckoned to the batman who was standing to one side still holding the basin and towel. "Put the thing down, Peters, and get me some tea. I am perfectly capable of dressing myself." Once the batman was gone, Wolfe found that his uniform and kit were not laid out waiting for him. "Oh bother!" Wolfe grabbed the towel and threw himself down on the cot. He fumbled the towel over his eyes and forced himself to breathe in a controlled, measured manner, perhaps to reduce the pounding in his head. He had actually achieved some small relief when he heard a polite cough.

"Is that you Corporal?"

"No, sir. It's Lieutenant Gray."

General Wolfe quickly sat up, wincing from the renewed throbbing in his sinuses. "What in heaven's name is being done to my wounded boys?" He dipped the towel in the basin and held it against his forehead, the water dripping down his face and wetting his grey jersey. He pushed his way past Gray and, pointing with his free hand at the transport moored just off Porte Frederic, he complained, "My boys are being off-loaded! They are being dumped on the pier like so many ..." Wolfe was searching for a proper description when William filled in for him.

"Just like so many bayonet practice dummies."

When General Wolfe glared at him for possibly attempting a joke at the general's expense, William hastened to add, "Corporal Jenkins was kind enough to give me the details of your concerns."

"Well then!"

"Our problem is, the harbour is very shallow near the main pier at the Porte Frederic Gateway. Apparently, the French used floating jetties or lighters to move cargo to the ships in the harbour. Unfortunately, we don't have any such equipment; it was destroyed by our guns or burned by the French. The plan was to move the transports in as close as possible to the pier and ..."

"Dammit man! If the ship had run aground, the navy shouldn't have put wounded soldiers on it!"

"She hadn't run aground, sir. Actually, she was riding high in the water when she approached the pier because all supplies and stores had been off-loaded. An extended jetty was built and the wounded were able to walk or be carried to the ship. Then it was planned to move her to deeper water to receive her stores, but she had touched bottom and no amount of towing would budge her."

"What is the navy going to do about it?"

"Well, now there is a new Harbour Master ..." William paused to see if that would have any effect on the general but he wasn't interested. "Some of the wounded will have to be off-loaded, as you can see."

"Dreadful!"

"Yes, sir, but with the surgeon's help, only the most able of the wounded are being chosen to be put ashore and then only as many as it takes for the ship to break free." William had been watching the ships as he had been speaking to the general. "If you will look, General, the transport has signalled she is able to move. See the men at the bow? They're rigging lines for a tow."

"How long will it take to embark my boys?"

"With this setback, general, several weeks. I am, perhaps, as anxious as anyone since *Sutherland* has been detailed to escort the first ships to return to Halifax."

"*Sutherland* will be the first warship to leave?"

"Aye, sir."

General Wolfe motioned to Corporal Jenkins. "Find Peters and tell him I would like to dress, now."

Jenkins moved away.

The general watched him go. "*Sutherland* was told to be the first of the Royal Navy ships to depart the site of a great victory while the celebrations are still continuing? Your Captain Rous is heartily disliked, Gray."

The general's batman, Peters, returned somewhat out of breath. Wolfe waved a hand at him, "Peters, get some fresh hot water. I would want you to shave the hairs off my neck." With that, the batman was gone again.

"You seem to have the same penchant for upsetting Royal Navy captains as does your dear Rous." Wolfe gave a slightly girlish-sounding laugh. "In fact, I think you are more skilled at it; *three* charges? That LeForey chap must have been severely aggravated. He charged you with looting? There were no surrender conditions for the French so how could there be looting?" Wolfe turned to re-enter the tent. "And what were the other charges? Just as bogus?" He sat on the edge of the bunk and looked up at Gray with a stern face and a steely eye. "If I were that displeased with your presence, I would have arranged for you to meet a pistol ball at the height of the attack," and then a lovely, friendly smile, "or do you wear a metal plate in the middle of your back, too?"

Gray had to step back as the batman returned with a steaming bowl of water.

General Wolfe allowed the batman to pass into the tent and then he stood up and extended his hand to the lieutenant. "I want to thank you, Lieutenant Gray, for your efforts on behalf of my boys." He sat down and leaned his head forward, exposing the back of his neck for the batman's attentions with the razor. "You have my permission, Gray, to return to your ship."

"Aye, sir." Gray saluted and walked away from the general's tent. Since he no longer had any gear ashore, having moved back on board right after his appearance before the Captain's Board, he decided to go to the waterfront and catch a bumboat back to *Sutherland*. At least that way, he might stay out of trouble.

"I say, Gray!" It was Major Inch, still showing signs of the continuing celebrations in his flushed face and unsteady gait. "What ho, Gray! Did you hear that I am taking ship with you to Halifax? We shall be, as you say, mates."

William saluted. "No, Major, I didn't hear that since I have been taken up with appearances before a Captain's Board."

"Jolly good fun as long as you aren't the accused." Inch put his arm over William's shoulder and drew him in closer so he could whisper some information. "I want to thank you for putting me in the hands of my little Jenny." In even more conspiratorial tones he went on, "Actually, her name is Genevieve but I will be calling her Jamie until we get her to Halifax."

"You mean the slave girl?"

"Sh-h-h-h, my dear boy! Mustn't let the cat out of the bag! I mean to take her to London where, with her vibrant looks and flashing eyes, she will be a sensation at court."

"Captain Rous knows about this?"

"Of course, dear boy!" Inch pulled William even closer. "Actually, I mustn't misrepresent his involvement in my little deceit. As the first warship to return to Halifax, he has orders to transport me and my manservant," here the Major gave an exaggerated wink, "so that we might catch the first ship home where I will personally report our huge successes to the King."

Major Inch released his hold on the lieutenant. "I must also tell Father what a jolly fine fellow that Captain Rous is," Inch poked William in the ribs, "assigning me a cabin for privacy on *Sutherland* where living space is so dreadfully limited."

The duty sergeant saluted as he called out, "There's a harbour craft at the pier, Major."

"Yes, indeed. Isn't that just our good fortune?" Major Inch took up the refrain of a religious song where 'the righteous shall always triumph' which he sang all the way to *Sutherland*, where his 'Jamie' waited for him in the privacy of Lieutenant William Gray's cabin.

Endnotes

[1] The final entry of the unknown officer's report on the siege of Louisbourg. "31st Admiral Boscawen sailed in and was saluted by the town."

[2] *H.M.S. Sutherland* was sent out on patrol.

Chapter Nine

"Through that notch and off to starboard is my home." William Gray was pointing to the break in the shoreline as *Sutherland*, on a starboard tack with a smart breeze, was having no difficulty passing the Ledges and Black Rock, making good time into the harbour itself.

Captain Rous nodded his head. "Aye, William. We won't have to stop for a pilot ... you still have your papers?"

"Aye, sir."

"That will save us time. The sooner I get ashore, the sooner I can shoot Bulkeley."

William took a quick look around to see if anyone else might have overheard the remark; however, they were quite alone at the rail and the noises of the wind in the rigging would have masked the comment even if there had been someone standing close.

"Sir, you're not going to shoot Richard. After all, he's your son-in-law!"

"I probably won't shoot him to kill him. No, that would be too easy and they might hang me for it. I'll shoot him in the ass so he won't sit a horse again, at least not in this lifetime."

"Goddamit, sir! Are you going out of your mind?"

"You watch your tongue, young man." Rous leaned on the rail, clasping and unclasping his hands. "He promised my Amy he would love her in sickness and in health. Well, that he ain't done." He stood upright and turned to look back out to sea. "I mean to have him suffer for the troubles he's caused her."

"What's he done?"

"First, the high and mighty Richard Bulkeley moves out of her bed. Then, he moves her, bag and baggage, out of the mansion into the old house and refuses to see her." Rous turned his

249

head away but William could still see the glistening of tears in the old sailor's eyes. "He says what she has is catching." He shrugged his shoulders. "It's only a cough; besides, we all get to die sometime."

"Could it be consumption?"

"What if it is? That's no way to treat his wife! At least, it's no way to treat my daughter."

William said, thoughtfully, "Poor Amy, she has everything in this world ..."

"Except a loving husband," Rous interrupted. "Now, I don't want to speak of it again, you hear me?"

"Aye, sir."

The two men—one tall and broad-shouldered, standing erect, looking ahead to the smoke of the settlement with eagerness, the second shorter and seemingly too small for all the gold braid and buttons that adorned the uniform of a senior naval officer—watched the shoreline close at hand and didn't look in the direction of Halifax at all.

Eventually they were abreast Point Pleasant where, in *Sutherland's* absence, more trees had been cut and several small homes with neat fences had been built. At George's Island, William commented on the lack of trees and the resulting bare look to the island, but the captain did not respond.

Signals from the King's Harbour Master indicated they were to take up a mooring opposite the site of the new dockyard. Captain Rous gave over the task to the duty officer who happened to be Lieutenant Adams, and went below. He did not return topside until all activity had ceased; even then, following the warning of 'Captain on deck,' he said nothing until Adams confirmed, by examining the dock with the glass, that there was a coach dockside sporting Bulkeley's green livery.

"Signal that officers will go ashore, Lieutenant Adams."

"Aye, sir."

Promptly the signal was raised, a harbour craft left the government pier and moved smartly toward *Sutherland*.

Rous watched the small craft slice through the water for a few moments. "Adams, the transports are assigned moorings?"

"Aye, sir. All seems well, Captain."

"Lieutenant Gray, you wish to join me ashore?"

"Thank you, sir. If Molly isn't on the pier already, she will soon be there. I appreciate your kind offer."

Lieutenant Adams called for the in-port ladder to be rigged on the side of the ship.

Captain Rous waved it away, making his way down the rope ladder with an ease that belied his years. William, thirty-five or forty years the Captain's junior, managed the descent to the open boat just as easily.

Sitting in the stern of the boat, they could see that it was, indeed, the Bulkeley coach. When they were within hailing distance of the pier, the door of the carriage opened and Amy Bulkeley stepped down, giving a small wave to the two officers. She wore a bonnet that covered some of her face and she seemed, somehow, to be subdued. She made no other welcoming signs until the men gained the top of the pier and approached where she was standing.

William felt a surge of admiration for the woman. Her dark, curly hair, mostly covered by the bonnet, not to be entirely restrained, framed her beautiful face with tight little circles. Her eyes, always large and bright, were a deeper brown than William remembered, her face wonderfully white as if it had never been exposed to the sun and the salt sea air.

Amy gave her father a warm embrace, all the while maintaining eye contact with William.

"Where is your husband, daughter?"

"Richard left for Boston, on business, I was told."

"He's not here?"

"No, Father. Richard is not here." Amy stepped back from her father's embrace. "I must speak with William."

"Yes, yes. When does he return?"

"I don't know, Father. He hasn't spoken to me in weeks." She reached for William's hand. "William, I don't ..."

"Doesn't anyone know when he will return?"

With fire in her eyes, Amy Bulkeley faced her father. "We have more important things to be concerned with than Richard's whereabouts!" Still holding William's hand, she put the other hand on John Rous's arm to soften her words. "Please, father."

"Yes, daughter."

Amy then turned all her attention to William. "You have a son, William. He is named James."

With alarm in his voice William demanded, "Molly! She is all right? She had no birthing troubles with Charlie. Did she have a problem this time?"

"No troubles. The boy arrived over two weeks ago. Molly and James were just fine."

"Then where is she?"

"Molly left the baby with me for a couple of hours while she took Charlie down to Granddad's boat. It didn't matter much if she was gone for a while since one of my maids, Rose, was still flowing from her baby; she would nurse James if he had a mind."

"What … happened? Amy! Tell me!"

"Molly took Charlie when she went out as crew for her father. By Rous's Island, a rogue wave carried away the boats on the deck, the father, Molly and Charles."

"Are they all right? They got back on board? They were rescued?" William had that same cold, dark feeling he had experienced when he had faced the Cambyse in Cormorant Cove. Death was near again.

As quickly as she could, Amy gave him the dreadful story. Molly's father had disappeared into the water. Like most New England fishermen, he had not learned to swim. William remembered the father saying, "Ya goes down right some quick with the boots and all. Better not to struggle in the water, she's so cold. Make it quick, I says." Yes, it would have been quick for John Ferguson. But Molly, she knew how to swim. What about Molly?

"For God's sake, Amy! What happened to Molly and the boy?"

"Molly held him tight. There were boats in the lee of the island. They reached Molly as quickly as they could. She handed Charles up. Charles was saved, William."

William knew the answer but he had to ask the question. "And Molly?"

"The fisherman passed the boy inboard but when he turned back to help Molly, she was gone. She just slipped under, William. Her body washed up two days later. She's buried in the settlers' cemetery."

"She's buried?" If Amy replied to his desperate question he obviously didn't hear it. William clasped his hands in front of his chest. "Oh!" His eyes wild with pain he searched the far end of the pier hoping that his Molly would appear. He knew she wouldn't, but he didn't have anything else to do with his eyes; they were useless if there was no Molly to see. His arms jerked as if he were trying to pull his intertwined fingers apart. Buckling at the knees he slowly sank to the ground, his torso supported by his arms outstretched above his head, his hands still clasped. William mashed his face into the rough timbers of the pier, soon drawing blood from his nose.

Both Captain Rous and his daughter reached down to help him, but a burly sailor lifted the stricken man upright and supported him.

Startled, Amy Rous demanded, "Who the devil are you?"

"It's all right, daughter." Rous gestured at the harbour craft at the side of the pier. "He's a *Sutherland*, come along to help William move his gear." Rous put his hand under William's chin, forcing the head up. Now there was a darkness in the eyes as if everything that was William Gray had been extinguished. Rous shook his head and stepped back. "Fink, I want you to take him to his house and look after him."

"Aye, sir." Able Seaman Fink slipped his huge arms under Gray, lifting him as other, lesser men might carry a sick child.

"Put him in my carriage, Seaman Fink." Amy Rous suddenly looked very businesslike. "I won't have him at Hollis Street, two men alone." She gestured at the carriage as she stepped forward to make Fink move. "Do as I say, Seaman!"

Rous sighed. "Do as she says, Fink."

Father and daughter watched as Fink placed the seemingly unaware Gray on one of the seats.

Rous wondered out loud, "Where are William's two boys?"

"At Richard's old house, in the guest room." Amy smiled at her father. "My maid is taking good care of them in the room next to mine." Extending her hand to Fink for assistance in mounting the carriage, Amy took her place on the other seat.

Fink closed the door. He stood, waiting for a signal from his captain as the carriage moved away off the pier and up the hill.

"Carry on, Fink."

Able Seaman Fink trotted up the hill, easily catching up with the carriage before it disappeared behind Carmichael's Tavern. The sight of the big, ugly sailor, keeping pace with the carriage, holding his hand on the side of the door as if to steady the vehicle to give a softer ride to his lieutenant, touched Rous.

Chapter Ten

December 31, 1758
The Old House
Halifax

"Richard has spies in the town." Amy Bulkeley listened to see if there was to be any answer from the adjoining room. She had become accustomed to William's silences and was not surprised at the lack of reply. She went on with her one-sided conversation. "No sooner is the *Sutherland* sent south on patrol ..." She repeated some of what she had said to herself, "the *Sutherland* ... I have been with the Navy too long ... gettin' to talk like 'em." Amy shook her head and started again, "No sooner is Father sent out on patrol than Richard shows his face in the town." She slipped a bed jacket over her shoulders since there was a chill in the room that the generous fireplace failed to dispel and looked in on William in the adjoining bedroom.

William, already dressed in his best blues, was seated by the fireplace. He was staring, not at the beautiful fire as one might expect, but at the window where the last rays of the setting sun were outlining in brilliant gold the tops of the trees that Richard had ordered planted around the house.

"Do you think Father has gotten over his urge to shoot Richard?" Amy accepted a beauty mark from the maid who had followed her into the room. She wet it with the end of her tongue. Placing the dry side of the little black spot on her finger she pushed the sticky side against her breast about a half-inch above her nipple. She pulled the ruffle from her undergarment over her erect and firm 'love buds' (she always called them love buds when she used to speak of love with her husband and she still thought of them that way). Her face was flushed; Amy enjoyed the arousal she felt when she dressed in front of William. There was something of a challenge in trying to make those dead eyes see life again.

255

"There!" She turned to face William. "It's the latest thing in Boston. It's called a beauty mark." She gestured to the maid. "I might put one on my cheek, too, Emily."

The maid selected another from the little pewter box, handing it to her mistress.

Studying her face in the mirror, Amy placed the black spot on her cheekbone. She looked through the mirror at William. There was no response, no interest in what was going on. Following an impulse, Amy walked over to William and grasped the hand of his good arm. She pulled her garment's ruffles off her breast and firmly placed his hand against her bare skin. Bending so that she could bring her face to his, she kissed him on the cheek and then the lips. She felt increased pressure against her breast; he was moving his hand! He was moving his hand away from her breast and out of her grasp. She studied his face. "William, are you there?"

"Yes," was the almost inaudible reply. He gave her a little smile. "I ... hear ... you."

Amy exclaimed, "Oh, William! We have all missed you so." She took his hand again and kissed it.

"I ... hear ... you, Molly."

Amy was so startled, she said, "I'm not Molly," before she could consider the consequences. As she watched, the spark of interest in his eyes faded and he was gone.

"Oh, damn!" was followed immediately by a deep retching cough, and then another, and another.

Emily quickly wiped the splatters of pink from the back of her lady's hand. "There, there," she said as she cleaned some pink spittle off her mistress's chin. "Come to the window, Missus Bulkeley. It seems to help when you have the fresh air."

"No!" Amy gasped. "The sun has gone down. The night air makes it worse!" She picked a small green leaf off a potted plant and put it between her teeth, biting down and crushing the mint taste into her mouth. The coughing stopped. "Oh, God! All I need is a coughing fit tonight of all nights!"

"It will be all right, Madame. Don't you fret so, it only makes it worse."

"Yes." Amy turned on her heel and re-entered her own

room. "Help me finish dressing and call for Fink to take Lieutenant Gray downstairs."

"Yes, Missus." Emily leaned out the doorway of William's room and called down the stairs, "Beverly! It's time to take the lieutenant down."

Fink bounded up the stairs, two or three at a time. He patted Emily's bottom as he whispered in her ear. "I told you, sweets. Never use me proper name when we're not alone. You call me Jake or Fink!"

Emily caressed the side of the homely face. "We're as good as alone, Beverly. She's in there pickin' a dress and he's," she tossed her head toward the silent lieutenant, "not here at all."

"Don't you no never mind, dearie, he'll come back." Fink pushed the girl against the wall. Leaning on the wall with one hand over her shoulder he bent down and nibbled on her ear as he whispered, "The Sea tried to take'im from the *Trent*, the French shot 'im near to death and the English came close to hangin' 'im. Then the Sea steals his Molly when he's not there to protect 'er." Fink gave a big sigh. "He's just takin' a rest, is all."

Emily twisted as if to go back into the bedroom but Fink's free hand held her, gently, by the throat. She settled back against the wall, her face upturned.

Fink tasted brandy as he kissed the girl and sought her tongue with his. He had a momentary picture of Emily helping herself to her mistress's liquors. He had been feeding her rum as a reliable 'leg opener' so he wasn't surprised she drank at other opportunities, but stealing from your shipmates was a flogging offence. He lost his concentration when Emily returned his kiss with enthusiasm, forcing her tongue into his mouth. She giggled and twisted away when he began to grope her breasts. Panting, she tossed her head in the direction of the other man and whispered, "What about 'im, watching."

"Don'tcher worry, luv! Right now he's restin' and he don't bother none the small stuff." Out of loyalty to his officer he continued, "But he's gonna be good, again. Just this mornin' we talked about the Cove …"

"Emily!" Missus Bulkeley sounded peeved. "I would appreciate your help, now, not sometime in the future, if you please!"

"Yes, Ma'am." Emily smiled over her shoulder at the sailor and went into the other bedroom, closing the door.

Suddenly self-conscious in the presence of his officer, Fink turned away to face the corner while he adjusted his penis to relieve some of the pressure, by unfolding it and pushing it straight up against his belly. He turned around again and said to the disinterested William Gray, "Time to stand up, sir. We're goin' to a party.'

Lieutenant William Gray stood up. "I'm ready to go, Fink."

Seaman Beverly Fink looked deep into the other man's eyes. "Are you there, sir?"

"Yes, Fink. I am here." William looked around as if he had heard something. "That's the recall signal, Fink. Ship's company to report."

Fink hadn't heard anything but replied immediately, "Then let's go down to the main deck, lieutenant." Fink took his arm and led him out into the hall. By the time they had descended to the foyer, Lieutenant Gray was silent again, no longer concerned with reporting to his captain.

Half an hour later, Amy Bulkeley descended the staircase, gorgeous in a red and blue dress that accented her pale complexion and haunting eyes. She accepted a heavy blue wrap from Emily and allowed Fink to drape it over her shoulders. Pausing in front of the hall mirror she asked the image, "Ready to take on your miserable fart of a husband, Madame?" Nodding her head in reply, Amy swept toward the door, where she waited while Fink opened it.

"When you have the lieutenant settled in the cab, Fink, run along and join us at the main doors to Carleton House."

* * *

"Good evening, Madame Bulkeley, and a Happy New Year." The manservant stepped back to allow his master's wife and her party to enter the foyer.

Amy Bulkeley gave the man a small, mean smile. "Let me explain, Able Seaman Fink," she said without taking her eyes off the servant's face, "the last time I came here, this man, following the shouted orders of my husband, pushed me outside and slammed the doors shut in my face."

Fink stepped forward but Amy put a restraining hand on his sleeve.

She widened her little smile. "Want a second bout, John? You'll have to get rid of my man, here, before you can resume your familiarities with my body."

"I'm terribly sorry, Madame, but the sailor cannot remain here. He will have to be excused." He lowered his head in a half bow. "The staff have orders that you are the mistress and to be honoured as such."

"And my man, Seaman Fink?"

"I'm sure, as the Mistress of Carleton House, you would want him to enjoy the comforts the staff can provide at the rear of the house, away from the invited guests." He beckoned to another servant. "See to it, Francis."

Amy Bulkeley nodded to Fink, who then followed the servant, Francis, toward the kitchens. Amy placed her hand possessively on the arm of William Gray. "And where is my husband?"

"He was expecting you to arrive with the lieutenant and requested that you meet him in the library." John bowed and indicated the direction of the library with his extended hand. "Allow me to …"

"I know the way, John."

Grasping William's elbow, Amy pushed past the servant. "Don't bother to announce us."

Seeming not to hurry, John reached the library door ahead of the couple. Knocking as he lifted the handle, John announced, "The Madame, sir, and Lieutenant Gray."

Amy entered the library, skirts and nostrils flaring as her eyes swept the room looking for her quarry. "My God, Rich! You look like an over-dressed maypole!"

"Close the door, John," was all the Colonel of Militia said in acknowledgement.

"Better still," laughed the carping wife, "you look like the aide de camp to the Spanish Ambassador!"

Colonel Richard Bulkeley smiled at the remembrance of how the two of them, in happier days, had made fun of the gaudy Spanish uniforms, but defensively he argued, "I had father's London tailor make this up in time for the party tonight."

"You should remove some of the brass braid …"

"Gold!"

"Some of the gold braid …"

Interrupting her again he exclaimed, "I didn't ask you in here to critique militia uniforms!" Richard turned his head and studied the quiet figure standing near the door for a moment or two before inviting him to be seated near the fireplace. "Warm yourself, William. It's a bitter night."

Husband and wife watched as William sat down close to the fire. When he was settled, without comment, Amy resumed the conversation.

"Why did you invite me here?" Amy moved to the other side of the fireplace and warmed her hands.

"It would be to our mutual advantage for you to be known as Mistress of Carleton House. I want you to move back into the main house."

"What's wrong, Rich? You having trouble with your other mistress, the Mistress of Orphan House?"

His face a flaming red, Richard stared into the fire.

"Is your dear Annie making things rough for the Honourable Judge?"

"The accounts of the Orphan House are being examined for … excesses …"

"Fraud?"

"… and I have severed my connections with the Mistress Wenman …"

"That must have hurt! I understood you were screwing her regularly …"

"You should talk, Madame! You have two sailors in your bedroom!"

Amy's mouth opened to say something but Richard continued, "I know, I know, Amy," he said in an apologetic tone of voice, "you don't even get a small rise out of the boy, but it's the appearances, right now, that can cause us harm."

"William's not a boy!" Then it dawned on her. "Emily! You get your information from Emily! She's *your* spy!"

Again Richard's face went red.

Amy stamped her foot. "I want that whore out of my service."

"Yes, of course, Amy."

"Tonight. Send someone and get her out of my sight."

"I'll have John see to it."

"Out of Halifax."

"What?"

"Send her away from Halifax. I don't want to see her again."

Richard pinched his lower lip with his thumb and forefinger. "I suppose my Mister Mauger could arrange to have her shipped to Boston as an indentured servant."

"Slave would be better." Raising her voice and pointing at her husband she shrieked, "And don't you send someone to spy on me again!"

"No, my dear, there would be no need once you are re-established here at the main house. We must reconcile our differences and set an example of propriety for the entire Colony to be proud of."

"You usually don't care what people think." Amy gave a mirthless laugh. "You didn't blink an eye when you stole title to Daddy's island."

"I gave him another island instead."

"Sure you did. Sambro Island. A lot of good that will do Daddy."[1]

They were both startled when William spoke up. "He stole that fireplace and mantel from the French governor's apartment in Louisbourg."

The Bulkeleys stared at the naval officer, who continued with a small voice, "Joshua Mauger and Amos Skinner did it …" His voice petered out. There was silence in the room.

"Christ!" Bulkeley threw himself down on the sofa. "How in the name of God did he find that out?"

Amy gave him a reassuring smile. "It doesn't matter. In five minutes he won't remember anything."

"Are you sure?"

"Perhaps ten minutes, at the most."

"Christ!"

Richard rang a bell.

John appeared as if he had been waiting outside the door.

"Escort the lieutenant into the parlour."

"No, Richard! He should have someone with him."

Richard held up his hand to silence his wife. "Please seat him by the side of the fire and have one of the servants look after him."

With William gone, Richard motioned for his wife to join him on the sofa. "It's better he isn't here for the rest of our little talk," Richard sighed, and continued, "because as any good servant of the Crown, I have taken advantage of opportunities ..."

"Daddy says you overcharge the Colony's ships for their rum."

"I do not!" Richard looked crossly at his wife. "Your father doesn't understand. I do a great deal of government entertaining. The spirits which we use to entertain guests of the Crown are charged against the ships' supply invoices."

"That's cute!" Amy studied the fire. Finally she asked, "So, what is troubling you so much that you get rid of your little Orphan House playmate and invite your legal spouse to return home?"

"It's not difficult, really. The Nova Scotia Assembly of Freeholders means to strip us of power and send us to the gaol."[2]

"By the word 'us', who do you mean?"

"Jonathan Belcher, Benjamin Green, John Collier, Charles Morris and me. Oh yes, and Governor Lawrence."

Amy gave a sigh of disbelief. "That's the Chief Justice, Provincial Treasurer, Registrar of Deeds ... what does Charles Morris do?"

"He's the Chief Surveyor and Registrar of Admiralty. Oh yes, and John Collier, as well as being Registrar of Deeds, is also Judge of Admiralty."

"I have to hand it to you, Rich, if you're going to be a highwayman, join a gang that has power."

Richard gave his wife a look of exasperation as he continued, "Our present troubles started because the governor believes his power rests with the soldiers of the garrison. It is, after all, the foot soldier who must put himself between the administration and any sort of threat."

"Go on."

"You heard about Hannah Price?"

"The washerwoman who was raped?"[3]

"We mustn't exaggerate, woman," Richard said irritably. "There was evidence that she was robbed of two shirts, one shift and three aprons, but there was no evidence of ..."

"She had just finished putting out the fire and candle when two soldiers burst in and threw her on the bed."

"Perhaps she ..."

"One of the soldiers drew his sword and held it against her neck and swore he would cut her throat if she made any noise."

"Merely her version ..."

"The other tied her hands and feet to the bedstead and helped to hold her down while she struggled against the fifteen or sixteen soldiers who lay with her." Amy grimaced. "Oh, yes, I know about Hannah Price."

Richard raised his voice to an authoritative level, "There could be little doubt that the soldiers she identified as her attackers were guilty of burglary, but she was well known to the men of the garrison and several hundred would have come forward and claimed intimate knowledge of the woman."

Amy gave another grimace. "I hadn't heard of the results of that trial. What happened?"

"There was no trial." Again using his authoritative voice Richard intoned, "The Governor of Nova Scotia, Captain General of his Majesty's Military Forces, saw fit to grant His Majesty's Mercy and return the soldiers to active service to the Crown."

"No punishment?"

"Returned to service with no penalty," Richard nodded his head, "and that was the beginning of our troubles with the Halifax Freeholders."

"I can believe that." Amy looked puzzled and asked, "By the way, is the soldier currently accused of raping the nine-year-old orphan girl going to receive His Majesty's Mercy?"[4]

"No. He's going to escape."

"This is unbelievable!"

"Governor Lawrence believes he must continue to seek the support of the garrison troops even though discipline is poor to non-existent. He cannot allow the soldier to be punished but, if he grants Royal Mercy another time, the Halifax Freeholders will ask the Assembly to submit memorials against the Governor to the Lords of Trade … perhaps to the King himself."

Richard smiled at his wife, "No, the soldier will escape. Probably has done so already."

"What if the Lunenburg Freeholders refuse to co-operate with the Halifax Freeholders? Isn't there equal representation from both areas?"

"You do have a grasp of the basics, my dear, but the reality is, we have lost any support we might have come to expect from the Lunenburg Freeholders."[5] Amy opened her mouth to ask a question but Richard carried on, "As far back as 1753, the German settlers were complaining that they were not receiving the supplies they had been promised. There was a disturbance in January of that year. A lieutenant colonel was sent to quell it which, mind you, he did rather quickly, but not without getting into an argument with one of the Freeholders, a Mister Hoffman."

"Who was the colonel?"

"Lieutenant Colonel Monckton. Monckton called the German a scoundrel and villain. Hoffman replied that he was no more a scoundrel or villain than the colonel himself, whereupon Monckton clapped the man in irons and shipped him to Halifax for trial."

"What has this to do with the …"

"Hear me out, Amy. The affair dragged on for years. Hoffman had been found guilty of misbehaviour to Colonel Monckton, fined one hundred pounds and sentenced to two years imprisonment. While he was serving his sentence at the Island Battery, all his goods and property were seized under the authority of Governor Lawrence and distributed to others. Since Hoffman then couldn't pay the fine, the Governor refused to discharge him at the end of the two-year sentence and Hoffman remained at the Island Battery."

"The poor man!"

"That's the reaction of the general population. The Halifax Freeholders took up a collection to pay the fine."

"So it's over?"

"No. Even with the payment of the fine, Governor Lawrence still refused to allow the man out of gaol until enough money was presented to cover a two hundred pound bond as surety that Hoffman would leave the province, never to return."

"My God! What an abuse of power!"

"Perhaps so, my dear, but the reality is you can feel the heat of the Lunenburg anger from here. I see no way around it. The Nova Scotia Assembly is going to recommend audits, surveys and investigations until one or all of the present administration are in gaol."

Richard stood up and turned his backside to the fire. "I intend to be a psalm-singing, charity-giving, public-spirited, model citizen and I need you by my side to make it believable." Richard took several steps to his wife's side. Taking her hands he pulled her upright. "Please stand by me on this." When she didn't respond, he squeezed her hands, pressing them to his lips. "We used to be good together."

"What else is there, Richard? You had better tell me all of it right now."

"That's all there is, my dear."

Amy pulled her hands free. She gestured toward the fireplace. "What about things like stealing this mantel? Any other juicy little things that might have just slipped your mind?"

"No, there aren't."

"Nothing more with the Orphan House?" When Richard shook his head, she demanded, "Or with the mistress?"

"No. Nothing." When Amy's faced still showed disbelief, he added, "The Governor's Council has appointed Mister Breynton to take over all of my responsibilities. I will have no further contact with the woman."

Richard was uncomfortable with this subject and wished it ended. He had, in fact, seen the comely Mistress Wenman in the last few hours and was afraid that his wife, who could read

him well, would discern the lie. Perhaps Amy had already concluded he was lying and that would be the reason for all of the
persistent questioning. He rubbed his chin as if he were being
pensive but it was really an affected mannerism he used in
court. "Against my better judgement I told the boys I would
take title to some of the Acadian lands." He held his hand up,
"Now, look, Amy! I didn't get any of the money for the Acadian grain and livestock ... at least none of it can ever be traced
to me. I'm clear of all that and I honestly tried to get out of
accepting the Acadian land but I was told I would have to take
title to some of it."

"Why in heaven's name do you have to take title to some
land you don't want?"

Richard shrugged his shoulders that he didn't know.

"How much land is it?"

"Not very much, my dear."

"How much," she added, "my dear," with sarcasm or irony,
Richard couldn't tell which.

"Two thousand one hundred and twenty acres."[6] Suddenly very proud of it, he said, "We will own over two thousand
acres of land as good as any in North America."

"Who told you that?"

"Charles Morris."

"The Chief Surveyor?"

"Yes."

Amy Bulkeley thought on it. "So be it," she finally said. "I
will move back in tonight."

"You will tell Father Rous that I am a good husband?"

"What about your talk that I was too sick to be a wife to
you? That you thought what I have is catching?"

"I will be a caring husband to you, my dear, in sickness and
in health." He extended his arm for his wife to take. "Gray will
move back to Hollis Street?"

Amy hesitated taking the arm. Finally she asked, "You will
still get rid of Emily?"

"Yes."

Amy took his arm and they walked toward the library
door. "What will I do about the Gray children?"

Just before they reached the door the manservant, John, opened it with a deep bow. "Some guests are here already and I ordered the quintet to begin." John looked directly at Amy. "I trust I did the right thing and Madame approves?"

"Yes, thank you, John."

Richard spoke to his manservant. "John, has Mister Breynton arrived yet?"

"He has, sir."

"Arrange for him to have a conversation with Lieutenant Gray and then tell him I want to speak to him about two more children for Orphan House."

Endnotes

[1] Sambro Island was deeded to Captain John Rous. He in turn deeded it to the province so that a lighthouse could be erected. When the lighthouse was completed, his brother was appointed lightkeeper.

[2] A memorial was prepared by the freeholders listing grievances against the colony's executive. They threatened to send it to the Lords of Trade or perhaps to the King himself. I don't know where it was sent, but a copy is in the archives.

[3] Detail from the list of grievances. "… a number of soldiers broke into the house of Katherine Whiston washerwoman in Halifax wherein were only herself and Hannah Price, who had been helping her wash. After putting out the fire and candle, the said soldiers threw the said Hannah Price on the bed and one of them drew his sword, held it across her neck …" The account goes on to say that the soldiers were found guilty but later pardoned by the governor.

[4] Detail from the report: "… a soldier was tried at the supreme court for an assault with intent to ravish a girl of ten years old … when it being proved that he did ravish her and gave her the foul (?) was found guilty and sentenced to be punished and was accordingly imprisoned but was suffered to escape."

[5] Another incident described in the memorial.

[6] According to the records, only Charles Morris, Chief Surveyor, took title to more land: three thousand seven hundred and twelve acres.

Chapter Eleven

April 17, 1759
Carmichael's Tavern

"Glad to see you're more your old self, my boy!" Captain Rous squeezed William Gray's shoulder; "We miss you on *Sutherland.*"

"Ship's company missed you, Lieutenant," Wimper said agreeably as he reached across in front of the captain to dip his fingers into the pork crackles.

"You'd take the last of them, would you Wimper?"

"Just so you would have the fresh ones all to yourself, Captain."

"But there aren't any crackles left, fresh or stale."

Wimper popped the crackles, one at a time, into this mouth and crunched down on them enthusiastically. "It's time some overaged, overpaid captain ordered some more."

Rous signalled to the barmaid for more crackles. "I can see you have been serving with me too long, Wimper. I have made you a rich man and this is the way you thank me."

"Aye, sir, I do have enough money and I'm thinking of signing off. It's time to go home to Handsworth," he stated emphatically.

Rous took another sup of his ale and explained to William in a stage whisper, "Handsworth is in England and if the English are smart, they won't let this little bugger back into the country." Slapping the manservant on the back with the flat of his hand Rous announced, "If I wasn't having so much fun being a pain in the backside to certain pompous asses ..."

"He means the admirals, Lieutenant," Wimper explained.

"... I would go home, too."

"Where's home for you, Captain?" William picked up his tankard, spilling more than half of it on the table. The three men rose to avoid being soaked by the spillage but the barmaid was right there with the plate of crackles and she wiped the mess up in a flash.

As the men settled down around the table again Rous answered, "Anywhere in New England near the sea." He gestured to the barmaid. "Bring another for the lieutenant."

"And a new arm for me, my dear," William joked.

"Still having troubles with your Louisbourg wounds?"

"Aye. That and the fact that I spent a lot of time recently feeling sorry for myself and just sitting around." William worked the arm back and forth. "The arm got stiff."

"What does the surgeon have to say?"

"Told me to keep trying to use the weak arm."

"Well, don't practise with tankards of ale until you get stronger, Lieutenant." Wimper lifted his tankard up and down several times as if doing some exercises. "It's such a waste to spill any."

"Aye, Wimper."

Rous leaned forward and asked, in a very low voice, "When you were ... sick ... did you have pain over the eyes," rubbing his hand over his forehead and then behind the ear, "here and here? Really bad, bad pain?"

"No, Captain, I didn't feel anything like that and, for the most part, I ..."

There was a commotion at the tavern entrance where a large number of excited men were pushing their way in, arguing and waving their arms.

Mister Carmichael appeared from nowhere, quickly making place for the two dozen new customers where, just a few moments earlier, there hadn't been room to swing a cat.

"I wonder what that's all about?" Wimper got up to go find out.

Captain Rous put out a restraining hand, "Wait on it, Wimper. Carmichael will tell us as soon as he has a moment."

The room got noisier, so much so that Captain Rous, gathering his cane and hat, stood up to leave.

Mister Carmichael must have seen the movement of one of his important customers and he hurried over wringing his hands. "I'm terribly sorry, my friends, but the lads have experienced a bad turn of events today and are riled up. The governor dissolved the Assembly!"

"The governor and his council will rule?" Wimper asked.

"There's no way of knowing at this time. The governor gave notice this morning that he considered the work of the Assembly to be petty and the actions of certain members to be self serving and contrary to the best interests of the province."

"He said that this morning?"

"Yes, but this afternoon, during the discussions concerning the Orphan House budget, an allegation was made about certain gentlemen making a profit from their official dealings. The governor entered not five minutes later and dissolved the Assembly. Told them he had given fair warning." Carmichael absentmindedly used a bar rag to wipe some remaining moisture from the table top as he continued, "According to the lads, Governor Lawrence was hopping mad."[1]

"You think he lost his temper and acted without thinking?" Wimper lifted his tankard so Carmichael could reach another wet spot. "It's the King what set up the Assembly. The governor can't undo what the King's done."

Carmichael stepped back, taking a good look at the table. "The governor can dissolve it. He has that sort of power."

"Then the freeholders will have the last laugh when the governor has to bring 'em back."

"No doubt! The Assembly is a royal creation and even though the governor might think himself a god, he ain't."

Rous snorted, "Lawrence is not a fool. He'll have a plan. You mark my words." Rous stared at his young friend who seemed to have swallowed his tongue. "What's the trouble, William? You havin' trouble breathin'?"

"My God!" was all William managed to say. His chair fell over backwards as he pushed himself to his feet and staggered toward the door. "My God! My God!" he kept repeating as he squeezed past the crowded tables to get to the door where several strangers were standing. "Jeremiah! It's you!" William threw his arm around a lanky individual who neither returned the embrace nor pushed William away. He just stood there until William stepped back a pace to take a better look at his old friend.

"I'm not ..." the tall man started to say and at the same time William blurted out, "You're not Jeremiah, are you?"

"No, I'm not." He extended his hand, "Although I gather you're a friend of his and I would be pleased to meet you. I'm Elkanah Smith and the nearest thing to old Jerry that you'll ever see. Often taken for him when he was in other parts, although my wife says I'm more handsome than he ever was."[2]

William didn't say anything. He took the proffered hand and shook it and then released his grip, but Elkanah held his hand. "You know that Jerry is gone? Taken with the pox last year, he and his young one. The family was in deep sorrow. Oh, yes. We're related. Cousins. Used to hunt and fish together 'til I got married and then Jeremiah went off to do his soldierin'."

Elkanah stopped speaking. He released William's hand.

The tavern had fallen silent as the clientele listened to the exchange. Captain Rous spoke from the corner, "Bring your friend over, William. Have him join us."

"Yes ... I didn't catch your name ..."

"Elkanah Smith, and I would be pleased to join you."

The tavern noise started up again. Mister Carmichael found a chair for the newcomer, who waved to his companions who were still at the door that they would have to fend for themselves.

"Sorry we can't manage more seats for your friends, Elkanah."

"That's all right, sir. They are shipboard acquaintances and not really friends of mine."

William was still not doing much of the talking so Rous carried the conversation for a while. "What brings you to Halifax?"

"As soon as my wife and I heard the French were gone from here, we thought this would be a safer place to raise our son."

Wimper spoke up, "Well, the Indians aren't gone."

Rous added, "And not all of the Acadians."

"Are they active?"

"Indians killed and scalped five soldiers at Lunenburg this month but there's always been Acadians in the Indian raiding parties. Yes, I think it's safe to say the Acadians are still active." Rous waved his arm for the maid to bring beer. When he had her attention he waggled his finger indicating a round of drinks. "Hope you like beer."

"I drink any given amount," Elkanah said with a grin. Then he was serious and asked, "In New England, the French always joined the raiding parties. The Acadians do the same thing here?"

"Maybe the French enjoyed being part of the murder and torture but it was different for the Acadians."

"How so?"

"The French governor in Quebec gave the order that Acadians would dress like Indians and go out on the raids. Maybe the Acadians liked being part of the raiding—maybe they didn't—but they had no real choice because the French governor told them they had to join in." Rous could see the question forming, so he posed it: "Why would the governor order that?" At that moment the barmaid arrived with four tankards and a bowl of crackles.

"Mister Carmichael thought you might want to treat your friend, seeing it's his first visit with us." She gave them all a big smile. "It's on the house!" And then she was gone.

Rous took a handful of crackles but held them in his hand, poised to pop them into his mouth as he explained, "The Acadians would rather be left alone. I don't think it mattered much to them which European country had power, France or England, as long as they could tend their land and raise their families."

"They wanted to be neutral?"

Rous dropped several of the crackles into his mouth and gave a couple of crunches before he continued. "I think so. And the French governor knew that. To bind the Acadians to their side, the governor used the Catholic religion, French traditions and language, but above all the English colonists' hatred …" Rous hesitated when he saw the reaction to his comments on the faces of his listeners, but then he pressed on. "Yes, the French governor believed our unforgiving hatred would keep the Acadians committed to the French cause."

Wimper, with his newfound feelings of financial independence, was quick to question his captain on this subject. "Why would the governor …?"

"When we saw some Acadians were part of the Indian brutality … we hated all Acadians. The French governor counted on us being just as cruel and barbaric right back, giving the Acadians little option but remaining loyal to the French cause."

William spoke for the first time. "I think Jeremiah was sweet on one of the Acadians. She made bread for us." The men waited for more of the story but all William said was, "I don't think she liked the English very much." Then he put his tankard to his lips and took a long drink.

"Did she like colonials?" Elkanah gave William a nudge with his elbow. "We're not the same as the English, you know."

William put his tankard down. "I am coming to believe that, Elkanah."

There was a lull in the conversation. Rous, making ready to leave, asked polite questions of the newcomer before he and Wimper left. William, interested in hearing about Jeremiah's family and friends, stayed behind to listen to stories of New England. When the two men realized it was near twilight, they decided to leave.

Once outside, and indicating a sloop tied up at the Government Pier, Elkanah said, "I'll be taking ship in the morning."

William grasped Elkanah by the elbow and led him in the direction of the vessel. "She's the *Yorke*. Let me show you something." As they walked toward the vessel, William explained that Captain Cobb had taken the *Yorke* up a little river in the Fundy to deliver rum to Jeremiah's militia company. Two French cannon crews allowed the *Yorke* to pass upriver before announcing their presence, at the same time as an entire regiment of French Regulars swooped down to attack from the trees. "We couldn't go back downstream because of the cannon and the French soldiers were coming at us from the banks of the river." William leaned out over the side of the sloop and ran his hand along the top of the bulwark. "I was standing right here when they fired on us. Feel the grooves in the wood? Made by musket balls—musket balls that were aimed at me."

"What happened then?"

"Jeremiah saved my life. He chased the French foot soldiers and cannon back into the fort."

"A whole regiment?"

"Well, perhaps there weren't as many as that and perhaps they weren't all Regulars," William said with a half smile, "but if it had been a regiment, Jeremiah would still have sent them off with their tails between their legs."

"Who's there?" The watch officer strolled across the deck. Recognizing William he said, "Good to see you again, Lieutenant. Would you like to come aboard?"

"No, thank you, Lieutenant Marsh. I was just showing my friend ..."

"Good evening, Mister Smith. I have good news for you; Mister Morris will be sailing with us in the morning."

Elkanah turned to William with a quizzical look.

"It is good news, Elkanah. Get the nod from Charles Morris and any site you pick is yours."

"How come?"

"He's the Chief Surveyor of Nova Scotia."

"I really don't know where to settle ... or even if we are going to come. I thought the Indian raids were finished and the French were all gone. Now I find scalps are still being taken as near as Lunenburg! I don't know if Betty will be willing to come."

"Betty's your wife?"

"Yes. New England is still suffering raids. She thought all the French and Indians had been cleared out of Nova Scotia and it would be safer here."

"Don't worry about it. Captain Rous is sailing this week to check on the ice conditions in the Saint Lawrence River as a prelude to the fleet laying siege to Quebec. Pretty soon there won't be any French governor to cause us trouble. General Wolfe will see to that, believe me."

"Where do you live?"

"Near the mouth of Halifax Harbour at Sambro."

"Could I get a land grant at Sambro?"

"Afraid not, Elkanah. There are no Acadian lands at Sambro." William turned away from the harbour. "I have to go along, now. I must drop by and see my boys."

"You didn't tell me you had a wife and family."

"My Molly was a fisherman's daughter. She and her Pa were swept away." William's eyes misted at the thought of

Molly. He cleared his throat and stuck out his hand. "I am pleased we had a chance to talk about Jeremiah and I look forward to seeing you again, Elkanah."

Elkanah took the offered hand and shook it warmly. "Perhaps we'll meet again."

"You never know."

The two men parted; Elkanah Smith boarded the sloop while William walked briskly up the hill to Orphan House.

William hurried. His appointment to see the boys had been for five o'clock. Usually he was right on time, the boys in the front room under the watchful eye of Mistress Wenman, the half-hour passing pleasantly with little cakes the Orphan House staff placed on the table near at hand.

He turned the corner. The front of Orphan House was in complete darkness. This late in the twilight, if the boys were still waiting for him, there would have to be a lamp or two. Should he knock on the door and try to attract someone's attention? He didn't want to raise the ire of Mistress Wenman since she had been good enough to take the boys in when they weren't actually orphans. Of course, William paid a fee for their care so perhaps he could be pardoned, just this once, if he was a few minutes—actually three quarters of an hour—late. He hesitated, not wanting to give up the opportunity of being with his sons but also not wishing to be in the bad graces of the Mistress. Perhaps if he went around the back of the house he could more easily get in to see them, but when he tried the side gate it was locked. He gave it a little push. The gate resisted.

Someone was knocking at the front door. William looked up at the house and could see the movement of a lamp as it was carried from the rear of the house to the front. *Good*, he thought. *There's another late visitor.* He pulled away from the gate but his coat caught on the latch holding him back. In his haste he yanked on the cloth but the coat was firmly caught. He had to look closely in the dark and move the material up and over the latch to free himself. Then he rushed to the front of the house in time to see two men being admitted. The nearest man, the one in a Ranger's uniform, he didn't recognize. The other, who was almost through the door when William first saw them, could have been Amos Skinner. The door closed and the holder of the lamp led the two men to the rear of the house.

William hastened to the door and rapped strongly. There was no answer. He doubled his fist, pounding several times. *Ah! Good! The lamp was returning to the door.* It was Mistress Wenman.

"What can I do for you, Lieutenant Gray? It is an hour past visiting time."

"Good evening Mistress. I hoped ... that is, since you are still receiving visitors, you might forgive ..."

"Visiting hours are well over, Lieutenant." A note of professional cheerfulness crept into her voice as she said; "A visit at this late hour would only excite the children and make it difficult for the staff to get them settled for the night. As a parent, I'm sure you can understand that."

A rising sense of anger overcame William's concern for good manners. "You just opened the door for other visitors, two men. One of them doesn't have ..."

"I can't see what business it is of yours, Lieutenant, but I have workmen and business visitors all times of the day and night. They do not visit with the children nor upset them at bed time which I assure you, with your tavern aroma, you would most certainly do." Forcing the door closed against William's upraised hand Mistress Wenman said, through gritted teeth, "You can visit at the normal hours but not tonight." Just before the door closed she managed a "Good night!"

"Damn it!" William stepped back and tripped over the mud scraper. He was floundering around, trying to get his balance, when the door snapped open.

"Take your drunken behaviour away from the front of this house, immediately, or I will call the patrol!"

Thoroughly cowed, William answered, "Yes, Ma'am. I'm going, Ma'am."

The door closed, quietly but firmly, and William was again left in the dark.

* * *

Three days later, Sunday afternoon, William was on time for his appointment to see his sons. He was ushered into the receiving room and told to wait by a tall, thin-faced woman who was wearing an apron. William hadn't seen her before. *Probably a nanny of sorts*, he thought. He waited, hoping that he wouldn't meet Mistress Wenman, not after his performance of the other evening. As it turned out, he was to be spared that encounter but was to have an entirely different kind of experience, instead.

The nanny returned, leading Charles by the hand and carrying the bundle that was James. She led Charles to one of the chairs. The boy climbed up and squirmed around so he could keep an eye on his father and on the door. Nanny handed the baby to William without a word. She left and then returned in several moments with a tray of muffins, placing them on a small table just inside the door. As she closed the door she said, "You have half an hour, sir."

William rocked the baby as he asked, "How have you been, Charles?"

Charles eyes were fixed on the tray of muffins. He didn't acknowledge his father's question.

The door opened and another boy of perhaps nine or ten years entered, timidly. William thought he looked frightened and unsure of himself.

Obviously Charles was concerned about his share of the muffins. He hopped down off the chair and raced to the tray before the older boy could take any. Grabbing one, Charles moved to the other corner as he devoured it, being very careful to cup his hand under his chin so there wouldn't be any lost crumbs.

What was the older boy doing here? It was unusual for a stranger to be in the room during family visits. "What's your name, boy?"

"My name is John George Pyke."

That answer sent shivers up William's spine. *This was the boy who had stood in the smoking ruins of Dartmouth and had made the same brave response to a British soldier. 'My name is John George Pyke,' he had said. 'Ma told me to stay under the bed until she came back. Then she went to help Da,' he had said.*

The mother hadn't come back. The Indians killed the boy's mother and father and they were most probably two of the bodies there on the beach when William told the sailmaker to put the final stitch of the burial shroud through their noses. William shook his head to rid himself of the thoughts of that ghastly night. *Of course, this Pyke boy is an orphan and he would be here at the Orphan House, but what is he doing in this room during our visit?*

Lower lip trembling, John George searched the room for someone else. "Am I in the wrong room again?"

"I think so, son."

John George's eyes grew large. "I get in real bad trouble when I come into the wrong room."

"Yes, well, mistakes happen." William didn't know what else to say to the boy but he added, "Nobody can get mad at a little boy who comes into the wrong room."

His lip trembling, John George Pyke shook his head, dislodging some tears. "I came in the wrong room and saw the soldier hurting Annie. He didn't stop." The boy sobbed. "Annie was bleeding from down there, between her legs. He didn't stop. I was crying but the soldier didn't stop."

William opened his mouth to say something but the little boy continued, "Then Mister Skinner was mad at me for coming into the wrong room."

"Who was hurting …"

"Later he gave me jam tarts and told me I was a good boy but Mistress said I didn't deserve tarts because I was a bad boy and it was me that got Annie hurt …"

The door opened. "John George! Are you talking to someone?" Amos Skinner came through the door and halted as soon as he saw William. "Shit! What did the little bugger say?" Amos didn't wait for a reply. "You can't believe anything that boy says." Skinner became less agitated as he explained, "You know, he saw his Ma and Pa killed by the Indians and the poor boy hasn't been good in the head since. Talks about blood and such all the time. We try to keep him …"

"Does he mean Anna Crowell, the orphan who was raped?"

"No! Of course not!"

"He saw her raped and you were there? Is that what he is saying?" Still holding James in his arms, William stood up. "Anna Crowell was raped by a soldier." William raised his fist at the other man. "You filthy bastard! The girl was here in one of these rooms when she was raped!"

"No! Not here! I didn't have nothin' to do with it."

"Were you waiting for seconds?"

A look of horror came over Skinner's face. "It wasn't me! I wouldn't ... It was Tambrow. I only ..." He jammed his hand in his mouth when he realized what he was going to admit.

The men stood there looking at each other.

John George ran from the room.

Charles, skirting around the centre of the room, went to the muffin tray and helped himself to another. He sat on the chair and nibbled away at the second muffin, still being very careful about the crumbs.

James began to fuss. William looked down at his son and jiggled him a bit to try and pacify him.

"You can't prove anything. I don't have to worry about the likes of you. Everyone knows you're touched in the head. Didn't even screw the Bulkeley woman when she was throwing it at you. Now, that's crazy!" Amos Skinner stopped when he saw the fury in William's face.

"I have friends in this town who will see to it that you are hanged for what you have done."

"I don't have to worry about your friends."

"Maybe so, maybe not." William's next words came from the depths of his soul. "There is no place you can hide. No one will ever see you without thinking of what happened to Anna Crowell, not in Halifax, not in Nova Scotia, not anywhere in the British Empire. You pig!"

The thin-faced woman must have heard the commotion. She entered the room, checking the muffin tray first before she looked anywhere else in the room.

"Keep this animal away from my children!" William carefully handed James to the nanny. When she had him safely in her arms he said, "I am going to get the Provost Marshal to come here and see what has been going on." William took steps toward Amos Skinner but Amos ran from the room and out the front door of the building.

* * *

Amos Skinner was right. The Provost Marshal was very attentive about William's account of the incident but not inclined to take any immediate action.

"See here, old chap," the Provost Marshal said, "we have all that information. Statements were taken and the culprit apprehended. Ranger Tambrow appeared before a Justice of the Peace and was remanded for trial."

"But he escaped!"

"Yes, he escaped and there is a twenty-pound reward for his capture. He will be found and punished. As for this Skinner fellow, you say he was involved ..."

"Of course he was!"

"We'll be on the watch for him. We'll bring him in when we find him." The Provost Marshal smiled, "There's not many places for him to hide."

"Ranger Tambrow is doing a good job of hiding. It's been a couple of weeks now and you've seen neither hide nor hair of the man."

The other officer pressed his lips together. He was clearly annoyed. Looking up from the file he was holding, he stared at William as if trying to memorize his features for some future case he might be called upon to investigate. Finally he said, "You're not on the Louisbourg beaches now, laddie, swinging your shillelagh, charging about like you own the place." He closed the file shut with a snap. "You mind your manners when you're in my town." He rose from his desk, "I told you what I was going to do with the case and now, sir, I have other things on my mind. Good day to you."

A corporal appeared behind William and very politely said, "If you'd be so kind, Lieutenant, to faller me, I can show you the way out."

Yes, it seems like Amos Skinner was right.

* * *

The next week's edition of the *Gazette* contained a news item.[3]

> Last Sunday night, a long time distillery worker by name of Amos Skinner, despairing of the Mercy of God and the Devil getting the predominance over him so as to persuade him to be an accessory in his own Death, which he effected in the following manner. By tying a small cord to the tricker of his firelock, with a loop at the other end in which he put his foot, and placing the muzzle of his firelock to the temple of his head, and by the movement of his foot, pulled the tricker; which in an instant put a period to his days.

* * *

William had given up wearing his naval uniform. Although he was officially on the sick list he didn't believe that he would ever sail again. Jake Fink had returned to *Sutherland* and she was gone to the Saint Lawrence, checking on the ice conditions so the might of the British Empire could soon be gathered there to strike down Quebec, the French capital in North America. Capture Quebec and starve Montreal was the grand plan.

He let out a long, long sigh as he stood on the steps of Saint Paul's Church and watched the activity on Prince Street. "Beached I am, in an unfriendly port."

"But not alone," a female voice said from behind him.

He turned to face Amy Bulkeley, who was standing two steps up from him.

"You mustn't be caught talking to yourself, sir, or the good folk will believe the scandalous tales about William Gray, the wild Scotsman, who catches naughty boys and girls after dark and spanks them with his shillelagh until they learn to behave."[4]

William had no response for that type of greeting so he kept his peace.

"Brown looks good on you, Willie."

William had purchased a brown coat, which he wore with his silk navy shirt and neckpiece. He had thought the jacket becoming, especially with the lace cuffs of the shirt extending down over his wrists. Butternut colour breeches, grey stockings and black shoes with gold-looking buckles made up the rest of his walking-out attire. William swept off his hat, in the manner of a grandee, and gave her a formal bow.

"Dear gracious me! Such an approach in my boudoir would have overwhelmed me but on the steps of Mother Church in broad daylight on a Sunday, I really don't know what to do, my dear Willie."

William hadn't realized, by performing his grand bow, he had placed his head at the level of Amy's pelvis. He recovered from his bow, his face scarlet.

Amy extended her gloved hand, drawing William up the steps to her level. Holding his hand she whispered, "If you have your shillelagh near at hand, I have the delicious inclination to be bad."

A bit of pressure and William was able to retrieve his hand from Amy's grasp. "You look lovely, Missus Bulkeley, although I might venture to say ..." here William hesitated long enough for Amy to be able to carry on for him.

"That I have changed my habit?" Amy ran her hand in a smoothing motion from her bodice to her hip. "Yes, it is homespun, although I didn't do it myself." She gave a delicate laugh. "I haven't progressed that far in our new lifestyle but soon, my dear Willie, you won't recognize us." William noticed that Amy wore no jewellery; her bonnet was of local manufacture and not from Boston or the continent, while the only touches of richness to her outfit were the small pieces of lace that had been sewn to the cuffs of her homespun dress. Amy fiddled with her neckpiece, a thin red ribbon, as she studied William's face for reactions while she asked, "Your boys are still at Orphan House? You have not been able to make other arrangements?"

"No, Amy, I haven't been able to arrange anything else."

"Well, you come to Carleton House tomorrow and we will speak about it."

"I shouldn't be coming to your home, Missus Bulkeley; Richard and I aren't on the very best of terms."

"Believe me, Willie, Richard is on the best of terms with everyone." Amy gave one of her throaty chortles. "Besides, Richard is in Boston buying an organ for the church."[5]

"I noticed that you were both singing in the choir ..."

"Richard isn't just singing in the choir; he's the choirmaster, and now he's buying an organ."[6]

"It will be a wonderful organ, if I know Richard," William said all too truthfully. "I remember when he bought the town's street lamps. He bought them by the hundreds. No one believed we would ever have enough streets to use them all, but now look at the size of Halifax!"

"Yes. Well, that's my husband." She placed a hand on William's cuff. "I want you to come tomorrow for tea," she said, as she withdrew her hand to gather up her skirts and prepare to leave, "at ten in the morning, please."

"It would be better to come at a time when your husband is at home, Ma'am," William called after her.

Amy took several steps back toward William. "At ten, tomorrow morning." Another couple of steps closer. "I will try to restrain myself." Then, sounding her chortle, she continued down the steps to Prince Street, where she met several people she knew and she again stopped to talk.

* * *

William had arrived at the door to Carleton House early. He killed a few minutes by closely examining the doorknocker which he recognized as being a mate to the one at the Old Mansion (as it was now called). Overhearing someone approaching the door from the other side, rather than be found skulking on the front walk, he hastily raised the knocker. Before he could allow it to fall, the door opened, revealing the lady of the house herself.

"Interested in acquiring a brass doorknocker, Mister?"

William gently released his hold on the knocker, allowing Amy to fully open the door.

"Please come in." Amy took his hat and closed the door behind him.

"I have told the servants to go to the other end of the house so we can have privacy." Exerting pressure on his elbow before William could react, Amy led him into the front room where a lady was already seated, sipping on some tea. "I want you to meet my friend, Margaret."

A very attractive young woman extended her hand for William to take.

"This is the William whom I have known forever, Margaret."

Margaret nodded her head. "I am pleased to meet you, Lieutenant Gray."

The throaty laugh. "Oh, please, Margaret, let's keep our tryst on a first-name basis." Before either of her guests could comment, Amy was busying herself with serving pieces and asking questions about tea preferences. Then she excused herself to fetch something from the kitchen.

When William became aware of the ticking of a timepiece in the room, he thought he had better say, "Have you lived long in Halifax?"

"My brother and I came in '50 from New England." She sipped for a moment or two on her tea. "You were on the staff of the first governor."

"Yes, I was. Been here since 1749," he added lamely.

"Was the first governor as devious as Governor Lawrence?"

That intrigued William. "Why do you think Governor Lawrence is devious?"

"He's devious because he dissolved the Assembly. Those freeholders were causing problems for his administration"—she snapped her fingers—"and out they went!"

Harking back to comments that were made in the tavern, William disagreed. "He made a bad, bad mistake. Lawrence had the authority to dissolve the Assembly but the members will have the last laugh because he will have to reassemble them."

"Ah yes, but with different rules."

What kind of different rules, William thought, *when the*

freeholders choose the members of the Assembly because the King said so. What could be changed about that?

"Let me explain," the bright-eyed woman with the curly brown hair said. As she spoke, William marvelled at her snowy complexion and delicate features, but he rapidly began to pay attention to what she was saying: he was getting a lesson in provincial politics. It amazed him as the information spilled from her heart-shaped lips. After a moment or two, he was just plain amazed at her knowledge. How did she learn all this?

"Remember before the dissolution?' she asked. "The King directed that the Assembly consist of twenty-two members." Margaret held up three fingers. "There were three groups: Halifax with four members appointed by the freeholders, Lunenburg with two members, and then the third group, the sixteen members representing the Province at Large chosen jointly by the freeholders of Halifax and Lunenburg." Margaret put her cup down and selected a scone to butter. "You can see that once the Assembly members turned against the current administration, there was no way for Lawrence to hush them. The Assembly was controlled by the freeholders, not the governor."

"That's the way the King meant it to be. Citizens of property would exercise an Englishman's inherent rights in a House of Representatives."

Margaret placed a scone on the plate and handed it to William. "And the governor and his council were supposed to heed their advice." She smiled, "There's lovely-looking jam, if you'd like some." When William said 'no' she continued, "Our governor and his high-handed henchmen were going to be investigated, audited, surveyed and just plain harassed until they were completely discredited."[7]

William smiled at the lovely woman who possessed such a thorough understanding of Halifax politics. "But! Our devious governor has done what? Tell me!"

"Governor Lawrence argued that changing times brought a change in the rules. He has reduced the number of members of the Assembly from twenty-two to twenty. Then he created five new Counties, each appointing two members."

"That's ten."

"Two new towns and Lunenburg appoint two members each."

"Ten plus six."

"Yes, and Halifax still appoints four members." Margaret sat back and crossed her arms. "Bearing in mind that the Acadians own no land, can you see how the governor got control back?" William slowly put his plate on the table to give himself time to think about it. "No, I honestly don't have any idea ..." Amy came back in the room. "You two are having a nice chat?"

"Yes, Margaret was telling me that the governor has gained control of the Assembly, somehow, but I don't really understand it."

"Wasn't he clever?" Amy said, agreeably, as she took a seat.

"All right, ladies. Let me in on it." The women smiled, knowingly, at each other but neither of them spoke. "The freeholders still appoint the members; that hasn't changed. So how does the governor get control?"

"The new towns and counties have no inhabitants except for the garrisons and their dependants." Margaret gave William a bright smile. "There are no freeholders."

"No freeholders other than men like my Richard who was granted two thousand acres of mostly cultivated land that qualifies him as a freeholder[8] in two of the counties and one of the towns." Any seemed delighted with herself. "My Richard gets to choose members on behalf of the King and to the benefit of the governor and his council." Amy sat down near the tea set. "More tea, William?"

"Back to my original question, William. Was your governor as devious as Charles Lawrence?"

Thoughtfully, William had to admit that Edward Cornwallis had been a babe-in-the-woods who had the heart torn out of his policies by the wolves like Mauger, LeLoutre and, yes, Bulkeley. "My governor suffered a recall to England. No, I guess he didn't do very well. He wasn't devious enough." William had the feeling that Margaret was pleased with the manner in which he had responded. That Margaret thought well of him gave him a sense of pleasure. William beamed.

Amy also seemed pleased and she let it show. "I didn't know what Margaret would bring up to talk about but I was sure you would be interested, William." She pursed her lips. "There are any number of subjects Margaret could have talked about because she keeps herself very well informed."

Margaret put her cup and napkin down. She pushed back on her chair and rose. "It's been very pleasant but I must proceed with my day, Amy."

"You just sit down, Margaret Skinner. I have things that must be said."

Her beautiful, light skin suddenly flushed with embarrassment, Margaret remained standing.

Amy, a trifle annoyed that she didn't immediately have her way, compressed her lips but her voice didn't betray her feelings as she said, "Margaret's brother died last Sunday. She no longer has a protector in this town."

Margaret interrupted, "I can look after myself, Amy!"

"Not really, my dear. Your late brother's associates will accept the notion that, since you are of the same stock, you are of the same inclination." Amy shook her head, negatively. "No, no, there will be men in this town who will see you as an easy target and seek to take advantage of you." Amy pulled on the sleeve of Margaret's dress, forcing her to sit down. "There! That's said. Your brother was Amos Skinner who died in a sorrowful way leaving you without family or much in the way of financial resources." Amy patted the embarrassed woman's hand and, turning to focus her attention on William, she pointed at him. "While you, dear, dear William, have two children at risk in Orphan House." Noting the alarm on William's face she repeated, "Yes, your boys are at risk in Orphan House." She wagged her forefinger at him as she accented her words, "There are people in this town who would like to see hurt done to you or yours. You have been a thorn in the side of Mauger and his boys and, once again, you have just cost them more time, more money and a dedicated worker. No, the sooner you get your sons out of there, the better."

Amy began collecting the tea things, arranging them on the tray this way and that, as she went on. "I thought the two of you might meet and see what nice people you both are." She dropped a napkin and she picked it up. "The little boys need looking after. The low-lifes of this town need to know that Lieutenant William Gray has an interest, nay, a concern for Mistress Skinner who is his children's nanny." She gazed at Margaret and then William. "That's the way I saw it when I invited you here."

Amy Bulkeley stood up. "Now, Margaret Skinner," she said in a mock serious tone, "you help me clean up enough so the servants don't think I am unable to manage without them."

Extending her hand to William. she drew him up out of his chair and gave him a gentle push. "You, William, go along now, and think about this. Let me know what you decide before midweek."

The servant appeared with William's hat. "My dear, dear friend has to leave now, John. Please show him the way out." Giving her guest a beaming smile and a little wave, she said, "Ta, ta, William. See you by Wednesday."

* * *

By Wednesday, an arrangement was made between Mistress Margaret Skinner and Lieutenant William Gray for the care of Charles and James.

June 10, 1759
Carleton House

"We have had our disagreements and a certain amount of testiness between us." Richard Bulkeley cast a quick look at William Gray to see how this approach was being received and then quickly dropped his eyes. *Not too well*, he thought. So he increased the humility in his voice. "And I know I am largely to blame for ..." a quick look but still no positive response on the other man's face, "... and I know I am to blame for that circumstance." *Nothing*. He let his voice trail off. He fixed his eyes on the younger man. *Perhaps silence would bring some response.* Richard sat down, holding his file of papers on his knees, apparently searching for a particular sheet.

Somewhere a child was playing. The tinkle of the laughter wafted through the open window, sounding out of place in the formal setting of the receiving room of Carleton House. Richard glanced up. *Nothing.*

William seemed as contented as could be, sitting with his legs crossed, gently manipulating his left arm and hand as if he were doing some sort of exercise.

God, he is stubborn, Richard thought. *Might as well get on with it.*

"It was good of you to accept my invitation to Carleton House." Suddenly Richard lost his temper. "Will you please stop doing whatever it is you're doing with your arm? I have some business to discuss."

"Well, thank you Richard. I had thought that you might have entirely disappeared into the cloak of respectability and there was none of the old Richard Bulkeley left! I couldn't believe it." William gave him an infectious sort of smile. "Glad it isn't so."

Richard smiled back. "I'm trying to change."

"You formed the ... what is the name of the association?"

"The Charitable Irish Society. Yes, all the members of Saint Paul's belong. It is our duty, as Christians to ..."

Laughing, William said, "Enough! I'll join, Richard, I'll join."

This is better, Richard thought. "You have a fine voice, William. Why don't you come out for choir practice?"

"I'm shy about things like that, Richard."

"What? The crazy Scot who scares bad children with his big shillelagh and turns them into sweet little angels ... is shy?"

"You know, Richard, if that story had any truth, it would be a claymore."

Nodding his head in agreement, Richard opened up the file again. "I have the latest reports from our fleet at Quebec. Would you like to know about them?" He picked out two sheets, "Rather, I have two sets of reports: the official one that has been passed to the Admiralty and the private report my man sends to me." He chuckled. "I don't usually share them with anyone, but you might find it interesting to get the same information from two different viewpoints." Without waiting for any further comment from William, Richard began reading from the official file.

"The report says there's two hundred sail, forty-nine of them Royal Navy ... more than half of them fifty guns or more." Richard scanned down the page. "It says the transports, ordnance and hospital ships, sounding vessels and provision tenders, etc. are in formation passing unopposed the length of the River Saint Lawrence." He flipped the page. "Just to give you an idea, William, there are 13,500 sailors and marines and 8,500 soldiers. The report says there is no enemy activity and the river is not fortified."[9]

"And that's the official report?"

"That's the bulk of it." He put the sheet down. "Here's what my man says. Yes, he confirms the figure of two hundred English ships but he says they are strung out in a line about fifty miles long. Whenever a ship draws close to one shore or the other, they are subjected to musket fire from partisans. As far as he has been able to witness, English casualties are very light. Let's see, morale is generally good. He has a report from one of the vessels transporting the women who will be working in the field hospitals; says there has been a discipline problem among the men who did not have access. Discipline was restored." He ran his finger down the page and then turned to the next page. "Here's an interesting point for you, ex-Naval Liaison Officer. He reports that General Wolfe exchanged words with the naval commanders when he found out the fleet had no reliable charts for the river ... and ... now get this, there's a thing called La Traverse which will not allow the larger English ships to approach Quebec Fortress."

"Any idea what it is?"

"My man made a note at the end of the report. Let's see ... yes, here it is." Richard read the footnote, "Near Orléans Island, ships must sail close to the north shore. At Madame Island, or thereabouts—my man wasn't sure—ships must cross to the south channel. The waters are turbulent and shallow. The channels are narrow. The area is tidal with a large rise and fall of water levels." Richard put the sheet down. "I wonder what my dear father-in-law said when he was told he wouldn't be able to take his precious *Sutherland* close enough to kill French?" William just grunted. It seemed to him that it was another case of the English trusting to luck, or muddling through, as he so often heard it said. He was about to comment on it but Richard asked him a question.

"How is Margaret getting along with the children?"

"The boys love her. She's good with them. I'm thinking about ..." Here William hesitated. "I might ..."

"So I heard. You're going to have her move in and you will build a shed on the back of the house for your sleeping quarters." When William stared at him in a surprised way, Richard hastened on. "Don't be surprised that I know. Amy told me. She tells me all kinds of things. Why don't you just marry the woman?"

Richard knew, from the set of William's mouth, that he wasn't getting any further along that track. "Well, then, do you want to know what else Amy told me?"

Relieved that the subject was being changed, he nodded.

The next issue of the *Gazette* will have no mention of Bulkeley indiscretions, nor Morris nor Belcher ... in fact, none of the Council members are mentioned."

"What happened?"

The citizens are concentrating their anger on our dear governor. Since he changed the composition of the Assembly, every social ill or political indiscretion is now laid at the feet of clay of our dear governor."

"Maybe you can still cancel the church organ," William said with a straight face. Receiving a malevolent glare from the First Secretary of Nova Scotia, William hunched his head between his shoulders to show that he had been joking.

"Some joke, Ensign."

They laughed together, William with no small sense of relief that the man facing him had taken the comment in good humour. *Christ*, William said to himself, *smarten up! This man has the power to crush you! Uncle Charles always said your sense of humour would get you in trouble. Piss this man off and you will find out what trouble is.* "You didn't call me over to brief me on the Quebec campaign, although I did appreciate it. What can I do for you, Richard?"

"Well, I have another file." Richard walked over to a desk. Dropping the two files he had been working with, he picked up a bigger, dog-eared file. "With everyone gone to capture Quebec, there are only two people in this town who have worked with the Acadians to any extent. There's the governor; he was the Commandant of Fort Cumberland and personally acquainted with LeLoutre and Beau Soleil."

"I suppose you're going to say that I'm the other one?"

Seeming to ignore William, Richard opened the file. "Someone has put numbers together for me. Sit down and listen." When William didn't move, Richard added, "Please."

William sat as far away from the man holding the file as he could. He crossed his legs and turned his head slightly, to look out the window.

"All right, William. That's part of it. You're sitting." Richard read from the file. "In the Restigouche and Miramichi, there are close to 1,300 Acadians." William tried to ask a question but Richard waved him silent. "Just listen! I'll tell you when I need for you to talk." He read from the file, tracing his place with his finger. "Evidence of the hostile designs of the Acadians is evident at Restigouche and neighbouring ports, where piratical vessels are being outfitted to cruise against His Majesty's subjects. The Crown is apprehensive for the safety of the settlements to be established at Chignecto, where the Acadians have induced the Indians to refuse to make peace."[10]

"There are Acadians at Chignecto?"

"There are about two hundred and forty Acadians at Chignecto."

"Where are they coming from?"

"We have over four hundred between Halifax and Pisiquid."

"And they are raiding again. I heard five soldiers were scalped near Lunenburg."

"No, that was an Indian war party. The two soldiers we lost on the Eastern Shore were at the hands of the Acadians."

"How can you be sure?"

"That's what I am told by people who should be able to tell the difference."

"No wonder he was worried about coming here."

"Who?"

"I met a friend of a friend ... his name's Elkanah Smith. He was an Indian fighter up Fort William Henry way. Indians almost got him last time out; got hurt pretty bad in the shoulder." William shrugged his bad shoulder and arm as if demonstrating where Elkanah was wounded. "Took him a year to recover and by that time his wife decided she wanted them to settle where there are no French left and the Indians have been pacified. They thought they would settle in the Fundy but when he got here, he heard about the scalping ..."

Richard opened another file. " He went out on the *Yorke* with Morris?"

"Yes, he did."

Holding the file toward the light from the window he read, "Elkanah Smith chose acreage on Sherose Island. One male, one female and one male child will be transported here." He sighed. "I'm surprised he is still coming. Usually if the settlers hear about the murders before they come, they stay where they are or, it they do come, they huddle around the forts and the burden on the Crown increases with no progress for the Province." He grunted. "If we had more"—he checked the name on the file—"Elkanah Smiths, we could force the Acadians into submission."

"Richard, not one of the Acadians ever made a voluntary submission. The only way we have made them bend is through threat of want or terror."

"You are right, of course. Forty Acadians of the village of Saint Anne have made no submission. They have no crops and we refuse to send them supplies yet they will not submit."

'How do they survive?"

"The Indians feed them." Richard sat in a chair opposite to William. "The governor's remedy is to gather up as many as we can find and ship them off again—back to France or off to England—anywhere but here, where they are interfering with the growth of our province."

"The governor will have to remember, we won't be able to trick them this time. In '58 they didn't have leaders. By now, they have had time to grow a crop of young men who would lead the resistance to the death." With Reine Cameron in mind, William added, softly, "The women would be more deadly than the men."

"Bloodshed?"

"Definitely. Some of their women have already taken up arms. I saw evidence of that at Louisbourg." He shook his head. "This woman I met, we took everything from her until she only had her man left. She fought by his side."

"Incredible!"

"It was a beautiful thing to see, the love that woman had for her husband. Only death will ever part them."

"We might have to arrange that, William."

The real Richard Bulkeley is never far from the surface, William thought. He rose. "Thanks for the chat, Richard. Hope I was of some help. Don't send for your man; I know my way."

July 12, 1759
Hollis Street

Margaret had been right; the baby's flannel was soiled. If I had believed that the little darlin' could poop again today I would have allowed her to handle it. She had volunteered to see why the baby was fretting, but no! Good-Hearted-Willie had said something about a long enough day with the children and he would handle the wet nappy. Sit down and read the Gazette, he had said. When he encountered the smell, he toyed with the idea of calling her to see if she would volunteer again, but he remembered advice Uncle Charles had given him; if you mean to do something, do it well. He opened the flannel and examined the cargo. "You little bugger, James, you must have heard Uncle Charles." There was so much of it, it was coming out of the end of the flannel and oozing down the child's leg.

"Willie!"

Margaret was calling from the front room. He responded, hopefully, "Yes, Margaret?"

"When you were last speaking with Amy's husband, did he discuss the Acadians?"

"Yes, I think that was the sole reason he had me drop by."

'I think he has been talking with John Bushell of the *Gazette.*"

"Is there an article?"

"Yes. Want me to read it to you?"

"Yes, please." In a moment of weakness he said in a half voice, "I'm up to my elbows in crap, you know!"

There was a rustle of paper. Was that a snigger he heard? Margaret began reading.

> "**The Acadian Menace Remains.** They have obstinately refused to take the oath of allegiance. They have induced many of our Foreign settlers to desert over to the French and have always supplied the French troops who have intruded upon this Province with provisions, giving them constant intelligence of all the motions of the English and have thereby forced the English to live on Garrison towns. Huddled as they be around the forts, the settlers were unable to cultivate and improve lands at any distance which has been the principal cause of the great expense to the British Nation and a means of more than half the settlers who came here with an intention to settle quitting the province and settling in other plantations where they might get their bread without risking their lives.
>
> "Even the numbers of Imperial Troops within our borders and the British Fleet in our Harbours and even in the presence of His Majesty's Admirals and to the highest contempt of the Governor and Council, they continue to refuse allegiance to His Majesty. And if this be their language while the Fleet and Troops are with us I know not what will be their style and degree of their insolence and hostilities when they are gone."[11]

"Tell me again, Margaret, did he use the word 'huddle'?"

A rustle of paper followed by that husky voice from the front room: "Huddled as they be around the forts ... yes, he used the word 'huddle.'"

'Then it's definitely Richard drumming up support for the governor to take strong action against the Acadians."

"Oh my!"

William finished with the baby and lowered him into his crib. Chucking him under the chin he called out, "That's two down." He looked around the room checking to see if all was in order. He picked up the lamp.

"Wash your hands, please."

There was definitely a snigger! He heard it!

"Use the soap I made. It's not so harsh and it will still take the smell away."

So she had known, all along.

The dry sink had been moved out of the little room because it was difficult having a separate room for Margaret when the shed hadn't been finished yet. As things were for the moment, Margaret used the one room upstairs, Charles and James used the room behind the kitchen, and William slept at the front of the house after everyone had gone to bed. It was a tiny house, getting tinier everyday as William and Margaret became more familiar with each other.

"There's someone at the door, William." Margaret came hustling to the back of the house. "I'm not dressed! Who do you think it could be?"

William slipped his coat on over the loose blouse he had been wearing. As he approached the front door, he reached behind the door and pulled his sword from its scabbard. He held it down by his leg as he asked, "Who's there?"

"Mister Bulkeley's groom, sir."

William still didn't open the door. "What do you want ..." he picked a name ... "Jake?"

"It's Adam, sir. Mister Bulkeley said to tell you it was very urgent."

The door unbolted, William opened it slowly. "Adam, at this time of night, Hollis Street isn't a great place to be. The town's changing, you know."

"I know, sir. That's why the Master sent the Watch with me." He gestured behind him and William could see three men of the Town Watch lounging against the street lamp.

"Would you please come to Carleton House as early as you can, tomorrow?"

"Yes, certainly. Do you have any idea what he wants?"

"Not really, sir, but he did receive word from Quebec late this afternoon."

"Thank you, Adam. Say that I will be there."

* * *

Richard Bulkeley didn't waste time with formalities but went straight to the point. "The news from Quebec isn't good, William. Come in, come in, and John close the door, that's a good man." He waited for the door to be completely closed before he opened the file. "Again, William, I have two reports: the official report and the one from my man."

"Excuse me, Richard. I don't understand what I am doing here."

"I think it will become obvious once you hear what I have to say. So, be quiet and listen." He started to read the file and stopped. He looked up at William and added, "Please," while giving his guest a pleasant smile. "You really have to hear this before you can see our problem."

William gave a nod of assent and clamped his mouth shut.

"Sixty big Royal Navy ships navigated La Traverse and were moored off D'Orléans Island by June 26; that put them much nearer the Fortress. *H.M.S. Neptune*, one of the largest ships, is sent downstream, past an Island named Aux Coudres, as a rear guard." Richard looked up from where he was reading and laughed. "I guess Admiral Charles Saunders didn't want to be caught unawares by any French fleet sneaking up on him."

"In the confines of a river, the *Neptune* would serve very well," William agreed.

"Now let me tell you what my man reported for that same period. At a Council of War held on *Sutherland*, General Wolfe expressed displeasure at the lack of Navy professionalism in not having a plan to get the bigger ships above La Traverse. Admiral Holmes said the matter was being looked into but, when pressed by the now irate general, was unable to be any more

specific." Richard gave a short laugh. "I'm going to read directly from the report so you don't miss any of this next bit. Here
goes. The captain of Holmes's flagship, Captain John Rous,
said there was a man in the fleet who would have knowledge of
the Traverse and he should be consulted. When Rous revealed
that Captain Killick of the transport *Goodwill*[12] might have
been in and out of Quebec Harbour as a Yankee trader, the
admiral said he would prefer not to rely on the likes of a Yankee trader for decisions involving the movement of His
Majesty's Fleet. General Wolfe made a comment that the possible uses of intelligence should outweigh any distaste for the
source. Admiral Holmes maintained his opinion that the Navy
would resolve the problem of the Traverse. At this point, Captain Rous suggested that not all donkey's asses were on don-
keys. Admiral Holmes was quick to ask what the good captain
meant by his remark and was not the least bit satisfied with the
muffled response. Captain Rous was doubled over in his chair
apparently suffering an attack of gout. Admiral Holmes
adjourned the meeting and, within the hour, had removed his
flag from *Sutherland*."[13]

"My God!" William could imagine the scene: *Rous's own
marines taking him into custody and leading him off to the brig.
No, worse than that! The admiral wouldn't dare leave the captain
on his own ship! The Sutherland in his own brig? Never. No, the
admiral would have to take him over the side to the brig of another ship.* "What happened? For God's sake, what happened to
the captain?"

Richard continued reading from his man's report. "Captain Killick did have the key to the Traverse. *Sutherland* was
one of the first ships to cross and take up a safer mooring off
D'Orléans."[14] Richard looked up from where he was reading.
"Now you know why my esteemed father-in-law was allowed
to live to sail another day."

"There's no further mention of the captain?"

"No. The next entry is for June 27. I'll continue. June 27.
Eight thousand five hundred men were prepared to land on
Beauport Beach, cross the Saint Charles River and attack
Québec. A fierce storm forced the retrieval of the landing

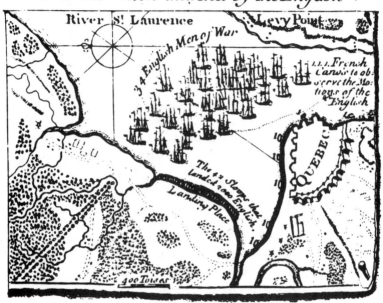

The Port and Environs of QUEBEC,
as it was when attack'd by the English .

Map of a Plan of Quebec.[15]

barges. Seven vessels of the fleet lost their anchors. A total of nine ships were driven aground, two unsalvageable. By the time the storm had passed it was night."

"What does your spy have to say about the 27th?"

"On the twenty-seventh he was with Wolfe on *Richmond*. From *Richmond* they watched as the landing boats loaded soldiers—"

William interrupted, "Does he say what kind of boats, how many sailors, what ships were going to be used to suppress enemy fire?"

"Matter of fact, he does give more detail than I would have normally expected. Probably because of how quickly the situation changed for the worse. Let me see. I'll start here." Richard had turned the page and was now following the text along with his finger. "Beautiful day, light winds. Flat bottomed boats rowed by twenty sailors each loaded sixty-three soldiers and assembled off the *Lowestoft* waiting for the attack signal to be raised on *Richmond's* yards."

"Your man is Navy!"

"Um, yes."

"And known to Wolfe."

"That's neither here nor there, William. Let me continue. A swivel gun was manned in the bow of each boat, drummer at the waist and the colours borne by a naval officer in the stern. Major General Wolfe and company took a longboat to the island and, from the north point, surveyed Beaufort Beach where the attacking force was meant to land. When he saw the storm approaching, Wolfe hastened back to *Richmond* to give the recall, which, somewhat belatedly, was given. The attacking force was recovered in time, however."

William sighed. "At Louisbourg, Wolfe said he didn't like the naval system: signals being given from the yards of the command ship." William smiled as he remembered. "He said he didn't want to wait upon some old fuddy-duddy on a man o' war to decide to give orders to *his* men. He preferred signals from the commander at the scene."

"I think you are beginning to see what the problem is, William, but let me finish these reports and then we can discuss it." He found his place in the document and read on. "Seven vessels lost their anchors. A total of nine went aground; two could not be salvaged. The storm passed quickly and then it was night."

"Nine went aground!"

"Yes. In a footnote, my man quotes Wolfe as saying that the Navy is so inept they can't get out of its own way even to save themselves. My last reports are for the twenty-eighth."

"Why is that? Oh, yes. It takes that long for the reports to reach here. So the last report they got before they left was about two weeks ago."

"Yes. The early morning of June 28th, the French loosed six fireships amongst the English Fleet moored off Ile d'Orléans. *H.M.S. Centurion*, the closest English ship to the approaching fireships began an effective cannonade the moment they were sighted. *H.M.S. Stirling Castle*, the flagship of Admiral Saunders, sent boat crews to tow one of the enemy ships to the shore, where it burned. No damage to the His Majesty's Fleet." Richard snapped the official file shut. "Wait until you hear what my man had to say about the fireships." Without waiting for an acknowledgement from his audience, Richard read the unofficial report with enthusiasm.[16]

"It was approximately six miles from Quebec Harbour to the British Fleet at D'Orléans. To be successful, the French should have waited until they were as close as a mile, but they fired up the ships too early. Still, they might have been successful for several reasons. One: it was a bad night with wind, rain and lightning. Two: several of the English ships had fouled their anchors, drawing attention away from the direction the fireships would be coming from. Three: the officer in charge of the lookouts had permitted several of his men to seek shelter, leaving only one man to watch the quadrant where enemy activity might be expected. Four: that solitary man was frightened by the storm and when he heard noises coming out of the night, shadows and sources of light, he panicked and fled, failing to raise the alarm."

"That's unbelievable!"

"It gets even better, William. During the Council of War

that morning, General Wolfe learned that the senior naval officers had been expecting the French to attempt a fireship raid—the French favour that type of thing and seldom fail to use the fireship tactic. The fleet wasn't ready for the raid." Richard closed the file. "My man says there can be no doubt in the mind of Major General James Wolfe that he and his men will be very poorly served by the Royal Navy during this campaign."

"My God, yes. I wish I were there to help."

"You mean, help like you did at Louisbourg?"

"Hell yes!"

Richard pulled out another file. "I have here the orders seconding ..."

"Do you have a file for everything?"

"... seconding you to General Wolfe and giving you the authority to act as Naval Liaison Officer."

Glancing at the document William observed, "Yes, but that was for Louisbourg."

Richard continued as if there had been no interruptions. "This document does read that you are seconded to a Brigadier where he is now a Major General and the intention was for this to be in the theatre of operations at or near Louisbourg, but it neither specifies that no does it have an expiry date. Yes, this is a valid document. I will have copies made and certified as true before you leave."

"Leave!" William almost laughed in the other man's face until he saw how serious Richard was. "I have but one serviceable arm!"

"Father-in-law will lend you that big ape of a sailor to look after you."

"There are the children!"

"There's Margaret." Richard grasped William by the shoulder, drawing him closer and speaking right into this face. "Wolfe said, 'let's use Killick,' but the pompous asses were willing to disregard him. Wolfe wanted to give his own commands even when it is an assault from the sea, but the pompous asses weren't listening. Wolfe has lost faith in the pompous asses. You can help them get along better."

Richard picked up a silver bell from the desk. "The communications sloop will leave on the tide ... around noon. You have no time to be coy. Do you want to go, Lieutenant?" William nodded his head.

Richard rang the bell. John entered, followed by two servants carrying William's seabag, sword and uniforms. "Missus Gray helped me pack," he said.

"She's not my ... that was nice of her. Tell her I appreciate her ..."

"We'll tell her, William. Now get going!"

William followed the servants out of the house.

Richard Bulkeley had a smug, self-satisfied look on his face as he listened to the clatter of his carriage taking the lieutenant off to war. He poured himself a brandy and sat down near the window and sipped his drink.

John appeared in the doorway. He grasped the door handle as he prepared to give his master privacy. He hesitated. "May I speak, sir?"

Bulkeley looked up but didn't say anything.

After a moment, John said, "You handled him well, sir," as he closed the door.

Nodding his head in agreement, Bulkeley savoured the aroma of his drink. "I did handle him well." He chuckled, "Pompous asses, indeed!"

Endnotes

¹ Microfiche at NS Archives: Governor Lawrence's correspondence was released to NS by New England Historical Society. When I wanted to know his state of mind, I usually found it in his correspondence.

² Elkanah Smith and Jeremiah Bancroft are as correctly represented as I could make them. Since I didn't know how the Smiths met the Grays in real life, I thought making Elkanah and Jeremiah cousins would be a good start.

³ An item about another poor soul as reported in the newspaper. I used it to exit Skinner from the story.

⁴ Emma Louisa (Gray) Schwartz often told the story about the boy who wouldn't go to bed on time. Before the Black of Night could catch the boy up past his bedtime, the last Gray of the Day (the Shillelagh Man) would try to help him reach the comfort and safety of his own bed. If the boy still dallied, all the Grays (even Granma Gray) would turn darker and darker until there was no hope for the boy.

⁵ Bulkeley did buy an organ for the church.

⁶ And he did become the choirmaster.

⁷ Taken from microfiche at the NS Archives.

⁸ The land acquisition figures are correct although I don't know how many votes he held as a consequence.

⁹ There were several accounts of how the English proceeded upriver. It was easy to create an "official" and an "unofficial" report for the purposes of the story.

¹⁰ These figures and sentiments are from a letter written on behalf of Acting Governor Belcher a year or two later. Used here to benefit the story.

¹¹ Taken from a government letter of an earlier date. Since they would not have had access to it, I attributed it to John Bushell of the *Gazette*.

¹² It was Killick who had the key to La Traverse and, eventually, his advice was followed.

¹³ I could find no historical reason why the Admiral changed his flag but this novel has one.

¹⁴ Leave it up to the great sailor; Rous took *H.M.S. Sutherland* across the Traverse.

[15] When I look at this little sketch, I imagine a French officer glancing to his right at the grand fortress of Québec knowing that it is the final objective of all the little boats approaching the French side of the river. Of course, everyone knows that the English cannot make a direct assault on the fortress because that would be suicide—they must first make a landing here, on the east bank of the St Charles River. The French officer pulls out his sketchpad. He draws the French side of the river to the best of his recollection and outlines the English shore for as far as he can see. He demonstrates his nautical bent by using 'toises' as the unit of measure (the French word for fathom). He makes a careful count of the enemy ships as they approach, noting on his sketch the part of the beach where the landing will be made. As he waits for the military action to commence, he adds details from his personal knowledge of the area: hills, forests, approach roads, fences, beach areas … when he looks up again, he estimates that already there must be some 2,000 English nearing the beach and over 40 little boats on the shore. He shades in the part of the shoreline where the English come ashore. He notes on his pad, "The forty-two sloops that landed the English." With a telescope he identifies the French canoes that are monitoring the movement of the English ships. He makes the notation on his sketch. When the storm comes and the English disengage, the French officer notes that 2,000 English had made the actual assault. He puts his pad away and continues with his duties.

What is interesting for us is that the English reported 8,500 men, mostly in flat-bottomed boats, were ready to make the assault but were recalled in time because of bad weather. This French map tells us that 42 sloops carried 2,000 English to the 'landing place.'

[16] The fire ship incident is as factual as possible.

Chapter Twelve

July 18, 1759
Fortress Québec

Du Pont Du Chambon deVergor[1] was resting his corpulence against a balustrade on the south wall of the fortress. *Splendid view,* he thought. Off to the left, seen faintly in the darkness, was the entire enemy fleet moored in the basin formed by Ile d'Orléans and the south shore of the Saint Lawrence River. He remembered gazing out over the basin on the day of his return from Lake Champlain where he had spent two years of purgatory for his performance as Commandant of Beauséjour. Losing his train of thought about the enemy fleet and the day of his arrival, deVergor's eyes glazed as he recalled the shame of the courtmartial right here, not a half-kilometre away, and the dire consequences if he had been found guilty.

Guilty! Of cowardice! Never! Of course, I was eventually declared innocent, although in the process I found out who my friends were. Yes, back in 1755, on the day of the Beauséjour surrender, I suspected that I might have less than total support from Chevalier deVannes, my second in command, and that was what I got at the Québec courtmartial—less than full support from deVannes, and the others. Fortunately, word of my difficulties reached Intendant Bigot in time for pressure to be brought to bear on the officers of the courtmartial board. He smiled as he thought of it; *and Captain Du Pont Du Chambon deVergor did not need any of his erstwhile Fort Beauséjour friends.*

Sensing a rising breeze, he set his hat more securely so that he wouldn't lose it over the balustrade.

It was fortunate for the future of the deVergor family that I had arranged the rendezvous with that duChappell woman so long ago! He inhaled, tentatively, testing the night air for traces of the cesspits of Lower Town. Reassured, he took a deep, deep breath, exhaling slowly as he considered his prospects. *One's future is certainly determined by one's past! I recall that very first*

*time; she was a courtesan but not readily available at the time
Bigot wanted her. Of course, it wasn't the first time I had interceded on behalf of Intendant Bigot to the benefit of his sexual grat-
ification and, hopefully, not the last. I am so lucky having a talent
that Bigot appreciates and avails himself of. I have enjoyed several
profitable appointments over the years because of my special relationship with that man.*

He raised his hand to his lips as he belched, deflecting the
breath so he could savour the odour of the partially digested
venison. *Wonderful meal! The meat had been seasoned to perfection!* He patted his belly, arranging his belt lower to a more
comfortable position.

*Yes, indeed! Several profitable appointments. Beauséjour net-
ted me over 6,000 livres! One more command like Beauséjour and
I will be able to purchase an estate near the Intendant and then,
let the pleasures begin and last forever and ever!*

Was there some movement in the basin? Perhaps not.

Leaving the distasteful memories of the Beauséjour surrender and the subsequent courtmartial, he redirected his thoughts
to that lovely day in July when he had returned from his Lake
Champlain exile to accept his posting at Quebec.

*Yes, it was July 12, or at least I think it was. The skies were
clear and blue and the waters of the river sparkling as if no one
had ever dropped shit into it. I remember that I had been startled
by the rocket that had arced the sky and my attention had been
drawn to the point of land that jabbed at the fortress from a kilo-
metre or two away. I hadn't noticed the English cannon when I
had been admiring the scene but they certainly had my attention
when they had belched in my direction. As I watched the shot land
in the Lower Town, I had the comforting thought that it was not
going to be anything like Beauséjour where I had been the sole target. No, here at Québec, there were others in front of me to absorb
the English shot, many others.*

"And I intend to keep it that way," he said, aloud.

He leaned over the balustrade. *Yes, there was some movement in the basin. One or two of the British ships were raising
canvas.*

* * *

"They probably change the guard at midnight." Captain John Rous looked up at the moon, which was bathing the world with a grey-white light. "Tonight's the night." He walked to the starboard side where he had a good view of the fortress. "Another half-hour ... give the new guard time to settle down, maybe make some tea, talk about their wives."

"Aye, sir."

Smiling at the first officer, Rous thought, *good man, Adams. I'll need his steady hand tonight. And I'll miss Wimper. This is my first action without him by my side.* "Have my man Ross bring my bandana and gauntlets." He turned away and isolated himself from the lieutenant by walking into the shadows cast by the moon through the standing rigging. He let his mind wander. *Admiral Saunders just wasn't going to do it. He said he would—get ships above the fortress—but he was coming up with a different reason every day for not doing it. Anyway, Saunders had contemplated making the attempt during daylight when all of the navigational hazards could be seen but there would have been no possibility for surprise.* "Tonight's the night," he said to himself, but louder than he had thought.

"You spoke, sir?" Lieutenant Adams wanted to know.

"No. Thank you, First. I'm old enough to talk to myself so don't you no never mind."

Rous remembered, *Wolfe had asked Admiral Saunders to get ships above the fortress because then the French would have to split their forces and keep a sizeable army upriver to counter the threat posed by the presence of the English ships. I thought Wolfe's proposal was sensible enough but I saw the stupid, pig-headed look on the Admiral's face ... that same pig-headed look he had worn when we had discussed the Traverse problem. The pompous asses wouldn't take advice from a Yankee. Well, I acted that time, leading elements of the fleet across the Traverse.* He rested his elbow on the bulwark. *Now, we're going to do it again.* He patted the wood, almost like a caress. *You're a gallant old girl, and tonight I'm going to take you up past the fortress. Tonight, we lead Diana, Squirrel and two sloops upriver, just like the General wants,[2] and to hell with the Admiral!*

"Pass the word, First. Get a hold of that drummer boy and don't let him beat to quarters! We need it quiet."

"Aye, sir."

Rous almost laughed when Adams spoke in a whisper to the Second. *Well, I shouldn't laugh, it can do no harm to be extra quiet.* Rous shuffled his feet, trying to sense if his dogs were telling him anything. *Nothing!* He looked down at his feet. *Maybe they don't know that the Admiral is gonna be some pissed, me sailing without orders. I'll be in deep shit come morning but I'll be above the fortress with two frigates and a couple of sloops. Won't that surprise the Frenchies.*

Rous listened as commands were whispered in the dark. Any moment now, Adams would report back that the ship's company were mustered.

One way or another, I'm approaching the end of my time in the navy. Richard warned me that the only reason I had been included in this campaign was General Wolfe expected me to be coming to Quebec. In fact, that was the reason Saunders had his flag on my ship ... Wolfe expected it to be there. Too bad we had the dust-up over the Traverse; I won my point and we got across the Traverse but Sutherland lost the flag. Wonder if I could have done it without insulting the man? My head hurt so bad—I just couldn't stand it no more.

"Ship's company ready, sir."

"Thank you, Adams. I want you to get the sand clock. When we are under way, and we have come abreast Pointe Levy, I want you to turn the clock. It's hard t' tell distances in the moonlight. We must not make the first change of heading 'til we have seven minutes on that clock."

Rous beckoned for his officers to join him by the helmsman. "Helmsman, I want you and the Buffer to listen, too." Rous saw the looks on his officers' faces. "I need all of us in this thing. I expect a lot of iron to come our way as soon as the fortress realizes what we are going to do. Since we are the leading ship, if we make a mistake, the others might make the same mistake. I don't expect them to do anything else because they will follow our lead to the other side. In the event of casualties, there's the normal chain of command but we will all know what must be done."

"We'll be close enough to the fortress, starboard guns double shot, sir?"

"We will not return fire. All cannon loaded with single shot but gun ports closed. Have the gun crews standing by but tell them no lit matches."

The small circle of men waited for their instructions.

"We haven't been beyond this point in the river and we have out-of-date charts, so it's unknown waters. I need a lookout on either side of the bow watching for swirls in the current. I want the man swinging the lead to work on the side of the ship nearest the shore. I don't want any calls until the iron starts flying. Use messengers. No shouts until we are discovered."

When he saw there were no questions, Rous said, "Send the first signal to the other ships."

* * *

Yes, there were a number of ships moving. If they come this way, they will be under the guns of the fortress. Too bad the English hadn't come under my guns at Beauséjour. I would have shown them! Instead, they had found our weakness. If help had been sent from here, I could still be making a fortune controlling the supply of firewood and wine. Oh, my friend Bigot had been so right. 'Profit, my dear deVergor,' he had said. 'Trim, cut ... as Commandant you have the power. You could soon join me in France and purchase an estate near me,' he had said. deVergor wiped a tear from his eye. *If only they had sent help from here to Beauséjour! He would have watched as French Regulars caught those damned New England militiamen from the rear and swept them off that little hill.*

He could see one big ship and several little ships now in a single file.

They wouldn't be attacking the fortress, would they? Up to now, that fellow Wolfe had contented himself murdering defenceless priests and children—if the reports are right, and I believe they are. Certainly, if I had the chance, I would exterminate all the English I could ... so why not the other way around? Well, I was told the English did make one raid: a raid on the Beaupré coast,

which was supposedly east of Montmorency although I'm not too
sure where Montmorency is. The English paid dearly for that little
incursion, about a hundred of them dead, some of them at the
hands of the Indians. He looked over the wall again. If they were
going to attack this fortress with those little ships, perhaps more
English would be killed. I would like to see that.
He walked down to watch the gun crews.
There are no gunners on the parapet. Where was everybody?
His nose told him there was a hot stew—*wine-based, I wager.*
There. Over there is a light and some voices.

Du Pont Du Chambon deVergor slowly walked to the
open door of a room under the staircase leading to the gun
parapet. He could see several men inside. It looked bright and
warm and comfortable. And the stew smelled wonderful!

* * *

"Seven minutes on the clock, Captain. The other ships follow
on, line astern."

"Thank you, Mister Adams. Hold this course."

"Aye, sir."

These were terrible moments for a captain. Committing
his ship to an action was one thing, but to do so in unknown
waters directly under the guns of the largest fortress in North
America … Rous kept his eyes on the gun platforms now so
close at hand that, if it were daylight, he would be able to see
the individual gunners serving their weapons. As far as he could
see, there was no activity! He beckoned to his first officer.
"Take up the new heading." He was turning *Sutherland* toward
the west as early as he dared, now sailing parallel to the walls of
the fortress.

Coming through first, *Sutherland* ran the risk of touching
bottom. At least, in that event, the other ships might avoid the
obstruction, leaving the grounded ship to its fate at the hands
of the fortress gunners. The last ship, the frigate *Diana*, had the
benefit of following the pathfinders, but would be under bombardment for the longest period of time as she would be the last
ship to pass out of range of the fortress's guns.

Rous looked up at the fortress. "My dear God, the place is immense!"

The minutes passed and slowly a wonderful sense of elation grew in Rous's breast. "By all the saints, we are goin' through!" He examined the fortress for activity but could see none. Looking back at his little flotilla, he saw all but one now sailing parallel to the walls, since *Diana* had yet to make the turn. No matter what the French did, at least *Sutherland* was above the fortress.

* * *

"There is no one on the parapet," deVergor said from the entrance of the little room.

Two young soldiers were bent over a pot of stew. The larger of the two, whom deVergor later found out was named André, took the spoon out of the pot and licked it off before standing erect and dealing with the newcomer. The second man, as tall as the first but much slighter in build, was already at attention, bug-eyed with fear.

"You have no tongue? Are there just the two of you?"

André swallowed whatever was in his mouth. "Our comrades are searching out plates and some salt."

"We have the bread," the thinner man, Jean Pierre, squeaked.

"I am not your officer but I would suggest he would be displeased to find there is no watch. You had better rectify the situation!"

"Yes, sir. Right away sir," they said in chorus but neither made a move.

"Well? Get on with it!"

André was not cowed. The officer didn't seem to be angry with them so he said, quite boldly, "We would, sir, but what does 'rectify' mean?"

It was at this moment deVergor knew he had better withdraw from the situation. If the English ships were attacking the fortress, everyone would soon know about it. If not, where could they go at this late hour? Besides, he simply refused to get involved in anything that might call up a courtmartial and this was starting to smell like a courtmartial situation. "Get your officer," he said as he withdrew from the little room. He took a deep breath of the night air to clear his lungs of the odour of the stew, delicious as it might have been, since he didn't want to have his appetite raised at this time of night; a full stomach would interfere with his having a good night's rest.

Entering the building where he had chambers, he heard voices raised behind him and the unmistakable trundle of cannon.

Ah! It begins, he thought. *And I must begin my plans to leave here and return to France.* He had known that even with his sterling connections, it was impossible to achieve a transfer directly from Lake Champlain to Paris. Now that he was here in Québec, it should be much easier to arrange something. He wondered where he would be assigned here at Québec while he made his arrangements to go home.

* * *

As he crossed la Place d'Armes and approached the quarters of the Governor General of all French possessions in North America, Le Chevalier Francois-Gaston de Levis, second in command of the regulars, had good cause to be worried. He had been summoned at this ungodly hour of the morning to answer for something and he could well imagine what it was. He adjusted his sash as he dismounted, pausing to study the windows of the château, hoping there would be a profusion of lights. All were dark. So. He alone had been summoned. "It was the promises," he grumbled to himself as he absent-mindedly returned the salutes of the guards. Everyone knew that an enemy force would not be able to sail past the fortress. The raison d'être for Québec was to deny the enemy access to the upper Saint Lawrence. "I merely told him what everyone truly believed; the English would not be able to get a single ship past Québec. Merde! Les maudits Anglais!"

A slave opened the door to the Governor's audience room and indicated that he was to enter.

Levis composed his handsome features and took a deep, deep breath. He entered. The door was closed, quietly, behind him. The room was well lit but there was no one there. He faced the three chairs at the end of the chamber: the ornate one in the middle for le Marquis de Vaudreuil, Governor; on his right would be the chair for Monseigneur de Pontbriand, Bishop of Québec; and the third, usually reserved for Francois Bigot, Intendant, the second most important man in New France. For the moment there was only Francois-Gaston de Levis, accompanied by his real fears as to what was going to happen to him, and he was sweating.

He glanced at the small door behind the dais to ensure he was still alone before he pulled a handkerchief from the cuff of his sleeve and wiped the perspiration from the back of the neck where it was probably staining the rolled collar of his tunic. Levis barely had time to return the linen to his sleeve when the small door opened and the Marquis de Vaudreuil came in, and padded over to the centre chair where, with a deep sigh, he sat down.

Levis held his breath but there was to be no Bishop, no Intendant, because the door was closed. No clerk for notes, no witnesses; this was to be a private audience.

The old man sighed again. He picked at the sleeve of his rich-looking tunic and, without looking up, he asked, "How many of the English ships passed the fortress last night?"

With a quaver in his voice, Levis said, "Several made the attempt. One of the frigates was turned back by the first salvo. No direct hits but it received some damage because it ran aground at Levy."

"So, how many of the English ships passed the fortress last night?"

"A ship of the line and a frigate."

"No transports, thank God!" The Marquis rose and slapped his thigh with the palm of his hand. "No transports."

Levis swallowed hard. With a lowered head he said, "I'm sorry, I thought we would be concerned about armed vessels. There were two sloop transports."

The Marquis scratched his head under his wig. He paced back and forth and then lowered himself, slowly, into the chair.

"Zut!" The Governor General raised his chin and stared at the military man.

Levis dropped his eyes, remaining silent.

"Well, I suppose I could detach Bougainville. Give him cavalry and some foot. Tell him to shadow the English transports if they go above the mouth of the Etchemin River."

"I regret, monsieur, but I must tell you that the Marquis de Montcalm would consider that as direct interference in his command."

Seemingly unconcerned, and changing the subject, Vaudreuil asked about the summary hearing for the soldiers who were to be disciplined for dereliction of duty.

"They will be found guilty."

"What about deVergor? I have no doubt he saw more than he admits."

"Yes. Can you imagine anyone taking a walk along there and not looking at the view?" Levis hurried on, "Yet he said he was out for a few minutes to take the air before bed, saw from below that there was no one on the parapet and suggested it be manned." Levis was feeling more and more comfortable with the direction the audience was taking and his voice became stronger, more assured. "At which time, the men saw the ships and called for their officer, who didn't believe them ..."

"At first."

"Yes, at first. When he saw with his own eyes that the ships were passing upstream, the officer sounded the alarm and they caught the last ship in a storm of iron."

"Our Captain deVergor says he saw none of it?"

"None of it."

The Marquis began pulling at the threads of his sleeve. "We dare not take any action against him." Vaudreuil hesitated but then proceeded, "He's Intendant Bigot's man, you know."

Emboldened now, Levis agreed, adding, "He's called other things."

"Does he have any particular skills?"

"Only the one."

"I mean, military skills."

"He is not well thought of. He lost Fort Beauséjour, which was the subject of a courtmartial."

"I want him out of my sight. I suppose with his rank, we have to give him command of something."

"A sentry post, somewhere out of the way?"

"Yes, give him command of a sentry post."

July 19, 1759
Pointe Aux Pères

The whaleboat crew had just pushed off from the shore to carry the English Commander in Chief to *H.M.S. Sutherland.* Wolfe was slumped in the stern sheets. There was a bit of a chop on the water. As the blades of the oars caught the tops of the wavelets, the spray was picked up by the breeze and carried back into the passenger's face. He pulled his black cloak closer to his neck, holding it tightly with his hand. He wasn't feeling very well[3] and he was suffering from the dampness of his cloak and the water on the seat from when it had been raining. His bladder was giving him great distress and he wasn't sure he would be able to reach the ship before he would have to pee again. When he cringed from a cramp, Corporal Jenkins asked if he was all right and should the boat return to the shore, which made the general even more irritable. "I'm all right, Jenkins, leave me be."

"Yes, sir."

In an effort to distract his commander from his physical problems, Jenkins held the eyeglass out for the general to take. "At the water line, sir, on that big rock. Something new since yesterday." Jenkins pointed toward the fortress.

"Eh? Something new, you say?" He took the glass and studied the shoreline where the grenadier had pointed. "A gallows?"

"Two gallows, sir."[4]

Wolfe adjusted the focus. "Yes, I see now; two of them ... and occupied. Soldiers, both of them quite tall it would seem." He turned in the seat. Before he raised the glass again to study the coast west of the fortress he mused, "One of them was a big man, the other thinner." He was silent as he studied the long line of cliffs high above the river to the west. "There's that plateau they say is called the Heights. It sticks up over the cliffs." Swinging around to face the other direction, Wolfe examined the mouth of the Saint Charles River for enemy activity and then swept across the basin between Ile d'Orléans and the Beauport cliffs. At the other end of the French line were the army camps at Montmorency Falls. He studied them for several minutes but, at this distance, there wasn't much to see. He swung back to face the fortress. He lowered the glass and handed it back to Jenkins. "Thank you Jenkins," he said, somewhat tiredly, Jenkins thought.

Wolfe sat quietly, looking at the fortress. Pointe aux Pères was less than a mile from the Lower Town so he didn't need the eyeglass; in fact, the face of the fortress, impressive at any time, seemed larger than life with its lines and angles etched with shadow from the afternoon sun. He stared at the fortress for a long, long time and then looked back at the rows of his cannon at Pointe aux Pères as they fired, one after the other after another, their shot landing in the Lower Town. He closed his eyes, listening to the cannonade.

Jenkins watched his commander. Several times he seemed to shiver from the chill of the spray, or was it a wince from the cramps? At least he was having a few minutes of rest. Too soon the boat arrived at *Sutherland*.

Wolfe roused himself and, refusing the chair, mounted the harbour ladder, somewhat slower than usual, to face the twitter of the pipes and the ship's company waiting to receive him.

"It's good to see you General," Rous said. "Ye'll have no ceremonial cannon today. Hopefully we'll have better use for the powder than killing a few horseflies and mosquitoes."

Not off to a good start, Jenkins thought, as the general screwed up his mouth, but maybe it was his sickness, because the general, wearing a grim little smile, acknowledged that it was better to use it killing French and Indians.

"Have ship's company resume regular routines, First."

"Aye, sir."

"Would you like to come to my cabin, General? We can talk there, privately."

Remembering how cramped and stuffy that cabin was, the general declined the offer, saying they should take the air for a bit.

"Have the crew give us space, First."

"Aye," he raised his voice slightly, "make space for the captain," which meant the two men would be given as much privacy as possible. Now, as the two of them strolled the deck, no crewman would allow himself to come within a dozen feet of the pair either on the deck or aloft.

Preparing to make the turn at the bulkhead, Wolfe noticed a ship being towed by four boats. "What happened to it?" he asked when he noticed there was damage to her decks and rigging.

"That's *H.M.S. Squirrel*. We passed the fortress and didn't lose a man although the *Diana* had her rudder knocked off and drifted ashore at Levy. The rest of us, including *Squirrel*, arrived here all in one piece."

Wolfe waited for the captain to tell the story at his own pace.

"Now she's being towed further into the mouth of the Etchemin River right behind us there. The enemy built a new battery at Samos, " he indicated the opposite shore with a toss of his head, "and they've been annoying the hell out of *Squirrel*."[5]

"So, in response to the presence of your ships here, the French have increased their fortifications?"

"Yes, there's the battery at Samos and new entrenchments at Anse des Mères. The feller in charge of the troops over there is Dumas. Then there's Bougainville runnin' around with a lot of cavalry and some infantry, too."

"There are new fortifications, there's cavalry and infantry, and there's cannon."

"And there's three or four French frigates what was sent up river for safe keepin' before our fleet arrived at Quebec. If we were meanin' to have the Frenchies divert strength from east of the fortress, we have succeeded."[6]

"Um, yes. That wasn't quite my idea."

Now it was Rous's turn to be quiet and listen.

"I have a number of attack options. The first is here, above Quebec, perhaps somewhere in that bay," he pointed at the Anse des Mères. "The most promising, and the one I have been discussing with Saunders, is somewhere between the Saint Charles River and the Beauport tidal flats, although I am less and less inclined to continue with Saunders and the tidal flats approach because of the manner in which that gentleman controls his ships." Wolfe seemed to be embarrassed by his admission but set his jaw and continued expressing what he was thinking. "On the other hand, you, my dear Captain Rous, are up here, where I asked you to be, ready to serve however I have need."

Rous interrupted the general, "Ready, aye ready, General."

Rous was almost shocked by what Wolfe had said. Not since he had been appointed a captain of the Royal Navy almost fifteen years ago had any Englishman every said 'well done' or 'that's a good job, Rous.' Not one. He had captured fourteen ships in one season, garnering plenty of prize money but not one 'well done' from within the Royal Navy. "You can count on *Sutherland*, General."

Major General Wolfe hadn't planned to pass a compliment and was taken aback that his statements of fact would be construed as such. As a consequence he didn't know quite what to say and was silent.

Rous thought the general was considering his options so he kept his mouth shut while a tremendous sense of pride welled in his heart, suffusing his face.

Finally, the general restarted. "There are several other attack options. I can attack at the far end of their line, near Montmorency, and roll up their flank."

Rous nodded his head, still tongue-tied from the general's praise.

"Or, I can storm the Lower Town from the harbour." Wolfe, now deeply engrossed in the tactical problems, shook his head. "No, the French would pick at us from above the whole time. No, not through the Lower Town."

"We could have a problem if ..." Rous meant to say that, from what he had seen, the river's north shore had a series of ledges. Some of those ledges weren't exposed even at ebb tide and would get in the way of naval support vessels. But since the general revealed in his following statements that he had discarded an assault downstream of the fortress, he didn't attempt to discuss the ledges again. Wolfe confirmed, "That's it, then. We attack upriver." His eyes flashing with the excitement of having decided upon a course of action, Wolfe was no longer a drab little man wrapped in a large cloak. He was going to be the Conqueror of Quebec. "You have a clerk, captain?"

"No, General, I don't, but my second officer does a fine hand."

"Have him join me in your cabin. I have orders to write."

It took a bit of time, but of course, while the general waited for the second officer to appear, Cookie served hot biscuit and tea. When all was in readiness—inkpot, paper, wax seal, pen and a very nervous second officer sitting at his captain's desk while his captain was standing—Wolfe dictated an order to Brigadier Monckton.

> "Brigadier Monckton;
> Our planned descent at Beauport, which we have been considering, is abandoned. We will attack the French above Quebec.
> July 20 you will embark as much of your brigade as can be accommodated in the flat-bottomed boats at our disposal and proceed to *H.M.S. Sutherland*. When ordered, your men will be rowed to the north shore, close to Saint Michel, where they are to secure a landing place, the ground above the village and the road that leads to Quebec.
> Your operational planning should be conducted within this framework."

There were other orders dictated that afternoon. The one to Brigadier Townshend, ordering his troops to come to the water's edge for eventual transportation above Quebec, were of considerable detail, such as: the troops were to be ready to march with two days' provisions, a blanket, thirty-six rounds of ammunition and two spare flints.

Major Dalling and his light infantry were ordered to scout above Quebec to find two or three places where the army could land and climb the cliffs without too much difficulty. If he found suitable structures that could serve as caches he should note their locations carefully.

Goreham and his Rangers were ordered to establish a post a few miles to the west of Pointe aux Pères on the Etchemin River.

With the written orders in the hands of couriers, Wolfe returned to the *Sutherland* quarterdeck and paced back and forth, up and down, back and forth, making it difficult for the crew to 'give him space.' He seemed to realize that he was accomplishing nothing. "Captain Rous!"

First Officer Adams jumped as if he had been scalded. "I'll send for the captain, sir." He nodded to one of the marines.

Major General Wolfe wasn't much into the spirit of chain of command this day. "Start whatever you do and take us up river."

"Aye, aye, sir." Adams looked over the general's shoulder to see if the captain were within sight yet. No, he could still see the top of the hat belonging to the marine who was still on his way to fetch the captain.

An impatient Major General tapped his walking stick against the bulwark.

The young officer was aware of the terrible quandary: General Wolfe had ordered the commencement of operations but there wasn't a possibility in this world that Adams could do so without his captain's permission. The general was already impatient with Adams' hesitation. How irritated would he be if Adams disobeyed? The lieutenant knew he couldn't disobey.

Adams spoke each word distinctly and slowly as if he were trying to clear his tongue of cold molasses. "How … far … up … the … river … do … you … mean … for … us … to …"

"What's wrong with your tongue, First?" There was a wicked gleam in the captain's eyes. "If it's going to be permanent, you'd better see ship's surgeon. Go along now. Second Officer Brown can look after this for you. Report back when your malady is cleared up." Obviously having heard the entire exchange between Adams and General Wolfe, Rous ordered the 'beat to quarters' without further comment. *Sutherland* was going upstream.

While the ship's company busied themselves getting under way, Rous had plenty of time to recall when Vice Admiral Holbourne had taken the entire British fleet to Louisbourg. *'Just to take a boo at what was going on,' the Admiral had said. Good for his curiosity but bad, bad for his fleet. Now Sutherland is sailing in confined, hostile waters with no reliable charts. As long as this Englishman doesn't say he's doing it just to have a boo!*

"Thank you, Rous. I thought I was having some difficulty with your man, making him understand that I want to go upriver to …"

"To have a boo?"

Wolfe stared at the naval officer for a moment to see if there was some sort of humour in the situation that he was not aware of. Since he was going up the river for just that purpose he answered, "Yes, that's it. I want to have a look for myself."

Sutherland moved majestically against the river current, a bone in her teeth. Whenever the ship came close to shore, north or south, she was subjected to musket fire.

"Can't see them!" Wolfe had the eyeglass and was searching for the most recent attacker but to no avail; the musket bearer was lost in the underbrush by the time the thwack of the musket ball, or most often, the noise of the musket discharge, was noticed.

"They can do little harm." Rous pointed at the main sail. "The ball doesn't have enough left to cut through the canvas. Makes a black mark, but doesn't come through."

"When I get back, I am going to have it proclaimed that if there is continued Canadian sniping, I will lay waste to the countryside." By Rous's face, Wolfe could tell that the old sailor wasn't in agreement. "It has the additional benefit, my dear Captain, that if the crops and livestock are destroyed, there will be less food for the garrison."

"But General, when we get to hold the fortress, there will be less food for our occupation troops. We will have to transport more food before the river freezes for the winter." Rous had noticed that the general changed the subject whenever he was finished with a topic. He expected it now and wasn't disappointed.

"Um, yes. I notice that the terrain rises steeply above the Saint Lawrence and is densely wooded. What is that point of land, Captain?"

"It could be Cap Rouge if my chart is correct. While you were working with the First Officer to get under way, I took a quick look at the chart."

"The shore is rocky."

Both men scrutinized the shore for openings or beaches, noting the waves crashing on the rocks and imagining what it would be like to approach it in the darkness. The few openings in the cliffs were mostly gullies engorged with this morning's rain, the water thundering and tumbling its way to the river.

"We might as well turn back."

Just as well pleased to return to the mouth of the Etchemin River, Rous gave the orders and *Sutherland* gracefully accepted the push of the river as she headed downstream.

The general continued to study the passing landscape. He came to an unhappy conclusion, although he didn't share his thoughts with the naval officer. *Probably, with a night assault, I could find a place to land unopposed. If my men gained the heights through one of those little gullies, they would probably find an enemy sentry who would give the alarm. I doubt, then, we would be able to hold our position long enough to get reinforcements ashore before we are driven into the river. Already the French have many troops in the area, some of them entrenched. And there's the Samos battery to contend with.* He stood alone at the taffrail deep in his own thoughts while the ship's company continued to give him space.

Despite the crew's efficiency in getting the whaleboat out and launched for the general's use, it wasn't fast enough for the preoccupied Wolfe. As usual, he declined the chair and hastened over the side. Before his head went below the level of the entry port, Wolfe nodded at Rous, perhaps as wordless thanks for the afternoon's work, perhaps as a way to avoid having to say anything.

"I look forward to supporting Monckton's troops, General."

"We shall see," was the enigmatic reply.

Sutherland waited for the arrival of Monckton's men, or a warning order giving them the details of their part in a proposed attack, or a note from the general telling them the attack was postponed or abandoned. Nothing. The general seemed to have changed his mind again, preferring a series of raids rather than a commitment to a major attack.[7]

July 21, 1759
Twenty Miles Upriver

The citizens of Point aux Trembles awoke to the noises of four hundred Highlanders and Rangers, ransacking the houses and barns, searching for an arms and ammunition cache.

Before dressing and going outside to meet the enemy, the local priest had the presence of mind to dispatch a messenger to Dumas, commander of the nearest French forces, telling him of the arrival of the English. Making little adjustments to his cross and chain as he strode to meet the invaders, he called out, "What do you want in my village?"

Colonel Guy Carleton, of the Highlanders, having served on the Continent, spoke French passably well. "Where are your soldiers who should be guarding this village?"

"There is nothing to guard here. The only soldiers here are harassing my people. I would ask you to put a stop to it."

Carleton smiled at the young priest but it was not a friendly smile. He was thinking that the priest was, perhaps, thirty-five and could be a soldier in disguise. "Check the church! Company strength!"

"Yes, sir," and a company of Highlanders moved in on the church.

If he wasn't a soldier, then he sure had a lot of balls for a priest! Carleton's smile broadened, as he considered the priest didn't have much use for balls ... *or did they? These French priests probably weren't much different from the English priests who came to Scotland during the years of the subjugation.*

Suddenly very polite, the priest asked, "Would you please ask them not to damage the church?"

"Priest, we have word that wagons came from Quebec to store things here."

"Certainly not military supplies."

"Then you know about the wagons?"

The look on the face of the priest told the colonel that wagons had brought something to this village ... perhaps for safekeeping? Gold?

"The church is clear," a voice the colonel recognized as one of his lieutenants could be heard from the direction of the church.

Musket fire on the road leading up the hill! English voices and then more shooting!

Carleton didn't budge. His men would look after it. "What did they bring? Gold?"

If this Englishman thinks there is gold here, they will destroy the village. The priest didn't hesitate. "I am the Reverend Jean Baptiste de la Brosse. Your name is?"

"What was sent here, priest?"

"The women of a number of influential families came to Point aux Trembles for safety. When the English withdraw before river freeze-up, the ladies will return to their homes in Québec. There is no gold. There are no military supplies."

A junior officer marched over and saluted Colonel Carleton. "Looked like a patrol. Killed three. Several more wounded but they withdrew. Perimeter is established, sir."

"The villagers are to be left strictly alone."

"And my church?"

Although Carleton already knew the church was clear, he asked, "Find anything suspicious in the church?"

"Nothing, sir."

"Leave the church alone."

"Yes, sir."

Reverend de la Brosse breathed a sigh of relief.

"Now, priest, gather up all of your visitors. I want them in the church in ten minutes."

"Sir, they are ladies ..."

"Half-hour from now." Carleton turned on his heel. Walking away, he beckoned to one of his ensigns. "Start rounding up livestock—cattle, sheep, chickens—and build a pen between those two buildings. Tell the boat crews we will begin transporting some refugees to *Sutherland* within the hour. Then they can expect to begin transport of livestock to all the ships."

It was more than an hour before the ladies were gathered at the church. The priest fretted about what the colonel would do to them because the colonel had been so abrasive when he had said a 'half-hour' but the ladies had insisted on dressing ...

The priest needn't have worried. When the colonel saw the gathering of fluttering French females, he was very charming and gallant with his new acquaintances, insisting on formal introductions all around, especially with the Joly sisters. Mademoiselle Couillard was overwhelmed by the gallantry of the Scottish officer. Madame de Charney couldn't take her eyes off the colourful uniform, the expressive hands, and the powerful-looking thighs. When the delightful colonel suggested a visit to an English warship, how could they refuse?

By noon the ladies were being introduced to the infamous Major General James Wolfe and the intriguing Captain John Rous. The officer who had been sent to take over naval operations above Québec, Admiral Holmes, was not interested in being involved in what could be interpreted as consorting with the French! Immediately following his introduction, he excused himself and retired to his cabin.

By two p.m., a Highland picket sighted a French detachment coming down the road from Québec, obviously intent on challenging the English presence. As Carleton deployed his skirmishers, he thanked his lucky stars that he hadn't accompanied the visitors to the ship. Flirting with the ladies had been fun but this, confronting the French, was his life! With a line of defence he hoped would give the sailors time to load the cattle, he waited for the enemy's approach.

By three p.m., with several men wounded and the cattle lost, the English returned to their ships.

Later that evening, seated at the head table in *Sutherland's* main cabin, Wolfe, Rous and Carleton entertained the ladies from Point aux Trembles, learning nothing of any significance other than that the wives and daughters of the enemy could make delightful dinner companions. Admiral Holmes chose not to attend, which severely limited the available locations where the officers might 'make space' for themselves after the dinner.

It wasn't until the next day, under a flag of truce, that the women were returned to the shore. As she was fitted into the bos'n chair, Madame de Charney sought solace from the assembled officers. "We must leave so soon? Please, may I have something to remember our time together?"

Carleton repeated the request in English. "She wants a keepsake."

A moment of indecision was resolved by First Officer Adams. "If I might suggest, captain, give her a spike."

Rous nodded.

Colonel Carleton looked around, searching for a 'spike.'

"Over there, by the cannon tarpaulin, Colonel. I'll get it for you."

"No, that's fine, I can get it." He picked up a spike, and gave it to the lady.

She grasped the spike and held his hand, just for the moment.[8] Then, with a flick of her wrist, she indicated to the sailors to haul away. She rose in the air enough to clear the bulwark. Before she was lowered into the longboat below she said, "Good bye, my friends."

The officers touched their caps.

July 23, 1759
H.M.S. Stirling Castle

"You can see without the eyeglass, that's the cathedral burning." Brigadier Monckton, along with the other two brigadiers, had been summoned to a conference on board *Stirling Castle*. As they arrived on the main deck, the fires caused by the bombardment from Pointe aux Pères were very much evident to the naked eye. "That's the Upper Town."

"I thought we could only reach the Lower Town with our shot."

"We put in a couple more rows of cannon, up the hill, with more elevation."

Usually not the one to make what he considered idle chitchat, Brigadier Townshend turned his back on the spectacle and proceeded to the main cabin where he assumed the conference would take place, leaving Brigadier Murray to make whatever reply was to be made to Monckton's observations.

"I would have all the popish houses burned if I had the chance. Therefore, I do not consider the burning of a cathedral to be significant."

Monckton accepted the comment. He found it hard to like Murray, who was the umpteenth grandchild of the Baron Elibank and, like most sons of noblemen who had no hope of inheriting, he was very conscious of any slight and filled to the brim with a sense of his own importance. Monckton, also a man of no small pride, disliked Murray, didn't trust his judgement, and found his manner offensive. Monckton didn't reply.

The brigadiers were not team players.

Wolfe, knowing the personal interplay (or lack of it) between the brigadiers, did not make any sort of welcoming statement. "We have fires in the Upper Town and that's where our cannonade will concentrate for the time being."

"I saw where the cathedral was burning," Monckton volunteered.

If Wolfe heard him, he didn't acknowledge the statement. "At five this morning, two more ships attempted to pass above the fortress. Concentrated fire from the French batteries forced them back. Consequently, I want more probes done here where we have good naval support. Brigadier Murray, I want you to put some men ashore at the mouth of the Montmorency River. Make it a reconnaissance in strength to force the buggers to come out and fight."

"Timing, sir?"

"I leave that up to you. Let me know your plans because I will want to go along to see the lay of the land and the fortifications on their side of the river. Any questions?"

"No, sir. I know what you want."

"Brigadier Monckton, I need you to prepare a plan for capturing a particular redoubt. Just west of the Montmorency River there is one in the open on the edge of the tidal flats. Stay in communication with Murray and plan for your assault the day after his probe. I have been assured that the navy can bring significant firepower to bear on that part of the Beauport flats."

"Yes sir! I have been working with Captain James Cook, who is modifying a transport that has shallow enough draft to allow it to sail within a hundred feet of the target. With the armed transport that close to the redoubt, it shouldn't take long to overcome the defences. But when the tide goes out, Cook won't be able to leave the transport there because it will be stranded and could be assaulted from the shore. The problem will be trying to hold the redoubt against a counterattack when the armed transport is withdrawn."

"I haven't looked that far ahead. If we capture the redoubt, if the French counterattack—or they could withdraw—those are the variables we will assess on the day. If I want to keep the redoubt, I shall."

July 29, 1759
H.M.S. Centurion

Admiral Saunders had moved his flag to the *Centurion*, the better to participate in Monckton's assault on the Beauport Flats, or so he said. Wolfe was reminded of the old adage: fish and visiting relatives create a stink after three days. Did it apply to visiting admirals? Rous and Saunders had a confrontation and the flag moved to *Richmond*. Then it was *Richmond* to *Stirling Castle*. After a short visit on *Stirling Castle*, it's *Centurion*. He toyed with the possibility of tormenting the old man about his changes of flagships, but Admiral Saunders struck first.

"Bad luck, that Murray episode, eh, wot! Lost a lot of good men, he did."

What the admiral was referring to was Brigadier Murray's probe at Montmorency River.[9]

Pressing his lips together, Wolfe made no immediate response: while one portion of his mind was contemplating what sort of mayhem might ensue if he throttled this naval dolt, the other reviewed the tactics that had cost the lives of so many men, so needlessly.

As I remember it, in the early morning, a detachment of Rangers and a company of Light Infantry had been transported to the eastern shore of the Montmorency River. We had reports that there were two possible fords, the first one about three miles above our beachhead and on the far side of a ravine. When Murray's assault force ascertained that the ravine was impassable to his artillery, Murray sent the gunners and their field pieces back to the beachhead.

Later, I went forward to view the enemy's positions, first hand. When I emerged from the ravine, I saw that the French positions on the other side of the river appeared to be very well defended. I remember thinking that perhaps we would have better luck at the second ford, reported to be about a mile upstream. I suggested the Rangers be sent to investigate.

"You didn't hear me, General? I said, too bad Brigadier Murray lost so many men. Indians, wasn't it?"

The Indians, emerging from the woods at the full run, caught the Rangers in the open—hacking and gutting them—hacking and gutting my men who had been ordered to advance without their support artillery. The standard response to an enemy frontal attack is to unlimber your field pieces and meet the assault over open sights. The Rangers had no supporting artillery because Murray had sent them back to the beach. Would I have ordered the Rangers forward if I had known?

Wolfe remembered the tinny taste in his mouth as he had watched the Rangers die.

Well, if I had been the local commander, I wouldn't have just stood there like Murray did, doing nothing to save his men. Wolfe sucked his teeth. *Murray was in shock, I suppose.* Wolfe swallowed, several times, to rid himself of the bad taste in his mouth. *Well, when Murray finally rallied his Light Infantry, it was too late for the Rangers who had been cut down to the man.*

"It was Canadians and Indians," Wolfe finally answered. "We lost men, yes, but we received no further interference and we now have an armed camp on our side of the Montmorency River. He swallowed again, "I say, your men did a splendid job yesterday with the fireship assault."

"Jolly good of you to say so." *If this young popinjay is going*

*to pass compliments, who am I to turn them aside? But then, it was
the lookout of the Stirling Castle, the ship carrying my own flag,
that gave the alarm.* "My men are trained for that sort of thing,
you know."

"Hazardous piece of work, all the same."

It was the admiral's turn for some introspection. *The
popinjay is correct on that point. The French had certainly con-
cocted a formidable threat to my fleet. A large number of small
boats and ships had been chained together and, under cover of a
heavy barrage from the fortress, stretched across the river and
allowed to drift down on my ships.*

*Our response was a well-organized, impressive piece of work
even if I do say so myself. My sailors rowed out into what looked like
the infernos of Hell, hacking the line apart and towing the ships to
shore, where they burned themselves out. The way they handled the
attack should serve as evidence, even to someone so untutored in
naval matters as this young popinjay, that the Royal Navy can
respond quickly and effectively even in the direst of circumstances.*

Recalling the event, Wolfe surprised himself by blurting
out, "You know, we should make Monkton's probe a major
assault!"

"I say, what?" the startled Saunders had asked.

"With effective naval support like that, we should be able
to storm ashore and establish a viable beachhead from whence
we can conquer Quebec!"

Flattered by General Wolfe's praise, Saunders had been
caught up in the enthusiasm of the moment. "I will personally
command the ships assigned to your assault force!" he said.

"Good! We shall have them!" Wolfe's face was flushed as he
raised an arm with a clenched fist, "We shall have them by this
time tomorrow."

* * *

Nature had the final word. The next day, July 30th, was hot and
still. There was no wind and the Royal Navy could not move its
guns close to the Beauport Flats. The assault had to be postponed.

July 31, 1759
H.M.S. Centurian

Admiral Saunders waited until precisely nine a.m. before he gave the signal. He was in full command and everything would move like clockwork or he would know damned well why. That meant punctual signals and exact responses. *So far, so good.* The 78th Highlanders at the Montmorency armed camp had been set in motion as if they meant to attack at the first river ford. Although it was pure trickery, the plan called for the Highlanders to make their threatening gestures, and he was pleased to see that they were doing what they were told and right on time. If the French were deceived by it, they would most probably reinforce the river and that would deplete the forces defending the redoubt.

The Montmorency feint wasn't the only distraction. At the exact moment the Montmorency feint began, the Pointe aux Pères guns, which had been bombarding Quebec, increased their rate of fire.

Superb! Clockwork. Yes, just like clockwork. Saunders rubbed his hands together with great satisfaction as the sails of the three warships, *Centurion, Three Sisters* and *Russell,* and the two armed transports, were raised in unison and filled immediately with the hot, dry breeze pushing them away from Ile d'Orléans and toward the Beauport Flats. *Yes! Yes! All together like a ball-room dance. Perfection!*

One of his staff officers handed him an eyeglass, suggesting that he sight behind the redoubt. He would much rather enjoy the spectacle of three powerful Royal Navy ships sailing in harm's way, challenging the enemies of the King to …

What? There's another redoubt? He swivelled about to ask the question of his staff, "Who knew there was a second redoubt?" but was met with a blank look by anyone who would meet his eye.

As *Centurion* sailed closer to the Flats, from his higher position on the quarterdeck of a ship of the line Saunders was probably the first commander to realize that, not only was there a second redoubt, but both redoubts were closer to the trenches than anyone on the English planning staff had believed. In the back of Saunders' mind there was the nagging thought that there was still time to … to what … *cancel? I can't cancel! There are three hundred flat-bottomed boats in the water between Ile d'Orléans and the Beauport Flats, where Monckton's entire brigade is waiting for the signal to dash ashore.*

Saunders clenched his teeth. No matter there was a second redoubt! The Royal Navy guns would smash everything before them. He consoled the dark voice in the back of his mind as he enumerated the amount of power he would soon unleash against that redoubt—those two redoubts. *Centurion had sixty-four cannon, Russell had twenty-eight and Three Sisters could deliver twenty-eight. Then there were the two armed transports that carried twenty-eight between them. That should be enough for a dozen redoubts!* He was running the total of his firepower in his head when he heard the shout, "The transports have stopped!"

Admiral Saunders was enough of a seaman to recognize the condition immediately; by the cant of their decks and the angle of the masts, he knew they had run aground.

"Helm hard down!" he shouted, instantly realizing this was not his ship and he had no right to give an order to any member of the crew in the performance of their duties, but he shouted again, "Helm hard down! Man the sheets!"

All three warships turned at the same instant, as though on the ballroom floor as Admiral Saunders might have repeated if he weren't so completely committed to scrunching up his shoulders waiting for the moment of impact.

It didn't come. The three warships had turned away in time; however, the transports were stuck—and very firmly they later found out—on one of the muddy shoals of Beauport Flats.

At the same time, General Wolfe was travelling to his battle on *H.M.S. Russell.* A total of four companies of grenadiers were available to him; the ones not carried on *Russell* were on *Three Sisters.* He was anticipating that, as soon as the naval bombardment was over, he would send in his grenadiers and the Conquest of Quebec would begin. *But the warships are*

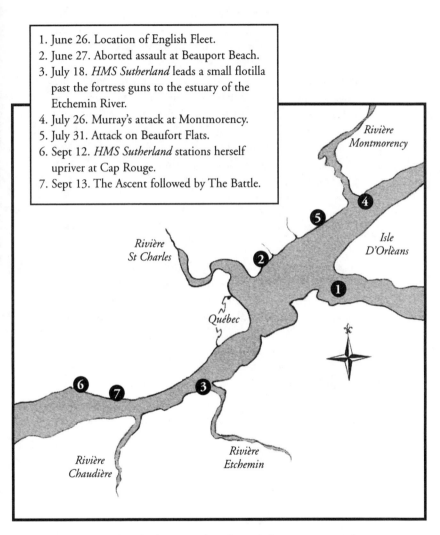

1. June 26. Location of English Fleet.
2. June 27. Aborted assault at Beauport Beach.
3. July 18. *HMS Sutherland* leads a small flotilla past the fortress guns to the estuary of the Etchemin River.
4. July 26. Murray's attack at Montmorency.
5. July 31. Attack on Beaufort Flats.
6. Sept 12. *HMS Sutherland* stations herself upriver at Cap Rouge.
7. Sept 13. The Ascent followed by The Battle.

Rivière Montmorency

Isle D'Orlèans

Rivière St Charles

Québec

Rivière Chaudière

Rivière Etchemin

I couldn't find a map that showed the action in and around Quebec. Using several sources, this map is a representation of the shoreline of 1759.

turning away! What's happening? The armed transports are still proceeding toward the Flats—or are they? Wolfe wasn't a sailor but even he could see that the guns on the armed transports had been put out of commission somehow. Then he saw that the ships had stopped moving but the force of the wind in the sails was lifting the stern or lowering the bow, he couldn't tell which, but the effect was to tilt the guns over and they were falling off their mounts. He watched as the crews dropped the sails to relieve the pressure, but the ships didn't right themselves. Those guns were out of the action.

"Captain Brown! What happened?"

"A miscalculation! It would appear that Captain Cook's calculations of the transports' gross tonnage and depth of the water were …"

"What does it mean?"

"It means, my dear sir, that the transports are hard aground and would appear to be out of action." Captain Brown lifted his hat, scratched his head, and then placed his hat back, firmly. "Probably, by the looks of it, those transports and their guns are lost to us. We will evacuate the crews, but the ships will be a total loss."

"How many guns?"

"Twenty-eight."

"Our fire power has been reduced by twenty-eight guns," Wolfe said more to himself than to the officers standing by him.

"And the warships will not be able to proceed any closer to shore than here."

General Wolfe stared at the captain as if he were speaking Chinese.

"We certainly won't be able to reach any of the expected fortifications on the shore …"

"My God!"

"Perhaps the redoubt will be within range of our guns. *Centurion* will be able to do better but, even then, the accuracy …"

"Enough, captain. I don't want to hear more of this right now." Wolfe strode to the bulwark and stared at the *Centurion*.

He wanted to get his hands on that admiral's throat! He shook his head to clear out thoughts of revenge on that stupid man. His mind raced through the problems now facing him.

* * *

Admiral Saunders could imagine what the army commander was thinking at this moment. *That little pipsqueak had better watch out what he says in the official reports. It wasn't my doing! That damned Captain Cook! He had obviously done his numbers wrong and now there wouldn't be a bombardment. Oh, there just had to be a bombardment!* "Captain Mantle!" He didn't wait for the reply from the *Centurion's* captain but gave his orders in a rush of words, "Make signal! The warships to close in and begin the bombardment as planned."

Captain Mantle saluted his commander. "Sir, it will be difficult for my ship to approach any closer. We will run the risk ..."

"Then bombard from here." Saunders could sense that the captain wished to present arguments about lack of accuracy, range and all that, but what was important at this stage of the assault was that there be a naval bombardment. "*Russell* and *Three Sisters* are to reduce their range to target before beginning bombardment."

"Aye, sir."

"And captain, there are English guns at Montmorency. Order them to bombard targets near the redoubt." He waved the captain on his way. No sense telling them about the second redoubt; they wouldn't be able to see it anyway. Now, let's see, the three warships plus the forty army guns at Montmorency ... *army* guns.

"Captain! Belay that last signal!"

Saunders waved the captain to return to his side. "Request the army commander ..." Saunders screwed up his eyes to assist his memory but finally had to ask, "Who is the army commander over there?"

The new officer on his staff, a long-in-the-tooth lieutenant, stepped forward from the huddle of his staff officers. He responded quickly, "Brigadier Murray."

"Captain, request that Brigadier Murray bombard the

redoubt as soon as possible."

"Aye, sir." The captain moved off to instruct his signals officer. He wasn't sure they had flags to pass the intention of the message—requesting an army commander (who didn't have a code number for identification purposes) that he discontinue his assignment under the army's official plan at the request of a naval commander (whose code number he wouldn't recognize). *While Flags works that out, I will send a courier,* the captain decided. "Boat's crew," he ordered.

And things were going so well, the little voice said to Admiral Saunders, *but the pipsqueak will put the blame on you.* "I need more guns!" he said loud enough for one of his staff, that new lieutenant, to hear.

"Your pardon, sir, there are the guns of Pointe aux Pères, twenty-eight of them. The first redoubt would be within their range."

"Yes of course. I would have thought of that." Saunders raised his arm to attract Captain Mantle's attention.

The lieutenant leaned forward so that only the admiral could only hear his comments. "I could arrange for a boat to carry your request to Major Dalling at Pointe aux Pères, sir. I suggest, sir, your interests would be better served by allowing Captain Mantle to bring the *Centurion's* guns to bear on the enemy as soon as possible."

"Yes, of course. See to it, Lieutenant …?"

"Lieutenant Campbell, sir, and grateful to be of service."

Saunders watched as Lieutenant Campbell arranged for a message to be written, a courier selected and a boat launched. In a very few minutes, the courier was on his way. *Finally, a man who anticipates my way of thinking.*

When *Centurion* lay parallel to the shoreline, one of her guns barked. Saunders recognized it as a ranging shot, soon followed by an entire broadside. *Ah! The bombardment begins.*

* * *

Wolfe heard the passage of the *Centurion's* shot overhead. He quickly fixed his eyes on the redoubt, hoping to see the entire thing disappear in a cloud of mud and debris. The destruction was impressive but the enemy position remained. As *Russell* gingerly felt its way closer and closer, a sailor in the bow swinging the lead, measuring the depth of the water, a cannonball struck the water about fifteen yards to the right and forward of the bow. Wolfe swung his head around. "Did anyone see where that shot came from?" Was it an English shortfall or was there a French gun, somewhere, getting *Russell's* range?

"It's French, sir."

Wolfe didn't have to turn around to identify the speaker. "Where is it, Jenkins?"

"I'm searching, sir." After a few moments he said, "There's a second redoubt, sir, and some trenches on the shore."

General Wolfe didn't say anything, just compressed his lips.

"I found the battery, sir. Look straight at the redoubt and then follow the shoreline to where the raw earth is."

A puff of smoke appeared to the left.

"There's more than one artillery battery on the shore."

Russell was turning. Captain Brown obviously thought his ship was close enough to be effective. Wolfe heard the anchors being let out. He didn't know it but the crew were working to set spring lines so the ship could be rotated somewhat to bring all the guns to bear on a given point.

The French shot splashed into the water dead ahead, fifteen yards.

General Wolfe thought, *this was going to be a long, long day.* He walked over to Monckton, who was chatting with Captain Brown. Monckton saluted. General Wolfe did not return the salute.

"Sorry, sir. When we are on a ship, it doesn't feel as if we are in the face of the enemy."

"That's all right, Brigadier."

"Captain Brown tells me his ship and *Three Sisters* will not be able to go any closer. They should be able to bombard the redoubt from here. They could also bring shot to bear on those guns on the shore. What is your preference, General, counter battery or softening up?"

"Those are small calibre guns potting away at us. Leave them be for the time being and have a go at softening up the redoubt."

"I've had some experience at this sort of thing," said the captain. "Eventually, old Froggie will figure out a way, move a gun onto the shore, use more powder or a better grade of powder, but he will drop some shot on us. He's only to increase the range by some fifteen yards and, at that time, we will have to do counter battery or withdraw."

"I understand, Captain. Please soften up that redoubt."

"Aye, aye, General."

The three men all looked toward the shore where there was a good-sized explosion followed by several smaller bursts.

"One of the Froggies just tried more powder," the captain said with a grim little smile as he went off to direct his gun crews.

"Load your grenadiers, Brigadier. Have the boats assemble to the rear of these ships. You'll have my order when it is time."

"Yes, sir!" Monckton almost gave a salute in his enthusiasm to get the show started but stopped himself in time.

For the next hour there would be constant movement on the deck of the two ships as the grenadiers were loaded into the flat-bottomed boats.

* * *

"Ahoy, the boat!" A ship's officer was challenging someone approaching *Centurion.*

Admiral Saunders shook himself out of his lethargy. *Who would be coming to Centurion?* He cocked his head to listen for the response but the reply was drowned by the rolling thunder from the guns of three warships, Pointe aux Pères, Montmorency and the French guns behind the redoubts. *It could be General Wolfe! The pipsqueak had better mind his manners!* Then Saunders had a simply delicious thought. *Wolfe could be coming to call off the assault! Wouldn't that be just ducky!* He beckoned for 'that lieutenant' to approach. "Find out who is coming, Lieutenant, er ..."

"Campbell, sir."

In almost no time at all Campbell returned and informed him that a Lieutenant Gray of *Sutherland* had requested permission to come aboard and permission had been granted.

Rous! Now, there's a son-of a bitch I can live without! Uncouth, no upbringing but …what do I care; the colonial is marooned up river on the other side of the fortress! The bastard had thought himself so clever—moving his ship above the fortress just because the pipsqueak wanted to see if it could be done—and there's no practical military advantage to it—so there he is, sitting out the campaign where his audacity has consigned both him and his leaky old washtub … and they could jolly well stay there, too!

Lieutenant Campbell was speaking to him. What was he saying?

"I said *Russell* has been struck by a ball or two!"

"Do you think General Wolfe was …?"

"No sir. He's just fine! See, he's pacing back and forth on the main deck."

"Yes, well, it's almost two p.m. and he should start his approach to the beaches soon or he will lose the daylight. The days are shorter this far north."

In the meantime, *Russell* had shifted it sights to the offending battery and it disappeared in a cloud of debris and smoke. In a minute or two, *Russell* resumed its bombardment of the redoubt.

"General Wolfe must have heard you, sir, because there they go." Campbell pointed at the dozens of flat-bottomed boats coming around the bows and sterns of the warships and heading directly for the redoubt. "The French are for it now."

"Yes. Better late than never." Saunders held his hand out for the eyeglass. "Brigadier Murray should be leading the 78th Highlanders against the enemy's left flank on the Montmorency." He studied the shore for a moment and nodded his head. "Yes, there they go."

Meanwhile, Lieutenant Campbell had been watching the progress of the grenadiers. The boats carrying the assault group were behaving strangely: eight boats abreast but stopped as if the French had drawn a line in the water and the English were not permitted to cross. He was about to mention it to the Admiral when Lieutenant Gray approached, asking permission to speak.

"What can you possibly want with me, Lieutenant?"

"Sir, I am Lieutenant Gray, sent from Halifax by the acting governor to continue my duties as Naval Liaison Officer for General Wolfe."

"Eh! Wot! What are you?" Admiral Saunders was flabbergasted! "Sent by whom? The governor? What for?"

Lieutenant Campbell interjected, "Sir, the assault boats are hung up on something in the water, maybe a chain just below the surface, but I can't imagine how the French could do that."

"It's more likely a ledge, sir" said the newly arrived Gray. "I reported to my ship the day before yesterday to obtain permission to present my orders to the commanding admiral. My captain ..."

"Rous," the admiral hissed.

"Aye, sir. Captain Rous told me to mention that there might well be a series of ledges along the river at this point. He said if our forces were experiencing any difficulty with ledges, there should be a break in the ledge anywhere there is a stream or a brook feeding into the Saint Lawrence."

The three officers all turned to look at the assault boats. They were being dragged off the ledges and were returning to the warships. One of them took a direct hit from the French batteries and disappeared as they watched. A grenadier hung on to a piece of the wreckage but the weight of his gear must have pulled him down, or perhaps he was injured, but he soon disappeared.

"Oh, I say!" There was a quality to the admiral's voice that both the lieutenants noticed. It was almost as if he was enjoying the army's setback.

Gray pointed to a break in the shoreline. "There's a brook! The boats should move off more to the left and they would probably pass through the ledge."

Admiral Saunders admired the manner in which Lieutenant Campbell seemed to anticipate his very thoughts when Campbell suggested that Lieutenant Gray, as the naval liaison officer, deliver the naval information about the ledges to General Wolfe.[10]

* * *

On *Russell*, try as he might, Jenkins was not able to get his commander to remove himself from plain sight of the enemy. "You're just tempting them, sir. They see you and they make every effort to get another gun on that point of land from where they can reach you."

Wolfe ignored the corporal. He grabbed a passing grenadier sergeant, who was wounded and consequently had not been able to take part in the assault on the Flats. "Have the Highlanders withdrawn from their assault on the Montmorency?"

"Yes, sir, I believe they have."

"You believe they have …. you *believe* they have? My God, man! Why don't you know?"

One of Wolfe's staff officers shouldered the unfortunate sergeant out of the way. "The 78th have withdrawn, sir."

"Good. Good." The sound of relief in his voice was palpable "Murray must have seen my signals."

"Yes, General, he must have."

Wolfe saw a naval uniform coming his way. "I don't need to speak with the navy." He took a second look and extended his hand in greeting. "Nice to see you, Gray. Jenkins! Look who's here! Your saviour."

Jenkins merely nodded his head at the lieutenant, although obviously delighted to see the naval officer again.

A dispirited Brigadier Monckton joined the group as Wolfe jested, "Well saviour, have you come to save the day for the rest of us?"

The welcoming smile died on Wolfe's lips as he put his hand on Monckton's shoulder. "You did the best you could, Robert. "What was it, a chain?"

"It's a ledge," William said. "Excuse me, General, but that's why the admiral sent me over here. I am to tell you there is a way around the ledge."

Monckton wasn't the least bit pleased with the suggestion that there might be a way around the ledge that he hadn't tried. "The only way past that ledge is to grow wings and fly."

William knew he was treading on some very senior toes. "With respect, sir, please permit me to explain my captain's suggestion."

"Rous?" Wolfe said.

Both generals were suddenly very attentive.

Wolfe said, "Proceed, Gray."

"He says there will be a break in the ledge opposite a stream or a brook that empties into the Saint Lawrence." William stepped to the bulwark and pointed to the break in the shoreline. "Over there, an opening in the ledge should be near the mouth of that brook."

Wolfe didn't hesitate, "Have your boys give it another try, Robert."

* * *

Admiral Saunders accepted a cup of tea from the steward. "You used honey?"

"Aye, sir, two dollops."

Saunders blew on the tea. He liked it hot but was careful not to burn his tongue. Over the brim he saw Rous's man returning. His initial reaction of distaste was replaced with one of curiosity. He signed that the lieutenant could approach. "Did the general appreciate our concern?"

"He is acting upon it as quickly as Brigadier Monckton can reorganize the assault forces."

"I hope he appreciated my advice?"

"He most certainly did," William lied. *Maybe I shouldn't have told the generals that the original information had come from Rous but ... done is done. No need having this old fart mad at me at this stage of the game.* So he lied some more. "The minute I said I was a messenger from Admiral Saunders they gave me immediate audience."

"Good. Good." He raised the eyeglass and studied the situation. "Why, there's Wolfe! Imagine the senior commander out there in an open boat under fire looking for a spurious hole in an underwater ledge!"

"I believe it's there, sir." *You do too*, William thought, *or you wouldn't have sent me*, but he didn't dare say it.

"I say! They are going through. The assault is on," the admiral shouted incredulously.

William recognized the uniforms. The Louisbourg Grenadiers

were the first to hit the beach. They formed up and waited.

"What are they waiting for?" Saunders swung the eyeglass back and forth, back and forth. There's nothing between them and the redoubt and the redoubt's empty! Why do they stand there?"

William could see with the naked eye that the French troops were retreating from the back of the redoubt. "Our grenadiers are being murdered."

Campbell, in hushed tones said, "They can't see the French from where they are. We can see because we're higher."

William made up his mind. "I must go tell Wolfe the redoubt is empty."

Campbell agreed, "Yes, as quickly as you can."

The Admiral, with his eye to the glass, told William, "I think that is the thing to do," but William was already gone.

It seemed to Campbell, who was watching from the *Centurion* quarterdeck, that everything went into double time. The Royal American Regiment arrived at the beach and formed up alongside the battered grenadiers. William's boat was approaching Wolfe who had remained behind, just outside the ledge. Campbell could see them conferring. Wolfe turned to signal his grenadiers but they had had enough. The grenadiers, bayonets levelled, charged the redoubt. They found it empty. Crazed by the constant shelling and frustrated by finding no Frenchmen in the redoubt to take it out on, they continued on, up the river slope, to attack the other redoubt and the trenches. Not to be left behind, the Royal Americans joined in but, by this time it had started to rain, turning the slopes into mud.

William and General Wolfe could see the men of the two regiments on the slopes of the riverbank. It was ghastly— British soldiers slipping and sliding all the while being picked off by the French who could be seen standing upright, nonchalantly choosing which struggling soldier to kill next.

Wolfe gave the recall. As soon as he could, from *Russell*, he ordered Murray to retreat from the western shore of the Montmorency River. He watched as the 78th Highlanders responded to the assembly but was bewildered when they stood there, facing the enemy, waiting for something.

William, always conscious of the sea and the tides warned, "If they don't move soon, they will be cut off by the rising tide!"

"Thank you, Lieutenant," Wolfe said, actually quite civilly when it was taken into account that he was beside himself with rage. First, the grenadiers thought they could take on an entrenched French army all by themselves and now a Highland Regiment was standing firm in the face of the enemy after retreat had been ordered. He was going to lose a regiment for some reason he couldn't fathom! He handed the eyeglass he had been using to the nearest person and turned his back on the spectacle. "I don't understand," he said.

William trained the eyeglass on the lonely-looking band of Highlanders. Yes, they were waiting. The French were forming up to force them into the water, which was getting deeper by the moment, but still the Highlanders waited. Sweeping the area with the glass, William found what they were waiting for.

A smaller band of Highlanders, carrying their wounded, was fighting to gain the shelter of the Regiment. Any Scotsman would know what was going on; the Highlanders were not going to leave any of their clansmen behind.

The French made a good effort to stop the smaller band from getting in behind the Regiment but the Highlanders persisted and gained temporary shelter.

"Sir, the Regiment would not abandon any of their clansmen. They were waiting for all who could hear the call to come to assembly." He handed the glass to the general. "They are moving into the water now."

"My God, the water's deep."

The wounded were slung across the shoulders of the biggest men, who stepped into the river and marched in the chest-deep water to the Beaupré shore. The rest of the Regiment maintained a fighting rearguard as they performed an orderly retreat to the British side of the river.

"That's why we will beat the French," William said. Several explosions, near at hand, had William ducking his head.

Wolfe, not the least perturbed by the light and noise, gazed at the two transports that were being destroyed where they had run aground. He pointed at the smoking and burning hulks.

"Not if we continue to have that kind of help from the navy."
Lieutenant William Gray was surprised when he felt a
surge of loyalty for his Service. "We will do better, General."

Endnotes

[1] The ex-Commandant of Beauséjour had recently arrived at Quebec
from the Lake Champlain area.

[2] I wasn't able to determine the names of the two sloops so left them
nameless.

[3] According to the *Dictionary of Canadian Biography*, Wolfe had written in December 1758, "I am in a very bad condition, both with the
gravel and rheumatism, but I had much rather die than decline any kind
of service that offers."

[4] A gallows did appear after *Sutherland* passed above the fortress.

[5] *H.M.S. Squirrel* had to be towed out of range of the enemy.

[6] The French dispositions are historical.

[7] The reference books say that during this time Wolfe seemed to dither
the campaign season away.

[8] The raid occurred, there was loss of life, the dinner party is a matter
of record, the ladies are reputed to have stayed overnight, but the hint of
impropriety is mine.

[9] The attack is factual but, to be blunt, there was so much indecision
on the part of the British during this time that I tried to make the story
line as short as possible.

[10] The records state that an unidentified naval officer in a small boat
delivered the information to General Wolfe that the ledges could be
skirted. I made him our Lieutenant Gray.

Chapter Thirteen

August 19, 1759
Québec Lower Town

"It is an impressive thing, the imposition of one's will upon an unruly lot whether they be French or English. A marvel to see," he added to himself.

Chambon deVergor was speaking of the English punishment parade that was being held at Pointe aux Pères. The beating of the drums, even from this distance, would have attracted his attention but the British, ever the ones to impose punishment with a flourish, had discontinued their bombardment of the town so that the sound of the lash would not be lost on the spectators. It was this sound, the sound of the lash cutting into human flesh, that had attracted deVergor's attention. "When I give punishment, I also give it very well."

His companion made no comment. He was busy figuring his commission from today's purchases in the market. Ensign deLangy might have lost several fingers at Beauséjour but he hadn't lost any of his skills as a negotiator. He was pleased that his old Commandant hadn't forgotten him and had asked for him to be assigned to the new Québec post.

deVergor had searched the Québec army lists for former confederates and he wasn't long in using his influence to have the men assigned to his new command. In all, he had found five soldiers who had served with him before, three of them from his time at Beauséjour: Ensign deLangy, Ensign deBaralon and Corporal Fortier. He sucked his teeth. *Too bad I wasn't able to have deBaralon transferred, but I don't have any cannon in my little command for deBaralon to serve. Not too little a command at that. A hundred men and, with the 'savings' I make on their daily allowance, I am doing rather well.*

Another well placed stroke from the lash! *I must hurry to a vantage point before the spectacle is finished.* "Come along,

Ensign. Put that purse inside your coat lest it be snatched! It is my money but it would be your loss."

Ensign deLangy knew his commandant meant exactly what he said. He secreted the purse in his peasant's blouse. He smirked. *I am not to wear my uniform when I go to market so as not to drive the prices up but all the vendors called me 'ensign' anyway.* It was no use explaining to his commandant. He was to wear the peasant's costume to market.

"Finally!" deVergor had found a rise where the building had been demolished which allowed them an obstructed view of the Pointe without having to go all the way to the harbour front. "It's not as bad today."

DeLangy wondered for a moment what deVergor was talking about but then he could see that there wasn't as much smoke in the river valley this morning. "Yes, there is less smoke."

Up and down the valley, during the beginning of August, the English had raided and burned anywhere they chose. The Canadians had fought back, skirmishing from the edges of the woods, but the more they fought, the more vicious the English were in their raids. Pointe aux Trembles, Saint Antoine ... as far down river as Baie Saint Paul, which must be all of fifty miles east of Québec.

"Perhaps they have stopped the raids?"

"Maybe so, but one thing we can be pretty certain of," — deVergor gestured to the other side of the river where the rows of scarlet uniforms were resplendent in the sunlight—"that devil, Wolfe, is still sick. When an army is inactive, it takes a very strong hand to maintain order. Less competent commanders use more whippings, so I would believe their General Wolfe is still sick." Having seen enough, he began walking back up the hill. "When he is sick there can be no assault. Let's go back to our home away from home." Climbing the hill was hard on a man of deVergor's girth. He stopped for a breath, but to disguise his distress he challenged his companion, "Delivery was included in this morning's prices?"

Not deceived, deLangy wore a worried look as he took his time with his response to give his commandant the opportunity to catch his breath. "Yes sir. I made sure of that."

August 31, 1759
Ile d'Orlèans

Admiral Saunders entered the command tent. The first thing he noticed, there was only one empty chair at the table. He nodded at Brigadiers Monckton, Townshend and Murray. He placed his hat on the table in front of the empty chair and unhooked his sword, handing it to Lieutenant Campbell. Campbell, who was now the admiral's primary aide, selected another chair from near the wall of the tent and took up a position where he could have the admiral's ear. Saunders was the only officer sitting at the table with an aide in attendance but, if anyone took note of it, they didn't comment.

"You are feeling up to snuff, General Wolfe?"

"Fine, thank you, Admiral. I called you gentlemen here to ..."

"Ah-h-h, I wanted to inform you that another five ships have passed above the fortress. We, the navy, now have control of the upper river."

"That's good news, and it fits in exactly with what I have to say, Admiral. I mean to abandon Montmorency and bring all of those troops to Levy for operations above the fortress. Brigadier Murray, you and Townshend, once you have your troops at Levy, will march them to the Etchemin River. That will be our jumping off place for the assault."

"And the assault will be above the fortress?" Townshend had curiosity written all over his face. When he saw the hesitation on Wolfe's face he pressed, "It's not a secret, where we are going, is it?"

"We won't be discussing where the assault will take place, at least not just yet."

"You haven't made up your mind?"

"I haven't made up my mind."

An uncomfortable silence prevailed until Wolfe began again, this time addressing Brigadier Monckton. "I expect it will take several days to get everything done, but when we are down to the last day, five battalions will remain hidden to give the Froggies a bit of a shock if they should attempt to interfere with our move."

"My men will spring the trap?"

"Yes."

"After the episode on the Flats, my boys would like to return the favour."

General Wolfe stood up. He paused as he watched the grizzled lieutenant whisper in the admiral's ear. Saunders listened and then raised his hand. "Ah, yes. Admiral Holmes will command the upper squadron. I will command the lower fleet as well as continuing as overall naval commander." Saunders stood up, assuming that General Wolfe would make an observation, but nothing more was said.

The meeting was over.

September 10, 1759
Saint Denis

The men of the Saint Denis sentry post knew that it wasn't long service or good service that qualified a soldier for the best appointments or early promotion. It was previous service with Commandant deVergor.[1] So far there were four men who were deVergor's Veterans and, by the look of the reception given to a young man at the door of the farmer's house that served as the Command Post and the Commandant's Quarters, that number was soon to be increased to five.

First of all, Corporal Fortier had saluted the new arrival and had personally taken the reins of his horse. Fortier, displaying his authority, most probably for the benefit of the visitor, shouted, "Cormier! Cormier you dolt! Come take the horse!"

Private Cormier ran to the front of the house and took the reins from the corporal's hands.

"Make sure she's rubbed down," Fortier ordered, somewhat imperiously.

Cormier's head bobbed up and down because it was safer not to make a reply. Cormier wasn't stupid. Just do as the corporal says and that is the path of least trouble. If he were lucky and kept his nose clean, he'd be a member of the inner circle on deVergor's next posting.

Finished with his subordinate, Fortier was all smiles to the visitor. "Come, sir. The commandant will be pleased to see you!" He rapped on the door and grabbed the latch but didn't raise it or push in on the door until he heard the word "Enter." The soldiers listened for the commandant's reaction. deVergor's hearty laughter confirmed the new arrival's status. Their view of the situation verified, the men around the command post went on about their duties.

Inside, Ensign deBaralon was led to the best chair and served a glass of wine.

"Some cheese and sausage?" Even though the ensign shook his head negatively, the commandant wasn't hearing of it. "Fortier, have the girl bring some cheese and sausage." deVergor winked at the younger man, "Her brother made the sausage and cheese, her father made this house and I," here he gave another wink, "made her this morning."

"The wine is very good."

"You should try the girl!" deVergor leaned forward and squeezed the ensign's knee. "You could, you know, if you had accepted a transfer here."

"That's what I came to see you about, Commandant."

"Really?" Suddenly cautious, since deVergor had already offered to bring the young man to Saint Denis and had been refused, "What is wrong at Québec?"

"There's nothing wrong at Québec that a transfer to your command wouldn't solve, my Commandant."

"I'm curious. What happened? Two weeks ago you had your battery and were ready to eat the British for breakfast."

"That's before I realized we aren't going to win this battle."

Commandant deVergor sat forward in his chair, eyes popped open, mouth agape, and asked, "The Marquis is going to surrender?"

"No, but a week ago yesterday the enemy commander ..."

"General Wolfe?"

"Yes, General Wolfe was seen in a flat-bottomed boat between Ile d'Orlèans and the Beaupré coast. Over a hundred little boats and canoes were in the water moving slowly across the basin. We had all the time in the world to mount an attack—to put gunboats into action—but we did nothing!"

deVergor disdainfully waved his hand at the ensign in contradiction. "Ah, you never know all the facts. There could have been a dozen reasons not to attack." To make the ensign feel somewhat better but not well enough to change his mind about coming to Saint Denis, he used his imagination. "It is a well-known military fact that the English need us to come out from behind our fortifications if they are going to beat us." He placed a piece of cheese, carefully, between his teeth. He chomped down on the cheese, spilling some down his shirt-front. "Because if we ever do come out, they will chew us up. Our defence forces must use the Canadians and Indians and they are not reliable. The English brought their Regulars and they are very reliable." He brushed the pieces of cheese from the front of his shirt; "They'd push us out of the way, just like they did at Beauséjour, and walk into our fortress with drums and those infernal bagpipes wailing."

"Then you agree with me."

"No, I don't. We will stay within our fortifications and the English will go away before freeze-up."

"They can attack anywhere they like! They have their main fleet off Beauport ..."

"We have Montcalm."

"There are over twenty English ships above the fortress!"

"Bougainville is up here with a large army. He will not allow the ships to just move around and deposit little soldiers anywhere they want. No, Bougainville is here and the English will stay in the river." deVergor stood up. "Come with me. The weather has been wet and miserable so it's been a number of days since I've had a peek at the English." He slipped a cloak on and put his hat on carefully. "With the cloak and hat, the men will not know that I am out of uniform. Which reminds me, why are you out of uniform, Ensign?"

"I didn't want to be recognized as an officer of artillery. There's no artillery out here."

"That's not correct, my boy. We have a battery at Samos now."

"I didn't know that."

"You could transfer to the Samos battery."

"No, sir. I would rather come here, to serve with you."

"Old loyalties?"

"Yes, of course, and"—deBaralon gave the senior officer what he hoped would look like an engaging smile—"the fact that Corporal Fortin was in town last week. He told me how much money you all are making. I thought, if the battle is to be lost, I might just as well be repatriated with some money in my luggage."

"That's good thinking, Ensign, but we aren't going to be troubled by the English." They had arrived at the top of the cliff overlooking the Saint Lawrence and within easy view of the mouth of the Etchemin River. "And I agree. You might just as well have money in your luggage under any circumstances."

Ensign deBaralon stepped to the edge to join the commandant. "Holy Mary!" He clutched at the other man's arm and pulled himself back from the edge. "That must be a hundred metre drop!"

"At least sixty. There was a narrow path but I had it filled in with trees and rocks." He lifted the eyeglass and scanned the river as he said, "It is unlikely the English would try to come this way and besides, I am here with a force of one hundred men."

"Only one hundred?"

"I could hold this position with a dozen." Putting the glass down in time to note a look of disbelief and, not wanting to say anything that might jeopardize the distinct possibility of adding a competent officer to his staff, deVergor hastened to add a note of humility. "We could hold until Bougainville arrived with his army. He's at Cap Rouge, you know, only ten or eleven kilometres distant. Besides, the English aren't coming here. Look at the top of that hill." deVergor pointed across the river. "The English are setting pegs in the ground. They are building another camp."

Both men studied the activity on the top of the hill opposite, deBaralon with the glass. "It certainly looks like a camp is being staked out. Barges are landing groups of soldiers at the bottom of the hill."

"Grenadiers," deVergor sniffed. "In every army there are soldiers who believe they are better than everyone else and they shall be named grenadiers." He looked up river and down river and, finding nothing of particular interest, seemed ready to go back to the command post.

The ensign was still interested in the activity on the river. "What is that large ship?"

"DeLangy found out for me. It's the biggest boat this side of the fortress: fifty guns, the *Sutherland.*"

A small boat left *Sutherland* and headed for the beach where the grenadiers were being landed. They watched it for a bit and then deVergor got bored or thirsty.

"Let's go back to the house."

"Take a look, sir. The first barge landed the grenadiers and they marched up the hill. The second group got off the barge and marched up the hill."

"Yes, that's what soldiers do, they march."

"The third group is walking."

It was true. The third group of grenadiers was taking their time walking up the hill to the site of the new camp. One of them stopped and put his hands on his hips while looking their way.

"Greatcoats! Those grenadiers are wearing greatcoats!" Ensign deBaralon thought he had discovered something significant. The English were practising some sort of ruse and, as French officers, the two of them should try to discover what it was. Small details could be evidence of a grand plan!

Not the least bit interested in great-coated grenadiers, deVergor sought commitment from the ensign that he would transfer to Saint Denis.

"I will go to the fortress and request your transfer." He waited a beat for the ensign to acknowledge the statement. When deBaralon didn't respond, deVergor looked at him sideways. *Damn! The little bugger was still looking through the eyeglass at the grenadiers.* "Grenadiers get sick the same as any other kind of soldier. Those men probably have the fever and are suffering the chills." deVergor put his arm over the shoulder of the ensign, drawing him away from the edge of the cliff. "Now we know what the English are going to have on that site—a hospital. I will arrange your transfer tomorrow?"

"I would appreciate that, sir. Thank you."

"Fine. Let's go have a drink to our mutually profitable future."

* * *

On the south side of the river, the army officers, used to walking over rough terrain, were having no difficulty with the slope of the hill but the naval officers were breathless after a few hundred yards.

Admiral Holmes was the first to complain. "Couldn't we take off these greatcoats now? I am melting in the heat of it!"

General Wolfe was quick to say no. "It isn't much further to Major Dalling's headquarters. See the farmhouse roof? That's where we are going and it's not far now."

"But this coat is so heavy!"

"We do not want the French to know that our War Council will be studying the north shore for our landing point. They must not know we are here." Trying to be tactful with the admiral in front of one of his subordinates, Wolfe appealed to the upper crust sense of team play. "Our grenadiers are up here play-acting in the hot sun. We must set them the example." Wolfe sensed that he had the support of Monckton and Murray but he could tell Townshend and Chads were chafing at the situation as much as Admiral Holmes.

Captain Chads, master of *H.M.S. Vesuvius*, had sweat streaming down his face and dripping from his chin. "I say! What are the boys doing? Are they laying out a pitch?"

"They are pretending to lay out a camp. If Froggie eyes are peering at us from the north shore, they will think our activity is associated with the building of a camp and not our inspection of their defences. Let's hope they believe what we want them to see." Getting a bit winded, Wolfe paused in his climb to gaze back at the northern shore. He noted the boat from *Sutherland* was approaching and gave no thought to the fact that they would have to wait, possibly for hours, while he settled the assault tactics before he would be free to go back to *Sutherland* for his quiet meeting with John Rous.

It was Brigadier Monckton who noted that Wolfe had fallen behind. The Brigadier made a barbed comment. "Getting a bit winded, sir?"

"Not at all, Brigadier." *Might as well remind Monckton who the major general is around here.* "I thought I had seen some movement on the cliff opposite but ..."

"By Jove, sir, you have a good eye! Someone is watching us with a glass. I saw the flash of the sunlight against the lens. Jolly good eye, sir!"

Wolfe stared at the cliff but could see nothing. His opinion of Monckton as a team player went up immeasurably. Perhaps Monckton wasn't such a short-tempered prick after all.

Monckton turned and briskly tackled the incline. "We are almost there, gentlemen. Then we can shuck these greatcoats!"

Major General Wolfe disliked Monckton all over again.

* * *

At six in the evening, General Wolfe took the boat back to *Sutherland* for his meeting with Captain Rous. They didn't talk about much as they shared a simple meal.

"The biscuits were excellent."

"Yes, they were good, weren't they? Cookie is important to this ship."

"Why does he stay? He could have a job almost anywhere."

"He could. My son-in-law asks him to cook at Carleton House every time we enter port."

"If I am not being rude, what makes him stay?"

"Prize money. I give him an extra share from my own." Rous blushed. "I don't know what made me admit to that. I haven't told anyone before." Rous munched on the last of his biscuit. "Not even my man Wimper knew that." He pushed at a couple of crumbs on the desk and then put them in his mouth. "My world is getting smaller as good comrades depart."

"You still have Gray."

"Yes, William has but one good arm ..." Rous shook his head as if driving away particular thoughts. "What did you think of Chads?"

"Seemed like a good man. You were right. Admiral Holmes has assigned your ship to Cap Rouge. You won't be anywhere near the attack."

"I thought I'd be pushed out of the picture as much as possible. That's why I suggested Chads. What kind of authority was he given?"

"Complete command of the landing."

"He will do you proud. Can you tell me what the general plan is?"

"We begin loading the troops tomorrow. On the twelfth, the fleet will sail higher up the river. I want the French to think that we are planning to attack further upstream. We won't go so far that we won't be able to drop back to Foulon after dark."

"Where in the Foulon Cove will be the exact landing place?"

"Your man Gray showed me a place on the north shore where there are two faults or breaks in the cliff. If there are two breaks above, he believes there will be similar breaks in any underwater ledge. I looked at it today from Major Dalling's observation post. The French have built an abattis in the fault with the brook in it—the brook of Saint Denis it's called. The other fault is much smaller but it is bone-dry."

"Defending forces?"

"Probably, but we won't really know until we try the ascent. If it's fortified at the top; we might catch them by surprise because it'll be four in the morning, it's two and a half miles from the fortress and the escarpment is steep, rising almost 175 feet. They won't expect us and might not be on their guard. Anyhow, unless something changes between now and the 13th, Saint Denis will be our landing point."

Wolfe pushed his chair back and stood. "If you would excuse me, I have some paperwork to do and then I would like to have an early night."

"Yes, of course. Good night."

September 12, 1759
Saint Denis

"The commandant didn't tell me! I don't know anything about day passes for you to harvest your crops."

Corporal Fortin knew quite well deVergor had given permission for more than half of the men to return to their farms but the commandant wasn't there right now. He had gone to the fortress on an errand.

Fortin knew that Ensign deLangy had slipped into his peasant costume and had walked up the road over an hour previously. The ensign was on an errand of mercy to relieve the boredom of one of the wives whose militia husband would not be home today. Therefore, Fortin reasoned, deLangy had taken advantage of the situation, so there was no reason why he, Fortin, should miss out. Oh, the men would get to work on their crops, but Corporal Fortin would have something for his trouble.

"What if you were mistaken? Why should I risk my hide for you? If the commandant comes back tonight—you are gone, and he gets angry, I will get the lash. By tomorrow our commandant would be kind and forgiving but tonight, in his anger, *I* would get the lash."

"If I say, on my word of honour as a sergeant, that the commandant gave permission, would a bottle of wine give you the courage to face him?"

Fortin didn't like the inference that he did not have courage. "I am a regular army corporal. You, Sergeant Mallard, are militia. I will hear the proper respect from you."

"Of course, Corporal."

"Two."

A gleam of satisfaction came to Mallard's eyes. "Two bottles, if we come back early tomorrow morning instead of tonight."

Fortin saw Cormier standing with the farmers. "Cormier has sentry duty on the beach after midnight. He must come back tonight."

"Three, and Cormier gets to spend the night at home with his children."

"And his young wife. Four."

"Done."

Corporal Fortin didn't wait for the men to disperse. He turned on his heel and strutted toward the commandant's house, anticipating some of that excellent cheese and a few social moments with the girl. He was feeling good about the day, very good indeed.

"Corporal!"

It was a messenger. Fortin hadn't heard him ride up. The man sat his horse well, so slim and straight. Fortin experienced a pang of regret. *I used to be slim*, he thought. *After a few years of good living as a corporal and now, lately, with the soft duty under my old commandant, I've gone flabby.* He lifted and straightened his belt over his melon-sized paunch and went to the gate to see what the messenger wanted.

"Tomorrow morning there will be supply barges coming downriver. Be on the lookout for them."

"How many?"

"How should I know? Barges they said and don't shoot at them."

"Good! Is that all?"

The messenger leered at the girl who had appeared at the door to see what was going on.

Fortin shooed her inside and closed the door behind him.

10 p.m., 12 September 1759
H.M.S Hunter

"What is it Buffer?"[2]

"Captain Smith, sir. I beg yer pardon fer talkin' to you like this." His head bobbing up and down as he said each word, the Buffer was obviously nervous.

Captain Smith was standing on *Hunter's* main deck. He had been searching the darkness because there were twenty-odd British vessels scattered from Cap Rouge to Pointe aux Trembles, most of them in the hands of good sailors like himself but, in a situation like this, with the level of the Saint Lawrence rising on the flood tide and the runoff from the recent storms, he liked to 'keep his pucker,' as the crew would say, and check everything twice. He had ordered absolute silence and was pleased with the manner in which his ship's company was maintaining that discipline. He turned his head from the darkness to the face of his Buffer. *Buffer is a good man, he thought, and had never crossed the line before, addressing me directly.*

"Yes, Buffer. What is it?" he asked, not unkindly but with the proper sternness in his voice.

"Seaman Stokes, sir ..." Buffer gulped or took a deep breath before he went on.

Captain Smith waited.

"Seaman Stokes says he thinks there's a canoe or a small dinghy off to starboard."

"Where is Stokes?"

"In the riggin', sir, mizzen mast."

Glancing up, Smith could see where Stokes was pointing into the darkness.

Smith could see them now—two men, French soldiers. The one in the bow put his paddle across the thwarts and raised his arms. The man in the rear continued paddling the canoe toward the warship.

Captain Smith had considered calling out his marines but he decided to maintain the silence discipline. "Get Baxter, he speaks French.'

"Aye, sir."

First Officer Baxter, using his own judgEment, had ordered up the marines. He and the marines arrived at the bulwark just as the canoe touched the side of the ship. "Take them into custody," Baxter ordered. "Sink the canoe. Get as much information out of them as you can. Tell me what you find out as soon as possible."

2300 hours, September 12, 1759
Saint Denis

Corporal Fortin knew better than to go to bed before the commandant returned from Québec. When deVergor did return he

shouted for Cormier who, of course wasn't there. Fortin took
the reins of the horse and said he would look after things.

deVergor slid off the horse, saying nothing. He stomped
up the path to the house, pushing so hard on the door to open
it that the door swung wide and slammed against the wall. He
left it open while he fetched a wine bottle and poured himself
a glass. He was cursing the mosquitoes when Fortin returned
from the stables.

"Did you close the door?"

"Yes, Commandant."

"Where is Cormier?"

"He was given the day off."

"The day off, yes, but not the night. Why isn't he here?"

"He begged to be allowed to be with his family, his children, tonight."

"You can't fool me Corporal. How much did you get for
it?"

Fortin sighed. When it came to squeezing the most out of
situation, there was no one as good at it as ...

"Well! How much?"

"One bottle, sir."

"I wager you got two." Seemingly bored with it all, deVergor blurted out the cause of his irritation. "The bastards won't
let me have deBaralon. He's not coming."

The corporal couldn't help but be a little pleased, although
he was careful not to let any of it show when he said, "That's
too bad, sir. The ensign is very capable," *and would have taken
a share of the profits we are making.* "Perhaps you can try again
after freeze-up when the British are gone."

Commandant deVergor poured himself another glass of
wine. He didn't offer to give any to the corporal. "Good night
then."

"Good night, my commandant." Fortin breathed a sigh of
relief that he could now go off to bed. He pushed down on the
latch but before he could open the door.

"The guards are set?"

"Yes, sir. Oh, yes. A messenger came by early this morning
to tell us there would be supply barges tonight."

"Good! Put three men on the beach so we will be sure to spot them. I am expecting some spices. I don't want to miss them."

"I have only one guard on the beach."

"I signed the roster. I know there are two scheduled. I want you to have three."

"Cormier won't be back until morning."

deVergor savoured the wine's bouquet. "Then, dear Corporal Fortin, you will have to pull guard duty for the first time." He waved his hand in dismissal. "Be sure to get my spices. Have a nice night."

Corporal Fortin lifted the latch. "Shit!" he whispered against the wood of the door.

Commandant deVergor heard his man but paid him no mind. He was feeling much better now, what with the second glass of wine and the expectation that in the morning he would have fresh spices to awaken his taste buds.

1 a.m., 13 September 1759
Cap Rouge

Now that it was approaching the time for the assault boats to be loaded, Captain Rous regretted all the times he had baited the Pompous Asses. If he had watched his mouth, been a trifle more polite, perhaps *Sutherland* wouldn't be stuck at Cap Rouge—but not likely. He had expected, nay, deserved being pushed off to the side on one of the most exciting days in the history of the New World, but it wasn't fair to consign his dear William Gray to the dustbin as well. He didn't dwell on it. If there is something that can't be moved then you go around. He still might get around the Pompous Asses as far as William was concerned. He would see.

There was lots of moon. At least he was able to see the activity all around; the flat-bottomed boats and longboats clustering around the schooner *Terror of France* and the *Sutherland* were filled with white, upturned faces. Soon the tide would be on the ebb and the flotilla of boats would be carried downstream the ten miles or so to attack at Saint Denis.

The companionway door opened. A drummer boy stepped out on the deck followed by the cloaked figure of Major General James Wolfe. *My! In the moonlight the black cloak made him look very tall. What was he carrying in his hand? A stick.* Rous was put in mind of Wolfe charging the beaches at Louisbourg—Cormorant Cove—he'd lost the hat but he had held onto the stick, using it as a road sign—'follow me'!

As if hearing Rous's thoughts, Wolfe put his hat on. He stepped closer to the old sailor.

"The biscuits were excellent, Captain. I intend to steal that man when I return."

"You are welcome to try, General. About my other man ..."

"Gray, I suppose."

"Yes."

"Wants to use his claymore on the French?"

"I don't suppose he has one," Rous laughingly said.

"Assign him to one of your boats, the one with my volunteers, if you like. They are in a *Sutherland* boat." General Wolfe was referring to the twenty-four men who had volunteered to scramble up the rocks to surprise whatever French troops were positioned at the top of the cliff while the rest of Wolfe's army, some four thousand five hundred men, assembled on the shore and made a slower ascent with their equipment.

Rous knew the volunteers were already on the water, but no matter. "I'll make sure he gets a position."

"Yes." Wolfe's mind had already passed on to other things and he followed the corporal grenadier over the side into the boat. The general, like everyone else, would wait in his boat until the signal to depart.

Captain Rous stood on his deck knowing what the skunk at the tea party must have felt: rejection. He could only stand there as several thousand men were on the move all around him. He knew the army was divided into two lines of battle. Brigadiers Monckton and Murray commanded the first line, which was being loaded now, while Brigadier Townshend would bring the second line into battle from the transport *Lowestoft*. Everyone had a role to play in this great endeavour and the job of Captain John Rous, Master of a Royal Navy fifty-gun man o' war, was to determine when the tide was full, raise two lanterns into the shrouds of his ship, and watch as it all happened. He felt left out. "Yessir! Like the skunk!"

He noted William going over the side with Seaman Fink right behind. *That's good,* he thought. *Fink will look after William, not let anything more happen to that boy.* Cookie brought a tea and biscuit. He missed Wimper but life goes on, he thought as he nibbled on the biscuit. He had finished the snack when his First Officer came to stand by his side.

"The condition of the tide, First?"

"Full tide, sir."

"Hoist the signal and may God bless 'em."

Rous didn't wait to see Captain Chads' lead boat row away into the darkness. As he went down the companionway he figured that since the river would run at about six knots, the first Frenchmen should die at four in the morning.

3:30 a.m., 13 September 1759
H.M.S. Hunter

The canoeists were deserters from one of Bougainville's patrols. They didn't have much in the way of information that the English didn't already know. They reported that Bougainville was at Cap Rouge with 600 soldiers and 200 cavalry. He had sent them out with orders to watch the big ship and to report any movement.

Captain Smith was pleased with what he heard. The English plan to pin Bougainville at Cap Rouge by leaving *Sutherland* there in plain sight while the attacking force sneaked downriver in small boats seemed to be working. Hopefully, by the time Bougainville realized that *Sutherland* had no role to play in the attack, it would be too late for him to come to the aid of Montcalm at the fortress.

One of the deserters asked if they could have some food since they had been on short rations for the last few days. They were expecting supply barges tonight but, of course, that would be too late for the deserters. Could they please be fed something?

Supply barges on the river? How many and when? As soon as Smith had the information, *H.M.S. Hunter* was moved from Sillery to a position about a mile off Foulon. If there were supply barges out there, they might run into the attacking force and sound the alarm. Captain Smith was determined not to let that happen. If the English were to have luck on their side tonight, *Hunter* would find the barges first.

"There!" First Officer Baxter hissed. "Off to the right." A boat came out of the darkness moving with muffled oars.

Captain Smith whispered, "Get ready to fire!" He raised his arm.

A figure in the boat stood to reveal himself. "Don't be gettin' too excited with the muskets, laddie!"

Smith's marines relaxed. That was not a Frenchman. It sounded very much like a Scot.

"Captain Fraser, 78th Highlanders, requests you identify yourself!"

Isn't that always like a Northerner, was the thought crossing Baxter's mind. *He's demanding that WE identify ourselves but he's the one ...*

"Well, laddie! Cat got your tongue?"

Trying not to show the irritation he felt, Baxter replied, "First Officer Baxter, *H.M.S. Hunter*. Come alongside. We have intelligence for you."

As soon as the lead boats were alongside, Captain Smith descended the harbour ladder to the level of the boats, where he explained to Captain Chads that French provision boats were expected to pass downriver. As far as *Hunter* could tell, they hadn't passed yet.

0350 hours, 13 September
Saint Denis

Corporal Fortier watched as clouds drifted over the moon. He shivered. If anyone had told him yesterday that he would be doing guard duty at four o'clock on a cold, damp morning, he would have told them they were crazy; he wouldn't have been able to imagine the circumstances that would take him out of his warm bed, unless, of course, the British were coming, and even then he wouldn't be down here. The commandant would have been ordered to move his men back into the fortress, leaving the English out in the cold and the damp ... *What was that?* There was a grating on the beach stones as if a boat had just come to the beach. *Another! Two boats!*

Fortier beckoned to one of the other guards. "Go see if that's the provision barges."

"Yes, Corporal."

Dumb militia bastards, he thought. *They do what they're told without considering the consequences.* Corporal Fortier realized that a younger Private Fortier had been like that at Beauséjour, but not any more! He was older and a lot smarter. Fortier took several casual steps away from the water so he could be closer to the trail going up hill, just in case.

"Who goes there?"

There wasn't an immediate response.

Fortier was at the bottom of the trail when the response came from the darkness. "France, and Long Live the King!" He held his place near the trees as the dumb militiaman, Hector Saunier, walking briskly back, happily reported, "They are our people with supplies. We can let them come."

The other guard, Paul Pageau, had joined Fortier near the bushes. Fortier had the fleeting thought that Pageau wasn't as stupid as he looked.

Pageau motioned to Saunier to return to the boats. "We had better get the commandant's spices before they proceed downriver."

The three guards stepped briskly to the water's edge.

Saunier was the first to die. He was watching his footing on the beach stones as he retraced his steps, so he had no idea what was going to happen to him.

The Highlander assumed the classic stance and thrust his bayonet through Hector's heart. Hector grabbed the bayonet with both hands, losing most of his fingers in the process. He went down, never looking up. His last view of anything on this earth was the boots and gaiters of his assailant.

Two other Highlanders hurried by their comrade who, by

this time, had his foot on the Frenchman's chest twisting on his musket to release the bayonet from the corpse.

Pageau had dropped his musket and was running for his life. He passed the dazed Fortier at top speed.

Mouth agape, Fortier thought, *Mother of God! Where did the Englishmen come from?* That dumb Saunier said they were French! His first instinct was that of the army regular, raising his musket and aiming at one of the Highlanders. One shot would alert the entire post! He'd shoot the one bastard and handle the other with his good bayonet skills, but there was no flash in the pan! His guts churned as he realized that it had been several hours since he had checked his powder and the river dampness had … but he had no time to think it through. He threw his musket at them and took to his heels. No one could catch Corporal Fortier on a good day! If he had understood English he would have heard the nearest Highlander say, "You take the fat one."

Both Scotsmen cast aside their muskets. As they pursued the fleeing Frenchmen, the one going after Fortier drew his claymore and threw it at Fortier's broad back. Fortier fell. He meant to roll over and raise his arms in surrender but he was pinned to the ground by the force of a knee in his back. In a moment the pressure on his back was gone. Fortier had a moment of hope. Perhaps he would be allowed to surrender? He died without realizing that his throat had been cut.

The Scot who had been chasing Pageau returned, wiping his sword on a handful of sea grass.

"Did ye get him?"

"Aye."

"Any trouble?"

"Nay. He tired on the hill. I didn't."

They heard the quiet call for assembly. They rejoined the ranks of their clansmen just as Lieutenant Gray was congratulating Captain Fraser on his ruse of using French to confuse the guards.

"Your French certainly worked with the guards on the beach," William said.

"Aye, I thought it might. It always worked with the mademoiselles on the Continent," answered a pleased Captain Fraser.

There was general laughter from the ranks, which the captain allowed for a few moments before he ordered, "All right, laddies, we have to take out that abattis. Sergeant! Get a move on." It began to rain.

While Captain Fraser and his men worked to clear the path that went from the base of the cliff to the top of the Saint Denis brook, Captain Donald MacDonald led his twenty-four volunteers and some light infantry, who wanted to go along, up the steep incline of the other fault some two hundred yards downstream from Saint Denis.

It was a difficult climb: the men, with their weapons strapped to their backs, pulled themselves up from rock to branch to tree trunk to rock until they finally reached the top. MacDonald knew that once the Saint Denis fault was cleared, Wolfe's main force would appear at the top of the cliff some two hundred yards to the west of where he was. His men assumed skirmish formation as they carefully advanced west along the edge of the cliff. Fortunately, it would soon be getting light. They would have no difficulty sighting enemy fortifications or sentries in the half-light.

0440 hours, 13 September 1759
Top of the Cliff

Sergeant Mallard had been back long enough to change into his uniform. He passed down the row of tents listening to the sleeping noises. Another fifteen minutes and he would rouse his men from their slumber.

When he looked in at the stables, a half-dozen of the boys were already back from their farms. It was warmer to wait in the barn with the animals so he was not surprised to find them there. That was good. He would send three of them to the beach to relieve the guards. He would bet it had been a cold, miserable night on the beach and now that it was raining ... he wondered, who had done Cormier's duty?

Stepping out of the barn, he cast a glance at the house. No smoke coming out of the chimney yet. The girl had better get to her chores, and then he smiled; she might actually be attending to one of her chores already. Anyway, that was not a concern of his. *Was that a man coming along the edge of the cliff or a deer?* His musket still slung by its strap from his shoulder, he increased his stride as he went to see. *It's a man. None of the boys would be coming back from that direction. Who could it be?*

* * *

Captain MacDonald saw the French soldier coming his way. He thought of Fraser's use of French and decided he would try to fool this Frog long enough for his men to get in better position. He could see the house, the tents and the barn. Yes, just a few more minutes. He spoke up, loudly, so his men would not shoot—not just yet.

"Good morning!" The French soldier was a sergeant but he wasn't reaching for his musket. That was a good sign. "Me and my men have been sent by General Montcalm to augment your forces guarding the Foulon."

"Yes."

"Please tell your officer that we are here."

"Yes, of course. He is at the house. Just wait here and I will get him." Sergeant Mallard had counted about twenty, twenty that he could see. Wait until he told the commandant!

The front door of the house opened and the girl came out with a chamber pot. She tossed the contents and stared, dumbfounded, at the soldiers coming out of the trees. Sergeant Mallard pushed her back into the house and closed the door. He ran to the window. More of them than before!

"Quickly, tell the Commandant the English are here!" He had to warn the men. Mallard pushed his musket through the partially open door and fired in the direction of the enemy soldiers. Now there was shouting.

"What is it, Sergeant?"

At least he had his pants on. "Commandant, the British are here. Most of our men are sleeping. We have five or six men in the barn but they do not have their muskets."

"Are you sure it's the English?"

Mallard regarded the commandant with disdain. "They

said they were from Montcalm and were sent here to help us defend the Foulon."

"Maybe they were. How do you know they are English?"

Several muskets were fired at once. A scream! In his imagination, Mallard thought he could recognize the voice as belonging to Cormier, one of his wife's cousins, the one with all the children. "They are English."

deVergor pointed at Sergeant Mallard and then at the door. "Leave now. Get the warning to the fortress. Tell them what you know. Go! Now!"

The sergeant opened the door and peeked out. Taking a deep breath, he lunged through the open door and ran toward the gate as fast as he could go.

deVergor considered the possible consequences of this episode. Damn! Damn! He was facing another courtmartial unless he did something to redeem himself.[3] Commandant deVergor slipped on his tunic and drew himself up to his fullest height as he stepped to the doorway. When he saw the Highland uniforms, he stepped forward, out into the yard, where he would be seen. He watched as Mallard went through the gate. Another hundred yards and the sergeant would be at the bend in the path. Maybe deVergor should have sent him to Cap Rouge. Would that have been better? This could be just a raid and that was what Bougainville had the cavalry for, to catch the sneaky English in their raids. A Highland officer was turning his way. *If he looks down the path he would be able to see Mallard.* It was then deVergor realized that he didn't have a weapon of any kind.

"You miserable red lobster! I challenge you in the name of my King to a duel!" He took a half step to the side to give the enemy a smaller target and slowly raised his right hand, sighting along his finger at the tall Highlander. "Well, Lobsterback! You won't fight! You don't have the brains to understand ..."

* * *

Captain MacDonald thought he had seen some movement on the other side of the gate. A French officer challenging him to a duel distracted him. By God! The man had assumed the position and was raising his weapon. MacDonald raised his pistol and fired. The French officer went down. MacDonald turned away and ran to the barn where prisoners were being taken. Word would have to be sent to the shore that the way was clear at the top of Saint Denis brook.

5:15 a.m., 13 September 1759
On the Beach

The Samos battery had the range. Huge spouts of water rose whenever they missed but most of the time the shot fell into the boats and ships crammed with English soldiers. The water was pocked with the debris of ruined boats and mangled bodies. Time after time, over and over, as the boats approached the shore, the Samos battery took its toll, but by five o'clock there were enough soldiers of the first division safely ashore that Wolfe began to believe that there might be a successful outcome to the day, after all. He began the task of organizing the remnants of companies into the semblance of fighting units. His instructions to his soldiers were brief and simple.

"Be attentive and obedient to your officers. We are professionals and our purpose this day is to bring the French Army into the field where we can destroy it. A determined body of soldiers is capable of doing great harm to five weak French battalions. Remember they fight as a mixed force of regulars, militia and peasantry. On the other hand, we—are the British Army."

When Wolfe was through speaking with one reorganized unit, he would gather another cluster of soldiers and work his wonders with them until it was the next group's turn.

* * *

Captain Chads was the first to get the word from the top of the hill. He sent William Gray to find General Wolfe in the noise and confusion that was the normal condition on the Saint Denis Beach. "It is all clear at the top of the trail. Tell the general that I am being rowed back to the *Lowestoft* to bring Townshend's second division to the landing place." He leaned close to William's ear to make sure he heard. "Ask him if there's something he can do about the Samos battery." He grinned as he left with the departing shout. "I'm sure he would if he could without me asking."

Wolfe wasn't too difficult to find. William passed the message and watched as Wolfe led the first of the division up the slope. He continued to watch for a while and, since he had no assigned duties, stepped into a break in the line between units and joined them as they trudged up the slope. The first time he slipped, he wasn't surprised to find Fink supporting him on his bad side.

"What ho! Fink! Where'd you come from?"

"The Cap'n told me that nothing was to happen to you, sir. Can't do that from the longboat if you insist on wandering about like a landlubber."

William saved his breath and accepted Fink's help. When they reached the top, William could see that Wolfe had already left the area. He noticed Jenkins standing near the door of a barn where some French prisoners were being held. "What is happening, Jenkins?"

"The general told me to stay here, sir, and wait for his return. He's gone to check the terrain."

Brigadier Murray had just formed up his men and was marching off to what William believed to be the west. "Where is the brigadier going with his men?"

"Vowed to put an end to the cannon still hounding the men on the water, the brigadier said."

"Do we have many French prisoners?"

"Not many, sir, although some wander in every now and then as if they had been on holiday. I almost forgot! There's one of them over there, wounded. General told me to take special care of him since he was the commanding officer, but he's too big for me to carry.[4] Could your man give me a hand to put him inside with the rest of them?"

"Come on, Fink. Let's give the corporal a hand."

"Aye, sir. Seems we're the only bods not doin' sumpthin'."

The French officer was sitting with his back against the front wall of the house. He glanced up when the three Englishmen approached but then looked away as if he wasn't the least bit interested.

William stopped, astonished that he would recognize the Frenchman. "He was the commandant of Beauséjour! I saw him when they were interrogating him about Ensign Hay's death."

deVergor heard the name 'Ensign Hay.' He didn't recognize William and soon lost interest, since he couldn't understand any of William's questions or comments. However, he quickly understood that they were going to move him and made a loud fuss about the pain of the wound in his hip.

It wasn't a great distance. Jenkins's plan was to have Fink lift the Frenchman enough that Jenkins could get him over his shoulder and carry him. They got him up and Jenkins carried him about halfway to the barn, when he had to put his load down for a rest.

Still supporting most of the commandant's weight, Jenkins looked past Fink and saw a man in peasant's clothing coming along to the barn. "It's another one of those holiday blokes. Someone will have to take his musket and put him in the barn."

"I'll do that," William said. "Fink, you help Jenkins with his load. Can't let him down to the ground; it will be too hard to get him back up again."

William unhooked his pistol and warily approached the peasant.

* * *

Ensign deLangy, dressed as he was like a peasant, had managed to avoid contact with English soldiers. He had seen where they were forming up on the plains near Butte à Neveu, about a mile from the fortress. There were hundreds of English troops between him and friendly forces, so he had decided to return to his post. The English were here too. Then he heard deVergor's complaints as the English were handling him. Was there anything he should do? Not really. He had pretty well made up his mind to surrender when he saw the Englishman with the pistol approaching him. Yes, deLangy believed he was going to surrender until anger rose in his heart and engulfed him. The Englishman with the pistol! He was the same man who had shot his fingers away at Beauséjour! There could be no surrender until he killed the man with the pistol! He raised his musket shouting "Revenge!"

* * *

William couldn't believe his eyes! He knew the man he was facing! This was the man who had tried to kill him at Fort Beauséjour, and by the look on his face he was set on trying again! Shit! Both Jenkins and Fink had left their muskets leaning against the side of the house and they were encumbered with deVergor. Oh God! Every time he got in trouble he had to rely on a navy pistol!

Fink saw the hate-filled eyes fix on his Lieutenant. Letting go of deVergor, Fink lunged at the peasant. The sudden shift in weight forced Jenkins to his knees, pinning him under the commandant.

William raised his pistol, matching the movement of the Frenchman's musket, and watched as his ball destroyed the face that was so filled with hatred. The Frenchman was thrown back and down.

William blinked a couple of times, so it couldn't have been right away when he noticed Fink standing in front of him with a crooked look on his face. "I think I took one, Lieutenant." He sat, quickly, his large body seeming to fold on itself as he went down.

It really unnerved William to see Fink all in a jumble like that. Fink was on the ground, sitting with his knees up to his chin, both hands open, palm up, flat on the ground, his large chin slowly dragging his head down. It reminded William of a gut-shot deer when the antlers seemed to drag the head down. Then he saw the blood. Fink had been gut-shot.

William dropped his pistol. He knelt and put his arm around the massive head, holding it against his chest. By this time, Jenkins had squirmed out from under the fat commandant. "I'll get a surgeon," he said as he ran off.

"I think my bottom parts are gone, Lieutenant."

"No, they're still here, Fink. How's the pain?"

"Less than ten stripes, more than a tooth, although my other end has a mind of its own and does pretty much as it likes. Shouldn't we be stoppin' the blood?"

"Christ, yes!" William looked around and then asked, "Can you hold yourself up?"

"'course!"

The only thing William could see to use as a bandage was the peasant blouse. He ripped it off the body and stuffed it against Fink's belly.

Fink put his huge hands over the blouse, pressing it against the flow of blood. "That feels better. Thank you, sir."

William sat next to the big man. "Lean against me, Fink."

"Oh, no, sir," he said but, as they waited, imperceptibly he leaned more and more against William as he lost strength.

"Here's Jenkins with the surgeon!"

"Your grenadier said you were shot, Lieutenant."

"It's not me, Doctor." William gently tugged Fink's hands away from the blouse.

The doctor scowled at Jenkins. "You told me it was the officer with the wound! I have enough wounded at the aid station without traipsing all over the ..."

"We are on General Wolfe's staff," an angry William interjected. "Look at his wound!"

The doctor opened his bag and took out a little brown bottle. "Give him all of this." He snapped his bag shut and rose to leave. "Keep pressure on the bandage at least until he passes out."

"Then what?"

The surgeon gave William an odd look. "Then I suggest you go on about your duties, Lieutenant."

None of this was lost on Fink but he sounded cheerful as he asked, "How's the battle goin'? I hear the guns ..."

"The last man I worked on told me we were lined up pretty thin ... in two rows instead of three, with gaps between the regiments so our battle line could be as long as theirs. The

French had fired their first volley. My patient had lost an eye from a shell splinter and walked back for help. He told me he thought our line was holding."

deVergor must have realized that the doctor wasn't going to look at his wound. He made protestations that he needed help but no one in the group understood French. His protestations got louder.

"Seems the Frog wants you to look at him," William said.

Before the doctor could reply, Jenkins added, "General Wolfe told me to look after him because he was the commanding officer."

"You had better look at him, doctor." William was lifting the cork off the brown bottle with his sailor's knife. "He's the general's special prisoner."

The surgeon took a quick look, manipulating the hip with his hands, much against deVergor's will. "The ball is still in there but in the flesh. Not much bleeding. He'll be fine when we get to him later."

"Anything we can do for him?"

"Don't give him any of the bottle. Your man will want all of it."

Fink watched the doctor walk away as a dog tied to a tree might watch his master until out of sight. William offered him the bottle. Fink took it all without comment, handing the bottle back as if he were asking the barkeep for another round.

A man Jenkins recognized as a messenger came trotting by. Jenkins waved him over. "What is the news?"

"The general said if I was to see you, to tell you to come up. He might have need of you."

Fink stirred himself. "How are things going?"

The messenger immediately recognized Fink as a dead man. He was almost tender the way he took pains to give Fink as much information as he could. "There's more of them than us so we're stretched pretty thin."

Jenkins pushed himself up. "I had better go. I guess the Frog officer is as good here as anywhere."

Fink laughed, "Sure looks like he ain't goin' nowhere the way he hollers ever' time he moves."

With an informal salute to Fink, Jenkins was gone.

"Well, what else?" Fink's head lolled to one side, but William gave it support with his arm. "What else happened?"

"Monckton on the right, Murray on the left with the old man in the centre. He ordered the entire line to load with two balls and not to fire until the Frogs was forty yards from the points of our bayonets. And we stood there, our bagpipes playin' a tune on our lines and our cannon playin' a tune on theirs."

Obviously getting weaker, Fink's eyes begged for more.

"Montcalm led by the centre and advanced. The Frogs fired a volley and our boys took it. Our line held. The Frogs advanced again. When they was forty yards, just like the man said, he gave the order to fire! Our centre fired at Wolfe's command. The left and right fired company by company. It was all dense smoke all over the lines. Wolfe gave the order to reload. Then he waited. After a bit he told me to run back and bring up the men who was attacking the Samos battery to reinforce the line. I found out Samos battery was captured and those men were already on the way."

"Did the French stand?" Fink had stopped asking the questions but William was sure he could hear and would want to know.

The messenger had been crouching so Fink could hear him speak. Now that Fink's eyes were closed, he stood. "I dunno. The smoke hadn't cleared when I left." He took a last look at the big sailor's face. "Sorry about him." As he left, William was sure he went out of his way to step on one of deVergor's hands, which deVergor was using to support himself. That led to a long string of French obscenities that lasted well after the messenger was out of sight.

William sat holding the big head against his chest until Fink stopped breathing. *What had Wolfe said? "Mustn't get too fond of any of them because it may be your duty to expend his life and the lives of a dozen more just like him." That's just so much shit, and the next time I see the general I'm going to tell him so!* He gazed at the still face and said, "I didn't expend your life, Fink! You bloody well saved mine!" He carefully lowered Fink's head to the ground. He was covering it with the blouse when Jenkins returned.

William's face was wet with his tears as he stood to face the corporal. "I think he's dead, Jenkins."

"How did you know?"

A little surprised and not really understanding Jenkins's meaning, he said, "I was with him."

"No! You were here." Then Jenkins realized that William was talking about the sailor, Fink. "General Wolfe is dead."

"Oh."

"A Canadian sharpshooter ... but we won the day. They run."

William was surprised at his own lack of concern about the death of Wolfe or the possibility of an English victory. "Good. I must return to my ship."

"*Sutherland*? It's at Cap Rouge, isn't it?"

"I need help from ship's company to look after ..." William indicated with a nod of his head the body of Able Seaman Fink.

"Not likely, sir. There's another French army between here and Cap Rouge. They might be attacking here. You'll not get back soon to your boat."

"But ..."

"Leave him to the Graves Detail, sir. They'll look after him right proper, sir."

Lieutenant William Gray put a foot one way and then the other, not knowing what to do.

Jenkins could see the hurt in the other man. He decided. "Lieutenant, go down to the beach; there'll be kitchens set up there by now. Get something to eat."

"What about Commandant ..."

"deVergor." They were both surprised when the French prisoner spoke.

"What about Commandant deVergor?"

"I will see he is cared for. Now, you go along down to the beach. Get something to eat."

As William turned to do as he was told, Jenkins patted him on the shoulder. "Now, that's a good officer."

William hadn't gone five paces when he heard Jenkins call after him, "You'd better take your pistol, Lieutenant!"

Gray walked on as if he hadn't heard. He was through with navy pistols for life.

Endnotes

[1] The Commandant was venal so I assumed that it would rub off on the members of his unit. Also, officers often "spoke for" subordinates who had served with them before. I thought our Commandant would follow the practice.

[2] The story of the capture of Quebec is so well known that I tried to give it a slightly different flavour without changing any of the incidents.

[3] The Commandant did send a messenger warning that the British were at his post.

[4] deVergor was actually wounded in the hand as well as the leg. For the purposes of my story, I had to have him so he needed assistance, so I gave him a hip wound.

Chapter Fourteen

"It's hard to believe, Margaret, sitting here supping tea with you, what those men went through."

Margaret Skinner had been overwhelmed with joy by the safe return of the father of her children. Yes, 'her' children because now there was no doubt in her mind where she wanted to spend the rest of her life. She had her Charles and little James, and now William had returned, safe, but somehow changed. She listened very intently to find what had changed in ... her ... her man.

William didn't sense the scrutiny of his housekeeper as he continued with his story. "They had to face the darkness of the river sitting for hours in those little boats. They were cramped and bum sore, being bombarded by fears of the unknown and then, at dawn's light, when they were discovered by the Samos battery ..."

"That would be French cannon?"

"Yes. The French had positioned their guns on a hill overlooking the river." William paused for moment as he pictured the sight in his mind. "The French dropped their shot into the river where there must have been several hundred boats at any one time in their range. It was like shooting ducks on a pond."

"Many died?"

"Yes, many." William placed another spoonful of honey in the tea and thought of Wolfe. "Wolfe led his men directly from the boats up a steep cliff and onto the field of battle where they faced an army much bigger than they. Actually, there were two French armies: one that could have attacked them from the rear at any time, and the one that was facing them."

"The French had the fort. Why didn't they stay inside?"

"Montcalm couldn't let the English bring their guns up. It would have been like Beauséjour all over again." William thought he should tell Margaret about Ensign Hay and the spy, Tyrell, and how the English got their guns on Butte à Charles … but perhaps not; it was an old story so, instead he said very simply, "The British put their guns on a little hill facing Fort Beauséjour and the fort fell. Wolfe did almost the same thing at Louisbourg."

"Almost?"

"When he placed guns on Gallows Hill, Louisbourg would have fallen. When we captured or destroyed the French warships in the harbour, Louisbourg was forced to surrender … but Wolfe already had them beat when he put his guns on the little hill."

"So, what happened at Quebec?"

"There was a hill less than a mile from the fortress. Montcalm probably was aware of Wolfe's tactics at Louisbourg and thought he had better destroy the puny little army before the guns came up. If Montcalm had any remaining doubts about whether or not to attack the English, his mind was made up for him when two of Wolfe's cannon began their serenade; he attacked."

"You said the French army was bigger. Why didn't they win?"

"British discipline. The French marched toward the British lines, halted and fired. The British did not return fire because Wolfe had told them there was to be no shooting until the French were at forty yards. The French reloaded and marched closer. Wolfe gave the order. The entire battlefield was covered in smoke from the gunpowder. Wolfe waited, patiently, for the smoke to dissipate. When it did, he ordered a second volley and the French broke and ran. He had gained mastery of the plateau and, by September 18th, the fortress had surrendered."

"The French general died, too?"

"Yes."

"Did you get to see Quebec?"

"No. *Sutherland* was sent back to Halifax.[1] Captain Rous was ordered to report for a new assignment. Don't know what it is, yet." William reached out and touched her wrist. "Margaret, I will not be going to sea again, at least not with the Royal Navy."

Margaret was not surprised that he would make a momentous decision. She had realized in the three days he had been home that something in this man had changed. Killing changes a man, her brother Amos had told her. William was just back from a war. Perhaps he had done some killing ... "Not even with your friend, Captain Rous? What if he receives an exciting posting, a bigger ship?" And the unspoken question, do you still want me here with the children? And with you?

"It was General Wolfe who made things clear for me. He said I shouldn't get fond of the men serving under my command because I might have to expend their lives."

The realist in Margaret agreed and she said so. "That's the nature of it, William. You shouldn't have been surprised."

A trifle testy at Margaret's reply, William retorted, "Well, one of those expendables saved my life!"

"He was expected to do what he did."

"Margaret, sometimes I could get angry with you. You don't know anything about it!"

"I'm sorry if I make you angry." Margaret Skinner put her cup down and stared into the eyes of the man she admired—and had come to love—more than any other man in her lifetime. "I have been in two Indian raids. The men went forward and fought to save the women and children. It was expected of them. I don't think they gave it a second thought. They were men. Jake Fink was a sailor. He ..."

"He followed me ashore. He told me Captain Rous had ordered him not to let anything happen to me."

"Then he did what was expected of him. I'm glad I had the chance to meet him."

"He was big and hairy." William smiled as he remembered. "He talked all the time and, every now and then, he would have the worst odour."

"A fart?"

"Er, yes. He said it was never his fault. It was his second brain that looked after things like that." William wiped at his eyelid. He looked out the window, perhaps searching for another topic of conversation. "Have you seen Amy?"

"Every day. If she isn't doing work at the church, she is

working with the children at Orphan House." Margaret remembered something and she hastened to add, "Do you remember that little boy you said survived the Dartmouth massacre? Well! He's been taken in by the Wenmans.[2] They are going to give him a home."

"Mistress Wenman?"

"No, Richard Wenman, a friend of Mauger." Seeing the distaste on William face she hurried on, "It's good the boy is finally going to have a family, isn't it?"

"I suppose so, although putting a boy in with Mauger's crowd isn't doing him a favour." William put his cup down. He glanced at the clock that had arrived from Scotland while he was away and now had the place of honour in the front room. Heavily ornate with a silver face and hands, it told him that he had twenty minutes to walk down to the harbour front to meet with Captain Rous. He stood and gazed at the clock. "I can't believe that Mother was able to bequeath the clock to me. She married an Englishman, you know. I am surprised he gave it up."

"And took the time and expense to ship it here." Margaret rose and patted William's collar flat. "Not all Englishmen are horrors, you know."

William took her hand and squeezed it gently. "I must go." He thought of something. "Why is Amy working at Orphan House? You did say she was working at Orphan House?"

"Oh, yes. Every good deed in this town has the hand of the Bulkeleys in it."

"I heard Amy say something about that before I left. What's going on?"

"There are going to be official charges of abuses in the management of the Orphan House. Richard, without a doubt, got some of the huge amount spent on superintending twenty-five children and will most likely be named in the charges. Amy is casting herself as an angel of charity, flitting here and there, doing good works absolutely without any thought of recompense. She's clever, but it will take a stroke from the Almighty to keep Bulkeley from being charged and publicly disgraced."

Margaret brought his cloak and hat from the rack in the

hall. "It will be cool when the town falls under the shadow of the Citadel."

"I'll carry the cloak, Margaret, but I don't think I will take the hat."

"Everyone wears a hat in town, William."

William's lower lip stuck out as he said, "I'm not a naval officer any more and I'll not wear a hat!"

Seeing the lip, Margaret, on a whim, kissed it.

Just as impulsively, William took her into his arms and kissed her warmly, his hands stroking her back lovingly.

They kissed.

"La, sir! You make advances!" Margaret pushed him back with both hands against his chest. She smiled broadly, as she jokingly pushed him to the door. "But be prepared to defend yourself, sir, after the children are in bed! Now, good afternoon to you, Mister Gray." She closed the door.

William Gray stood there, savouring the breathtaking feel of the woman. She would, he knew, give of herself, but that would mean a commitment from him that ...

The door opened and Margaret Skinner handed him his hat, stuck her tongue out, and closed the door before he could respond.

William stepped onto the street. Being careful not to look at the house, he jammed his hat on his head at a ridiculous angle, but he did try, out of the corner of his eye, to see if she were watching from one of the windows. He was sure she was, so he cocked his head until the hat was level and then staggered down the street, one shoulder up, one leg dragging, and one arm seemingly longer than the other, but the hat was level.

"Lieutenant Gray! Is that you?"

A young couple, the man carrying a child, were standing uphill of William, the sun behind their backs. William couldn't recognize them, their faces being in the shadow. He self-consciously stood erect and reached up to put his hat on properly. Shielding his eyes from the sun's glare, he searched the woman's face for some recognition. She was lovely—flashing eyes, her smooth-skinned face framed by the neat bonnet she wore over dark hair. No, if once he had seen this woman, he would never forget her. He did not know her.

The man spoke again, drawing William's attention.

"If I didn't know you were a family man, Lieutenant, I would seek redress from you, sir!" He spoke with a broad smile. Shifting the young boy to balance on his hip, he extended his hand. "Elkanah Smith, at your service, sir, my wife Betty and my three-year-old son, Joseph. We caught you at a delicate moment?"

William pointed at the door, "My ... the lady that ... my housekeeper ..."

Now quite serious, Elkanah apologized, "We don't mean to embarrass you, Lieutenant. We are here several days and can make ..."

Regaining some composure, William hastened to assure them that he had been entertaining his children who had, by now, returned to their play. No, he was delighted to see them and what were they doing in the town? William learned the Smiths were settled on Sherose Island and had come to Halifax to buy a ship, hopefully a French seizure.

"I'm on my way to meet my captain at Carmichael's Tavern. You remember the place?" William lifted his hat to Missus Smith. "Beggin' your pardon, Ma'am," he gave her a small bow, "Elkanah, why don't you come down and talk to him?"

Elkanah gave Betty a swift look and then apologized, "I'm afraid I can't leave my ..."

"You go ahead, Elkony. The Hursts are just around the corner. You go ahead. Joey and I will take some air and then go back, no trouble at all."

Both men raised their hats as Betty left them.

William expressed his surprise. "You are staying with Gerald Hurst?"

They matched step as they went down the hill to Carmichael's.

"Yes. I was surprised. He is senior clerk to the chief surveyor. Offered to put us up whenever I came to town because he knew I had to come back to buy a ship. The chief surveyor was just as thoughtful."

"Enjoy it while you can. Our provincial officials aren't always so nice."

"What do you mean?"

William was about to explain why government officials were scrambling to put a Christian glow on reputations long tarnished by greed and avarice, but they arrived too soon at the door of the Inn. William leaned down on the latch and put his shoulder to the door. Checking the captain's corner as the door swung open, he saw that Captain Rous had already arrived and was hunched over a drink, his face a thundercloud.

William stopped Elkanah with his hand. "It looks like the captain has news that doesn't sit well with him. Don't be surprised if ..."

"William!" Rous made a wide gesture with his arm. "Don't dawdle, my boy! There are biscuits and crackles and beer. Bring your friend to partake of my munificence!"

In an aside William confided, "I tell you one thing, Elkanah, he talks that way when he's in the cups." He put his arm around Elkanah, steering him through the tables to the corner. "Captain, do you have news?"

"We'll have more beer, Mister Carmichael!" Rous, using the flat of his hand, pounded on the table to attract the tavern owner's attention.

Carmichael waved from the taproom but it was easy to see that he was upset with the captain's behaviour toward him.

Rous must have seen it, too. In a befuddled manner, he shook his head and shouted, "Sorry, old man!" Not satisfied, Rous pushed away from the table to go to the taproom, probably to make his apologies directly to Carmichael, but William assisted him back into his chair.

"Carmichael understands, Captain. He understands." When William was certain Rous would remain seated, he took his hands off him and restarted the conversation. "You have news, Captain?"

"I most certainly do! I get to convoy the mast fleet to England!"[3]

William couldn't believe it. "They didn't give you this year's convoy!"

Elkanah Smith wasn't quite sure what a mast fleet was but he knew that to have command of a convoy would be a great responsibility. "That must be a great honour, sir." He started to say more but the looks on his companions' faces told another story.

"It's not an honour, Elkanah. When a captain is about to be placed on the retirement list, he is given one last task that returns him to home waters. The mast fleet is the usual way to …"

"… Get rid of a captain from Halifax station." Rous's voice quavered. "I suppose it was Saunders who arranged that. I shouldn't have called him a horse's ass." He quaffed the rest of his beer.

Neither of the younger men spoke. It seemed he had more to say and they waited for it.

"Only been to England the once, you know, in '46 when I took back the news of our first victory at Louisbourg. These are home waters for me."

"*Sutherland*?"

"I was relieved this morning."

"I saw the mast fleet in upper harbour."

"We sail tomorrow."

There wasn't much said around the table as they drank their beer. Once, Rous said something like, "Going to see Wimper," or perhaps "Going out with a whimper," William couldn't tell and didn't ask.

Elkanah and William were wondering how they would get the captain home when six *Sutherlands* entered the inn. They didn't have to look around to find their old master, coming straight to the corner. First Officer Adams explained to William as the others led the captain out the door, "We have his kit. There's a carriage outside. We'll make sure he gets to where he now belongs."

"I'd like to go with him, see he's …"

"You're not *Sutherland* any more, Mister Gray. Leave it to us."

Captain John Rous didn't say anything and didn't look back.

Elkanah sat down and picked up his beer. "That was a sad thing."

"Yes, it was." William couldn't decide whether to sit or go outside. He finally sat as Elkanah asked him other questions.

"What did they mean you're not *Sutherland*?"

"There are many ways to depart a ship and still be thought of as being one of the ship's company. All the acceptable ways are beyond your control: sickness, death, promotion, transfer, retirement, but not resignation. I left the Service for personal reasons. I put 'Self before Service' is the way they think of it. They would always remember me fondly but I am not part of the brotherhood. That's what they meant."

Elkanah was naturally curious about the old captain and it gave him the opportunity to change the subject. "What's the story of Captain Rous?"

"John Rous was Master of the Boston privateer *Shirley*. His exploits during the capture of Louisbourg in 1745 earned him promotion to captain of the Royal Navy, probably the only colonial to achieve that rank." William considered telling Elkanah how many French ships Rous had captured, or maybe mention the names of some of them that easily sprang to his mind, but he didn't want to make it a speech. Instead he spoke only of the time he had known his old captain.

"I first met him in 1750 when he was returning to Halifax with a captured brigantine, *Saint Francis*. He had taken *Saint Francis*, which was a bigger, more heavily armed ship than his *H.M.S. Albany*, with the loss of only three men: two sailors and one junior officer. He was a remarkable tactician, Captain John Rous. However, getting a replacement officer proved to be more difficult than capturing French ships, so when I volunteered, he accepted me as the replacement officer. I served with him when he was commander of the naval forces during the assault on Fort Beauséjour." William raised his voice with pride, as he announced, "In the history of the Royal Navy, there had never been such a successful amphibious assault and envelopment."

The noise in the tavern abated as more of the customers listened to what William had to say. Maybe he was making a speech! He blushed but continued.

"Rous knew what had to be done to capture Louisbourg. He had been there before but the Royal Navy senior officers— Captain Rous called them Pompous Asses—" there was general laughter in the tavern, "—wouldn't listen to him. So he sailed the old *Sutherland* around deliverin' death to the French wherever it pleased them to stick their heads up, until the Pompous Assess finally did it his way and captured Louisbourg."

Now the tavern was absolutely still. There was only William's voice.

"Oh, the Pompous Asses took him along to Quebec but only because General Wolfe said he wanted the old man there."

Some cheers rose from the very attentive crowd.

"General Wolfe wanted to get closer to Quebec Fortress. The Pompous Asses said they would look into it. Captain John Rous took him there."

More applause broke out, which William stilled with his raised hands.

"The French didn't believe the big ships of the Royal Navy could pass by the guns of the fortress. Neither did the Pompous Asses!"

More good-natured laughter filled the tavern. William waited for it to subside.

"Mind you, this is the biggest fortress in the New World we're talking about. It has more guns than … Gibraltar! Maybe John Rous shouldn't have been able to sail upriver past a fortress that has more guns than Gibraltar …"

William paused and the men waited.

"… but nobody told John Rous that!"

William beat down the cheering with his voice. "The *Sutherland's* daring passage above the fortress sealed the fate of the French in North America! Because of *The Sutherland*, Wolfe captured Quebec."

The men in the tavern began to cheer, but hushed as they saw William had something more to say.

"Well, our John Rous won't be around for the capture of Montreal."

"No!"

"Why not?"

"Where's the captain?"

"Because the Pompous Asses always have the last word, Captain John Rous is being sent into retirement."

"We can change that!"

The call, "We'll go to the governor!" drew general laughter.

"You can't go to the governor for anything unless you've got lots of money or your name is Bulkeley," was the jest from the back of the room.

Mister Carmichael tapped a ship's bell that was hanging at the door to the taproom. The bell was only rung when there was an important announcement, such as a declaration of war or someone was going to buy everyone in the house a drink. He stood, allowing the noise to subside.

"I suggest we raise a glass to an able seaman and an old friend, Captain John Rous. If ye empty yur glass in his honour I will have it filled." Carmichael raised his glass. "To John Rous! May the wind always be at yer back ..."

"... And the road come up to meet you," was the deep-throated response from the tavern patrons.

"John Rous."

* * *

The way seemed steeper than usual for the two drinking companions as they climbed the skirts of Citadel Hill.

"My ballast keeps shifting," Elkanah gasped as he staggered to the old tree. Unbuttoning the front flap of his breeches, he prepared to piss against the gnarled and scarred bark.

William, moving as quickly as his unreliable legs would allow, attempted to protect his tree but arrived too late. The stream had commenced and, by the girth of the flow, was judged unstoppable by his fuddled mind. He placed his hands on his hips. "Dammit, Elkanah! That's the tree I saw when Governor Cornwallis sent me ..."

"What? What do you want?"

William giggled. "You piss like a horse!"

"Indeed sir, I can mark a territory to rival the wolf." He squinted his eyes to see William's face in the lamplight. Failing, he looked down so he could be assured he was fastening his flap properly. "I did just that at Sherose."

"Did what?"

"Marked my land so the wild dogs would know."

"What with?"

"Oh, shit, William. You're drunk!"

"In good company."

Both men heard the sounds of running feet at the same time.

"Boots!" William felt a moment of relief as he said to Elkanah, "Could be the patrol!" He experienced a thrust of ice into the pit of his stomach as he realized it could also be Mauger's bullyboys bent on revenge against him. "Do you have a weapon, Elkanah? I have enemies in this town."

They could see shadows pass near the farther street lamp coming toward them.

"There must be a half-dozen of them!" William turned to look at Elkanah. He was struggling to get something out of his cloak. "Unclip the damn thing!" William drew the only weapon he had, his sailor's knife.

Elkanah pulled William off to one side so they were behind the trunk of the old tree. Elkanah had a pistol. He was coolly checking its prime as the running men approached to where they could be seen and identified.

It was the patrol.

Self-consciously William slipped his knife back into its sheath. "What is the trouble, men?"

The patrol didn't stop. Several of them spoke at once as they passed. "The governor is dead! Lawrence is dead!" As the pounding of their feet retreated into the sounds of the night, William realized they were going in the direction of Carleton House. Of course! Richard Bulkeley would be one of the first to know!

Elkanah had put his pistol away and was straightening his cloak. "Who will be governor?"

"Richard Bulkeley suggested there should be a succession policy … passed the Assembly last week.[4] Judge Belcher, as far as I know, will be governor. He's a friend of Richard's."

"Well, it's nice the province continues to be well served by its public officials."

William couldn't tell, in the lamplight, whether he was joking or not.

"I think I will call it a night, my friend."

"I will too, although I feel like I've just had a cold swim in the harbour!"

"Nothing like some excitement to sober a man up."

"You're right! Good night."

"G'night."

* * *

"Good night and thank you." Richard Bulkeley closed the door at Carleton House.

From the head of the stairs Amy called down, "Who was that, this time of night?"

"The patrol." Richard fancied a bowl of stew. There might be some in the kitchen, set back on the hearth. He ambled off toward the kitchen.

"Aren't you going to tell me what they wanted?"

"It was the patrol. I'm going to have some of that stew. Want some?" He heard the squeaks on the stairs as she came down. He sighed but kept walking down the hall past the library.

He was leaning into the hearth, pushing the pot crane closer to the heat, when Amy came into the kitchen.

"What was it, Richard! Now, don't you play any of your games with me."

His voice had a rich resonance from the hearth as he said, "The patrol informed me that Lawrence took sick and died." He stood up and lost the deep timbre to his voice. "John Belcher is interim governor. You sure you don't want any of this stew?"

Amy stared at her husband. When it became obvious he wasn't going to say any more she asked, "What did he die of?"

"Don't know, my dear. He took sick and died."

"My Lord, Richard, did you have him killed?"

"I don't want to hear talk like that, especially from my wife. Now, either have some stew or go to bed!"

"I'll have some stew as soon as it's hot."

They both pulled wooden chairs over and sat by the fire.

"I'm not a fool, Richard. There's something going on and you would be in it up to your eyeballs."

Richard Bulkeley inclined his head and steepled his hands in front of his mouth but remained silent.

"Well, if you won't tell me, let's see: your friend, Belcher, becomes governor. Assisted by the First Secretary, who has an intimate knowledge of the workings of this government, Jonathan Belcher will investigate and speedily report to their Lordships on the shortcomings of the late Charles Lawrence, Governor of Nova Scotia."[5]

Richard smiled.

"In fact, the new governor wouldn't be at all surprised if the esteemed Richard Bulkeley, the church-going, choir-mastering, organ-playing First Secretary, recommends laying all the problems of the colony at the clay feet of the conveniently dead Governor Lawrence."

Warming to her story, she listed what she called Lawrence's Liabilities. Amy counted them on her fingers. "He encouraged and protected the disorderly conduct of the military. That's a good one to start with. Then you would charge he was implicated in bribes—no, much better to say abuses—in contract procedures, don't you think? Of course, it was Lawrence who granted lands contrary to official instructions. Wasn't he involved in the Indian trade? Then, he diverted public funds into the Indian trade ..."[6]

Richard got up and moved the pot crane away from the fire. "I think the stew is warm enough." He gave his wife a veiled look. "Don't forget the mismanagement of the public funds of Orphan House. No, mustn't forget the inordinate expense of superintending the children."

"Aha! You and your little doxy! You're right, Richard! Mustn't forget to get you off the hook for that!" She watched his back for a moment or two as he fussed with the stew pot. "You weren't involved in his death, were you?"

"Must you ask, my sweet?" Richard ladled two bowls of hot stew, handing Amy one of them. "Let's have our stew and then off to bed. The night air isn't good for your cough, my dear."

19 October 1759
Government Pier

The ships loaded with fresh masts for the Royal Navy were making ready to leave Halifax. Lower sails were set and, occasionally, when the direction of the wind allowed, the sound of a fiddle found its way to the people standing on the Government Pier.

"Why are they playing music, William?"

William fixed his eyes on the face of the woman who was shielding his younger son against the chill of the harbour breeze. She had asked a question that his Molly would have known the answer to—or Amy Bulkeley—but Margaret? She was not from seafaring folk. How could she be expected to know?

"Hauling the anchor from the ocean floor is hard work. A man plays a pipe or a fiddle to make the work go easier."

A voice he immediately recognized as Amy's chimed in from behind him, "Or it could be the man with the fiddle just wants to play and get out of the hard work."

"Good morning, Missus Bulkeley; you are right in the sense that the man who plays is usually one of the oldest men in the ship's company."

Both women exchanged little words and made a joint fuss over the boys.

"That would be your father's ship, Amy. The one flying the signal flags would be the convoy commander." William studied the ship far out in the main channel as she came abeam the pier; a fifty-gun like *Sutherland* but even older. "We should wave now, ladies."

William, not wearing a hat, raised his arm and moved it back and forth, slowly. When Charles scampered to the edge of the pier, William had to rush to pick him up. When he returned to the women, they had stopped waving.

Wistfully Amy asked, "Do you think he sees us?"

Despite the fact that Rous didn't like using the little brass telescope, he probably had one to his eye this morning. If Wimper had been there, he would have found one of those old, single-piece 'bring 'em nears' that Rous liked, but the way things were, he was probably using the telescope. "Yes. He sees us. He will let us know that he does. Wait for it."

"What will Father do, William, change the signal flags?"

Just then, a puff of smoke appeared near the bow of the ship, followed quickly by the sound of the cannon.

"My God! Father is not supposed to do that in the harbour!"

"You're right, Amy! The Queen's Harbour Master will make an entry in his log noting the time and date of the infraction. The very next time Rous enters Halifax Harbour, he will be summoned to the Harbour Master's Office to atone for his crime."

Amy's eyes fluttered and her bosom rose with excitement as she asked, "You truly think he will be coming back with a new command?" When she looked into William's eyes she knew he had been joshing. "Oh, you!" She hit his arm with her fist. "You mean that he won't ever be bringing a ship back so he doesn't care about their silly regulations. You are terrible, William."

"Men are all the same," acknowledged Margaret.

William wasn't going to allow the two of them to get started. "He might still be able to see us. We should wave good bye."

They waved until the ship had sailed down harbour enough to be the same comparative size as George's Island.

"Father knew you would be here. He said to tell you he has given his island to the province."

"Sambro Island?"

They turned away from the harbour. They chatted as Margaret and William walked Amy to her carriage.

"Yes. He heard you say a lighthouse was needed there. Well, Father negotiated with Richard. If Father gave the island to the province, Richard would arrange for a lighthouse to be built."

Margaret was smiling as she said, "That's wonderful! We are going to live at Sambro, where William will be a pilot again. A light at Sambro should make it a lot safer, isn't that what you said, William?"

"Yes, most certainly." William gave Amy a kiss on the cheek.

Amy cast an anxious look at Margaret and then blushed. "What was that for?"

"Next time you see your Father, you can tell him how pleased I am." He took one of her hands in his. "The lighthouse will be a monument to John Rous, a way to remember his name forever."

Amy shook her head slowly in disagreement. "They'll call it Sambro Lighthouse and that will be the end of that. No, Father didn't want a monument; he just wanted you as safe as possible."

Her servant opened the door to the carriage. William gave her a hand up. The door was closed and the servant climbed up to sit by the driver, who waited for the word from his mistress to move off.

"Will Richard be able to get approval for a lighthouse now that Belcher is in control?" William asked.

"Yes. If Richard supports Belcher on his pet project, then Richard should be able to have a beneficial item like a lighthouse at Sambro."

William's curiosity was aroused. "What pet project could Belcher have?"

"The first chance he gets, he's going to deport as many Acadians as he can round up. Belcher is single-minded about that. They are a threat to all settlements with their raids and now their piracy and there are more and more of them every day. Judge Belcher says they are coming back from as far away as North Carolina. They must be gotten rid of."

"He won't be able to do it without bloodshed. The Acadians have leaders. Any attempt at deportation and, this time, they will fight!"

"Oh, I don't think so. The Judge already has one of the priests tied to his apron strings right here in the town: Pierre Maillard. Then there is Paul Laurent whom I met the other day. Richard says Laurent is going to use his influence with the Indians to convince them to make peace."

Margaret said, "That would be good because the Acadians need the support of the Micmac. An Indian peace treaty might make the Acadians easier to live with."

"And there's more! Belcher believes he will have Abbé Manach in custody by spring. So, William, that doesn't leave many leaders to cause trouble if Belcher finds an excuse to deport them. As I said, he has the plan for deportation. All he needs is a good reason and he will deport as many as he can lay his hands on."

The baby, James, whimpered and then began to cry. Amy gave Margaret an understanding look. "We will see you Sunday, at Saint Paul's."

"Most assuredly," answered Margaret for the family. "We are going to spend the winter at Hollis Street because it is far too late in the season to open the Sambro house. We will be attending regularly."

Amy flipped her hand at the driver. "Then we shall see you more of you both. I shall advise Richard to place you on the invitation list at Carleton House." As the carriage moved off she said, "G'bye," and made little waving motions at Charles.

"She is a lovely person." Margaret was hushing James by bouncing him in her arms. "I like being with her."

"We probably won't see as much of her as you might hope."

"Why is that, William?"

"Despite what she or Richard might say, Richard is uncomfortable with me around because I remind him of the days when he was a flunky for Cornwallis."

"Amy said she would put us on the invitation list."

"Well, we shall see, my dear."

The Bulkeley carriage had disappeared up the hill. William took Charles's hand and led him toward their cab-for-hire which had been waiting for them at the end of the pier.

"I hope you aren't disappointed, Margaret."

31 December 1759
Carleton House

William made a great pretence of studying the familiar lion's face doorknocker as he and Margaret waited for their knock to be answered. He had been afraid that he would be reminded over and over of Molly here, since they had visited so often in other days, but Margaret wasn't allowing any fits of depression to overtake her William.

"I want you to take that scowl off your face, William. Next year we will be at Sambro and won't be mixing with the Halifax elite."

"So-called elite," William corrected her but he did so with a big grin. "Don't you worry, my sweets, I will be the soul of discretion and sobriety."

She smiled back at him as she joked, "I don't want you to carry good behaviour too far. Just be polite and appreciative to Colonel Bulkeley."

The door opened. John looked down his nose at them as he ushered them into the front lobby.

"You know, John, if you held that nose of yours any higher we'd be able to count the hairs in your nostrils."

"William!" she whispered, "you promised."

John carried on with handling their cloaks as if William hadn't been disparaging, but his nose did settle significantly. "The mistress asked that you join them in the front reception room."

"Thank you, John." William noticed that Margaret was fussing with her hair and seemed upset at not being able to freshen up before joining the party.

"Don't worry, Margaret. As soon as we get in the front room, Amy or one of the girls will whisk you off somewhere. Isn't that right, John?"

"Most certainly, sir."

William leaned as close to Margaret as her wide skirts would allow and whispered, "Besides, this is the way Bulkeley receives his special guests, the ones he wants to honour or the ones he wants to get a special favour out of."

"Which are we?"

"Have to wait and see, my pet," William managed to whisper before they were ushered through the door into a room where seven men were standing in a circle listening to Richard Bulkeley.

Margaret smiled, gratefully, as Amy rescued her and led her away to an anteroom.

In the meantime, William was welcomed most graciously by the host and introduced around the circle. Most of the men William recognized as being Bulkeley cronies. The only man he didn't know was the one introduced as Captain Sutherland of the 77th Regiment of Foot.

Richard was in fine form, giving a deep bow in the direction of the army officer as he announced, "Actually, Captain Patrick Sutherland is our guest of honour tonight because, tomorrow, he becomes Major Patrick Sutherland and will never be seen again in polite company."

There was some laughter and congratulations which Richard allowed to take its natural course and then he added, "Patrick felt he would be an utter stranger here this evening so I invited another Louisbourg veteran, William Gray, hoping they might have met in that theatre of operations or, at the very least, they could entertain each other with their exploits while we, gentleman, make up to their ladies."

Good-natured laughter filled the room as the ladies rejoined the men and they all proceeded into the main reception room.

Later in the evening, William found himself standing next to Patrick and they exchanged pleasantries until William mentioned one of the Acadian leaders who hadn't yet been captured, Beau Soleil.

"Have you seen him?" Patrick asked.

"No. I consider myself very lucky not to have run across him. He's vicious, I'm told."

"Had him in my sights at Louisbourg."

"I find that interesting. Would you tell me about it?"

"I was commander of a small outpost at North East Harbour.[7] It was the only time the Acadian Irregulars attacked us at Louisbourg and, of course, they had to pick my post. But we were ready for 'em." Patrick looked into William's eyes to see if he was being bored.

"Please. I am interested, very interested."

"You probably know how it is. One minute there are these birds making a racket and next there are Indians swarming all over. Up jumps this Indian, almost on top of us. I was startled, let me tell you! Of course, I had my pistol but the damn thing misfired. My boys were ready for 'em with bayonet ..." he paused. "The Indian nearest me, all war paint and glaring eyes, was taken out by my corporal and, while he was clearing his bayonet, I was left to contend with the next warrior who actually looked like a freckle-faced English boy. It looked like his face had been scrubbed clean of everything Micmac to reveal one of us."

William interrupted. "Tell me again?"

"If you took away the headdress and Indian clothing, he looked quite English. Funny what strange thoughts you have when you are facing death. I am certain I would have had the biscuit but for a poor shot by that fellow Beau Soleil."

I am not going to interrupt again, William told himself, so he held his tongue and didn't ask the questions that popped to his mind, but he couldn't stop himself for long. "How do you know it was Beau Soleil?"

"Oh, I knew it was him, all right!" Sutherland took a sip from his glass.

William kept his mouth shut. He wanted to hear the story about a freckle-faced Indian because it could have been Robert Cameron.

The army officer continued. "I had seen him before at a raid down Lunenburg way. He's not a Micmac, you know, but a renegade Inhabitant, bigger than the warriors and very commanding in his presence. When he is on the field, you can't mistake him. Anyhow, back to my story about Louisbourg, Beau Soleil makes a poor shot and brings down Freckle Face instead of me and saved my life. If I ever see him, I'll have to tell him how much Missus Sutherland appreciated his poor marksmanship." Patrick Sutherland chuckled at his humour.

"What happened to Freckles?"

"That was rather strange. As soon as Freckles fell, another, smaller Indian came forward, right under our noses, and picked him up. The second Indian was so small by comparison, I don't know how he found the strength to carry Freckle Face, but he did. That's when I got Beau Soleil in my sights."

"Please tell me."

"We were reloading while the little Indian picked up Freckles. By the time he was labouring with his load going back the way they had come, my corporal had finished reloading. I became impatient with my pistol and took his musket. I had the little one in my sights"—the Captain held an imaginary musket and aimed it—"leading him just a little, when I realized that Beau Soleil was doing the same thing."

"Beau Soleil was going to shoot one of his men?"

"I don't know." He scratched his chin. "Probably not, but here was an opportunity I couldn't pass up; Beau Soleil was exposed and I had the chance to bring him down. I switched targets."

"You sighted on Beau Soleil."

"Yes, but the minute I had the bead on him, he knew it! I swear he felt my eyes on him because he snapped off a quick shot and then threw himself to the right. I had anticipated movement to the right and hit him just above his eye."

"You wounded him?"

Patrick nodded yes. "Before I could reload, he stood. He scowled at me! That's when I got a really good look at his face. I had caught him over his eyebrow—probably tore away part of it."

"So he lived."

"He would have had a miserable headache but that's about all." Patrick took a sip of his drink. "And, of course, he would only have half an eyebrow." Somewhat embarrassed that he had monopolized the conversation for so long, he asked the polite question. "I say, did you have any Louisbourg adventures?"

"Certainly nothing like yours. Most of my time was spent sitting in boats being cold and miserable."

"Pity. We can't all share in the fun."

Quite some time later, William had an interval when he could think about what he had been told. No matter how he worked it through, there was no sense to it. The only Indian with freckles would be Cameron. The little Indian was Reine, who would overcome anything to save Robert. And what about Beau Soleil? Why would he want to kill or wound one of his own men? It was a riddle with no answer.

Margaret left a circle of admiring men and collected William from his thoughtful interlude. "It's time we left, William. Did you have an interesting time?"

"I did, Margaret, most interesting."

"Did you find out why we were invited? Was it as honoured guests or as a pawns in one of Richard's schemes?"

"Probably for the first time since I have known Richard he was acting socially with no thought of advantage." But in his mind William thought, *maybe, maybe not.*

20 March 1760
Carleton House

"I'm truly sorry, Margaret, we don't get to see more of each other."

Margaret Skinner entered the sun-dappled sitting room and paused as she took a moment to enjoy the harbour view.

"Please sit down opposite me, Margaret. John will fetch some tea."

"Is Richard going to allow that tall building? Won't it spoil your view?" Margaret sat where she was told. "I thought Richard is …"

"… Is not all-powerful." Amy pointed at the table where she wanted the serving girl to place the tea tray and then dismissed her. She waited until the girl had left before continuing. "If Richard could have his way, the Lords of Trade would have confirmed Jonathan Belcher as governor instead of Henry Ellis."

"Ellis? Where will he be coming from?"

"Henry Ellis is currently Governor of Georgia."

"They never last long when they come north." Margaret accepted sugar, two servings, and then sipped her tea appreciatively. "He'll get sick and go home to England. Maybe he won't even bother to come."

"M-m-m-m. That's good tea. You can never be sure of the quality of the teas. I must speak to Richard and get more of this." Amy put her cup down and picked up a small plate with nicely shaped cookies. "They're called butterfingers. Our new cook is simply marvellous! He sailed with Father."

"Have you heard from Captain Rous?"

"They had an easy crossing. Arrived December 26th. When his ship was decommissioned, he immediately went to Whitehall but, up to the date of his letter, no one had given him a hearing."

"Hearing?"

"Well, Father calls it a hearing but it's really an interview or a debriefing and then he receives his new orders. Anyway, he hasn't had it."

"Richard must have friends who can help Captain Rous."

"Father doesn't need help. He will be fine."

"Well, I'm certainly glad you told me about his safe arrival, at least. William will want to know."

Amy changed the subject. "Is William still working in the Chart Room?"

"Yes, it kept him busy over the winter. He told me the new lighthouse is a landmark on the Admiralty Charts. William made the corrections."

"I understand that better glass has been ordered from England."

"William says the lighthouse is very much appreciated. It was a wonderful thing your father did."

" I have been working on Richard to have it named Rous Light ..."

Margaret hesitated but went ahead with what she meant to say anyway. "William said it is Sambro Light on the charts."

Amy's faced shaded a rose colour. "I imagine Richard forgot or he would have arranged it for me. He has so many things to keep track of and everything is moving so quickly ... like those buildings you spoke of. Richard said the town is growing up around us and he couldn't keep track of everything." Amy offered more tea and butterfingers, which Margaret accepted. "Besides, Richard couldn't stand in the way of progress."

Margaret realized that something had changed in Amy Bulkeley when the subject of Margaret's relationship with William was broached, unkindly. "Will he take you as his wife?"

"I don't know, Amy." It was Margaret's face that turned pink, this time.

"If he can plough for free, why buy the land, eh, Margaret?"

"Amy! He is still mourning Molly. I love the boys ... and I ... love ... William, but I am the housekeeper." Realizing that she had rankled the wife of the most powerful man in Nova Scotia, Margaret sipped her tea as she thought of ways she might make amends for whatever she had done. She tried bringing up subjects that would be impersonal but of mutual interest. "The Priest Manach will be sent to England?"

"Of course! What do you expect Richard to do with him? Manach was found inciting the Acadians and Indians to resist the provincial government. Abbé Manach has been placed in the brig of *H.M.S. Fowey* and will be delivered to the Lords of Trade for their disposal."[8]

The sun-filled room seemed to darken after that. Margaret tried several subjects: how was Amy's cough, schooling for the boys, the move to Sambro, all to no avail.

Amy Bulkeley went through the motions of a private tea party but the friendship that had existed between these two women was gone. At the appropriate time, Margaret was escorted from the premises by the Mistress of Carleton House, the door being closed behind her before she had gone two paces down the front walk.

When she told William most of what happened at the tea, William wasn't surprised.

"Amy has a streak of cussedness about a yard wide and she made a deal with the devil when she went back to Richard's bed and board. He can't or won't give her what she really needs: love and affection." He put his arm around Margaret and hugged her close.

While William was saying, "Don't you worry about the Bulkeleys; we won't have much to do with them again," Margaret was enjoying the closeness (however fleeting) of this man whom, she realized, she loved with her entire being.

7 July 1760
Government Pier

Out of the corner of his eye, William Gray watched as Richard Bulkeley descended from his carriage. Other than his green liveried manservant and his driver, he was alone. Perhaps the rumours William had heard were true: the Mistress of Carleton House was terribly sick.

William turned, ever so slightly, to keep Bulkeley in his view, watching as he strutted across the pier to the knot of people who were preparing to take ship to England. William witnessed the handshakes, smiles and a kiss for Missus Mauger. Yes, Richard had come down to say goodbye to Joshua Mauger.

Too bad Cornwallis couldn't be here to see this but, in a way, I'm here for him, not to say goodbye, but to satisfy myself that the bastard Mauger actually leaves Halifax.

Several more carriages arrived. William identified the men, no accompanying wives, as Michael Francklyn—he strained his head to see around one of the others—Issac Deschamps and Butler. He had forgotten Butler's first name but he knew that they were all heavily in debt to Mauger.

"Some more of Mauger's boys."

"What did you say, William?"

In his preoccupation of watching Mauger's group, William had lost sight of Richard and here he was, standing by his side, close enough to hear William talking to himself.

"A man who talks to himself has a poor audience."

"Hello, Richard. How have you been?"

"I have been fine, in fact, never better. Unfortunately, I can't say the same for my wife."

"What has been wrong?" *It's probably her consumption getting worse*, William thought. He believed his suspicions were confirmed by Richard's initial reply.

"It's her cough. Been really bad the last week since she received word."

With a feeling of dread, he knew there was more to it than Amy's cough. "Received word?"

"Yes, I don't mean to keep you in suspense. It isn't good

news, really, and arrived about ten days ago. Struck my wife heavily and she went to bed. She hasn't been up since, the poor dear."

"What struck her?"

"The news concerning her father."

William felt as if he was going to knock the bastard down but had to keep being attentive and patient or he wouldn't find out what happened to Rous. *Maybe Rous received an assignment to the Pacific. A man his age would find that terribly difficult. Going round the Horn to reach the Pacific was …*

"As you probably know, he arrived at Portsmouth the day after Christmas. His ship was …"

"I know about the ship, Richard! Tell me what is going on with your father-in-law."

"Nothing much now. He was buried in Saint Thomas's Churchyard on 3 April."[9]

"For God's sake! How did it happen?"

"He lost his patience waiting for his new orders. Every day he would ask for an interview. Every day he was sent away." Bulkeley made several 'tsk—tsk' noises between his teeth. "Terrible treatment for a man of his record, but he was not without his faults and not without his critics."

William didn't know what to say. He knew his mouth was hanging open but didn't care. Captain John Rous had died outside the office of some clerk who was following the orders of some mean-spirited man determined to have revenge on the great John Rous. "They tormented him until he couldn't take it any more."

"I believe that to be a safe assumption," Richard's smugness infuriated William. "And what was bound to happen, finally did happen where it was recorded and became part of his file."

"What was put on his file?"

"That he challenged Whitehall authority in the guise of an Admiralty Clerk, uttered unintelligible noises and fell, drooling, to the floor where his tongue protruded, further and further, as he died."

"I can't …"

"He was accorded the funeral of a captain of the Royal Navy and a cemetery plot was provided at Saint Thomas Church."

"At least you couldn't take that away from him."

"That's right, but I don't think he cared much by that time, so it mattered naught. I must excuse myself, and return to the little farewell. Mauger is leaving us but his influence will continue unabated, as you can see by his retinue. Joshua is buying a seat in the English Parliament and I wouldn't be the least bit surprised that he will arrive at a position where he chooses Nova Scotia governors from that little group: his entourage, as they say in London."[10]

Bulkeley waited for a response. When there was none forthcoming, he touched the brim of his hat and said, "Ta, ta, William."

13 January 1761
Government House

William hoped that Margaret wouldn't worry too much. *Pilot Schooner* had come to Government Pier for supplies and the plan was to return to Sambro Harbour before dark. Of course, Margaret would understand that when Governor Belcher summoned him to Government House, he would have to go, but there was no way to tell Margaret. Hopefully she was used to his absences by now.

He stopped breathing for a moment so he could listen to noises down the hall. Yes, that was Belcher's voice. Maybe he was coming! He kept hearing the voice but it wasn't getting any closer. He tiptoed to the door and opened it. From down the hall, where someone else had also opened a door, he could hear Belcher in full argumentative bloom. Boy! Was Belcher mad! Curiosity overcame him and William went down the hall a way to better hear what Belcher was talking about.

"They are inflexibly devoted to France and the Romish religion and by intermarriage with the Indians their power and disposition to be mischievous is more to be dreaded ..."

He's talking about the Acadians, I bet, thought William.

There had been some shuffling of papers and William missed parts of Belcher's argument.

"… they will never sincerely submit. Were our province filled with people well established and if the Acadians were judiciously distributed, they might be kept under control with our normal governmental practices …"

Someone kept shuffling pages. Perhaps Belcher was dictating to a clerk?

"… and after the 1755 expulsion, many returned from as great a distance as South Carolina and not only opposed but actually attacked the King's troops at …"

A chair scrape followed by the sound of a door being closed cut off Belcher's voice in mid-sentence.

William realized that Governor Belcher—still governor since the man from Georgia, *what's his name*, hadn't come to Nova Scotia—was drumming up support to deport the Acadians again: the ones missed the last time and the ones who have returned to the province. William hoped that he had not been called in to participate in that exercise. *If I were, I wouldn't, nosirree! Not going to get involved in that kind of thing again.* He went back into the office and sat down in the chair. He sighed a long sigh and closed his eyes. Sooner or later the governor would return to his office. William would find out what he was wanted for and he would go back to Sambro. He looked out the window. *It's getting dark. Well, I guess I won't be gettin' back home until tomorrow, then.* He leaned back and closed his eyes.

By the time Governor Belcher returned, it was night.

Governor Belcher made no apologies and went right to the point. "I ordered your ship to wait. You were involved in our actions against the Acadians in 1755 more than anyone still here at Halifax. You were also at Louisbourg. Would you be able to recognize the renegade called Beau Soleil?"

Recalling his conversation with Major Sutherland on New Year's, William said he probably would be able to recognize him.

"*Probably* isn't good enough. I must know, without a doubt, that I have the scoundrel in custody. First of all, the man I have in custody claimed he was Joseph Brossard. When a priest identified him as Beau Soleil, he changed his story and became Beau Soleil. I want to get rid of these people, once and for all. I mean to start with the leaders and I must know if I have Beau Soleil!"

"Sorry, Governor." William stood up, "Nothing else you want me for?"

"If you can't help me in this, then, no. I wish to thank you for your time."

William had a thought. "What about Major Sutherland? He would be able to identify him for you."

"He was my first choice but he is selecting new town sites the other side of Merligueche and is not available to me."[11] Belcher shook his head from side to side in disbelief. "No white man should be in country during winter but he enjoys it because there's …"

Both men said, "No flies or mosquitoes," at the same moment and laughed, self-consciously.

William warmed to the man. "I would be able to ask the prisoner questions about Louisbourg that only Beau Soleil would know."

"With certainty?"

"Absolutely."

"Fine. Please come with me. I will have you taken to see him."

* * *

In the dark, William couldn't be sure it was Artz Street but he thought it might be. The carriage stopped in front of a row of little houses that had been built since William and Margaret had moved to Sambro so there were no landmarks he could identify to verify his guess.

The corporal let William descend first.

"It's the house with the sentry, sir. I will join you right away as soon as I gives the driver 'is instructions."

The sentry was alert and responded to William's approach by shouldering arms and turning to face him. "I'm sorry, sir. You must wait to be escorted before you can go any further. These houses is out of bounds to the public."

"At your ease, Hudson. Mister Gray is with me. Which house is for the governor's special guest?"

"C, corporal."

"Very good! Carry on!" He beckoned to William, "Foller me, sir, if you please," leading William to the front steps of the third doorway in the row. He rapped twice and then three times. The door was opened inward by another redcoat who, recognizing the corporal, stepped back out of the way to permit entry.

"Inform Mister Brossard that Mister Gray is come t'see him."

"Yes, Corporal."

In short order, a tall, erect man with tied-back hair, broad shoulders and an imposing manner filled the little archway into the room.

He spoke in French. A voice from behind the arch said, "He says he is Joseph Brossard and wants to know who you are."

Brossard stepped into the room, revealing a much shorter man dressed in priest's robes.

"My name is Pierre Maillard and I was summoned to help in the interrogations."

"This is no interrogation! I merely wish to speak with him." William motioned to the English soldiers that they should be left alone.

"Then you have need of my services because Joseph speaks little English."

"We will be outside the door if you have need of us, sir."

"Thank you, Corporal."

William fixed his eyes on the priest's face. "When he speaks with me, his words must not be repeated."

"I am his priest."

William wasn't quite sure that was good enough for him, but if the Frenchman didn't mind, what did William care? "Are you Beau Soleil?"

"He says he is Joseph Brossard but, if the English wish to call him Beau Soleil, he would be proud to carry the name of a fine warrior."

"Tell him to answer straightforward, one warrior to another. I was at Louisbourg and Quebec."

"He says he is Beau Soleil."

"Ask him if he led the raid on North East Harbour."

"He was the leader of the attack on North East Harbour."

"How many of his warriors did he shoot in the back at North East Harbour?" William believed he was going to be throttled by the man, but Brossard restrained himself and answered the priest.

"He shoots no one in the back."

"I have a witness who saw him shoot the Acadian known as Carrot Top."

"He says the English officer lies."

"How did he know it was an English officer?"

The priest searched his face for a truth when Brossard didn't answer. Slowly the priest dropped his eyes and said, quietly, "He doesn't make a reply!"

"It was the same officer who wounded you above the eye,"—William raised his finger as if to touch the scar on Brossard's forehead—"taking away part of your eyebrow."[12]

Brossard struck William's hand down.

"I will ask you questions. If you continue to lie to me, I will tell your friends about North East Harbour. They might believe me." William didn't wait for a reply. "Carrot Top had a companion. Give me the name."

Brossard turned to look out the window at the dark of the night. "Claude," he said.

William rose from his chair. "So, you do speak English. Thank you, Beau Soleil."

Still with his back to his interrogator, he asked, "You speak to Governor?"

William smiled. "Yes. I will speak with him in the morning."

He turned. "Tell him," Brossard paused and continued in French which the priest translated, "I will charter a ship and take as many of my people as I can to Saint-Domingue, if he will let us go."

"I will take the message." It had been nagging at William ever since he had watched the Camerons walk away from the Louisbourg Gate. If he didn't ask now, he would never know.

"What happened to Claude and Carrot Top?"

"They were caught and killed by the British."

"Where?"

"On the Bras d'Or. You will give my message to the governor?"

"I give you my word."

With relief, William closed the door behind him and stood in the shadows. The two soldiers made a move as if to come to him but he waved them away. "Not just yet," he said. William leaned against the wall as he collected his thoughts about what he had just been told.

Well, Jeremiah, you can look for her in Paradise if French Catholics and English Protestants ever get together in the hereafter without fighting. Shit! That poor woman did everything she could to be with her man. A caring God would have allowed them some time together, away from the English.

The door opened and the priest came out. He almost bumped into William in the darkness, muttering his excuses as he passed and stepped onto the street. Pierre Maillard hesitated as if he didn't know which way to go.

"I have a carriage, priest. You can join me."

"No, thank you, my son, but I need to speak with you."

William indicated they could go back inside where it was warm, but Maillard pointed at the street. They matched step as they slowly paced up the hill.

The priest was quiet.

William could see, by one of the older houses, that this was indeed Artz Street.

"Joseph did not tell the truth."

"I thought you said you were his priest," William blurted.

"Yes, and I will be reproved by my confessor if what I do is not the right thing." He sighed. "My confessor is old and doesn't listen." Again he sighed. "He is old and doesn't listen ... and ... I lose heart when I hear such things as in there."

Pierre Maillard halted and put his hand on William's sleeve to turn him in the darkness. "Robert and Reine Cameron live." He squeezed the muscular arm: "They live in the east of Île Saint Jean near a river teeming with fish. They have a son, named Robert. I baptized the boy. Joseph knows this but he lied twice in there. I wanted you to know since you gave your word to speak to the governor and expected truth as payment. Now you have it."

William felt a sense of joy and elation that almost overwhelmed him. He felt, deep in his heart, that God was in his place.

"You will tell the governor that Beau Soleil wants to leave Acadia and take as many Acadians with him as he can?"

"Yes. I gave my promise."

"Good! It is better Acadians leave Nova Scotia and find happiness elsewhere."

"Like the Camerons did."

They shook hands before they parted.

* * *

In the morning, William still carried with him a feeling of well-being and contentment that must have shown on his face in Belcher's office.

"You spoke with Brossard and liked the result," the governor said.

"Joseph Brossard is Beau Soleil, without a doubt."

Governor Belcher was going to speak but William had the temerity to stop him. "Just hold up a minute, Governor, there's some news you will probably want to hear. Joseph Brossard will charter a ship and take away as many Acadians as are willing to Saint-Domingue."

"He'll take a whole boatload?"

"Yes."

Belcher hit his palm of one hand with a fist. "Got 'im! Keep 'im! Keep him locked up until our next treaty with France and then let him go with all his friends."

"Does he have family, sir?"

"Why, matter of fact he does. They were the reason we caught him. The bugger came into Fort Cumberland to get food for his children." [13]

"We could let him live with his family until it is time to let him go."

"No! He would cause trouble that way—get in touch with the raiders and incite the Indians. No, I want him put away somewhere, locked up."

Remembering the desolation at Cinq Maison where all of the Inhabitants had definitely been taken away, William suggested, "Put him with his family at Windsor. There aren't any French there and he is a long way from the borders of the province where he might have contact with the French."

"And under the eyes of the Windsor garrison. Yes indeed." Belcher pulled at his lower lip as he thought it through. "We could do that."

Governor Jonathan Belcher stood up, giving the sign of dismissal to William and the clerk who had been sitting in the corner making notes.

"I didn't ask, Mister Gray. Why were you sailing into Halifax?"

"*Pilot Schooner* was coming into the harbour for victuals."

"Pretty rough seas, this time of year."

"Not rough enough to stop me from going home to be with my family."

"That's nice. That's nice. Pass my compliments to your good wife."

"I will, sir."

27 April 1761
Pilot Schooner

It was the kind of spring day the crew of *Pilot Schooner* liked: scudding clouds, bright sunshine and enough wind from the north-east to cause brave captains to seek the help of the pilot rather than attempt harbour entry on their own.

Francis Peters, Master of *Pilot Schooner*, surveyed the ship they were approaching. "She's big enough," he said to Ship's Pilot Gray.

"This is her second charter trip. She stops in Halifax to pick up supplies for the settlers and then, a couple of days later, takes them to their new settlement. Last time they went to Onslow."

"Boat crew, make ready!" Captain Peters called out, the order being repeated and the men moving about smartly to obey. *Pilot Schooner* was a happy ship and a happy ship came from the ship's company knowing their work. The five men on this ship were professionals.

"You got pretty wet this morning, William. Did you get a chance to dry out?"

"Margaret packed extra clothes for me so a quick change and I was right as rain."

"If you don't mind my saying, that Margaret is a wonderful girl."

"Don't mind at all, Cap'n. Soon as the circuit minister comes, she has promised to be my wife."

"I wondered, William ..."

"You wondered what, Captain Peters?"

Both men knew, in a village as small as Sambro, it was common knowledge that William slept in the front room while the housekeeper used the master bedroom. Yet there were still the uncharitable who wouldn't believe that a man and woman could live under the same roof without having carnal knowledge of each other. One such uncharitable woman had made snide remarks about Margaret during a quilting bee. Margaret had come home in tears. Again, in a small village, it was an open secret that the incident had happened.

"I mean, that Hiltz woman had no call to ..."

"I really don't want to talk about my affairs, Captain."

"You are a good man, William Gray, but you need some advice and I'm set to be givin' it to you."

His lower lip forming what could be called a pout on a child but on a grownup it passed as a glower, William waited to hear what his captain had to say.

"It won't stop with Missus Hiltz. There will be others, now, who will get their jollies from hurtin' Margaret."

William turned away, presenting his shoulder to the captain.

"You can turn away if you like, but you will hear me out, Ship's Pilot Gray." Captain Peters was encouraged when his pilot swivelled to face him. "We go into Halifax for victuals in two days. While we are in port, go to Saint Paul's and make arrangements for a wedding. Then, two weeks later, on our next victuals run, we can take Margaret in with us and you can be married."

William felt as if he could spit grape shot instead of words but he took a deep breath. "I appreciate you mean well, Cap'n. Margaret won't do that because she wants the wedding at Sambro where all her friends and neighbours will be witness to the ceremony."

"And Missus Hiltz?"

"Especially Missus Hiltz."

By the set of William's jaw, the captain believed the conversation was over, so he was surprised when William went on to explain the situation in the village of Sambro.

"Missus Hiltz is a widow lady who took a special liking to my wife Molly, and she always thought of herself as a grandmother to my boys." William looked out to sea, still explaining to the captain but avoiding any sort of eye contact. "Edith Hiltz was as shocked and saddened by Molly's death as ... well, she was as shocked as I was. Then, when I went home to Sambro bringing the boys back to her, I also brought an outsider who seemed to ... well, who appeared to ... who lived in the house with the children and took Molly's place." The last words all came out in a rush.

"Boat ready, Cap'n!"

William squared his shoulders. "It's been hard on Missus Hiltz ... and on Margaret." William hitched up his belt and turned to go. "It has been especially hard because Margaret is a spinster woman."

Peters placed his hand on William's shoulder. "And every day there will be another Missus Hiltz, taking a slice off Margaret, just for sport. How long do you have to wait for that circuit preacher?"

The sailors had opened the entry port. The oarsman was already in the dory, his oars at the ready, the dory suspended two feet above the ocean swell. *Pilot Schooner* had passed ahead of the transport, taking up the same course. The dory would be dropped and would manoeuvre to be as close as possible to the transport as it sailed by.

"A few more months." William leapt into the boat. He swiftly positioned himself on the stern sheet. "Ready?"

"Ready!"

"Away the boat!"

The dory dropped into the ocean and immediately fell astern of the schooner. The oarsman turned the dory to put them in the middle of the wake of the *Pilot Schooner*. The transport, under reduced sail, came up the wake, seemingly to run the little boat down. The oarsman worked to place the dory in the path of the transport and, at the last, backed off enough to let the prow slowly pass them.[14]

The oarsman had taken in his oar on the side next to the ship and with skilful manipulation of the other oar, kept the dory parallel to the ship as it passed. "Careful!"

"You're telling me?"

Most often, ships would heave to when they took on the pilot but, for ship's masters that William had served before, he had set up a signal that told them to reduce sail and do a pick-up. Today was a good sea, and William wanted to save time and get back to his Margaret. He had signalled for the ship to do a pick-up.

Now they were very close to the slowly moving wall that was the hull of the ship. A boarding net was hanging over the side. William stepped forward and grabbed the net. Travelling away from the dory on the side of the ship, he glanced over his shoulder to check if the little boat was all right.

The oarsman was merrily rowing away from the transport's wake to be picked up and brought inboard by *Pilot Schooner*.

William clambered up the net and through the entry port where, with the captain's permission, he proceeded to take the ship into Halifax Harbour.

With the ship again under full sail, William took a look around. There were the usual passengers on the main deck taking the air but he was surprised to see a man and woman, well dressed, not more than thirty years old, standing on the quarterdeck. Most captains were fussy about passengers wandering onto the quarterdeck, but this ship's captain, Captain Oland, was particularly strict about passengers staying out of his way. *Who could they be?* He decided to find out.

It took but a few words of conversation to realize that they were very well-to-do and had probably paid a premium to the captain, over and above the government passage allowance, to travel as first class. William learned that Samuel Brewster, a man of the cloth, and his wife Agnes, had read Governor Lawrence's proclamation inviting non-Papists to settle on lands that had been vacated by the Acadians. Imagine the opportunity, the Reverend enthused, a community, all of one faith, having the opportunity to leave behind the worldly sins and begin anew! It was a challenge Samuel Brewster couldn't resist. They had left their affairs in the hands of family in New Hampshire and were traveling to Cornwallis to meet their destiny.[15]

"Won't the Church of England send priests?"

"Oh, there are already a number of ministers but they speak German," Missus Brewster explained, "and yes, the governor will probably bring Church of England priests, but they won't do for our flock."

Mister Brewster grasped the taffrail as if it were the railing of a pulpit, "We are Dissenters," he said. "It rests with us to make the church a part of daily living and not just a Sunday House, rife with ritual, layered with gold and silk and served by a caste of godlike priests."

"Samuel preaches a fine, fine sermon," Agnes Brewster said glowingly.

"We must guard against prideful thoughts, Agnes."

"Of course, Samuel."

"You ... marry people?"

"Yes, of course. Well-intentioned men and women, wishing to be joined in matrimony, are the basis of a rock-solid church. That's what we will be doing in Cornwallis, building a church."

William had an idea. "It will be several days before your supplies will be loaded and you depart for Cornwallis."

"Yes, so I understand."

"I live just over there." William pointed at the lighthouse. "I have two children. The circuit preacher won't be coming for a month or more." The words were spilling forth, faster and faster. "I wish to marry my housekeeper. She's been looking after my children since my wife departed ..."

Samuel Brewster leaned forward and lowered his voice. "Departed, as in ... ran away?"

"Oh dear, no! My Molly was drowned."

It was the turn of Agnes Brewster to lean forward. "House-keeper, that means you live in the same ..."

"House! I have no knowledge of Margaret. I love her deeply and ..."

Samuel smiled at Agnes. "We understand your needs and are relieved that you have not yielded to the temptations of the flesh. Physical love between man and wife is one of God's great gifts and should be tasted with fervour," the Reverend waggled his finger, "but only within the bounds of matrimony."

"Will you please come to my village? I will make sure you do not miss your ship to Cornwallis. Please?"

"If there is no possibility of missing our ship when it is time to depart Halifax, we would be pleased to perform the wedding ceremony."

Agnes Brewster touched William's cheek with her gloved hand. "We are grateful to be able to help such an upright man take his place as a proper husband and father."

* * *

Two days later, Sambro Village was awakened to the sound of the emergency bell on the pier. Of course the men responded as quickly as possible, followed by the children and the sleepy women, to learn that Margaret Skinner was to be wed to William Gray that very day.

Excitement overtook the village almost immediately as the preacher and his wife were introduced. Within a very few minutes, Agnes Brewster was assigning tasks. The men off-loaded the supplies William had brought from Halifax. Since it was such a lovely day, the churchyard would be the site of the wedding and the feast following. Chairs would be collected from the homes by the older boys and arranged according to a little plan that Agnes had drawn up. Cooking was placed in the capable hands of Missus Hiltz, who gave the soon-to-be Missus Gray a big hug. Everyone was excited and had a wonderful time and, eventually, before the setting of the sun, William and Margaret were married.

In their home at last, the children tucked away, Mister and Missus Gray had their first quiet moment alone. William put his arms around Margaret and untied her apron. He threw that item of clothing on the floor. Next …

A sleepy voice from the children's room asked, "Daddy, you and Margaret shouldn't be making so much noise."

William nuzzled his wife's throat as she answered, "Why is that, sweetheart?" William was tickling her. She held his hands, afraid that she might laugh out loud. "You have been up so late, Charles. Time that all good children were quiet and asleep."

"I know, but if you aren't quiet and in bed, Mother Margaret, when the sun goes down, the Shillelagh Man gets you."

Margaret suppressed a giggle. "Don't you worry the least bit, Charles. Good night."

William took her into his arms. "I'm going to get you," he whispered.

Endnotes

[1] As usual, Sutherland was dispatched to other duties as soon as possible following the action.

[2] Several times I found reference to John Jacob Pyke's mother dying and one reference that she did survive the Dartmouth massacre and married a Wenman, giving the boy a family after all. For the story, I had her nobly die at Dartmouth.

[3] John Rous commanded the mast convoy. He died in England and was buried there.

[4] The timing was strangely fortunate.

[5] The actions of the dead governor were examined minutely.

[6] All laid at the feet of the dead governor but, when Belcher was eventually called upon to pass judgement, all of the old-time executives, including the governor, were found not guilty of any crimes.

[7] Captain Sutherland was in charge of the outpost. It was the only point where the Irregulars attacked the British.

[8] Incidents like the one quoted in this story are historical.

[9] According to the records.

[10] Which is exactly what happened.

[11] It is recorded that Major Sutherland was out searching for new town sites.

[12] The shooting incident and this interview are fiction but the governor would have wanted to be sure that the man he had in custody was the man known as Beau Soleil.

[13] Beau Soleil was permitted to live with his family near Windsor.

[14] The Gray family story is that generations of sons rowed their fathers out to the ships off Sambro.

[15] In a later book of the series, *Abuse of Power: The Planters,* Samuel and Agnes Brewster arrive at Cornwallis Township to take possession of the prime farmland made vacant by the Expulsion of the Acadians. Not all the Acadians are gone. Richard Bourgeois, who escaped from the transport ships at Minas in the storyline of *The Acadians,* Book 1 of the Abuse of Power series, has survived all these years in the forest.

Epilogue

In April 1762, the Nova Scotia House of Assembly chose Joshua Mauger as the Colony's London Agent. In that capacity, Mauger carried on a bitter fight against Governor Jonathan Belcher; Mauger wanted control of his old fiefdom. Michael Francklyn and Isaac Deschamps, cronies of Mauger, became governors in their turn. For many years, nothing could be enacted that was against Mauger interests.

October 1762, the French captured St. John's, Newfoundland. Major Patrick Sutherland commanded the battalion that recaptured St. John's. In the meantime, the news of the initial French success in Newfoundland inspired the Nova Scotia Acadians to demonstrate what Governor Belcher described as "unacceptable insolence." He implemented his deportation plan, sending many Acadians to Massachusetts. Boston refused them so they came back. Belcher had to be content with seeding the Acadians among the established English population in Nova Scotia.

After the Treaty of Paris was signed in 1763, Joseph Brossard was arrested at Pisiquid and found to be in possession of a letter written by the Ambassador of France in London. As far as Belcher was concerned, the letter proved that Beau Soleil was active again, working with a foreign power against the interests of the English Crown. In 1764, Joseph Brossard was permitted to charter vessels and take six hundred Acadians, including women and children, to the French West Indies. The climate overcame many, and Brossard is believed to have taken the survivors to Louisiana in 1765.

Margaret and William Gray lived in Sambro until the end of their days. Their sons, Charles and James, following in their father's footsteps, took to the sea. Samuel and William worked the bitter soil and were fishermen in the season. The middle son, Thomas, went to Halifax one morning and was not heard from again.

MEMBER OF SCABRINI MEDIA

Quebec, Canada
2004